*Crooked Pieces*

*Crooked Pieces*

# SARAH GRAZEBROOK

First published in Great Britain in 2007 by
Allison & Busby Limited
13 Charlotte Mews
London W1T 4EJ
*www.allisonandbusby.com*

Copyright © 2007 by SARAH GRAZEBROOK

The moral right of the author has been asserted.

'When You Are Old' on page 429 by William Butler Yeats, in
*W.B. Yeats: Selected Poems* edited by Timothy Webb
(Penguin Classics, 1991), used by kind permission of AP Watt Ltd on
behalf of Gráinne Yeats, Executrix of the Estate of Michael Butler Yeats.

A CIP catalogue record for this book is available from
the British Library.

10 9 8 7 6 5 4 3 2 1

ISBN 0 7490 8183 X
978-0-7490-8183-6

Typeset in 11/16 pt Sabon by
Terry Shannon

Printed and bound in Wales by
Creative Print and Design, Ebbw Vale

SARAH GRAZEBROOK exchanged a career as a television actress for one as a writer following the birth of her second child. Her first novel, *Not Waving*, won the *Cosmopolitan* Fiction Prize and she has written six others. She wrote a monthly column, 'Notes from the Garret', for *Kent Life* for four and a half years and contributes to a variety of satirical radio programmes. Sarah has wide experience of teaching creative writing for the Arvon Foundation and at Macon in France. She now lives in Deal, Kent.

**Also by Sarah Grazebrook**

*Mountain Pique*
*Foreign Parts*
*Page Two*
*A Cameo Role*
*The Circle Dance*
*Not Waving*

*For David*

*I'd like to thank everyone who has put up with me during the long incubation of this novel and, most particularly, Professor Irving Benjamin for his invaluable information regarding force-feeding, and Kirsty Fowkes and Dr Andrew Palmer for all their advice and encouragement.*

*'Man is the whole world and the breath of God;*
*woman the rib and crooked piece of man'*

*Religio Medici*, 1643
SIR THOMAS BROWNE

# PART ONE

## 1905

Well, we have been walking for close on an hour now, half across London, I reckon, and *she's* not said a rotten word. No more have I. I am so…rankled. 'Rankled.' I am, truly. Much good it does, for if I said to her, 'Ma, I am rankled with you,' she would probably smile. Think I was grateful. She is so dull. She knows nothing. Except how to make a cabbage and a scrag of mutton feed six mouths, then seven, then eight. Seven again now, for she has shot herself of me. Just when Frank is coming home and with a present for me, for certain – a ribbon, maybe, or some carved wood thing. And now Lucy will get it. Once he brought an orange. Ma said it was too beautiful for eating and kept it from me for days and days till the skin withered all up like Mrs Carter's from the laundry who's dying.

Ma says, 'Maggie, keep up. Do you want to be late your first day?'

I do, as a fact. In truth I do not want to go at all. Why must I act glad for something so…? Reverend Beckett told Ma I was the cleverest of any he had taught in Sunday School. I can read; I can write; I can say nine psalms off without failing once. 'She is a clever girl, your Maggie. You will be proud of her one day, I'm sure, Mrs Robins.'

'I thank you, Reverend Beckett.' Twitchy little smile. 'I am proud of her now.'

So proud she has fixed me up for a skivvy, which you need no reading or writing for. Just bones like a brute to carry coal and lay fires and scrub and clean and polish till you fall down dead of weariness.

He will be angry that I am gone, Frank. I know that. I am his best girl. Better than all the shiny ones with skirts made of flowers and the yellow ones with feet smaller than a thimble, *and* the ones with two heads, one black and one white. He says so. 'Maggie, you are my best girl and if I could I would marry you.' I am glad he cannot. Being married is a fearsome thing.

'Maggie, it's not far now. Try to do well there. They are good people. This is such a chance for you.'

'Chance for what?'

She is silent. 'To get away.'

I say nothing – kick a stone with my newly polished boots so that Ma's face goes all worried and unhappy. Now she knows what it's like.

The house is mighty. There is a room for Mr and Mrs Roe and one for Miss Pankhurst and all her painting and foulness, then two more, one for eating and one for not eating, and a place for me of my very own that is mighty, with a bed and a shelf and my own candle. I have never slept in a bed by myself before. At first I was frightened and feared the Great Red-eyed Rat would come creeping in the bottom and gobble my feet, as Frank always says it will if I don't lie right close to him, so I piled all my clothes and my best boots and the chamber-pot on the cover so there was nowhere for it to get in. There is hardly room for me but that is not new, and I sleep a lot better for having company, though boots and a chamber-pot are not so warming as brothers and sisters.

Downstairs we may wash ourselves inside the house, and the kitchen has a great range and stone sink and next to it there is a 'pantry' where the food is kept – meat and sometimes a piece of silver shiny fish. Cook is horrid and makes me watch her doing the food and then to wash the pans after.

Mr and Mrs Roe are kind but very old and must surely die soon. Then what? For two such old people they eat prodigious much. Soup, then a dish of meat with nearly always potatoes and then some cheese or maybe a pudding of suet and currants. And this they do every day, with bread and eggs at breakfast and more bread with sugar sprinkled on it at four in the afternoon, and in the evening, a pie or cold bacon with some beer. Cook found me scraping off their leavings on my first day and chided me wicked. I thought she would tell the mistress and I should be sent home, but instead she sat me in the kitchen and put before me a great bowl of stew and bread, cut thicker than a fist and a mug of beer, all my own. I was so stuffed I feared my skin would split. 'You're nothing but bones, girl. Thin don't make good workers.' Well, if that be so she must be the finest worker ever, I fancy, for two grown men could not get their arms round her.

My work is hard but not so bad as I had feared. I must rise at six to lay a fire in the eating room, and then put water to boil for Cook to make the breakfast. In the morning I sweep right through the house and wash the steps and polish them. I wipe the furniture over with a cloth and on Mondays I help with the washing. We boil a great tub of water and then Cook takes a bar of soap, thick as a brick, and rubs it on the dirty clothes and plunges them up and down till the water turns muddy. Then we mangle them. The handle is dreadful hard to move but Cook says I must keep at it to make my arms strong. I say they will fall off first, but she just laughs and if I do it well she gives me a great big spoonful of sugar.

Miss Pankhurst is very plain. She has a beautiful name – Sylvia. I heard Mrs Roe call her so. It does not suit her. Her clothes are all brown and sloppy and soiled with paint which is very hard to get out. My fingers are raw from scrubbing at them. Her hair is brown, too, rusty and not at all neat. She has big sad eyes like a cow and always seems to be thinking. Cook says she is an artist and can draw anything in the world and you would swear it was real. I say, can she draw me a big bowl of sugar then, and I can swallow it straight? Cook just laughs and says I 'will do'.

Miss Pankhurst eats with the Roes, but not so much. Sometimes there is quite half her food left when I am sent to clear. Cook says I must throw it out and am not to touch one bit of it, for don't I get enough and more? This is true but it makes me very angry when I think what Ma would make from such wasting. Although she vexed me all the time when I was there I sometimes think Ma has more sense than all these fine folk, for she would never waste a morning putting flowers in a jar, as I have seen Mrs Roe do, or spend an evening pushing ivory figures round a board.

I have been here a month now and heard nothing from home. Frank will be gone again. I wonder how they are all going on without me. If Alfie is keeping up with his letters now I am not there to help him. If little Evelyn is over the croup. If Will still wakes every night howling. How is my nan's cough going along? Has Pa got work still? Does Ma still go singing round at the Black Prince on a Saturday night with that rotten tattered ribbon in her hair that made me die for shame? I remember when it was new. Blue like the sky. Now it is the colour of rat droppings but still she wears it. She was so beautiful then. When I was little. Plump and rosy and always laughing. Sometimes I wonder where that Ma went. Did she creep away one night and leave this Ma behind her? I wish, in a way, it was so, for rather that than see what she has become. And us the cause.

I wonder who watches the little ones now when she's out? Not Lucy, for sure. Did Frank give Lucy my present? I'm sure he would not for she is not his best girl and anyway, too young for such things. He will be far away by now. With all his other girls. I shall be quite forgotten. Forgotten by everyone. Even my own ma. Well, her first of all, for it was she who sent me here. 'To get away'. From what? From her? I know I was a trial to her sometimes when I would not speak, or fought with Lucy or spent the whole of dinner saying psalms. I would not do that now. I promise. Does she miss me at all, I wonder? And shall I ever be allowed to visit? I know I am better here, and 'fortunate' and 'favoured' as Reverend Beckett declared, but if I am never to see my family again it will be very hard. Even Lucy that I do not like.

Miss Pankhurst found me crying and spoke very kindly to me. She said her mother and sister live hundreds of miles from here and she misses them badly. We are to be friends, she says, so that we need not be lonely. I am to call her 'Miss Sylvia' which she likes a good deal better than 'Miss Pankhurst' and she is to let me look at her paintings on Saturday. She is not so plain as I thought for she has a lovely smile and no spots at all that I can see.

Mrs Roe says I may go home next Sunday and need not come back till night. She and the master are to visit her sister for their dinner and Cook has said she will manage very well alone, so I shall not be needed. I am so excited. I have two shillings that I have saved to give to Ma, and Mr Roe says I may take some apples from the tree, as many as I can carry. I told Miss Sylvia I was allowed to visit when I took her her clean linen. She gave a little nod as though she had known it all along. 'And will you still come and look at my paintings tomorrow?'

'I shall be honoured, miss.'

She laughed and said, 'Well, I don't know about that. I'm only a student, you know.'

I didn't know what to say so I just laid the linen down and asked if I should close the curtains.

I have two spots now. It is so unfair. Just when I am going home and all the street will be out to look at me. Also my dress is very tight. I shall have to keep my shawl about me all day long and it is so hot it is bound to make my spots stand out on my head like a watchman's beacon. Cook says I must put some vinegar on them and they will go. She says I must not keep eating sugar, but it is very hard. There is nothing so beautiful as sugar.

Miss Sylvia's paintings are very fine. She has the skill to make a person look happy or sad or fat or thin – all with a brush. How can you do that? I wish I could. She asked me what I thought of her work. I could think of nothing worthy of it, so I said, 'It is wondrous as the feet of Sheba,' and she looked at me very strangely then began to laugh. I was very ashamed. When she saw that she stopped at once and became serious again. 'I am not laughing at you, Maggie,' she said. 'Don't ever think I am laughing at you.'

Ma is with child again. I knew it would be so, for when she came with me first to Park Walk her eyes were bruised like a rotten potato, all purple and yellow. I am thirteen now and should know what life is about, but if the getting of babies is done always with pain and fighting, I do not understand how there are so many. Reverend Beckett said the last queen had nine children. Surely, if she was wed to a prince, he would not keep hitting her for royal people should not go on like that? I only know every time Ma has a cut face or an arm she cannot lift, there is another on the way. I will have no children. Frank says they grow inside your belly and only men can put them there. He told me once that he had put one in me while I slept and that it would grow bigger and bigger till it burst out of my front, dragging my heart behind it. I screamed and screamed for terror and Pa came running down the stairs. Frank said it was just a game we were playing so Pa gave him a clout for waking him up. After, Frank said he would pull the baby out again if I lay still and left off crying. He did it with his finger. I didn't like it.

It took me above an hour to walk to my street. I was so warm with my shawl that I nearly put it by, but then I saw Joe Rice who drives the ragman's cart and I was afraid he would mark how tight my dress was, so I carried on. I don't think he knew me till I was right by him, for he made to tip his hat, but when he saw who it was he just sort of gaped like the great donkey he is.

When Ma caught sight of me she just gazed like she had never seen me before. She was standing in the kitchen, stirring the dinner with Will under her arm and him trying to pull her hair. I said, 'How are you, Ma?' and she just sort of opened her mouth and closed it again, and then she set Will down so he straightway started yelling and said, 'Oh, Maggie. It's only broth'. And I thought she would start out crying too, for a moment, but Ma never cries – not like Mrs Carter who's dying, and half the other women in the street who are not.

I said, 'Well, it will be better than that, Ma, for I have brought you this.' And I reached in my pocket and gave her the two shillings, and she just stared at them there in her hand as though they were sovereigns not shillings, and then she said, 'Well, hang up your shawl, and go and fetch Evelyn from the yard, and if Lucy's there you can send her down to the alehouse to tell your Pa you're home. And then you can help me with your nan. She can't get out of bed just now and the nurse says she must be turned every hour.'

'That's not all I've brought.' Then I showed her the apples which had nearly weighed me to my knees I'd picked so many, and best of all, a loaf of currant bread which Cook gave me just as I was leaving. 'You might as well take this. ''Twill be stale by tomorrow and I can't eat it on my own.' That's what Cook's like. She always acts as though she don't care and it's nothing to her, but I think inside she has quite a good heart. Ma took it from me and said, 'Oh, that looks nice,' and put it at the back of the cupboard as though every day she got given a currant loaf and apples.

'Where's Alfie?'

'He's gone off wandering. Comes back soon enough when he's hungry.'

'Is he working at his letters like I told him?'

Ma sighed. 'He… Maggie, your brother will never…' Then she sighed again and said, 'He's a good boy. Now go and find Evelyn for me. I need to wash her hands.' And I thought, it's just like I've never been away, but when Pa saw me he gave me a great big kiss and said, 'Lord, Maggie, you're a fine sight. More like a woman than a girl, I'd say. Isn't she, Ma?'

Ma shrugged. 'She looks well enough, that's true.' Lucy, of course, had to spoil it by pointing out my spots. 'What's that on Maggie's forehead, Ma? Are they boils like Mr Hill has on his nose?'

Ma said they were not and would very likely be gone by the morning.

'I'm glad I don't get them.'

'You will if you live to be as old as I am.' I don't know why I said that. I was just so vexed. Anyway, there was nothing wrong in it, but Ma's face creased up as though someone had stuck a knife through her. Just then Alfie came in, very muddy. He was so joyful to see me and gave me a big hug which put mud all over my sleeve, but I didn't mind for I know how to get mud off and it's easier than paint, for sure.

Pa let me hand round the apples so I made sure Lucy got the smallest. Evelyn was so excited she choked on hers and had to be held upside down and shaken. But she still ate it. Will got none as he has no teeth. He cried mightily so Ma gave him a little crumb of hers and he put it in his ear, which was a waste. Nan couldn't manage hers. I don't think she knew what it was. She kept turning her mouth away, even though I cut it up real small for her, so I gave it to Alfie which meant he had two although he thought he had ten because of the pieces.

When it was time to go Ma busied herself with the plates and when I went to kiss her she looked all flurried and said her hands were wet and I should mind not to get water on my dress. Since it already had mud and apple and Evelyn's spit from choking, I did not think a drop of water would harm it greatly, but she turned her face away, so I just said, 'Goodbye then, Ma. I will come again soon, I hope.' And she said in a crackly sort of voice. 'God bless you, Maggie.' As she doesn't go to church, I thought this strange.

Miss Sylvia wants to paint me. She said it when I was fetching back her breakfast things. I still had my Sunday dress on as it was so dirty from going home I thought it better to save my other for after I had cleaned her room. Though I like her now and we are friends (she says) she is still quite fearful dirty with her oils and things and it is a great chore to clean them all up, knowing full well it will be back again as bad an hour after I have finished. I was just putting her cup on the tray when she said out of nowhere, 'Maggie, would you be willing to let me paint you, do you think?' I was so shocked I nearly dropped the tray.

'Not now, I don't mean.'

'I don't know, miss. I've not been painted before.'

'All the more reason, then. You could sit for me on Saturday afternoons for an hour or so. I promise not to keep you long. I could get some cake for us. How would that be?'

Cook says I may as well as I am free then. She has given me

some bicarbonate for my spots because we do not think they would look well in a picture.

Miss Sylvia is very strange. I had put on my Sunday dress (clean now, but it took much scrubbing) and brushed my hair a hundred times so that it sparked and Cook said she would roast a chop on it and when I knocked on Miss Sylvia's door she said, 'Oh, Maggie, you look far too clean.' I did not know what to say. Reverend Beckett and, more particular, Mrs Beckett told me God hated dirty people. I know this to be true for he certainly hates the people of Stepney or why would he let them die so, and be ill and hungry?

'I'm sorry, miss.'

She smiled. 'No, don't be sorry. *I'm* sorry. I didn't mean it to sound like that. I just meant... No, never mind. Come in. I've got the cake. It's ginger. Do you like ginger?'

I was not sure that I would, as it is what Ma gives my nan for down below and she is prodigious smelly after.

Miss Sylvia does not talk when she is painting. She wears a smock which makes me wonder how she gets so much paint on her clothes. First she held up a pencil and looked at it till she was goggle-eyed, then she started to scratch away at her canvas like a mad thing. I sat as still as I could but my spots were troubling me, although they are better than they were and Cook says if I leave off the sugar bowl for just one day they will go like magic. She had dressed my hair so that it sort of slops over my brow and you cannot see them. I asked Cook if she had ever been married and she said, yes, she had but that her husband had died very soon after. She didn't say why. I think she is lucky because if a husband dies you do not have to keep having children and being hit.

Miss Sylvia will not let me look at the painting till it is done. I would dearly love to see it, if only to tell if she has put my spots in.

Today I told her how I am teaching Alfie his numbers. She says she has a brother, too, called Harry, and she loves him very much. I said I love my brothers much better than my sisters, and she looked right up at me over her brush as though she understood. Maybe I will tell her about Frank next week.

To stop me fidgeting she asked if I would like to look at a book. I said I should like it very much and she gave me one with only pictures and them very silly. After a while she asked if I did not like it and I said I thought it very fine but where were the words? She looked a lot surprised and said, 'Do you read then, Maggie?'

'Yes, Miss. And I know nine psalms.'

She looked mightily ashamed and went immediately to choose me a book with words. It was fat and dull, about what I do not know and after a while I was back to shifting about. Miss Sylvia set down her brush and fetched me a beautiful book full of animal drawings, with words under of where they lived and what they liked to eat.

There is a big stripy cat called a leopard that can eat a whole man, and another with spots that lives in trees and can run faster than a locomotive. Miss Sylvia had two times to ask me to sit up for I was so bent over the book I had forgot why I was there.

I hate Cook. She has shouted at me all day long and now it is to come from my wages and I do not know how I can ever take money home again. I was to do the silver and she told me to take a cloth and some powdery stuff and rub it all over the spoons and knives and forks and anything silver I could find and then to polish it off. She said it was a salmon and now no one could eat it without dying of poison and it had cost over a shilling. And when it was dinner time I had to take in the cold pie that was nearly gone from yesterday, with potatoes and a cabbage, and Mr Roe looked so grieved and made a humphing noise. Afterwards Mrs Roe came down to the kitchen and said, 'Mrs Jenkins, did we not decide on fish for today?' And Cook's face went all stiff with vexation and she said, 'Yes, ma'am, indeed we did, but young Maggie here has put an end to that, I fear.'

'Oh?' said Mrs Roe, looking mightily surprised.

'The girl has only polished it.'

'Polished it?'

'Thinking it to be silver, ma'am. I've said it will come from her wages.'

Mrs Roe gave a little start and put her hand to her mouth, then hurried away back to Mr Roe, and soon we heard a great deal of laughing, though I don't know why.

Today I made a *glace*. There was company, and Cook said we must make something tasty as it was all ladies and they might like something cooling. First we took bread which I chopped very fine, then some sugar and *two* eggs and a pint of best cream which the man said I could not have if I did not give him a kiss, but Cook heard and hit him with a big spoon so I did not have to. She said if he says that again I am to tell her and she will hit him with a copper pan, which made us laugh so much. Cook is not so bad.

The ladies were very noisy. They arrived all together, four of them, chattering like starlings, and hardly a word for Mrs

Roe who was waiting to receive them, but straight into the parlour (as the not eating room is called). There they made more noise. I was sent to tell Miss Sylvia and down she came, looking quite neat with her hair all smoothed and a big white collar and dark blue dress, although I did see she had paint still under her fingernails.

I asked Cook if the ladies were artists also and she rolled her eyes upwards and said, no, not at all, and she wondered if some of them were even ladies from how they went on, some of them. I thought best not to ask any more.

After a while Mrs Roe came down to say they were ready for refreshment so I took up a tray with lemonade and the *glace* and they all whooped and cheered and quite fell upon it like the animals in Miss Sylvia's book.

At a little after five the ladies came rushing out and went running off down the path like the bobbies were after them. When I went into the parlour Miss Sylvia was still there. She was scribbling away at a piece of card with a stick of charcoal and, of course, had got some on her collar! I asked if I might clear and she said, 'Of course, Maggie. I'm sorry we've made such a mess. We didn't realise the time. I hope they haven't missed the omnibus.' I thought, I hope they haven't, too, or they'll be back here and there's no more lemonade or time to make it. Then she held up the card that she was drawing on and said, 'What do you think of this, Maggie?' It was of a woman, just the outline, but very soft and wavy, with one arm stretched upwards and the other clasping a book with 'Victory' writ across it. I said, 'It's very fine, miss,' not wanting to make myself foolish like the last time. She nodded. 'It would be, Maggie, if it were so. And it will be one day.

That I'm certain of.' Then she set aside the drawing and said, 'Maggie, will you tell me something?'

'If I can, miss.'

'Do you think men have bigger brains than women?'

I stared at her, thinking she must have very little brain at all to ask me such a thing.

'Maggie?'

'I do, miss, yes. For they are bigger altogether so must have.'

'Yes, but elephants are bigger by far than men. Does that make them cleverer?'

No answer came to me.

After supper was cleared and the dishes washed Cook told me that Mrs Roe says I am to have a new dress. It seems the ladies had marked that my skirt is high above my ankles now and that, owing to fatness round my chest, the bodice is frightening tight. She will speak to her niece who teaches sewing at a poor school and see what can be done. I am so excited. For best I would like it to be red with flowers all over like I saw once on a lady at the Black Prince. She was much whistled at by the men which I should not like, but it was a very pretty dress and her chest was very fat, so perhaps mine would not notice.

Miss Sylvia says I may see my picture next week. It is nearly finished. I could, if I wished, take a peek when I am cleaning, but then she might ask me, and it would be a wicked thing to lie to her when she has given me so much cake.

I told her I am to have a new dress. She said she was glad for me, but did not ask me one thing about the colour or cut or anything.

She is very happy because her mother and sister are to visit. I wonder when I may go home. Mrs Roe says I need not pay for the fish but I must ask Cook before going my own way again. She is a lady. Mr Roe has quite taken to smiling at me and keeps asking if I have polished the sausages or the beef or whatever he is eating at the time, to which I reply, 'Please, no, sir,' which makes him laugh mightily.

I am teaching Cook to read. She caught me looking at the master's paper and asked me what good staring did when there was work to be done? I said I did not stare.

'What then?'

'Reading.'

She laughed and said, 'Then read me something.'

So I did. At first she thought I was making it up but then I stumbled on a funny name so she knew it must be true. 'I'll teach you if you want it.'

She said no, never in a thousand years. She'd got this far without. But next day she called me over and told me to read her some more, so I read her the price of currants and how to make a jelly from cows' brains and she said it was a disgrace to charge so much for currants, but I was to read her out the brains again so she could put it to her memory. I said, 'If you could read, Cook, you would not need to remember', so she made a huffing noise and said, 'Maybe. I'll think about it.'

Since that I have read her a little every day and given her a letter to learn, though on Friday there was nothing about food, so I found a little patch about a man who wanted the men to vote for him and he would give them jobs, he said, but before they could decide two women shouted out and asked why they should not have a vote as well and the man was very angry and would not speak to them and they were carried away by two policemen.

When I had finished I saw that Cook's face had gone all white and pink. I thought she was vexed with me again but she just said, 'Is it true? Are you making it up?' I said, how could I be, for I knew nothing about such things and cared a good deal less? Then she took my arm real hard and said, 'Do you not know who those two women were?'

'It does not say.'

She spoke so low I could scarce hear, 'That is the sister of Miss Pankhurst, and her mother, maybe, too.'

Mrs Pankhurst and Miss Christabel Pankhurst visited today. I was never so frightened in my life. I had my new dress on, which is the most horrible thing in the world. It is brown without so much as a stitch of another colour. Just brown. I hate brown. It is the most horrible colour in the world. The only thing I do not hate is it does not squeeze my chest and my ankles are covered. Miss Sylvia asked me in the morning why I looked so wretched but I said nothing, knowing it was wicked of me to feel so rankled when it was done from good feeling and kindness. But *brown*! If there really is a heaven I hope there may be nothing brown there. Not even sugar or sausages.

Mrs Pankhurst is the most beautiful old person in the world. She does not look old at all, but must be for she has two grown daughters and more besides. Her cheeks are high and rounded like doorknobs and her eyes are like violet jewels. She is so clean. It is hard to think how Miss Sylvia can have so much hair falling down when her mother is like a perfect picture of tidiness. Still, I am very fearful of her. She is like a great power that is silent till roused forth like a mighty lightning.

Miss Christabel Pankhurst is the most beautiful person in the whole world. She is beyond the riches of Sheba. Her hair is dark as currants and wound round so it glows like an angel's halo. Her skin is pale and pinky with little dots round her nose and her eyes shine like blue stars. Her voice is low and strong and she wore a most beautiful white blouse with tiny flowers in blue and yellow all over it and a black skirt. I felt like a muddy puddle beside them.

Cook had told me they were to take tea with Miss Sylvia in the parlour, and I must be sure to cover the tray with a linen cloth, and not to slop the tea. A little after three a cab drew up and out got two ladies. Cook said, 'You'd best make haste or Mrs Roe will be there before you,' so I ran up the stairs from the kitchen and opened the door and there they were, stately as queens. I almost thought I should curtsey but luckily Miss Sylvia came hurrying down the stairs just then and they were too much taken with greeting each other to see if I had or I hadn't. I took their coats and that was when I saw how fine their dress was, especially Miss Christabel's – much finer than her sister's – and I wished with all my heart I had had on my old one which was grey and at the least did not make me look like ditch water.

I showed them into the parlour, thinking how different they were from Miss Sylvia's lady friends that had run off to catch the omnibus. I cannot imagine Mrs Pankhurst ever running. Rather she would glide like a swan, and Miss Christabel would soar like an eagle.

At five o'clock Cook sent me to clear the tea and I was just piling up things on the tray when Miss Sylvia said, 'You can leave those for a minute, Maggie. I've something for you to see.' At which Miss Christabel leapt up and said, 'Something for us all to see. Lead on, fair sister,' and she flung open the door and marched out into the passageway. Mrs Pankhurst rose very gracefully and followed and Miss Sylvia called out to them, 'Straight to the top of the stairs and turn left. Come on, Maggie. I need to know what you think.'

Well, I did not know what to think except that whatever it was I should not dare let it out of my mouth in such company. Up we went. I was glad to see Miss Sylvia had tried a little to make the place tidy. In one corner, nearest the window, was her easel. It was covered with a cloth. In a moment I realised what was to happen and felt my stomach come right up into my mouth.

She pulled back the cloth and there I was, sitting, looking far away as though I could see forever, but instead of a book in my lap she had painted a cloth for polishing and beside me some rusty pans.

Mrs Pankhurst went right up close to it and gazed and gazed. 'What do you think, Mama?' Miss Christabel asked. Her mother nodded her head very knowingly and said 'Hmmm' in a thoughtful sort of way.

I feared this might mean she did not like it, but Miss Sylvia looked so tickled with just that one 'Hmmm', that I knew it must be the highest form of praise. Miss Christabel, too, was much taken with the picture and said it showed my soul. And then they all three fell silent and I knew they were waiting for me to speak. So, thinking it the finest thing that was ever done – so like me I could have been looking in a mirror, except that, Lord be praised, I was wearing my grey dress – I dragged up all my courage and said, 'Hmmm', as loud as I dared.

They all three fixed their eyes on me as though I were quite the quaintest creature they ever had come upon, and then Mrs Pankhurst simply burst out laughing and then Miss Christabel and Miss Sylvia, too, and Mrs Pankhurst laid her hand on my arm and said, 'Maggie, you are a singular girl. A very singular girl.'

I did not know if this were good or bad, but she smiled so sweetly at me that I guessed she meant it kindly, so I said, 'Thank you, ma'am. I'm much obliged.' Then Mrs Pankhurst took out a beautiful silver watch on a chain and said, 'I think we must be going, Sylvia, my dear,' and so we all went downstairs again and just as I was fetching their coats, Mrs Roe appeared and was greeted like an old friend. 'And we are to come to you on Wednesday, Mrs Roe, if that is agreeable still?' Mrs Pankhurst asked. Mrs Roe said it was. Mrs Pankhurst thanked her heartily. 'We shall be about ten in number, I think, but you are not to think of refreshments. Sylvia will attend to all that.' I thought it not a good idea to leave Miss Sylvia in charge of such arrangements and she clearly thought so too, for she gave a little smile and said, 'In which case I shall ask Maggie to help me, if Cook can spare her at all that day.' Mrs Roe said she felt certain Cook would. I was not so sure but after our supper when Cook and I were sitting together and I trying to teach her the difference between 'E' and 'F', I said, 'Miss Sylvia would like me to help her next Wednesday if I can be spared.'

'Help her what?'

'To provide refreshments for ten ladies.'

Cook rolled her eyes. 'Let's hope they are more ladies than the last lot.'

It being two months since I had visited, Mrs Roe said I might go home on Sunday. It was raining and by the time I reached our house I was dripping like a gutter. Ma came to the door. She looked ill, but when she saw me her whole face brightened right up. I said, 'It's me, Ma, and I have brought you some biscuits.' They were ginger which will either cure my nan or kill her. Ma is well gone with the baby now, and I never knew her to look so worn. Her skin is yellow like a candle and her eyes ringed with dark. I gave her my wages – four shillings all but three halfpence which I had spent on some ribbon for the collar of my new dress. It is green. I wanted yellow but it was a farthing more. Cook showed me how to sew it and a wicked business it was. My fingers were so punched full of holes I felt like just wiping them over the dress till it was red. She says she will teach me properly when there is more time, but that I do not have a natural way for it. I could have told her she does not have a natural way for reading – it is weeks now, and she still cannot remember beyond 'J', and usually only 'I'.

Pa gave me a big squeeze and said because it was me, he would light the fire. I think he meant because I had brought so much money, but I still felt proud that he should do it.

Ma sent Alfie out to buy some faggots for our dinner. She gave him a sixpence which was far too much but he came back without any change. I chid him hard and said he must go straight back and ask for the tuppence that was owing but he just threw his arms about and went and sat in the corner. Ma said not to fret and she would speak to the butcher come the morning. I knew she would not, so while she was tending to Will, I put on my cloak and ran all the way to the butcher's which was just on the point of closing.

'What can I do for you, miss, in such a hurry? You'd best be quick. I'm on my way to church,' he said, all smarmy smile.

I said, 'You can give me back the tuppence owing that you forgot to give my brother.'

He looked real surprised and angry and sort of squinted at me over the counter. When he realised who I was he smiled again, all smarmy still. 'I wouldn't have known you, Maggie Robins. All grown up in your fancy gown.'

'Well, you know me now, Mr Green,' I said, 'and if you could hand me the change of the sixpence Alfie gave you, I'll be grateful.'

He glared at me long and hard, then reached below the counter and brought up a black tin box. 'I was going to call round to your ma's on my way home,' he said, handing me the tuppence. 'She hadn't ought to send your Alfie out on errands where there's money. What if he'd lost it? Where's your dinner then?'

I was so vexed that he should try to blame Ma that I just smiled all frosty at him. 'You being such a good churchgoer, Mr Green, I expect you'd've given it him for free.' I turned smart on my heel before he could think to reply.

After dinner I decided I must give Alfie some teaching. Although I do not like Mr Green who thinks himself so close to heaven he would have an angel to polish his wings, I fear it is no help to Ma if Alfie cannot tell how much to pay and get back when she sends him to the shops.

I sat him down by me and told Lucy to go away for she, of course, wanted to hang over his shoulder giggling at each mistake. She made a face like the madam she is and slumped down by the window where she set to drumming her fingers on the sill like a rat in the rafters. Little Evelyn sat at my feet quiet as a lamb.

At first Alfie would not try at all, would not speak – just kept shaking his head and rolling his eyes around but then I whispered that I had brought something for him that he should only have if he did well. Then he tried very hard. First I took a book and showed him the letters that we had worked on before I went to Park Walk. He remembered some – no worse than Cook! But it was when I asked him his numbers that he got in a dreadful fret. I said them over slowly and told him to say them after. He could not do it. A full hour I sat with him and at the end we were both near to screaming, I think.

Ma came in. 'Maggie, that's enough for now. Alfie is tired, and you have a long journey home.'

I stared at her. 'This is my home.'

Ma came over all hot and bothered. 'Yes, yes, I know. I only meant…' Just then Nan called out and she went to her. Lucy, the little worm, stopped her drumming and wriggling about and said in a sneaky little voice, 'You see. It's not your home any more.' I felt near to throttling her but would not give her the pleasure of seeing I was rankled.

'It is,' I said coldly. 'Same as it is Frank's. Homes are homes. We don't have to be here.'

Lucy gave a funny little choky sound. 'Frank's here more than you are now. See what he gave me.' She reached down inside her dress and pulled out a tiny heart made of some shiny stone and hung around her neck on a bootlace.

'When did he give you that?'

'Last time he was here.'

'It was meant for me. He didn't know I'd be gone.'

Lucy gave me a real funny look. 'No, that was the first time,' she said. 'He's come back again since then. I'm his best girl now.'

I stood up and fully meant to slap her but just then Alfie flung his arms round me and begged me to give him his reward for all his learning. I was so angry – God forgive me, I never meant to do it – I pulled out the apple I had kept by for him and just flung it in the fire. Poor Alfie burst out with a mighty sob and rushed to get it back. I seized hold of him and clung with all my might, screaming at Lucy to fetch Pa. Ma came running and between us we pulled Alfie away before he could burn, but he was crying and throwing his arms around and several times we both took blows from him. At last Pa arrived and lifted Alfie clean up in the air and shook him like he was a sack of feathers till he had ceased howling. Ma threw a bucket of water on the fire lest he would try again.

And all that for an apple.

I took my leave, for I could not bear to think of what I had done, and most particular, that they had lost the fire. Ma came with me to the door and laid her hand on my shoulder. 'Maggie, you are not to fret. Alfie cannot help it. He's a good boy, but life is hard for him. Try to understand.'

I thought, my life is hard, too, but who understands that? Who understands me? Of course there is no need, for I am Maggie Robins. The clever one. The fortunate one. The favoured one.

The door closed. I stood in the dark street outside the house that was no longer my home, listening to the voices of the family I was no longer part of. I thought, yes, I am Maggie Robins, and I am clever and fortunate and favoured. But most of all, I am alone.

The Wednesday of the meeting I thought I should go mad. First Cook had a turn and could not walk for feeling dizzy and feverish. Mrs Roe said she should go to bed and she would make her a poultice. I was desperate I should have to cook the lunch and dinner *and* help Miss Sylvia, but Mrs Roe said I need not do so. She would fry up some chops for herself and the master and they could make do with the cold bacon and some pickles for their supper. I was heartily grateful for Cook had said I must be sure and polish the fender in the parlour and lay a neat fire and wipe the windows over with vinegar and water as well as all my usual chores.

At four o'clock Miss Sylvia returned from college. When Mrs Roe explained that Cook was ill the very first thing she did was boil a kettle and take her in some beef tea, although Mrs Roe had twice sent me up with soup and some porter ale, which Cook had drunk to the last drop, declaring all the while that she would be dead by morning. I did not think this likely as she asked if I could bring her some of the visitors' jam pastries, for she fancied they might cool her head.

Then Miss Sylvia and I set to making sandwiches, enough

for an army. There was paste and beef brawn and chopped egg
and salmon. Next we made scones and some syrup cakes and
a great jug of lemonade, and I laid out plates and glasses and
little pretty bits of cloth for them to wipe their hands on. Mr
and Mrs Roe dined early and retired to the parlour which was
a great blessing, although Mrs Roe kept coming out to see if
we needed anything and kept suggesting things, till in the end
we wished she would go away and leave us alone to our
muddle.

At seven o'clock the doorbell chimed. Miss Sylvia ran up
the stairs to change her dress and came back within a minute
but it was all buttoned wrong.

The first lady to arrive was very old. I thought she might
have been a queen or something once for she was so stiff and
noble and wore only black lace in her hair which was quite
white like a snowball, and her hands were all crinkly and had
brown spots on them like a tiger. I was very afraid, but when
she had been shown a chair and was settled she seemed
contented enough and took a glass of lemonade. Next came a
very smart lady, though somewhat stout, who spoke most
kindly to me, asking my age and how many children my
mother had at home. I replied, 'Four, ma'am, with one in the
grave and one in the making,' at which she gave me a very
kind smile and said she hoped I was happy here.

More ladies came, most old like Mrs Roe but a few of Miss
Sylvia's age. They wore fine pretty garments and all had hats,
though some were smarter than others. Last of all came Miss
Christabel and Mrs Pankhurst and with them a tiny woman
in very dull clothes but with the most sparkling dancing eyes
and a laugh like a string of cans clattering.

At nine o'clock I took up the refreshments. The ladies looked mighty pleased to see me. I do not know what they had been speaking of, but they were very pink-cheeked and Miss Christabel leapt up from her seat when I entered, crying, 'Manna from heaven, eh, Maggie?' To which I replied, 'I'm sorry, ma'am, it's mainly sandwiches.' Everyone laughed and I wished I had never spoken. Miss Sylvia came to my side and said in a nice still voice, 'Maggie has positively slaved to get this ready for us. I am very grateful for her help,' whereupon they fell quiet and gave me many smiles. I think, perhaps, ladies are nicer than men.

Three Wednesdays the ladies have now met at our house. Cook is recovered and we have served them anchovy toasts, as well as stuffed pigeons' eggs and meat pâté with mustard and lemon sherbert. I think maybe I should cease reading so many recipes to Cook as she is getting more and more wild in her endeavours and sometimes poor Mr Roe looks quite bilious when I put a dish in front of him.

I asked her once what she thought the ladies talked of in their meetings and she screwed up her face and said it was mad things and not something I should be concerned with, but she is softer now since I gave her the jam pastries, and so I asked her over and over, and in the end she confessed that the meetings were all to do with votes. I was not overly sure what they might be, but Cook explained that men could choose who should govern them, but women could not. And Mrs Pankhurst and her daughters were foremost in protesting this. Then I thought back to how Miss Sylvia had asked me about brains, and it seemed to me that maybe she was not completely mad.

Last evening a strange thing happened. I had taken in the spiced pork tartlets and kippered slices and was about to fetch more lemonade when a discussion amongst the ladies burst into quarrelling. I had taken no heed of the talk till all at once they grew so heated. Miss Christabel uttered something of working women, whereupon Mrs Despard (she who, I think, was once royal) said firmly, 'But do you not see, Christabel, that these women are useless to the cause? They cannot reason, they cannot debate. They simply work, give birth and die. How can they advance us in any way?'

Miss Christabel rose to her feet and looked Mrs Despard strong in the eye. 'Without them we are nothing.'

Then another lady with a very fine hat trickled her fingers into the air. 'Christabel, think. Think how hard we have tried to persuade these creatures to stand by us. I agree with Mrs Despard. They are useless. They cannot think, they *will* not think. All our efforts are wasted in that area, as well you know.'

There was a horrible silence, then Miss Sylvia who had not spoken till then, held up her hand. 'I should like, if I may, to ask Maggie why she thinks it is that working women will not support our cause.'

I felt quite sick, and held my peace, staring all the while at the tray I held. All fell quiet and I continued in silence, hoping mainly that I might die on the instant and so not have to answer.

Miss Sylvia, seeing this, rose and came to my side. 'It's all right, Maggie. You have nothing to fear. These ladies would like to know why so few working women – women like your mother, perhaps – are not interested in furthering their rights.

In making a better world for themselves and their children.'

One of the ladies clapped. 'Exactly. How can they not see how much their support is needed? Why are they so…feeble?'

I looked at her, with her fine hat with soft grey feathers and thought about Ma with her yellow skin and the bruises rising from where Alfie kicked her.

'I think, ma'am, perhaps they are very tired,' I said.

Miss Sylvia wishes me to attend the next ladies' meeting. Cook looked very black when I told her and muttered about how was she to feed so many and make dinner for the master and mistress on her own? Was she a miracle worker? No. I said I would do all my work in time but still she rumbled on till I began to think it would be simpler to tell Miss Sylvia I could not go. I do not know that I would like it anyway. Particularly if I am to be questioned and held to account, but it is hard not to be a little interested for they are all such lively glittering souls; even Mrs Despard who looks as she could saw through iron with just one glance.

It is my belief that Cook fears I will be persuaded to the ladies' thinking, but how could I be since I understand nothing of it, apart from men being cleverer than elephants, but even that I wonder about, since the animal book said elephants could remember for a hundred years and I'm sure no man alive could boast as much. Pa cannot mind where he has put his pipe ten minutes ago, and Mr Roe is forever asking where his slippers are.

Just when I had decided I should not attend, Mrs Roe came trotting into the kitchen and said, 'I hear you are to be with us this evening, Maggie. I am so pleased,' after which neither

Cook nor I could dispute it, but it was a heavy day for me in the kitchen.

The evening was quite the strangest of my life. First of all I opened the front door to the ladies and took their coats as usual, all wet and smelling like mouldy cats for it had been pouring rain all day; then when they were settled I had to hurry up the stairs and join them. My heart was pumping ready to burst but Miss Sylvia drew me to a seat between her and the tiny lady with the clattery laugh, who immediately clasped my hand saying, 'Well, Maggie, welcome. I am Mrs Drummond.' She had such a funny way of talking that I feared she spoke a foreign language and, knowing none myself, stayed silent.

Mrs Despard talked a great deal in a fine ladylike voice and I understood not a word. It was all of education and ideals and symbols and the like and it seemed to me that some others of those present were also a little confused.

Just when I was wondering whether I could slip away unnoticed back to the kitchen, there was a heavy knocking on the door below. I hurried down to open it. There stood a woman, not old but drably dressed. Before I could ask her business she pressed past me, flung off her cloak which was drenching wet, and rushed up the stairs. I hastened after her, not knowing if I should first call the master for I did not think I could manage to force her out myself.

When I arrived my shock was even greater, for the person was being warmly embraced by Miss Christabel and several of the company. Miss Sylvia led me towards her. 'Maggie, this is Miss Annie Kenney. A true friend of the cause.' The person turned, smiled at me a great flashing beam of a smile and shook my hand like she was wringing out the washing. 'Pleased to meet thee, Maggie,' she said. 'Looks like you and me are in it together.' I had no faint idea what she might mean, but she seemed so cheery and had hold of my hand so hard, I thought it best to smile back at her for fear she would twist it off.

When everyone had settled once more Miss Christabel rose. 'I have some excellent news. Sylvia has pulled it off. We have tickets for the Albert Hall. James Keir Hardie has excelled himself.' She waved some slips of paper. 'Annie here and Teresa Billington are to represent us. And, better still, Annie is to sit in a minister's box.' There was a general murmur of delight and admiration. 'Now, who can lend her the clothes?' Various of the ladies offered to produce whatever was necessary. I listened amazed, for it seemed to me a very strange thing that a poor working woman, as she plainly was, should be given tickets to the play and dressed up like Cinderella by ladies who would, you suppose, walk past her in the street.

Then came the biggest surprise of all. Miss Christabel turned and gave me a wonderful sparkling smile. 'Of course Annie will need a maid,' she said, looking straight at me, 'and who better than Maggie? She will be quite perfect, I'm sure.' My mouth came open like a codfish. The other ladies all nodded their heads approvingly. 'Good. That's settled then. We'll discuss the details later. Sylvia, how are the banners progressing?'

Miss Sylvia said they were all but finished but her room was now so packed full she had no more room for storage. I thought if ever I were called on to speak, it should be to agree on that score, but I was not and it seemed I had been forgotten

again, for they went on to talk about letters to the Prime
Minister. Mrs Drummond said she could lay hands on a
typewriter which made the ladies squeak with joy. Frank has
seen one and says it is the finest thing. Nearly as good as a
gun.

There was much talk of rallies and again the ladies began to
complain about supporters. I feared I should be examined
again, but luckily Miss Annie quite snuffed out their moaning.
'Leave it with me. I shall sort out a regular crowd,' she said,
all purposeful, and Miss Christabel nodded and looked most
satisfied.

When the ladies had left Miss Sylvia helped me put the
room to rights. After a while she asked, 'What did you think
of the meeting, Maggie?' I said I was not sure.

'Are you happy to go with Annie to the Albert Hall? You
do not have to, you know.'

I was surprised at this for I had thought Miss Christabel
required me to most positively. As if she guessed, Miss Sylvia
added, 'My sister can be very pushy when she wants
something done. You are under no obligation to put yourself
at risk, however slight.'

'What risk would that be, miss?'

She shrugged her shoulders, 'None, really, since you would
not be involved and so could not be blamed for whatever
occurs.'

My heart ran cold. 'Is it a...bad play, miss?'

Miss Sylvia looked truly confused. 'What play, Maggie?'

'That we are going to see. At the Albert Hall.'

She began to laugh. 'It's not a play, Maggie. Although it
may end up like one. It's a political meeting. There, I've told

you enough. The more you know, the more you are complicit, and we have no right to drag you into something you do not fully understand.'

'I don't understand it at all, miss, but I should like to go to the theatre with Miss Kenney, only...'

'Yes?'

'Miss Kenney is to wear fine clothes to the Albert Hall.'

'Yes, indeed. She is to sit in a minister's box.'

'And am I to sit in it, too?' thinking it must be a very large box.

'You are.'

'So must I wear this dress?'

Miss Sylvia fair shook with laughter. 'Don't worry, Maggie. We'll find you something nice, too. Fit for a lady's maid.'

I was never so happy.

Next day Cook, although pretending not to care, asked me what had occurred at the meeting. I was not sure how much I should tell, although no one had said I must not and Cook has been very kind to me, for all her black days. I said there had been a great deal of talking of things I could not follow, but there was to be a visit to the Albert Hall and I was to go in attendance on one of the ladies. I did not say it was a dressed-up working girl for I know Cook would sniff herself blue at the very thought.

Miss Sylvia looks very tired. She works long hours at the art college and then late into the night in her room. Now my portrait is done I cannot sit with her on Saturdays, although she lets me read her books still and sometimes when I am choosing one she asks me what I thought of the last. At first I would say, 'Very nice, miss,' or 'I liked the pictures,' – dull things like that, but then she would ask me what I liked about them and I would have to think. Sometimes, after I had thought, I realised that maybe I did not like them so much after all. They were too plain or too fussy, too unreal, even. Then Miss Sylvia's face would light up and she would nod happily, as though it was a good thing not to praise everything just because someone has made a book of it. So little by little I am learning, not just about dresses and ribbons and all the things I used to dream about, but a whole new world, for there is so much stuff in them. Birds and animals, kings and queens, foreign lands, stars, oceans... Words, so many words, like a great road stretching before me into a distant land, a road I long to travel.

If ever I do marry I shall make certain my man can read, else we shall do nothing but quarrel and make babies, like married people do.

I wonder how Ma is going on. Although we did not agree on one thing when I was living there, I find there is so much I should like to ask her and speak to her about. My chest is nearly like a woman's now; even with my new dress, it shows out. The bread boy tried to feel it when I opened the door to him the other day. I hit him on the ear and he swore something awful. I don't know what I shall do if it gets much bigger. Cook's is down round her belly and I do pray that will not happen to me. I have wound a length of muslin around me, back and front, but it is wicked tight, and besides I shall have to return it come Thursday for that is when Cook plans to make her jam.

This Wednesday only Miss Kenney and Miss Christabel

came. I was sent for to hear of the arrangements. Next Friday Miss Sylvia will take me in an omnibus to Kensington Gardens and from there we are to go in a *cab* to the Albert Hall. I cannot believe it. I am so jittered. I was never in a cab. I asked Cook what it would be like and she sniffed and said it was nothing particular, which makes me think she has never tried it.

Miss Sylvia is to lend me her blue dress with the white collar and I am to have a cape and a hat from a real maid that works for the stout lady who asked about my family. I have polished my boots like mirrors and Cook says she will fix my hair like a real maid's for she has seen how it is done when she worked for a duke one time. I am surprised if that is true for she never mentioned it before.

Today has been the biggest of my life. It snowed all morning and Cook kept grumbling at me for first I could not get the fire to blow, then I forgot to take the master his eggs so they were near cold. All day I had the trembles and could not think of one thing but that I must go in a cab to the theatre that very night.

At five o'clock Miss Sylvia came home. She looked pale as a sheet. Cook had brushed my hair into a giant roll and pinned it to the top of my head. In truth I thought she had nailed it, but she said I must not fuss and did I want to look neat or did I not? Miss Sylvia's blue dress fits like it was made for me. Even she remarked it. 'You look perfect, Maggie. Just right, doesn't she, Cook?' Cook said she thought I would do. Mrs Roe came out when the hat and cape were on and positively clapped her hands, saying, 'Maggie, I would never have known you. You could be a nanny.' This upset me a lot as looking older is one thing, but my nan has no teeth and her hair is like clumps of moss. She fetched Mr Roe who gave me a very gallant bow and said, 'I don't know about a lady's maid. More like a lady,' which almost made up for the mistress.

It was bitter cold when we left the house. We walked quickly to the omnibus stop. There were a lot of people on it and I could feel them stare at me in my fine clothes. Miss Sylvia said we should go upstairs, but it was full of working men all smoking and spitting, so we came down again and sat opposite three women who goggled at us like we were circus freaks. I stared them right back and all but one – very fat with a shabby brown shawl – looked away.

We got off by a great tall building all lit up like a palace and Miss Sylvia said we should go along to the corner for that is where we were to meet Miss Kenney and the other lady, Miss Billington.

I swear I should not have known them as they stepped towards us. Miss Kenney had on a coat of finest black wool with a collar of soft grey fur. Her hat was black with deep red feathers like ox blood. Miss Billington had on an outfit of rose pink velvet and round her neck a gingery dog with gnashing teeth and bright green eyes. Dead, for sure, but I still felt an awful panic for I am not fond of dogs and would never wear one round my neck.

The ladies seemed as taken with my looks as I with theirs and said I was 'the very thing'. Then Miss Kenney said, 'We must get on. It would be a disaster if we got spotted.'

Miss Sylvia nodded. 'I shall see you after. Clement's Inn.

Good luck.' She turned to me. 'Stay close to these ladies, Maggie. They will look after you.' Then she was gone. I felt suddenly that the ground had disappeared from under me. Miss Kenney grasped my arm. 'Don't frct, Maggie. We shall look after you fine. Say nothing and stay by me close.' With that, they led me to thc cabstand. A cabman immediately leapt down to hold the door. Miss Billington and Miss Kenney climbed in, although Miss Kenney stepped on her hem and nearly fell nose first. I feared the same would happen to me but the cabman put his hand right on my bottom part and just shoved me, saying, 'In you go, lovely. I wish you were riding with me.' I thought this very annoying and was about to spit at him but remembered in time that I must not speak so probably should not spit neither.

The cab was very strange. It made me think of when I had a ride with Joe Rice, the ragman's father. I cannot mind how old I was but Lucy was the baby then, and Samuel still alive, so maybe five or six. Frank sat by mc holding my hand for fear I would fall out. I wished tonight I had him with me, then nothing could frighten me.

As we rode I could see other cabs trotting past us. They were full of gentry, thick with furs and finery. At last the cab halted and the cabman came round to hand the ladies down. He was very smarmy with his oily two-tooth smile. When it was my turn he tried to put his hand back where it had been before but I was wise and jumped right down on his toe which made him gasp for I screwed my heel right into him.

The Albert Hall was bigger far than any theatre in the world, I think, and full of lights and steps. There was such a throng I feared if I looked away one second I would lose Miss

Kenney and Miss Billington, who seemed as settled to the
company as they had lived all their lives amongst princes.

We had not been there a few moments when a very old man
with a beard came charging towards us and shook Miss
Kenney's hand. 'Good evening, Mr Hardie,' she said. 'Will we
do?' At which they both laughed and Mr Hardie winked at me.
I had thought to spit at him, for winking is very forward, Ma
said, but I held myself back and simply frowned at him with
all my might. He looked mightily chastened and we proceeded
up a thousand or so steps past lines of rich dressed people, all
with hats and canes and looking very sober. I wondered if I
should like a political meeting as well as the music hall, for
there we had roasted chestnuts in a little bag and when the fat
man came on we threw the shells with all our might.

A man in a black jacket looked at our tickets and directed
Miss Billington to a seat in the circle, but us he led all the way
to a heavy wood door. He tapped and, receiving no answer,
opened it most cautiously, then stood aside to let us enter.
Miss Kenney nodded to him most gracious and in we went.

Well, it was beyond imagining. There were chairs all
covered in velvet, red as blood, with wavy gold ribbon around
the edges, and curtains of the same. Six seats were laid out,
four in front and two behind and from them we could see all
round the theatre. I glimpsed Miss Billington across from us
and would have waved, but Miss Kenney slapped my hand
down quicker than lightning, whispering most urgently, 'You
don't know her. You don't know anyone. Remember, you are
only a maid.'

Just then there were voices outside and the door opened
again to admit a vastly fine gentleman and with him two

others of similar smartness. Following on came a lady with curly gold hair and a gown of butter yellow silk, quite the most beautiful you ever saw. I could not leave looking at her, though she paid no heed to me, or Miss Kenney. The gentlemen, however, nodded to her before taking their seats in the front row. I think they thought to seat the lady next to them, but, quick as a flash, Miss Kenney sank down on the end, leaving her nowhere to go but behind them. There remained one chair which I thought must be mine but just as I was about to take it, the door opened again and in came a real lady's maid, all in black, and tall as a pikestaff, with a little tray on which rested a glass of cordial and the tiniest pastries you ever saw. She glared at me as though I had fallen down her chimney and, without a word, set the tray down beside the lady, who took no notice at all and was twittering at one of the men as though she had left her brain in the cab that brought her.

The pikestaff stepped back and, folding her hands, stood silently behind her mistress without further movement. I did likewise, praying with all my might that she would not speak to me or ask me where Miss Kenney's pastries were. Fortunately I was saved, for amid much clapping and hoorahing a man walked on to the stage where several chairs and a table were laid out, and began to speak. About what I know not, for he kept clearing his throat and fiddling with his necktie, and I was thinking all the time how he reminded me of Mr Green in the butcher's. After he had talked for a while some more men, all dressed as for a burial, came on to the stage and sat behind the table, ahemming and pouring themselves water from a great jug.

When the first man had done, another of them got up and said some more, and so on through all five of them. The pretty lady sat nibbling at her pastries and peering all round the theatre at anywhere but the stage, and all the while her maid stood clamped behind her like a gate-post, without so much as blinking. I tried to do likewise but my boots felt tighter every minute passing and my legs ached and I began to think how long it was since my dinner, although Cook had given me a plate of bread and dripping before she dressed my hair.

Just when I thought I should sink to my knees with weariness, there was a noise from the side of the stage and the first man, looking mighty relieved, held up his hand and said, 'And now, ladies and gentlemen, I am happy to present to you, our leader, the Prime Minister, Sir Henry Campbell-Bannerman,' whereupon there was a great cheering and on to the stage came a very old man, older even than Mr Hardie, waving his hand as though he were the King himself.

When the noise had died down he started speaking in a great hooty voice, saying how much he would do for the country and the people and the working men and all that, on and on like he would never stop. Miss Kenney shifted in her seat once or twice and I half hoped she would say it was time to leave, for a duller speech I had never heard, for all the beauty of our surroundings.

I think the gentlemen felt the same for one of them was looking at his watch. Just as he did so Miss Kenney sprang to her feet and cried out in a clear quavery voice, 'Will the Prime Minister tell us what is his party's policy with regard to granting women the vote?' There was a silence, deeper than the darkest trough, then suddenly people began to shout and wave their fists. I was frozen like an ice stick with terror and could not move but, quick as a flash, Miss Kenney reached inside her beautiful wool coat and pulled out a scroll of paper which she flung down over the rim of our box. I could not see what it said, but those that did began to yell even more fiercely. Miss Kenney then shouted her question again above the din, and at that very moment Miss Billington flung out her arms, uncoiling a great broad banner with *Votes For Women* writ in huge black letters. It was upside down but still they bayed and roared like angry animals. Straight off, two ticket men came marching in and positively dragged her away.

I saw no more, for the gentlemen by us were of a similar mind, it seems, and hustled Miss Kenney from the box most brutally. The pretty lady was shrieking like a mad thing, her maid fanning her all the while with a hat. Well, I knew the cure for such fitting, for Ma has had like trouble with Lucy in the past so, meaning to help, I smacked the lady hard across her face. She stopped her crying instantly. All there looked at me astonished. I had thought they might thank me, but it seemed not, for the man with the watch raised his hand as he would strike me too. Before he could do so, a great peel rang out from an organ, so thunderous it might have been the end of the world and I, fearing for me it was, turned on my heel and fled as fast as I could, all the way down the thousand steps and out through a great wooden door into the street. I did not cease running till I had reached the corner and then, for lack of breath, I stopped and saw that I was altogether lost. Never in a hundred years could I have found my way back to Park Walk, and even had I found an omnibus and by some mighty miracle, it going to Chelsea, I had not a farthing for the fare.

Wet snow was slapping at me and my cape, for all its style, kept not one shred of coldness out. Never have I wished so truly for my home and Ma to comfort me. Not by speaking, for she seldom does, but just to be. My tears came pouring.

Next I know a bobby is at my side. My heart jumped for I knew he must have come from the theatre to take me for smacking the lady. I thought to run but he was between me and the road.

'What's this?' he asked. 'What's amiss, miss?'

I cannot tell why, but this made me smile. He smiled back with big white teeth and eyes all crinkled. 'Well, I am glad to have stemmed your tears, miss. But I've yet to know what caused them.'

I stared at him, praying perhaps he had not come to lock me up.

'Are you lost? You look a bit lost.'

'I am altogether lost, sir. I don't know how it happened.'

'Perhaps you dropped off a star?'

I had not known that bobbies could be mad.

'No, sir. I'm from Park Walk, Chelsea.'

'Well, that it is a long way from here. No wonder you are lost. Should you like me to arrange your return?'

Just when I would have fallen at his knees in gratefulness, out of nowhere appeared Miss Kenney and Miss Billington, neat again for all their battering.

'Ah, officer. You have found my maid for me,' says Miss Kenney, quite like a lady.

'It seems so, ma'am. I think she is very cold.'

'Yes, yes,' said Miss Billington. 'It is a very cold night. Would you be kind enough to direct us to a cab?'

The bobby bowed his head. He led us to a cabstand and immediately a man came hurrying. I was glad to see it was not the oily person, but a snow-haired man who showed great humbleness and soon we were safely seated.

'The ladies are going to Park Walk, Chelsea,' the bobby told the man, whereat Miss Kenney rose up fast and said, 'No, no, we're not. Take us directly to Clement's Inn. Near to the Aldwych, if you please.'

The bobby stepped back and touched his hat but he gave me a real strange glance. I, not knowing what to do, just shook my head in hopelessness and suddenly he smiled, a great golden smile, then we drove away, but I felt monstrous warmer.

When we arrived at our destination – a huge high house with lights in half the windows – the door was opened by one of the Wednesday ladies. 'Oh, you are here. Thank goodness,' she fairly squeaked, and led us up two flights of stairs to where Miss Sylvia and several others were gathered on the landing to receive us.

With much excitement we were led into a handsome apartment – a big wide room with a fire blazing like a furnace in the hearth. I would have loved more than anything to rush straight to it and toast my hands like muffins but, there being so many present, I knew that I could not.

The stout lady, kind as always, came hurrying towards us. 'Annie, Teresa, come in, sit down. Tell us how it went. And little Maggie. Poor girl, you look frozen. Come over here and sit by the fire. Move up, ladies. Make room for a heroine.' One of them leapt out of her chair and bade me settle myself in her place. I did not think I should, but just then Miss

Christabel came springing out of the next room. 'Sit down, Maggie and warm yourself.' And she fairly pushed me into the chair.

All eyes turned to Miss Kenney and Miss Billington. The others listened, one minute silent, the next fair snorting with aggravation as the ladies unrolled their tale.

'And what did our great Prime Minister do when you asked your question?' enquired the stout lady.

Miss Kenney stood up and, placing her hands in her skirt as she had pockets, opened and shut her mouth like a great codfish gasping for air. The ladies fell about with laughter, and so did I for I had seen it, and indeed he had looked just as she showed him.

Miss Billington then told how she had lowered her banner, forgetting to say that it had been upside down, and how she had been manhandled out into the street.

The stout lady said they had been superbly brave and all agreed and clapped their hands and sang, 'Fight the good fight', two times through. After that, the lady went out and shortly after a little round woman with a very jolly face brought in refreshments – lemonade and sliced pork pies, quite the best I had ever tasted and I wondered if I might ask how they were made, to tell to Cook. A thousand times better than those silly snippets the maid had brought her lady at the theatre. After a while I noticed that no one else was eating, so I made to stop, whereupon Miss Christabel called, 'Maggie, you are to finish all these, or Mrs Pethick Lawrence will be very angry with you', whereat the stout lady gave me a great big smile and said, 'I won't at all, Maggie, but it would please us all to see them gone.' So I ate them.

As I was finishing Mrs Pethick Lawrence suddenly frowned and I feared I had done wrong and she had only been tempting me like Jesus in the wilderness, but she said, 'How did Maggie escape the Albert Hall, Annie?'

Miss Kenney went a tiny bit pink and said, 'I think she was right behind me. Is that so, Maggie?'

I nodded. 'Except for the lady.'

Mrs Pethick Lawrence asked, 'What lady, Maggie?'

'The one in our box who was fitting, ma'am.'

'Fitting?'

'She got all screechy, ma'am, when the banner was loosed.'

'And?'

'Well, ma'am,' I could feel myself reddening like a radish, for all eyes were upon me, 'my sister, Lucy, who is very spry and aggravating when she cannot have her way, will often fall to a fit, and Ma has had to slap her mightily to bring her back to sense again.'

There was a silence like the Day of Reckoning.

Mrs Pethick Lawrence came and sat down straight opposite to where I was. 'Are you saying, Maggie, that you slapped the lady in the box?'

I felt my heart and belly changing place. 'Yes, ma'am.'

'You slapped her?'

'To stop her fitting.'

'And what happened then?'

'The gentleman was not too pleased with me.'

'What did you do?'

'I ran, ma'am.'

There was more silence, then suddenly Miss Christabel began to laugh. She laughed and laughed and clapped her hands. 'Maggie, you are a true heroine. A true heroine.'

The other ladies laughed, too – so loud they might have burst. Only Miss Sylvia looked at me with a quaint gentle smile, as though she wished it might have been otherwise.

Shortly after Miss Sylvia returned to the north, and Miss Kenney with her. The Wednesday meetings ceased and I forgot all about votes and rights and the like. Cook was teaching me to knit and I was working up a little coat for Will and a blanket for the new baby.

I had not been home since I threw Alfie's apple in the fire and, truth was, I feared it, not knowing how I should be received. Still, having saved near six shillings I was glad when the mistress said I might visit two Sundays on.

The day before I was to go, Miss Sylvia and Miss Kenney returned, mighty sparky and full of plans which they seemed to think I should like to hear about. It being Saturday I was sat with a book and my knitting in the corner of the kitchen while Cook snored in the carver. Miss Kenney came jumping down the stairs. 'Oh, there you are, Maggie. Will you take a cup of tea with Sylvia and me directly? We've something to ask you.' She was gone before I could answer.

I made the tea and carried it up. Miss Sylvia took the tray. 'What's this? Two cups? Stay here while I fetch another.' I dared not think what Cook would say.

When she returned we sat all three and Miss Sylvia insisted on pouring. 'Well, Maggie, how have you been?'

'Very well, miss.'

'We have had a remarkable time. Quite remarkable, have we not, Annie?'

'We have that.'

'Do you still read the paper to Cook, Maggie?'

'Sometimes, miss. The master asked she should go back to plainer food, so she's not so keen as she was.'

'So you won't have read about the by-election?'

I tried to look as though I might have.

Miss Kenney burst in at this. 'Sylvia, of course she's not. Poor lass, give her a chance. Now, Maggie, here's it in short: we have been away rousing the women of the north to fight for their rights, and come out bold in asking for the vote. We done so well we put the frighteners into the Liberals' man, Churchill, and near lost him his place in Parliament with our protests. Now we must do the same down here.'

She stopped and took a sip of tea. As did I, for else I would have had to speak.

Miss Sylvia leant forward and spoke quietly but with great force. 'Maggie, Annie has been sent to stir up support amongst the working women of London. What I would like to ask you – and remember, I'm asking not ordering – would you be willing to introduce her to your own mother, so that she could talk to her and maybe some of her friends? Nothing more. Just to talk to them.'

Well, I fear my mouth must have been working like the Prime Minister man's. The two of them sat quietly while I sought around for my thoughts then Miss Kenney said. 'Happen the next time you go home, I could step along with you. I shouldn't stay long, not to get in the way of your visit.' She looked so hopeful – pleading, almost. What could I do?

'I'm to visit tomorrow, miss, but my ma is fair gone with a baby. I doubt she'll be thinking much about votes and that.

And my pa can be a bit funny with strangers.'

She laughed so happily. 'As can mine, believe me, duck. Trust me, I'll not bother your ma above ten minutes.'

So it was. Come nine o'clock next morning the two of us set out. We took an omnibus to Whitechapel which Miss Kenney would pay for, though I doubt she has much more savings than I, and walked from there. She asked me to call her Annie, but it didn't feel right, so we settled for Miss Annie which she said made her feel like a milliner! It was a fine day and for once I was neither too hot nor cold, although as we turned into my street I felt my hands begin to clam up for I knew not how we should be greeted.

Outside our door we halted. I was set to knock when round the corner trots Lucy. She stopped and fair stared at Miss Annie, then on goes her Sunday School smile, all coy and gooey. I said, 'Lucy, this is Miss Annie. Will you tell Ma she would like to speak to her.' Lucy went round the back and after a few moments Ma came back with her, holding Will who had a bruise like a plum on his forehead. Ma looked worse than before. For all her belly was blown up like a carter's wheel, her face was thin and yellowy still. She never looked so bad with Will and Evelyn. The others I don't remember.

I said, 'It's me, Ma. And this is Miss Annie Kenney.'

Ma nodded. 'Excuse me, ma'am. I must go round and open the door to you.'

Miss Annie would have none of it. 'Mrs Robins, I've come in back door all my life. With your permission I'll do so still.' And she gave her her great sparkly smile. I could see Ma was nervous, but she made no objection.

Evelyn was playing in the yard and she fair whooped when she saw me, although she was shy of Miss Annie and hid herself in Ma's skirt.

'You'll have to excuse my kitchen, ma'am,' Ma said. 'This is my son, Alfie. He's...'

Alfie was sitting on the floor picking at a potato with his nails like he was scratching for gold. He showed no sign of heeding us. I would have gone and spoke to him but Ma caught my eye and shook her head. Fearing another storm, I stayed put, but it was hard to see him so.

Ma sent Lucy to bring a stool from the front room. I wondered she did not show Miss Annie through, for it is a far better place than the kitchen, but I guessed she did not care to in case Pa came in. She looked fair put about with worry. 'You must excuse me, ma'am. I must get the broth on for our dinner. I had not known Maggie was coming and with company.' But Miss Annie would have none of it.

'You seat yourself down here, Mrs Robins. Maggie and I will fix the broth between us, eh, Maggie?' I was so flummoxed I could only nod, and Ma more so than I, for she fairly flopped on to the stool. 'Your Maggie is a capital cook these days, did you know?' Miss Annie went on, all the while scraping the potatoes and piling them in the pot. I did like with the carrots and Ma just sat there with Will on her knee, looking for all the world like she had landed on another planet.

When all was done and the broth brewing Miss Annie wiped her hands and, leaning on the bench as though she had lived there all her life, started to ask Ma about when the baby would come, if she was well with it or ill, who would deliver her, and so forth. Ma was stiff to start but Miss Annie has such a way with her, you cannot but answer and not mind her way of questioning. Soon they were smiling together as though they had been friends or even sisters for years, for Miss Annie is nearer Ma's age than mine, though she says she's much too simple for one who has lived so long!

The two of them being so thick in talk I made my mind to hurry to the butcher's and see what I could buy to liven up our dinner. I had hoped Mr Green might be about his prayers but he was there, all slimy smile and fingers knitting. 'Ah, Miss Maggie Robins. Quite the lady now. Gracious of you to grace our premises, I'm sure.' I felt the spit rising.

'I'll take two slices of your finest ham and a half pound of sausages,' I said, cool as water.

'Your Ma must be glad you are earning so well,' he said as he took my money. 'Another mouth, soon, if I'm not mistook.'

I said nothing but waited for my change. He made a great to do of finding a threepence and in the end handed me a load of farthings. I counted them out to see if he would try to cheat me again, but it was all there, though a great nuisance in farthings. On the way home I stopped at a stall and bought a loaf and some cheese and used them all up, then I walked along by the river for a while for I was nervous of what Miss Annie might say to Ma and was wishing I had never brought her.

When I got back she had set up the big tin bath and was pouring water into it. Will was sat on Evelyn's knee while she struggled to get his clothes off. Miss Annie laughed when she saw my face. 'I'm giving Will a bath, then little Evelyn's going to let me wash her hair, she tells me.' I thought this very unlikely for Evelyn would rather drown than have her hair wetted. Just then Lucy came in with a pile of rags for drying them, all sweet as if she were a nice girl and not the little spider she is.

'Where's my ma?' I should have said it better, but I was so unsettled to see Miss Annie, sleeves rolled up, just like any worker woman in the street, that I forgot what was owing to her in manners.

She put her finger to her lips. 'I've sent her to lie down. She's fair slattered and so near her time. Your brother, Alfie, I've asked to fill the buckets. And here he is,' as Alfie, grinning like a monkey, came staggering in with two pails filled to spilling. 'Thank you, Alfie. I'll ask you to put them on the stove for me.' This he did and stood by, still grinning, as he was waiting for his next orders. I thought her mighty bold to trust him near the fire, but then she wasn't to know how Alfie can be sometimes.

'I've brought some ham and sausages,' I said. 'To have with the broth. And bread and cheese for after.'

Miss Annie smiled. 'A regular banquet you'll be having.'

I shouldn't have said it. I knew I shouldn't, but it was out my mouth before I could stop it. 'You are mighty welcome to join us, miss, if you don't mind poor folk's fare.'

Her face went all stern and I thought she was vexed at the liberty, but she shook her head. 'There is nothing I should like better, Maggie, but I cannot take food from those who need it more. Here's a growing family.'

'If my husband will agree it, we will be honoured to have you eat with us, ma'am.' Ma was standing in the doorway, her face all flushed but looking better than I had seen her for a long time.

Miss Annie, who had just taken Will from Evelyn, put him down again. He started to howl. 'Mrs Robins, it's very kind, but really I must not. What food you have you need for yourselves.'

Ma bent over, so awkward with her great belly bulging, and picked up Will. I took him from her and dumped him in the bath so he shut up. 'If we are to fight for better times, ma'am, we must fight together. I have spoken to my neighbour, Mrs Grant, and she will stop by when she has visited her daughter.'

'Mrs Robins, that is wonderful. Perhaps Mrs Grant's daughter could be persuaded to join us, too?'

Ma sort of smiled and shook her head. 'Mrs Grant's daughter is in the graveyard, ma'am. She was burnt pulling her son from a tallow vat. She and the lad are buried together.'

Miss Annie put her hand on Ma's arm. 'Maggie and I will make do here. Go and rest now. If your husband agrees it, I will stay, but it is no matter. I have done what I came to do.'

Ma did as she was told and between us we got Will washed and Evelyn, too, for it seemed she would do anything for Miss Annie and scarce cried at all at the tangles in her hair. Alfie lifted the buckets so carefully he hardly spilt any, well, not for him.

All the while my heart was churning – part for fear of what Pa would say, but more to know what had passed between my ma and Miss Annie. That Ma should go out and speak to Mrs Grant and bid her come by the house was just so…strange for, though they are neighbours and like each other well enough, they are not close. At half past midday I heard Pa's footsteps. I ran to meet him in the yard. He was glad to see me and gave me a great hug and lifted me in the air, then made out I was heavy as an elephant and that he would fall with the weight of me. Although he seemed merry enough, still I hoped somehow to save myself from what I must ask. Indeed, I was saved, for at that moment, out ran Evelyn, polishcd like a new penny. 'Pa, we've got a new ma. Come and see.'

This did not seem a very good way of sorting things, but Pa was so confounded that he had no timc to be vexed. At that moment Miss Annie, sleeves rolled down, stepped out of the kitchen and made him the most fetching bob of her head. 'Mr Robins, forgive me. I am a friend of Maggie's and she was kind enough to bring me home with her and introduce me to your fine family. I'll take no more of your time, sir, and I hope you'll forgive the intrusion.'

Pa lookcd as he would forgive anything she desired, for it is true, Miss Annie is powerful handsome with her soft brown hair and dancing eyes. I took my chance. 'Pa, if it does not unsettle you, I would like Miss Annie to eat dinner with us. Ma is agreeable. I've bought ham and sausages and cheese and a loaf.'

Poor Pa did looked quite perplexed. I did not understand how he could delay, but Miss Annie, who is not simple at all, it seems to me, lowered her eyes and said, 'Your Maggie only bought the goods as we knew you were not expecting us, Mr Robins.'

We had a very jolly dinner. Pa sent Alfie to bring in two jars of porter and when we had done he asked Ma if she would sing for us. She said she could not for she had no voice, but Pa and I rebuked her and she sang a very fine ballad about a maid at a fair who was spurned by her lover and went mad. We all clapped and cheered and then in came Mrs Grant, looking very sad and would not take a glass of porter, so I asked Pa if he would walk with me along by the river and show me the salmon leaping as he did when I was little. So he and I and Evelyn set off, leaving Alfie, who could not take his eyes off Miss Annie, and Ma and Will and Lucy.

We walked for half an hour and Pa carried Evelyn on his shoulder so she was higher than any of us and kept reaching up for the branches. Hardly a word passed between us, yet we were happy. At last, as it grew dark and we turned to go home, Pa said, 'Your Ma is not well with this baby, Maggie.'

I said I thought she looked more tired than usual.

'Tired? She's worse than that. I never saw her so... Not even with little Samuel. She's hardly strength to wash the clothes. She keeps no eye on Alfie when I'm out. He has the run of the street.'

'Perhaps once the baby is born she will be better again.'

Pa gave a sort of laugh. 'Maybe. I hope so, Maggie, for if we should lose her, I cannot mind what's to follow.'

A cold wind – more than cold – a wind of brick-hard ice seemed to have wrapped me round. That my pa could hold such a thought.

'Ma will be well,' I said, clenching my hands together. 'Once the baby comes.'

'And there's another mouth to feed.'

I know not what stirred me but I could bear it no more, his complaining. 'Pa, do you not put the babies in Ma? Why can you not stop?'

We both stood still and Evelyn, who was cold, began to squeak.

Pa stared at me, quite blank with fury. I knew then how Ma

must feel when he takes his hand to her. He raised his arm and Evelyn, wobbling on his shoulders, caught hold of it and squeaked the more. He lowered his arm again and turned away. We walked home without a single word between us, having seen no salmon.

When we got back all the pans were washed and the dinner things away. Mrs Grant had gone and Ma was sat in the front room with Will tearing at her hair. If ever I have a child I will shave my head, I think, for there can be nothing worse than to have it dragging at you every moment.

Miss Annie said we should leave soon if we were to take the omnibus as Sundays are difficult. Ma came with us to the door. 'I thank you, ma'am, for all your kindness today.'

Miss Annie shook her head. 'The kindness is yours, Mrs Robins, to listen to me and spare me your time.'

As we walked to the stop I wondered if she would tell me what they had spoken of while Pa and I were out walking. She seemed deep in thought but once we were settled on the bus she turned to me. 'Maggie, I cannot thank you enough for today.'

I was surprised, for it seemed little of a day to me, to be at someone's house washing their children and cooking the dinner.

'I have talked with your ma and Mrs Grant and they will speak to the other women in the street.'

'What about, miss?' I asked, feeling very dull.

'There is to be a rally. On February 19th – the day Parliament re-opens – as many women as we can muster will meet at Caxton Hall in Westminster to hear if the King's Speech contains a bill for suffrage – giving women the vote.

Mrs Pankhurst will address the assembly, and Miss Christabel, too, with luck. It will be a mighty occasion. But I have been charged with stirring up the women of London and it is not an easy task. Your ma can help me talk to some I would not otherwise meet and we must hope they will spread the word about.' She wiped her hand across her brow and for a moment looked very tired. 'Oh, but it is a big job and no mistake. A mighty job. Still,' she squeezed my arm and again looked very chirpy, 'we have made a good start, you and I, today.' Though I had not understood one word in six of what she had told me, I felt exceeding proud.

Miss Sylvia and Miss Annie have been rushed off their feet these last few weeks. Ladies have come and gone bringing leaflets and posters, all to be stacked in Miss Sylvia's room till it looks like a paper factory. Once, the old man who we saw at the theatre, that winked at me, came. He showed no such impudence this time, I am happy to say, or he would have found mud on his coat when it came time for him to leave. Miss Sylvia seems very fond of him and listens to him with great respect.

The Wednesday meetings are back and this week we were all given handbills about the rally at Caxton Hall. I did not know what to do with mine so showed it to Cook who made a 'tch'ing sound and put it straight on the fire. Though she does not say so, I think she is vexed with me for spending so much time above stairs, yet the mistress truly encourages it and is herself much occupied with writing letters to the newspapers.

Miss Sylvia asked me to help her with rolling up her posters but I spent so long admiring them that in the end she did it all herself. She did not seem to mind. When I told Cook, she said if I had nothing better to do she would find me something and made me unpick two whole rows of Will's new coat. I had better make haste, else it will be too small. The baby's blanket is finished. I do not think I can ask to go home again yet, for it is less than a month, but if Miss Annie is really to talk to the women in our street, perhaps she will take it for me.

Well, thank goodness for Mrs Drummond. Just when Miss Sylvia and Miss Annie seemed fit to drop and everything an utter muddle, arrives Mrs Drummond *with* a typewriter. I am ashamed I did not believe her the first time, for then it seemed impossible that she should have use of such a thing. Now, after three days of her sweeping in and out, I think there is not one thing impossible for her, except, perhaps, to speak English that I can fathom.

Every morning she is up when I am, breakfasts off a piece of bread and some butter, then off to the omnibus, her arms fair dropping with bills and posters. Back in the afternoon, a cup of tea and a cake, then off again to knock the doors and wheedle the women into promising their attendance. From what Miss Sylvia says, a good few of the men have given permission for their wives to go. It would be brave man could refuse Mrs Drummond, I'm thinking, for though she is not fierce like Cook, she is very firm and does not like to lose a fight.

First Cook did not like her at all, for she came bustling down to the kitchen and tried to instruct her in a Scottish gruel with oats and salt and water. Cook sniffed mightily and said she thought she was above serving slops to her employers, but Mrs Drummond just laughed till the tears ran down her face and said, 'That's me in my place,' (according to Cook, who speaks a morsel of Scottish) and after that she begged Cook's pardon and said it was just that she was sad sick for her babbies and the gruel would make her think herself back home. The next we know, Cook is making a great tub of it and it is vile indeed, although if you stir some sugar in, it is much improved.

Mrs Drummond came back all white like a statue this afternoon. Cook asked if someone had thrown a bag of flour over her, but Mrs Drummond just laughed and said, no, she had been chalking all over the pavements to tell people about the rally. I wondered how she had got away with it. When I asked her she just gave me a great big wink and said, 'I hae my ways, little one,' or something like that.

Miss Annie told me she would be seeing Ma this morning and had I any message for her? I asked that she would take the blanket and tell Ma I am working a coat for Will. Also I gave her three shillings to give to Ma and a ham bone that Cook had left for throwing out, as too small to make a soup of. Poor Miss Annie looked like a Hebrew slave, so weighed down was she when she left.

Miss Annie says Ma is feeling better. She sent thanks for the money and the ham bone and says Frank was home last Sunday as his ship was docked at Tilbury. I asked Miss Annie if she had seen Pa but she said, no, he was working. Alfie, too, which is good to hear. He has employment shifting coal for Mr Turner – a shilling a day. I only hope he will not lose it coming home. Miss Annie said Evelyn begged to have her hair washed but there was not time. She has promised to do it soon. Will has another tooth. I asked about my nan. 'She is not so well, Maggie, but I gave your ma some mint leaves for her to ease the bloating.'

'How could you know what to take her, miss?'

Miss Annie laughed. 'Maggie, before I go out each day, I skim the garden. There is always something will serve and it's cheaper than the apothecary.'

'And did you talk to many women, miss?'

'I did. Your ma is a regular recruiting sergeant. She took me from house to house and at every one of them we got a cup of tea. I tell you, Maggie, by the time we were done I was fair bursting for the lavvy.'

'And will they come to the rally?'

Miss Annie shrugged. 'Some will, I'm sure. I'm to talk to another group on Friday night – friends of your ma that she sings with, and some others at the wash-house. Oh, we shall get there by and by, but it's a long ladder we're climbing. Still, when I see women so wretched and worn down with work and child-bearing...' She stopped and I knew she feared to have hurt my feelings.

'If anyone can make my ma's life better, I would do all I could to help them,' I said.

She smiled. 'I never doubted it, Maggie. And you wait. Things will get better for women soon, and it'll be the likes of thee and me and your poor ma they'll have to thank.'

On the day of the rally we were all up early. Me to light the fires and get my chores done, for Mrs Roe said I must certainly go to the meeting, though Cook made faces like a thundercloud and muttered all day about giddy-gaddying and wasting good working time and how I should have to make it up come Saturday.

When it was time to go she gave me a slice of currant cake wrapped in paper and threepence. 'For your fare. Mrs Roe may do as she pleases, but you must come back and finish the pressing afore you go to bed.' I thanked her and said I wished she was coming too. She went bright pink and said she couldn't be doing with such nonsense and any woman with any sense should know better than to leave her family and go flibbertigibbeting all over town. Since I have done reading recipes to Cook she has taken to hearing stories from *The Ladies' Home Journal* and her words are becoming wondrous fancy.

Such a building is Caxton Hall! It is vast like a palace and full of wooden seats – row upon row – in a great space like a theatre, and corridors and mirrors and stairs leading off all over the place.

I was charged to put a programme on each chair, while a dozen or more ladies unrolled posters and pinned them to the walls and round the stage, on which was set a table and some chairs, much like at the Albert Hall. I greatly feared we were to hear more speeches of the kind delivered there and wondered if I might creep away when I had done my work and walk about outside till the meeting was over.

In the entrance we set up trestle-tables which we covered with great white cloths and then piled high with leaflets and handbills. We uncoiled flags – glorious blood red – and hung them round the walls and over the entrance, then back to the main hall to dress the stage with white and purple banners.

Miss Billington was fixing one. She asked me if it was straight. I nodded. 'And it's the right way up this time, miss.' She gave me a very funny look.

By noon the hall was mostly ready and we went into a room behind the stage where lemonade and bread with potted meat and jam pastries were spread out all along one side. I did not think I should be allowed, but Miss Sylvia spotted me and led me right up to where a huge lady with the biggest hat you ever saw was pouring tea. 'Mrs Montefiore, may I introduce Maggie? She has worked like a Trojan to help us get ready for today.'

The huge lady held out her hand. 'I'm very pleased to meet you, Maggie,' she said. I bowed my head, thinking she must surely be a royal person with such a hat, for all she had a foreign name.

At two o'clock the doors were opened and ladies, two or three at a time, began to wander in. By half past two the hall was but a quarter full. I could see Miss Annie and Miss Sylvia in earnest talk with Mrs Drummond who, as always, looked exceedingly cheerful and kept shaking her head and laughing as though it were the simplest thing in the world to fill the place to bursting.

As I was helping to lay out teacups there came a flurry of voices outside and through the door swept Mrs Pankhurst herself, so fine in a lilac coat and hat to match.

'Where's Annie? Find her for me, please, and tell her I must speak to her at once.' A lady rushed off, returning with Miss Annie who looked very down and harassed.

Mrs Pankhurst embraced her kindly. 'Well, Annie, how have you done? Where are all our workers? We can't just preach to the converted.' Poor Miss Annie looked as though she wished the ground would swallow her.

'Mrs Drummond and Sylvia and I have been about every single day, talking to the women. We could get no firm promises, but I truly thought more would be here, Mrs Pankhurst.'

Mrs Pankhurst gave a little shrug. 'Well, it cannot be helped. A few are better than none. And those that hear Mr Keir Hardie will go home converted, I am sure.' At this moment they were joined by Miss Sylvia and Miss Christabel who seemed a little displeased with each other.

Miss Christabel fair pounced on Mrs Pankhurst. 'Have you seen this, Mother? What Sylvia and Annie have achieved between them? If there are two hundred people out there I should be surprised. And all of them belonging already, I'll be bound.'

Miss Sylvia, distressed, I could tell, murmured, 'I'm sorry, Mother. It hasn't been for lack of trying. We have all been working like dogs.'

'Dogs would have done a better job,' snorted Miss Christabel.

Mrs Pankhurst put a hand on her arm. 'We must make do with those we've got, Christabel. We have the hall, we have an audience, we have our speaker. And we have the Press. Let's see if we can't rouse a few headlines, come what may.'

Just then one of the younger ladies came hurrying in and handed Mrs Pankhurst a letter. She read it, folded it, put it in her pocket. We all waited. 'Mr Hardie sends his apologies, but regrets he is unable to attend this afternoon.'

There was a veritable gasp around the room. Mrs

Pankhurst raised her shoulders. 'Perhaps it is just as well, seeing we have so small a gathering for him. Annie, you will speak as arranged and I will say a few words. What they will be will depend on the King's Speech.'

'Well, whatever it is, Mother, please make sure it raises their appetites.'

I had never heard Miss Sylvia speak so sharply.

'Oh, I shall endeavour to do that,' said her mother. 'I usually manage something of the kind.'

'Good,' replied Miss Sylvia, 'for we've five hundred currant buns to dispose of before anyone goes home.'

Miss Christabel burst out laughing. 'Oh well done, my sister. No recruits but you've sorted out the eating arrangements. Perhaps that's what you should stick to. It's plainly what you're best at.'

Miss Sylvia said nothing, but she bit her lip hard and walked clear out of the room. Miss Christabel seemed very little unsettled and set about ordering those remaining to various tasks. Me she sent out to the front to direct latecomers to their seats.

I was not halfway there when there came a sound – a sort of murmuring like distant bees, then, as it came closer, more like voices, women's voices, then voices raised in song.

I raced to the entrance hall. If I had not seen it...

Outside the great glass doors, all across the road for as far as I could see and right round the corner, came women, red flags swirling, singing for all their hearts. Beside them on horses rode bobbies, some laughing, others looking quite brain-lashed with bewilderment. Up the stairs the women came, into the hall, like a great brown wave, for their clothes were poor and shoddy and hardly a strip of colour in their hats. Some had babies squawling and blabbing, others were grimed and oily from work. Old, young, and every shade between. Up the steps and into the hall. I had to press myself against the wall for fear of being trampled, then ran as quick as I could, back the way I had come.

I burst through the door. 'Oh, Miss Annie,' I cried, not daring to address Mrs Pankhurst. 'They have come.' Miss Annie came hurrying across to me.

'Who, Maggie? Who has come? Is it the police?'

'No, miss. Well, only a few on horses. But the women... Hundreds, miss. And babies and all. They are...like the lilies of the field.' I was not sure that this was quite right, but Miss Sylvia seemed to understand, for she leapt up and ran to a little side door that gave on to the stage. Opening it a crack, she beckoned wildly with her hand. All rushed to look, even Mrs Pankhurst, though she is very little and could scarce see past Mrs Montefiore and her hat.

Miss Sylvia shut the door. 'Perhaps we shall need those buns after all, Mother.'

Mrs Pankhurst nodded gaily. 'I think we may, my dear. Well done. And well done, Annie and Mrs Drummond. Your efforts have borne fruit. Now it is up to us to ripen it on the bough.' I thought this very beautiful and made a grand effort to put it to memory.

'Maggie, what are you doing here? I thought you were to show latecomers in. You'll not find many round here.'

I blushed purple and back again. 'I'm sorry, Miss Christabel, ma'am... I only came to...'

Miss Sylvia stepped in. 'It was Maggie brought us the

news.' Miss Christabel gave me a lovely smile. 'Thank you, Maggie. You are a clever, useful girl. Now hurry back to your post.'

It was on my way back that I saw Ma. She was leaning against a wall, eyes closed, the baby riding so high in her she could scarce find space for breathing. Mrs Grant was with her and looking more than anxious. I fought my way across to them. 'Ma.'

She opened her eyes and tried to smile. 'I thought I might see you, Maggie. Miss Annie said you would be here.' She took a great gasp of air.

'Ma, you must sit down. Have you been walking all the way from home?' I did not see how she could.

'Miss Annie arranged that we would come on the Underground,' Mrs Grant told me. 'But it is a perilous long way up from it and your ma so near her time.'

Wrong though it was, I felt a stab of envy that Ma should have been on the Underground train when I had not.

'There's tea,' I said. 'And buns. Miss Sylvia bought five hundred.'

'Enough to feed an army,' Mrs Grant declared.

'An army is what we are.' It was Miss Sylvia. 'But an army that needs a chair.'

'Please, Miss Sylvia, this is my ma,' I said, wishing Ma had not looked so done in.

Miss Sylvia held out her hand. 'I'm so pleased to meet you, Mrs Robins. Annie cannot sing your praises high enough for all the help you've given her.'

Ma straightened up. 'I thank you, ma'am, but I've done little enough.'

'I'm sure that's not so. And Maggie here has been quite excellent. You must be very proud of her.'

Ma made a snitching sound as she does when praise is offered. 'I hope she will always do her best.'

'That and more. Now will you come and take a cup of tea and something to eat before the meeting begins? You must be weary from the journey.'

Ma began to say that she required nothing, thank you, but I knew why. 'Ma, you must. It's free and if you don't eat a bun, and Mrs Grant, too, and everyone here, we shall be living off them till Christmas.' Even Ma laughed.

I cannot mind when I have seen so many people all in one place, jam-packed together, munching on those buns like their lives depended on it. At last someone rang a bell and everyone made their way into the grand hall.

I sat with Ma and Mrs Grant near the back. Ma looked so tired I could tell she would rather not be there. I wondered who was minding Evelyn and Will. Not Lucy, I hoped, or they would both end up drowned or worse.

After a few minutes Miss Billington and Mrs Montefiore and some other ladies I did not know came on to the stage and everyone fell silent. Miss Billington thanked the women for coming so far and at such trouble to themselves. She then called upon Miss Annie to address the meeting. As she stood up there was a great roar from all the women she had talked into coming, as though she was one of their own.

She told how we must await the end of the King's Speech in Parliament. On that depended our next action. I was not sure what this meant, but everyone clapped and cheered, so I did too, and Miss Annie went on to say how more than half the people of Britain were women and it was monstrous that they should have no say in how they were ruled. More cheers. She told how where she came from in the north, women would work a ten-hour day, six days a week, for half what the men alongside them were earning. And was this right? Was this just? Was this Christian?

'No,' we all cried, even Ma, who looked much sparkier than before.

Was it right that married women should depend on their men to vote for them, and unmarried girls have no one at all to champion their cause?

'No. *No*. *NO*.'

Were women too stupid to know what they wanted? Were they too lazy to walk to the polling station? Did they not care what happened to their children? Was not this great nation founded on the toil of men *and* women?

'Yes. *Yes*. *YES*.'

I think if the old grey man from the Albert Hall had stepped on to the stage at that moment, he would have been torn to pieces before our eyes.

Miss Annie made to continue when, suddenly, came a sound from the side of the stage and Miss Christabel fair leapt on to the platform. Those who knew her raised a mighty cheer, but she held up a hand to silence them. 'Ladies, we all know why we are here today. It is to see if the Government has at last come to its senses. Today is the opening of Parliament.' She paused, dipped her head, then solemnly raised it again. 'It is with great regret I must inform you that no mention whatsoever was made in the King's Speech today regarding a bill for women's suffrage.'

There was a silence. More than a silence. A sort of damp despair curling over us. Then, quick as a flash, Mrs Drummond jumped up on her seat and cried, 'For shame! Shame on this government of weaklings and bullies.' The cry was taken up like a great chorus and rang round the hall till, had it been trumpets, the walls would surely have fallen. And into all this wildness stepped Mrs Pankhurst. Still, tiny, but like a flame in the darkness.

'My dear friends, this is a disappointment indeed. More than a disappointment. A blow to the heart of our frail bodies. But let us remember that it is but a blow. One blow. A harsh one. But not a murdering blow. It has hurt us. It has wounded us. It has not killed us. Nor will it *ever*. For while there are women such as you – true, loyal, honourable, brave, deserving – prepared to fight for what should be theirs by right, we shall *never* be beaten. We shall fight on. Till we win the glorious day.'

Such cheers as rose would have lifted the roof and carried all the way to the King himself if there was any justice in the world.'

Mrs Pankhurst then proposed that all those willing should make their way to the House of Commons and demand to speak with the Members of Parliament. The hall emptied. When we got outside a wicked cold drizzle was falling. I told Mrs Grant to take Ma home. Ma started to protest but Mrs Grant would have none of it. 'You've children at home need their mother, Mrs Robins. Your man's done well by you to let you come. Don't give him cause to rue it, for this will be a long hard struggle, to my reckoning.'

I had to ask. 'Is Pa looking after the littl'uns?'

Ma nodded.

'But what about his work?'

'He has a free day.'

'How? It's not Christmas.'

Mrs Grant looked at Ma. 'Shall I tell your Maggie?'

Ma shook her head. She took a deep breath, as deep as she could with the baby squeezing her like an accordion. 'Your nan's gone, Maggie. We buried her today. Mr Bailey gave your pa the day off, else I could not have come.'

I stared at her. 'You came here, today? With my nan dead?'

'I did, yes.'

'But...she was your ma.'

Ma turned her head away. The baby kicked her, you could see, right through her smock, then she looked at me. 'I can't help her no more, Maggie. You and Lucy and Evelyn, maybe I can. And this little blighter inside.'

'If it's a girl.'

'It's a girl, all right.'

'How do you know?'

'Girls kick harder.'

I walked with Ma and Mrs Grant to the Underground. It seemed strange to watch them disappearing down into its black gob. It struck me then, perhaps I should not like to try it after all.

The crowd was marching up the street and I was carried along with it, not knowing where we were bound except for 'Parliament'. The rain was lashing at us and I wished I had worn my workaday shoes, for my boots, though smart to the extreme, were leaking water like muslin.

I asked a woman how far it was to go. She shook her head.

'Bloody miles, my love, but worth it to see their faces.'

I could have told her it was not, for I had seen the Prime Minister's before, and very dull it was. I took to thinking about men's faces as we trudged, and it seemed to me that they are mainly plain. Mr Roe, though jolly, has a very red nose and a big pot belly on him. I have heard my Pa called handsome, but I cannot see it, for his nose is bent and his skin worn brown like a saddle. Frank is handsome, with his dark eyes and gleaming teeth and soft fine skin. Frank is not like an ordinary man, though, for no one can refuse him anything he asks. He is too winning in his ways. Of ordinary men, the only one I minded that was tolerable was the bobby who found me the night of the Albert Hall. He was tall and strong with greeny brown eyes and a brave warm smile. *He* had gleaming teeth. I do like fine teeth in a man. Mine are good. Many have remarked on them. They are the best thing about me, but what good is that, except for gnawing beef bones? I cannot spend my whole life smiling or I will be sent to the madhouse, I suppose.

As we turned down by the river there, ahead of us, suddenly rose up a palace. I thought the plan must be changed and we were to visit the King himself, for so marvellous was the building, all swirling stone and windows and towers. My stomach fair curdled with fear, in case His Majesty should come forth and ask me to explain myself. I hung back as best I could but with such a crowd it was not possible for long. We moved forward like a great tide, and well nigh wet as one.

As we came to the great gates, cries of 'The Strangers' Entrance. Round to the Strangers' Entrance' reached us, so we all swooped about like a flight of starlings and headed off down a side street. I did not think it likely the King would come to a side door and felt much the happier for it. Nor would it have mattered if he had, for when we got there the place was quite barred with bobbies, two or three deep and looking very stern with their feet spread like ducks, hands clamped behind their backs, and every one of them frowning.

Mrs Pankhurst marched right up to them. 'We wish to speak with our representatives in Parliament.'

A sergeant stepped forward. 'I'm sorry, ma'am. We are ordered to admit no one.'

'How so?'

'Those are my orders.'

'Who has delivered such an order?'

'That I can't say, ma'am.'

'You do not know who issued it?'

'Not as such.'

'But still you obey it?'

'I do, ma'am.'

Mrs Pankhurst smiled. 'Well then, officer, suppose I give you an order rescinding that order? What will you do then?'

The sergeant looked very hot and unsettled. 'There is to be no admittance.'

'On what grounds? It is our right to speak with Members of Parliament on matters concerning us.'

'Not today, it isn't.'

'Today or any day. It is enshrined in the constitution, as you will be well aware.'

The sergeant became quite sticky. 'I will refer the matter to my superior, ma'am. I must ask you to wait here while I do so.'

He marched away, coming back minutes later. 'I have been informed the Honourable Gentlemen are prepared to receive a deputation, ma'am.'

'Thank you, officer. We are that deputation.'

'Of twenty women.'

'Twenty?'

'Yes.'

'I see. Did the Honourable Gentlemen by any chance say which twenty they would like to receive?'

Everyone screeched with laughter and even some of the bobbies grinned. The sergeant went redder than boiled beetroot. 'Twenty, ma'am, and that is it.'

Mrs Pankhurst nodded. 'So be it.'

After some discussion, it was decided that the Wednesday ladies would serve the matter best and in they went, fine hats dripping. We stood on in the rain, half-frozen but somehow cheery. A woman near me said it was good to see someone so young making a stand, and the others around agreed and said I was a fine girl and an example. If my boots had not been leaking so I would have felt quite warmed by their praise.

After about fifteen minutes the ladies returned, looking mighty cross. It seems the Honourable Gentlemen had behaved as mean as unhonourable ones and quite refused to keep their promises. Mrs Pankhurst, however, had obliged them to receive another twenty ladies. There being some hundreds of women in the square and all of us very wet, I hoped the choosing might be quick.

It was, for immediately Miss Sylvia took over, saying, 'Now it is the turn of the workers. Let the Honourable Gentlemen

take note, our movement touches every corner of the realm,'
and instantly began to select who should go, from fishwives to
shop girls. Miss Christabel was unhappy and declared
someone of knowledge must go with them for fear they would
stumble on their words, to which Mrs Pankhurst replied, 'Let
Sylvia take them in then, my dear.' So Miss Christabel agreed,
although she did not look truly persuaded.

Next I know, there are a bundle of women, all oily and fishy
and I know not what, thrusting towards the gate, Miss Sylvia
herding them like a sheep dog. As she passed me by she caught
my arm. 'Come on, Maggie. This will interest you.'

I struggled to say that it would not at all, and I really quite
liked being wet, but such was the speed the group was moving
that I was inside the palace before I knew it.

What a place is a palace! High, high ceilings, higher than a
house or twenty houses. Stone and marble and all sorts.
Voices clanging like bells off the rafters. Men dressed in the
strangest garb like something from a panto, shuffling around
and stamping their feet. It was all I could do not to laugh, for
why would a man want to wear such frills and stuff and not
be on the stage?

We were led along a great corridor into a hall and there we
stood, steaming. After a few minutes a very sniffy gentleman
with his hair smoothed flat like boot wax came to tell us that
we might proceed to the Chamber. This we duly did and there
stood, elbows on the mantelpiece, several gentlemen in black
coats.

Miss Sylvia stepped forward. 'I would like to direct a
question to Sir Edward Grey.'

There was a slight stirring of elbows before the greyest man you ever saw speaks out. 'What is your question?'

'Good afternoon, Sir Edward. I would be grateful if you could tell me why there was no mention of women's suffrage in the King's Speech today?'

The grey man barely moved. 'I am not responsible for the content of the King's Speech, madam.'

'Are you not, sir? Then how is it composed?'

'It is a combination of those bills deemed most beneficial for the nation as a whole.'

'And the nation excludes women, who number the greater part?'

'It is not for me to decide these things.'

'No, indeed, Sir Edward, but may I ask if you are still willing to lend your support to the cause of women's suffrage?'

A long pause.

'Times change, madam. Priorities change. I am not aware of any great desire amongst the general community for such a bill.'

Miss Sylvia gazed at him. Had blood run through his body and not rainwater, he would have shrivelled. 'Times do indeed change, Sir Edward. And those who fear to change with them may find themselves forgotten when history is written.'

The grey man at last looked provoked. 'I think, Miss Pankhurst, when history is written there will be little doubt whether my name or yours will be the most remembered.'

Miss Sylvia gave him a quaint dark smile. 'I agree with you entirely, sir.'

\* \* \*

I asked Miss Annie later if she was sad at the Parliament's refusal. She said, yes, but not surprised. 'If I'd thought it could be done in a day, Maggie, I'd not have stirred from my warm bed. No, it's a long road to freedom.'

Miss Sylvia, too, seemed undeterred by her treatment. In fact she looked happier than I'd seen her for a long time, though that may have been getting all those buns eaten, for it would be a sorry thing to have to throw them to the ducks.

Mrs Pankhurst spoke as of a great victory. I could not see it, for it seemed that nought had been gained except perhaps a few hundred head colds, mine being the very worst, I venture.

Cook was of like opinion as she mixed me a mustard footbath and boiled some sage leaves for my throat. 'I knew no good could come of it. Giddy-gaddying. And now look at you. No good to man nor beast and lucky not to be in the infirmary.'

But she let me off working my Saturday and in fine sent me back to bed, not to get up till I had ceased sneezing and coughing.

Miss Sylvia, when she heard, was exceeding sorry and brought me a hot stone wrapped in a shawl to warm my bed, and some lemonade to cool my fever. I was by turns so boiled and frozen that I knew not what should become of me.

I lay four long days with wicked nights full of bad dreams – one when my ma came to me clasping a squealing baby, that when she unwrapped it, was a piglet and she said we would eat it for dinner if I didn't finish its coat that I was knitting. I woke up screaming. Miss Sylvia came hurrying, for hers is the nearest room to mine. She wiped my head with a cool cloth and told me never to fear a dream for they cannot come true whatsoever in this life. She stayed with me till I slept again and in the morning the fever had gone and I was much myself, although weak and a whole lot thinner which truly I did not mind, but Cook said, 'What's all this, Miss Skin and Bones?' and made me eat a whole bowl of oxtail which truly I did not much fancy. Afterwards she gave me some syrup pudding and straightway my strength began improving.

Mrs Roe, too, came down to the kitchen to look at me and said I should not do anything strenuous till I was fully recovered. Cook turned all thundery and sniffy and when the mistress had gone she said she thought she knew not to overtax an invalid, she thought she knew *that*, and hadn't she sat up brewing me beef tea *and* cast off all the stitches to Will's coat and sewn it up while I was lying upstairs in bed?

I said I was sure Mrs Roe had not meant to be interfering and that I was very grateful indeed for all her care of me and truly believed I should not have got well without her. I told her, too, that I wished my ma had such a fine soul to nurse her and did not have to give birth in a hard cold house such as ours is.

Cook went quite quiet at this. When she spoke again it was as though nothing had passed between us. She asked me to gather some parsley for a sauce and when I came back she had laid out Will's little coat, all beautifully finished, as from a quality shop, with red buttons all down it and a pocket added that I could never do if I knitted a thousand years.

*  *  *

Miss Annie came round tonight. After supper while Cook was drinking her porter in her room, she came down to the kitchen. Ma has had a girl. Mrs Grant attended her and, though the baby lay crooked and had to be pulled out with the tongs, it is not harmed much and Ma is gaining strength. She cannot feed it properly yet, so it must have cow's milk boiled which is a great burden and expense for them. She sends her love to me and wishes I may go home soon to see my new sister.

I asked what they had called her, thinking it would be May, after my nan. Miss Annie looked down, quite awkward, which she rarely is. 'I hope you will not mind, but your ma says she would like to call her Ann. I am to ask you first, she said, and send word soon.'

Well, I thought, there are no Anns in our family, but things change. So many things change. So I said, 'If she will grow up as brave and kind as you, miss, it will prove the best name in all the world.'

Miss Annie smiled greatly, then she told me how since the rally hundreds of ladies have signed up to belong to the women's movement, and how they are so overcome with letters she has persuaded Mrs Pethick Lawrence to take over the management of it all and the money.

'What money, miss?'

'Well, that's the problem. There is no money just at present, and what there was I spent on buns and rail fares, and altogether made a fine mess, so it is a huge mercy that Mrs Pethick Lawrence will undertake the task. We shall move our headquarters to below her apartments by and by, for there are offices to let and it will be impossible to continue to gather in the Roes' dining room.'

'So there will be no more Wednesday meetings?'

'Not here, at any rate.'

I don't know why, this saddened me. Perhaps because I had enjoyed to see so many fine hats and clever ladies. And to be asked what I thought about things, stupid though my answers always were.

I realised that Miss Annie was looking at me very hard and was afraid I had put on a sour face. At length she spoke.

'Maggie, I have something to ask you. You need not answer now. Indeed you must not. You must think very hard about it, because you are young and bright and I know that Cook thinks you have the makings of a lady's maid if you set your mind to it. And Mrs Roe would be very sorry to lose you, although she understands the reasoning behind it.'

My heart stopped. 'Am I to lose my position, miss?' All I could think of was Ma and the new baby needing cow's milk, and if I were to lose my wages what would become of us all? 'Was it because I was ill? I will never be ill again, I promise.'

Miss Annie shook her head. 'No, indeed, Maggie. It is not to do with that. You are highly valued here and, indeed, you would not have been ill at all if you had not walked so far in the rain with us that day. That is why...' Again she stopped. Whether it was my light-headedness from the fever or what, I felt like someone falling off a cliff they never climbed. 'Please tell me, miss. What is afoot? If I am to lose my place I must try to find another at all speed.'

'Maggie, calm down. I should not have mentioned it to you before you are fully well. I beg you not to agitate yourself this way. See, I will tell you, but as I said, I want no answer from you till you have fully thought it through, and whatever you say... Well, it will be as you wish.' Then she told me.

It seemed that with so many women wanting to join the movement they had need of someone to work in the office, noting the names of those who applied, posting replies, sending out information of meetings and the like, and Miss Sylvia had suggested *me*. With my reading and writing, she said it was a waste that I should only sweep floors and make beds, for all the Roes were the kindest people in the world, and Mrs Roe herself had said it would be a grand step up for me though she knew not where to find such another. Thinking how I had polished her salmon, I thought she was likely right, but I could not think of leaving them without a great wobbling fear in my belly, for all it was the grandest hope of my life to make use of my learning one day.

That night I swear I slept worse than with the fever. I tossed and turned and every time sleep came near I would jolt awake again, thinking of an office, and writing and reading for my living, then jolt some more for fear there was no wages and so I must turn it down. But surely Miss Sylvia would not put me forward if there was to be no payment, knowing how I am placed? But then, she does not seem to care about money and indeed, some of her clothes are close to shabby.

Oh, how I rolled about that bed, half of me wishing I had never been asked, the other half singing with exaltation. Let God decide for He is mighty and a Great Warrior. I wished I believed in Him a bit stronger for that would have been a great help – 'a very present help in time of trouble'.

Mrs Roe sent for me the next day and when I entered the parlour she told me to close the door and sit down. Then she said, much as Miss Annie had, that she would not like to lose me, but she would feel forever guilty if she stood in the way of me bettering myself. She said how could she lift her head for the Cause if she had denied her own servant advancement? I said I did not know, and she had always been kind and a good mistress to me and I would do whatever she advised so long as there was some payment in it, for I could not afford to be without. She assured me that that had been thought of and said, if I was principally willing, she would ask Miss Sylvia to furnish those particulars, that I might know what was offered before I told my folk of it. I thanked her and said I was willing.

Twelve shillings a week! And my board with a lady off Oxford Street. Ma could not believe it when I told her. If I had not known better I would say she was close to crying.

The baby is quite rosy and sweet. She does not cry much and when she does it is a strange cold little piping sound – not like Will who could outpeal the Bow Bells with his bellowing.

Ma still looks weathered, but it is scarce a month and that is a bad time always, I recall. Her milk is not coming proper yet, and so there is still some to be bought. Still, with twelve shillings a week in my purse I shall have no trouble aiding her. Mrs Roe had sent word if Lucy would like to take my place, but Ma says she is too young and she has need of her at home still to mind Will and Evelyn. I am glad, for she would sulk and pout and be lazy and Cook would think ill of us all for sending her such a dullard.

I am to start as soon as Mrs Roe has engaged a suitable girl. Cook says nothing. I had thought she would be angry with me and call me stupid and ungrateful to leave such a household for – what? I tried to ask her her feelings, but she just turned away and started skinning a rabbit. She knows it makes my stomach turn and how I have to go outside till it is over. That is all very well, but if I ask her every hour she cannot peel a dozen rabbits a day. I would be so glad to know her heart in this matter.

The girl is found. She is fourteen (looks ten. I saw her through the tradesman's door). The child of some gardener's groundsman and sister to the bakery boy, so at least she will not get her chest felt by *him*. Not that she has one, that I could see, and all the luckier for it.

I am to leave on Saturday when I have finished the dinner plates. Miss Sylvia says she will go with me to my new lodging and then to buy two white blouses and a black skirt which she will pay for, to come out of my first week's wages. I am sick with exaltation. Today I bought a little book of recipes for Cook. It is plainly writ so I think she will manage. Mostly pies, which she knows how to make anyway, but it was the best I could afford and has a lovely picture of a salmon on the front, its head poking from the pastry and a sprig of dill weed between its jaws, so perhaps she will think of me when she sees it. Inside I have writ: 'To Cook, who will always be in my thoughts. From Maggie Robins.'

Miss Sylvia gave me some paper and let me use her coloured pens to make a card for Mr and Mrs Roe. I drew a picture of a house and me with a big bag walking away up the path and inside I writ: 'To My Kind Master and Mistress. Goodbye. From Maggie Robins.'

* * *

Today (Saturday) I had thought to be the best of my life, but when it came time to leave all I could do was blab. Mrs Roe was very kind and said it was not the end of the world and I would always be welcome to call, and Mr Roe kept humphing and in the end gave me a whole sovereign which was all clammy he'd been pressing it so hard in his palm. I didn't know what to say for gratitude, so I just curtsied to him and cried some more. Then Mrs Roe said if I didn't stop, they'd all be at it, including the new girl whose name is Jane and just stood there staring at me like I was a mad thing. Then Miss Sylvia came down and said, 'If you're ready, Maggie, we had better make a move.' I asked if I might just say goodbye to Cook who had gone into her room after dinner and not come out. I tapped on her door and there was a sort of grunting noise, so I called, 'Cook, it's me. Maggie. I'm to go directly with Miss Sylvia.'

I could hear her crossing the room, then she opened the door and said, 'Gracious, girl, you look half drowned. Be so good as to water the parsley on your way past,' which made us both laugh. Then I gave her my book and she looked at it and just glared so I was afraid she was offended, knowing how to make pies already. 'I've writ in it,' I said. She opened it up and frowned all the more. I think she was struggling with the letters. At last she closed it again, nodded. 'Thank you, Maggie. You had no need to go spending money on me, you know, girl.'

I said, 'I know, Cook, but I wanted to.'

She turned away and picked up a package, wrapped in the paper she lines her tins with. 'There. Take this. It's nothing much. Just a bit of idleness.'

Inside was a perfect knitted blue shawl. The softest, prettiest ever made, I swear. I held it to my face.

'And don't you go crying all over it, or you'll have a blue face too,' she said, all gruff. 'Now off you go. I've things to do with this new girl to teach. Fingers crossed she's not as dull as you were, Maggie Robins, when you came through that door.'

She made to turn away but I on the instant just threw my arms round her and hugged her so the air fairly hissed out of her. 'Goodbye, Cook.'

'Goodbye, Maggie. And you keep yourself dry now on those mad marches you go on, girl. Dry and safe, that's all I ask.'

# PART TWO

## 1906–1909

I cannot fathom how my life has changed. Scarce a year ago I had not spent one night away from home, if you don't count when Pa lost his post at the smoke-house and the bailiffs came and threw us on the street for not paying rent. My nan and grandad took us in then, but it was a sore squash. That was when Samuel caught the measles.

I must not think about those times for they make me sad and I am as happy now as it is possible to be. I have a room – quite the finest room in the world, with blue curtains and a cupboard for my clothes. I cannot bear to lay them in it, for they are so smart and excellent that I will not be parted from them, even for a minute. A black skirt, down to my ankles, made of gabardine, the lady in the shop said, and 'durable'. My shirts are purest white with a high round collar and buttons (white) all down the front and long sleeves and cuffs.

When I tried them on, Miss Sylvia inspected me most carefully and said I looked like a proper secretary. She says Mrs Drummond's typewriter is in the office where I shall be

and that I am to be taught how to work it. If she had said I
should have a magic carpet I think I could not be more
excited.

Mrs Garrud, in whose house I lodge, is truly kind and jolly.
Her husband is somewhat quieter, but very generous in his
behaviour. He brought a hammer straightway to fix my
window which his wife said was rattling, though I could not
hear it, and nods most courteously if he meets me on the
stairs.

I take my meals with the family when I am home. They eat
a lot of fish which pleases me for I have heard that fish can
grow your brain and I would like so much to be cleverer than
I am, for all I have come on a deal since Reverend Beckett's
Bible class.

Mrs Garrud teaches fighting. She says it is not exactly so, it
is 'self-defence', but I have seen some photographs of her
classes and the students have a mighty ferocious look to them.
They wear white floppy coats with the widest sleeves ever, and
are bound about in the middle with criss-crossed belts. They
have no shoes on, which is just as well because their feet are
high in the air as though to kick a man's head. Some of her
pupils are ladies, and she said she would teach me for free if I
wished, but I have no floppy coat, which is a shame for there
are some heads I would dearly love to kick – the Parliament
men's for a start.

From my very first day there has been nothing but
excitement. Mrs Pankhurst had written to the Prime Minister
asking to speak with him and, when this was refused, had
gone with several ladies to see him anyway. She had been
turned away and told to write again if she wished an

interview. This done, she received a reply that he would not see her at all!

Mrs Pankhurst, on learning of this, stood very still in the centre of the office, her face unmoving, then, with a quick nod of her head, tore the letter into a dozen pieces and flung them into the waste paper basket. 'We shall see about that. Sylvia, spare me a moment, my dear, if you would be so kind.' She swept into the next room, Miss Sylvia following. The door was closed. After a few minutes it opened again and they both came out, Mrs Pankhurst looking a great deal more cheerful, her daughter less so.

Although Mrs Pankhurst is so tiny, it is quite terrifying to see her when she is annoyed. Not that she stamps or shouts or does anything at all, really, but her quiet fury seems to seep into every corner of the building, and all the way to Parliament, for aught I know. I have heard that there are magicians can make people rise into the air and float across a room, merely by the power of their thoughts. I had always disbelieved it up till now, but I truly think if Mrs Pankhurst were so minded, she could make a whole audience take flight. Certainly she can lift their hearts higher than the sky. She has such a warm wise way about her. Even when she speaks to me who knows less than nothing, she makes me feel as though what I say is of importance to her. It is a wonderful skill, I think, to make people feel they matter.

Miss Sylvia says her mother has decided that another deputation must be sent immediately to the Prime Minister's very door. Miss Annie composed a letter to our supporters and I copied it out eight times while Miss Kerr, who is the office manager, typed as many again on the machine, and then

Miss Lake, her assistant, took over and did twelve! Very pleased with herself she looked, too. I shall ask Miss Sylvia if I may stay late each evening to make myself better on it, for my wrist ached wickedly with all that writing.

The letter gave notice that all who could, should gather at Westminster Bridge station the coming Friday morning. I went with Miss Annie to meet them and there were above two dozen easily, all chattering and laughing as they were on a church outing, not off to change the laws of England.

From the station we walked all the way to Downing Street which is not so very smart but has bobbies up and down it like they were guarding a prison. I was glad to see Mrs Drummond already there. She was ribbing the constable who stood outside and for all his frown, I could see he was trying not to laugh. There were several men in hats gathered nearby, all hung about with black boxes. I asked Miss Annie if they, too, were after getting the vote, but she said, no, they were from the newspapers, come to take our picture. This was wonderful indeed, and I was very glad I had on my newest blouse and my hair wound in a coil under my hat. I took to thinking what Cook would make of it if she should see my face on the front page of the master's journal.

When we were all arrived Mrs Drummond, Miss Annie and another lady went up to the shiny front door of Number Ten and struck the knocker boldly. After a while an ancient man in black with a white high collar and a very sour face came to the door and asked their business.

'We wish to speak with the Prime Minister,' said Mrs Drummond and gave him a huge winsome smile which only made him look the mouldier. He went away and was gone for so long that we took to singing 'Fight the Good Fight', Mrs Drummond conducting. The bobbies carried on walking about.

At last two men came to the door and said there was to be no reply from the Prime Minister and with that, slammed the door shut in our faces. One of the ladies started to batter on it with her fist, shouting, 'Freedom for women,' loud enough to wake the dead and Miss Annie hopped up on the step of a big black car and began to make a speech. As she did this a bobby pulled the first lady away from the door-knocker, but Mrs Drummond took over and I don't know what she did, but suddenly the door sprung open and she rushed inside. She came out pretty soon after in the arms of the two cross men, and she, Miss Annie, and the lady with the fists were escorted away by bobbies.

I thought I had better get back to the office to tell everyone what had happened, but when I got to the end of Downing Street I realised I had no idea which way to go. For someone who has lived in London all her life, I seem to be forever getting lost.

I waited a few minutes to see if it would come to me, but when it did not I knew I must ask, so I went into a tobacco shop on the corner and said to the man, 'Excuse me, sir, but would you be so good as to direct me to Lincoln's Inn?'

He squinted at me, sort of funny, and said, 'Why would you be wanting to go there, may I ask?'

I replied, 'It is where I work. In an office.'

I thought that would make him mind his manners but he just plucked at his flabby lips and said, 'Oh yes? And why should an office girl from Lincoln's Inn be so far from her desk at this time of day?'

I drew myself up tall as I could. 'I have been to call on the Prime Minister, if it is any of your business, sir.'

He started to laugh then suddenly his face went all purply and he positively roared at me. 'I know what you are. You are one of those stupid troublesome females that would set wife against husband with all your wicked ideas.' And, throwing up the flap in his counter, he came charging out at me. I turned and fled, right out into the road and would have been flattened but for a hand catching hold of me and dragging me back on the pavement.

I was so shaken I could scarcely think what had happened, till a lady handed me my purse that I had dropped and another, the man who had saved me, asked if I was all right. He was a rough sort, and very dirty and I saw that he had a broom in his hand for sweeping up the rubbish. I thanked him greatly and said that I was, at which the tobacconist monster, who was watching from his doorway, called out, 'You should have left her. We've no need of her sort, here or anywhere. Nor yours, for that matter.' The man looked right angry and I think would have answered him but just at that moment round the corner came a big tall bobby, at which he shuffled away and continued with his sweeping.

I would have thought the shop man would have scarpered, too, but he just stood there, arms folded. 'Good day, Constable.'

The bobby touched his hat.

'If you're looking for them women, there's one of them there.'

The bobby turned to me and I felt a great wobbly thud in my heart. It was the very same one I'd rushed into after the

Albert Hall. I looked away fast, hoping he would not recognise me for, besides all else, my sleeve had dirt on it from the road sweeper, and my hair was straggling down from under my hat.

If he did, he said nothing, but merely nodded to the man and, taking my arm, said in the gentlest voice, 'Come along with me, miss, please.'

'A night in the cells might knock some sense into her,' the beast bellowed after us, and I felt a sudden dreadful panic that that was what was intended. We walked along silently for a few moments. It was a big wide road with trees on either side with just the beginnings of blossom. The sky was blue as silk but it could have been darkest night for the sickness and jumping in my belly. I dared not ask where we were bound.

At last he stopped and looking down at me, all serious, said, 'This is a long way from Park Walk, miss.' I stared at my feet. 'But so was the Albert Hall.'

I could not believe that he would remember all of that.

'Will you not speak to me?'

'I live somewhere else now, sir,' I mumbled, thinking he must find me the stupidest girl alive.

'Do you so? But not in Downing Street, I venture?'

It struck me then he must be stupider than I, but when I looked up I saw that he was smiling so I smiled too.

'No, sir. But very near as nice, to my thinking. Argyle Place, though my work is in Lincoln's Inn.'

He raised his eyebrows. 'Is it not all offices there?'

'I work in an office.'

The bobby looked mightily impressed. 'Do you, indeed? I

thought last time I saw you, you were in service.'

I was not sure how to answer this. 'Yes... At that time... That is...' He waited. 'It was decided with my reading and writing, I would be better occupied in an office.'

He nodded. 'Pretty *and* clever. I am sure you will go far.'

I could feel myself turning pink like a boiled crab. 'I know nine psalms,' I said, as this always cools me down.

'That's eight more than I do. Perhaps you'll teach me them some time when you are not busy.'

I could not see why a bobby should want to learn psalms but as he asked it so civil I said I would do my best if such a time should ever occur. He seemed satisfied with this.

'Well, I must let you get back to Lincoln's Inn for I am sure your employer feels the want of you, miss.'

'Yes...'

I know not if he guessed, but without exactly saying, he remarked that his duties took him in that direction and asked if he might walk along with me. I was never so grateful.

He told me he had been a bobby a year come April. I asked why he had chosen it, thinking it might run in his family, but he shook his head. 'No. My father thinks it a bad choice. Truth is, all my family do.'

'But why?' I thought how proud Ma and Pa would be to have a son in the police.

The bobby shrugged his shoulders. 'They are Quakers.'

'Is that an illness, sir?'

He burst out laughing. 'Some might say so. I don't think my father would consider it such.' Seeing my confusion he went on, 'They do not believe in taking oaths, which you must do to be a constable. You have to pledge your loyalty to safeguard the King and his people against villainy.'

'I can see very little wrong in that,' I told him. 'It is a fine thing to protect people from villains.'

'Yes, I think so too. But my father is very set in his beliefs. There are so many things he disapproves of. He doesn't like music or plays or very much reading, apart from the Bible.' He sighed. 'And I do.'

'I do, too.' I said.

Soon I began to recognise the buildings about me and knew that we were close. Outside Number Four I stopped. 'This is where I work.'

To my horror he took out a pencil and paper and wrote it down.

'Why do you do that, sir?'

'It's my job.'

'But why? What have I done wrong? Am I to be arrested? Oh, please don't write me down, sir.'

He looked at me hard, then gave a quick nod. 'Very well, miss. But if I have cause to bring you here again, I shall be forced to enquire your name.'

'Oh, yes, no...thank you, sir. Thank you.'

He touched his hat. 'Good day to you then, miss.'

'Good day, sir.' I hurried up the steps and rang the bell.

'And my name's Fred Thorpe,' he called just as Miss Kerr opened the door.

I was much ribbed for being brought back by a policeman. Mrs Drummond, Miss Annie and Miss Miller (with the fists) had been taken to Cannon Row and there made to wait a full hour till word came from the Prime Minister that they should be freed, but even their experience was considered second to my own.

'Fancy! Your very own private escort, Maggie. That's more than the Prime Minister's wife has when she goes shopping.'

I tried to explain that he had been on his way to another duty but this produced still more laughing. Mrs Drummond said she wished her bobby had been half as handsome and Miss Miller said all policemen were ugly on account of they were all violent.

I had to say then that this was not so, for mine had specially told me he disliked to use a truncheon and had never done so, for all he had often been provoked.

They giggled some more at this, which I thought pretty foolish for grown women, then Mrs Pethick Lawrence came in with a grand piece of news. The Prime Minister had agreed to receive a deputation in the 'near future', so everyone cheered and declared victory was just around the corner.

Later Miss Lake asked me if I was dreaming about my bobby. (I was just resting my eyes a little from the typewriter and happened to be gazing out of the window.) I said, sharp as I dared, 'That I'm not, miss. If you asked me I could scarce describe him.'

She nodded. 'I thought his moustache a little droopy.'

'He had none.'

Then Miss Miller remarked she thought him too short for a constable. I told her he was a clear head and a half above the sergeant guarding the Prime Minister. 'Well, maybe, but he had red hair and I never like that.'

I had to tell her how very fair he was, with not a carroty strand to his head.

'And you've quite forgotten his eyes, I daresay?' asked Miss Lake.

I said they were greeny brown, as far as I recalled.

'Tall, fair, clean-shaven with greeny brown eyes. Yes, I can see you've forgotten all about him.'

I was just glad they had not heard him call me pretty, or I think I should have been teased till my dying day.

The office is a very busy place. Being in a room at their home, Mrs Pethick Lawrence is forever popping in and out with fresh instructions and ideas for the Cause, as it is known.

Although there are just three of us working there, Miss Kerr, Miss Lake and myself, there are always a half dozen or so ladies milling around, collecting posters and leaflets or bringing news of what is happening in the Parliament and such, and all the time wanting to know what to do next. If you cannot tell them on the instant they take it upon themselves to find a task and generally this causes more muddle than if they just sat in a corner and chatted, or better still, went away!

Poor Miss Kerr was close to tears the other day when she found one of the helpers had taken all her files and rearranged them in date order, when she had come in over the weekend specially to sort them by letters.

Another of the ladies decided we would work much better for the accompaniment of music, and sat a whole afternoon playing on a black wooden pipe till we all felt like throwing her and it out of the window, her only knowing one tune and getting that wrong more often than right.

Because they mean so well it is difficult for anyone, even

Miss Sylvia, to say anything. In fact I think she finds it hardest of all for she has such a gentle nature and does not like to see people offended or hurt in any way, but this often leads to misunderstandings. It would not matter so much if we were left to ourselves to sort it out, but we are always in fear that Mrs Pankhurst, or worse, Miss Christabel, will make a flying visit and we shall not be able to lay our hands on what they require.

This would be worse than dreadful for I know I long for their good opinion above all others and I am sure the others do too. Miss Lake goes quite quivery when Miss Christabel is by and so do most of the helper ladies. One good word from her and they are glowing like buttered muffins, one frown and they are low as mud. Fortunately Mrs Pethick Lawrence always comes to our aid, knowing just where to find lost files and who was meant to do what, and what they did instead, and how we can best undo it. Sometimes when the muddle is too terrible even for her, she flops down in a chair, clasps her head and murmurs, 'Give me a moment, ladies. Let me take this in.' Then comes up with the most brilliant suggestion that we all wish we had thought of first, and truly I have heard some repeat them as though they had!

My duties are various. Every morning I spend thirty minutes at the typewriter learning how it is done. At first I thought I should never work it for the letters are higgledy-piggled all over the place and not in any order to make sense. I asked if it was a German one, for we all know they are not to be trusted and might easily make the letters foreign to cause mischief. Miss Kerr laughed mightily and said she had not thought of that. Miss Lake made a tutting sound and one of the ladies rolled her eyes upwards and glanced at her friend.

She did not say anything but I could see she thought me very stupid. I hate it when they look like that. Why can they not say to me, 'Maggie, that is mad,' as they do to each other? 'Enid, you are quite potty.' 'Alice, where did you leave your brains this morning?' But to me, nothing. Eyes rolling upwards. How many of them know nine psalms, I wonder, and have a bobby wanting to learn them from them?

One day when I was waiting for Miss Sylvia to bring me a letter for typing one of the helpers, a very pretty girl with hair the colour of chestnuts and pale speckly skin, sat down on the edge of my desk. 'Does your father not mind you working here?' she asked.

I said, no, he was very pleased for me to have come by such a position. She seemed most amazed. 'Mine doesn't know anything about it. He'd go dippy if he did. Mama knows but she says I must never breathe a word of it at home. You are lucky, having the pater on your side.'

I said I thought so too, not having the faintest notion what she meant. Just then Miss Sylvia came in with her letter so I was able to get on with my work. I heard the young lady say to her, 'Why does Maggie talk like that, Sylvia?'

'Like what?'

'Well, I don't know. As though she was common?'

I have rarely seen Miss Sylvia angry. I'm not sure that she was angry then, but her face seemed almost to freeze for a second, then she said, as calmly and kindly as ever, 'Maggie Robins is the least common person I have ever met, Marion. Now, have you got enough pamphlets or shall I try and rake out a few more for you?' I felt like crying, in gratitude to her, but mainly for shame of myself.

Maybe I should have stayed where I was with the Roes. Ladies will smile at you while you are serving them tea, but lift yourself to be like them and they will very quickly put you in your place. I wonder what 'equal' really means.

I am also in charge of the post so each day I spend a good hour putting leaflets into envelopes and stamping and addressing them – to such places as you would never believe: Homesby Manor, Clarendon House, Chesterfield Hall. I am surprised there is not one to be sent to Buckingham Palace. None to Turnpike Lane, Stepney, but who there could read it, now I'm away?

Incoming letters I file from A to Z in a great wooden box which Miss Kerr has fitted a lock to! At noon I go to the post office and when I return there is usually a plate of sandwiches and cups of tea laid ready for everyone. This is one task the ladies are very good at for many of them are from rich families and bring all sorts of delicious treats for us to try. I think it is a competition between them, for though they always swear that whoever has made the food that day has exceeded all others, it does not stop them popping up with something even more fancy when it is their turn. One lady, a Miss Haythorne, brought some horrid little black pellets which she spread on slices of toast. The others 'ooh'ed and 'aah'ed mightily, and seemed to think it the finest food on earth, but to me it tasted like salty jelly so when no one was looking, I spat it down the sink and had to make do with dry toast for there was nothing else that day.

In the afternoon we write more envelopes and Miss Kerr and Miss Lake take it in turns to type out replies and requests for money, which Mrs Pethick Lawrence usually signs as she is very well liked and can get people to open their purses.

At four o'clock everyone gathers to say what has been done and what needs doing next – planning meetings, letters to the press and the Prime Minister, who shall make the next speech... Miss Annie is champion at this, although she herself swears she is nothing to Miss Christabel who could 'turn water into wine'. I have yet to hear her, but it would not surprise me, for she is so altogether brilliant with the shiniest hair I ever saw. Except for Frank's and he, too, can persuade a soul to anything with just one smile.

Mrs Beckett said beauty was a curse, sent by the devil to drag you from the paths of righteousness. Well, she had no cause to fear on that account for more warts I never saw on a chin and some of them joined together. I should so like to be beautiful. I know it is a vanity, but it would not be altogether bad, for fine looks are a powerful weapon, it seems to me. Truly, people will follow a handsome person when they turn up their noses at a plain one, though I think they would follow Miss Christabel if she came tinkling a bell, shouting, 'Leper'. Oh, to be like her! To be one of the handsome people. To lead. I would so love to lead.

I asked Miss Sylvia why her sister did not speak at all our meetings. 'She'd be hoarse within a week. Besides, Mother is most particular we fit the right speaker to the right occasion.'

'Surely our message is the same, whoever brings it? "Women should have the same rights as men".'

'Yes, but there are many ways of coming by it. Think, Maggie, what good would it do to send Mrs Despard, say, whom we both know sounds like the Queen of England,

amongst poor starving women in the East End, or Miss Annie
to talk to the aristocracy? Firstly, they would not understand
a word and secondly they would undoubtedly object to being
lectured by someone with no experience of their problems.'

'Except the nobs don't have problems, miss, do they?'

'Well, not so many, certainly, but they think they do, so it's
the same thing.'

I could not help myself from laughing. Miss Sylvia nodded.
'I know what you are thinking, Maggie and, of course, you
are right. Deciding which hat to wear to the rally is hardly in
the same class as wondering where your next meal is coming
from. But some of our girls have awful family problems. You
heard yourself how Marion dare not tell her father of her
involvement. It is like that for a lot of our supporters.
Husbands and wives torn apart, brothers and sisters, fathers
and daughters... It may seem nothing to you, but to them it is
everything, so try to be a little patient with them when they
make silly comments or unfortunate remarks. Just think, it is
they who are ignorant, not you.'

'I shall try, miss.'

Miss Sylvia laughed. 'Well, don't try too hard for some of
them could do with a dressing down, believe me. Would you
like to see some pictures I've had framed? I'd love to know
what you think of them.'

I thought they were sad and dreadful and beautiful and
brave. Miss Sylvia had been away to the north of England and
spent weeks going round all the workplaces up there, just
painting and sketching the women as they laboured. Pit
women dragging great carts of coal along tunnels scarce high
enough to house a donkey. Weavers, eyes swollen like red pus

balloons, noses shrivelled for lack of air as they sweated a ten-hour day in front of their looms. Factory workers slumped across their benches, seamstresses blinking by candlelight to sew black on black in the black, black night. Women yellow from lead poisoning as they dip and dye cloth for the gentry.

I asked, 'How could you bear to draw such ugliness, miss?'

She was silent for a while. 'I don't know, Maggie. I'm not that good with words. Not like Christabel or Mother. This is all I have. My way of saying it cannot go on.'

I said, 'If you cannot think what to say, why do you not just show the people these pictures?'

She smiled.


Miss Sylvia is requested everywhere. Her paintings have moved people more than a thousand speeches, I would venture, but also they have given her the courage to speak out and tell the women what is happening to their sisters.

Sometimes she will draw shouts from the crowd, telling of their own bad fortune. She replies that that is why they must fight. Fight to save their children from such a fate. From being thrust up chimney shafts and down coal pits till their poor young spines are twisted from crawling through tunnels scarce wide enough to take a dog.

I heard Miss Christabel chastise her once. 'Remember, it is the women we are after, Sylvia. If you lose sight of the goal you undermine the Cause.'

Miss Sylvia shook her head. 'The women will fight for their children before they fight for themselves and if the way to do that is through the vote, then that is the path they will surely take.'

Miss Christabel looked vexed but said no more on the matter.

Every night I take home a pamphlet to study in the hope of understanding the Cause a little better. It is easy to see that the world would be much improved if everyone had enough to eat and a good warm hearth to come home to, but I find it hard to fathom how voting for some stiff grey man with a top hat and his own carriage is going to change things. Miss Sylvia is very patient with my endless questions though she must think me very dull for it always comes back to the same one. 'Why should such people care about me?'

'Maggie, I agree. Many of them would not, do not. But you are just one. Think if every female in the country were to rise up and demand the vote? Half the country – more even, for there are more girls born than boys. Did you know that?'

I said I did not but it would not surprise me for there are a powerful lot of ladies wandering around our office most of the time, and hardly ever a man.

'If women refused to cook or keep house till such time as they were given the vote, think how they could influence the framing of the laws. Why should a government of men decide how taxes paid by men *and* women should be spent? Why must our money go to making guns and sending men to war, rather than building hospitals and schools? Why should not every child receive a decent education? Why are boys taught chemistry and mathematics while girls are made to sew and polish doorsteps? Is that fair? Is that what you want? Is it what you want for your children if you have any?'

'No, but...'

'But what?'

'How can you make all the women agree to stop cooking?'

Miss Sylvia smiled. 'Well, let's hope it does not come to that, but do you not see, Maggie, the very knowledge that it is within their power to do so may give them the strength to fight for their rights. Women are only powerless if they allow themselves to be.'

I have thought about that. I understand that if there are more women than men and they all stand together surely they should be able to force the men to do their bidding, but men are bigger than women and I know that if Ma refuses Pa one thing he slaps her hard across the head and makes her nose bleed. So I think we have a long cruel battle ahead of us. I said so to Miss Annie.

'You are right, Maggie. But it is a just one so God will be on our side. Always remember that.'

I think she must have forgotten that God is a man.

At last! Mr Hardie sent word that there would be a reading of a bill for us in the Parliament. Mrs Pethick Lawrence nearly danced when she heard. Miss Miller declared it was a vital step and we must all go to hear the debate so, late in the evening, we set off.

We had to climb more steps than Jacob's Ladder until at last we entered a dusty place, dark and manky – not at all like the room the grey men lounged about in.

At the front was an iron grille and for a moment I feared we were in a prison cell, but then Miss Sylvia showed me how we could look down on the Parliament as they talked, so we settled ourselves down and listened for what seemed like forever as the men made speeches to each other, about I know not what. No more did they, I reckon, for I saw more than one asleep on his bench, and some of them seemed outright tipsy. I looked all around for my bobby but the constables there seemed as old as the stonework they guarded.

The room was quite packed with ladies, many of them in evening dress, and others like me, in work clothes so that we must have made a quaint sight, jammed together like sprats.

I was just thinking how glad I would be to see my bed when a door at the back opened and Miss Annie rushed in. 'Now,' she whispered most urgently and all the other ladies, many of whom looked quite as droopy as did I, stirred themselves and began to murmur.

I looked down and saw entering the chamber old Mr Hardie, although amongst the others there he looked quite spry and I was glad to see his beard had had a trim.

'This is *it*,' whispered Miss Sylvia and clasped my arm so hard I nearly squealed.

Mr Hardie began to speak, saying that sex should be no bar to having a vote, whereat one of those who had been asleep rose to his feet and said, it should be no bar to having a family either, at which there was a great whoop of laughter from all those present, many stamping their feet and shouting, 'Hear, hear', which of course no one could.

Mr Hardie continued that it was unfair and unjust to expect women to pay taxes and receive nothing in return. Another man called out there should be a tax on their tongues – more laughter – and another, a very silly man who could hardly stand for bandiness, cried out that women were the cause of all Man's troubles and so it had been since Eve had struck her bargain with the serpent. This, it seemed, was the funniest thing ever said, or so you would have thought to see the gentlemen fairly rolling around the chamber. For myself I have heard far better at the music hall and still seen cabbages thrown.

Again Mr Hardie rose to his feet, saying the behaviour of the Honourable Gentlemen was such that he began to think women, and women alone, should order the affairs of the nation, at which a voice (Miss Miller's, I would lay good money) cried out, 'Hear, hear'.

A dark silence fell. The Honourable Gentlemen began to mutter amongst themselves and then a very ancient person who positively flopped in his seat, signalled a constable.

'Justice for women!' came another cry and out comes Miss Billington's banner, she trying with all her might to thread it through the grille. I know not how it looked to those below but it struck me it could do with a good washing from where I sat.

Next we knew, the door again flew open and in rushed a herd of constables like bulls and began hauling off the ladies, many clinging to their seats till they were fairly dragged away. I could not believe what was happening. That ladies with fine hats and fans and everything genteel should be so mauled about. Indeed I had not thought that any man could behave so roughly to a woman if he were not married to her or on the drink. I ran for all my might before they got to me, down the stairs and back into the courtyard where a great pile of coats and wraps were lying, some badly torn, that the bobbies had ripped off as the women fled.

It was wrong of me, I know, but seeing them there, it came to me how many women in my street would give a week's rent for just a touch of such soft fine garments, for all they were torn and muddied.

The next day there was a great turmoil at the office, for the newspapers were all full of what had happened, although I do not think they got it right for they said it was the fault of the women, and not the Parliament that seemed to me more like a bear garden than a place for making laws. They have named us the 'suffragettes' to set us apart from men who also want the vote. I venture they would not be so hard on them! Still it seems our efforts were not lost. The Prime Minister has decided he will receive the ladies on May 19th.

There is to be a great rally in celebration. Women are to come from all over the country. Every kind, rich and poor, high and low, old and young. I have worked my fingers dizzy typing. Miss Sylvia was going to order more buns but her mother advised against it, saying the time for buns would be when they had the victory. Miss Sylvia remarked they would be stale by then, but Mrs Pankhurst said if that were her only worry she would die a happy woman.

I understood her reasoning, but I think Mrs Pankhurst, and Miss Christabel, too, do not entirely understand what a difference a little food may make to a hungry woman. It is all very well for the helpers to have lemonade and potted meat and pastries when they have but put out a few tables and hung the banners. That could be left. But when a woman has walked an hour to the starting point and must walk another two in the procession...

I cannot complain. I am fed like a queen at Mrs Garrud's. She says she has found an old coat that I may borrow to learn the fighting in, so I have no excuse! I am to go on Tuesday evening for an hour to see how I like it.

\* \* \*

I do like it! At first I thought I would not, for the hall was full of the most fierce-looking creatures I ever saw. They were huffing and snorting and whipping their arms around like they would slice through a brick wall if it stood in their way, but Mrs Garrud calmed them down and introduced me to each of them and they all shook my hand and said they were glad to know me, and generally made me feel so welcome, by the end of the lesson I was slashing and wheezing away like I was born to it.

Mrs Garrud says it will make me strong as a lion and twice as flexible. I looked that up. It said: *'will bend without breaking'*. We shall see.

Such a rally! Women – more than the eye could see – from every rank and trade, all along the Embankment cheering their very hearts out. Brass bands playing; costumes of every hue – shawls, clogs, purple gowns, the leather aprons of the tanners, – oh, so many different garbs, so much colour.

Off marched our leaders, heads held high like a conquering army, banners flying in the breeze, the traffic forced to stop and make way. I could have burst for pride to be a part of such a day, for all I had done but little towards it. I was there, and that was enough.

We waited and waited, all hopeful and gay in the spring sunshine, for we truly believed no man and no Parliament could ignore such a throng. We joked and laughed and took turns to say what we would vote for first. I said, 'Sugar', and a woman by me said, 'enough money to bury me babbies decent', which seemed a bit of a waste. Another wanted a straw hat with ribbons, and another, a smeary broken-looking woman with dark cracks in her skin, said, 'Daylight'. I thought to myself, no one should have to ask for that.

At length came word that the meeting was over. We clambered to our feet, breathless, hardly daring to speak, dizzy with excitement. Even the bands fell silent, cymbals raised.

They never sounded. The meeting was indeed over. And *nothing* achieved. It seemed although this Sir Henry, this Prime Minister, had owned himself in favour of the Cause, he durst not go against his fellow ministers. I wondered what sort of a leader he could be that was afraid to force his will on those beneath him.

A sort of dull emptiness spread over us.

The ladies came back very down, except Miss Annie who looked crosser than I ever saw her. 'We are not going to stop for this,' she cried out, as they came near. 'We are going on with our agitation.' All who heard her cheered for she has a way of lifting people's spirits. Nothing ever dismays her for long. She is like a rubber ball. You may throw her down from the greatest heights but she will bounce right back again, and higher than before.

So we did not give up. We marched to Trafalgar Square. Not an inch of pavement was free. Bodies everywhere. Even the great stone lions had mill girls draped about them like they were no fiercer than factory tom cats.

The traffic had to stop all over again and some of the cabmen who started off yelling at us gave up and joined in, many swearing it was better than the vaudeville.

Speaker after speaker.

'Are we to take this? Are we to accept that our words, our

wishes count for nothing in the eyes of this mean and cowardly government?'

'Look about you. What do you see? Hundreds, nay, thousands – from every part of the country, come here today to demand justice. The right to be heard.'

'If God had not meant women to speak out he would not have given them voices.'

'He slipped up there,' yelled a man from the back of the crowd. Lucky he was at the back or he would have been hung from the nearest lamp-post judging by how the mill girls turned on him.

One old lady told how she had been fighting to gain the vote for forty years, and swore she would go on another forty if that was what it took. I was much moved by this for though she was bent and crippled in her body, her eyes were like a young girl's, spilling over with hope.

So many came forward and such a mix – governesses and fishwives, carders and clergymen's daughters. How odd to think that people who would pass each other in the street should stand together on a wooden platform and swear that they are sisters.

Then at last, Mrs Pankhurst, her voice, so low and calm, carrying to the furthest reaches of the square (I swear, even the pigeons heeded her) urging us on – never to give up, but to fight for what should be ours of right, to work day and night till our goal was met and only then to look for just repose.

'Remember always, we women are the mother half of the human family. What family can survive or thrive without a mother? We are its very spine, its heart, its life-blood. Without us the human race would cease to exist, and yet we are denied our place in society as though we were no more than animals, pets, and irritating ones, at that! Indeed there is one gentleman in Parliament who, I am told, has likened the female species to rabbits. I wonder how his mother feels about that. Or indeed, his wife.' Waves of laughter echoed round the square. 'I am also told by those who consider themselves to be experts on the matter, that what distinguishes a human being from an animal is a sense of humour. It is some time since I heard a rabbit laugh as you have just done.' That set us off again. 'But I must, in all fairness, point out that none of the gentlemen we met this morning so much as mustered a chuckle throughout our visit.' Her face grew serious. 'I know today has brought its disappointments. I, too, had nourished great hopes for our meeting with the Prime Minister. No one more than I had longed to stand before you this afternoon and cheer our victory, but patience, good friends. If this bright morning has turned all too suddenly to dreary night, remember still that tomorrow a new day awaits us. So I say to you all, let us take courage and together, arm in arm and shoulder to shoulder, stride bravely on through taunt and difficulty towards the dawn, united as ever, in hope.'

How I would love to have the gift of words – to make strangers stand out in the open and heed me. More than that, to cheer me and clap and stamp their feet, and go away persuaded, for such is Mrs Pankhurst. That Prime Minister could learn a lesson from her, that is afraid of his own party.

Miss Annie says that Mrs Montefiore (with the great big hat) has refused to pay her taxes till she has the vote. She has locked up her gates so that the bailiffs may not enter. We all went to see and surely she is a very brave lady. High on a wall was nailed a huge banner: *WOMEN SHOULD VOTE FOR THE LAWS THEY OBEY AND THE TAXES THEY PAY.*

After a few minutes she came to a window wearing a fur hat with a tassel and holding a noisy little dog. She shouted out to us that if the Parliament men were against us they were wrong. She mentioned one in particular: 'Asquith'. Such a strange name. I think he must be foreign and if so, maybe a spy, for why else would he be in our government? She said his house had windows, which I thought a little mad, for most houses do, but if she is locked up all alone with only a yapping dog it is possible she has lost her mind, just for now.

More newspaper men were there, which was good for we had brought banners and posters to drape on the fence and some food for Mrs Montefiore, although I did not think it likely she would starve with such a big house and so many hats.

Miss Annie is in prison! It is a terrible thing. We had heeded Mrs Montefiore's word and gone to this Asquith man's house, for it is said he is our worst enemy and so must be brought round above all others. He had twice refused to show his face but we were forty strong and quite settled we would not quit till he had spoken with us.

As we arrived a crowd of bobbies (but not mine) came charging at us and fairly ripped our banners away. Miss Billington, who is very attached to hers, as we know, tried to grasp it back, whereat one of the bobbies, a very mean-faced creature with a crooked lip, struck her hard across the face and, next we know, she has slapped the man full square across his scabby cheek. At this another leaps upon her as she were

a wild tiger and near throttles her. A big round woman tries
to pull him off and is herself quite slit about by his nails. The
police fight like rats and not as men should do, is my opinion.

In all, four were arrested: Miss Annie, a little lame woman
who tried to free her, and a poor old woman who did no more
than shake her fist at the windows. Also Miss Billington. They
have been sent away to Holloway prison for six long weeks.

I cried mightily when I heard it, but Miss Sylvia and Mrs
Pethick Lawrence said I must not fret for they had done it for
the Cause and it was a mighty blow for freedom. I cannot
think how being shut up in a cell can make for freedom, but
they seem to think it is so. I wonder if they have ever seen the
inside of a prison. I did once, when my nan was there for
selling flour mixed with chalk, only to make it stretch and so
to sell more bags. Prison is a wicked place, full of coldness and
holiness, which I think lie side by side together.

Miss Kerr visited them. She told us they were well and
bearing up and the old lady was even enjoying it, for it was
years since she had had a decent rest and a room to herself,
with enough to eat and not much to do but knit socks for the
other prisoners. I thought of Ma and wondered how she
might like it.

I will go home soon. I know it is wicked, but I like my life
so much now, with my fighting and typewriting and clean
smart clothes, I hold back, for it always brings me down to see
how rotten is their life, even with what Frank and I can send.

It is near eighteen months since I saw Frank. I wonder if he
would recognise me now, for I am so tall and every way
different. Or am I? To look at, yes truly, but in my heart? In
my head? In my resolve? Here I am safe, but I cannot run

away forever for if I do... I know I must speak to him, tell him...beg him... Not Lucy. It is different for me. God's punishment. I will not think about it any more. My eyes are closed.

Since Miss Annie has been in prison I have given much thought to all I have learnt about the Cause. I own at first I cared for nothing but my wages and fine new clothes. I believed myself near enough to heaven just to be paid to write letters and then take them to the post office. Perhaps if I had not read the leaflets, not seen my friends arrested, I would have stayed of that opinion. Happy and stupid. Sometimes I wish I had.

All the time my mind is churning – Why? Why? Why? Why is a man paid more than a woman for the same labour? Why can a woman not decide for herself who should rule over her? Why, when work is scarce must a woman be the first to lose her post? I have read how some are forced on to the streets, merely to feed their children. Others are humping sacks of coal – breaking their backs, for women were never made to carry such weights. What is it in us that lets us be so used? All this is whirling in my mind when I sit down at a meeting, and yet I say nothing, though sometimes I could scream with aggravation.

I do believe the ladies mean the very best, but how can they ever know what it is like to live in wretched damp lodgings, with a child coming every year and half of them dead before walking? They can easy talk about a vote for each woman in the land, but will that bring her food or coal for the fire? I know very little, but I do know those grey men care nothing for the likes of us – man, woman or child – and if it is for them we must vote, so they can live in a palace and lean their elbows on a great marble mantel, while women like my ma stand in the rain and beg for a minute of their time, then where is the point in this struggle?

I asked Miss Sylvia if she truly believed their minds could be turned. She was quiet a long time. 'I do, Maggie. In the end. If only because we have men like Keir Hardie to fight for us. Ten years ago he was fighting for his own right to have a voice in how he is governed. He has told me himself how many times he felt like giving up, slinking away, "burying himself", he said, so that he need not face another day of battling against the arrogance and stupidity of those around him.'

'So what made him keep at it?'

'Belief. Pure and simple. If you truly believe in something then you must fight for it, whatever the cost.'

'That's easy said, miss.'

Miss Sylvia looked quite down. 'I know what you think, Maggie. You think this is just a game for women who have nothing better to do with their time. Am I right?'

I shook my head. 'I don't know why the ladies do it, miss. I only know it is a world away from the likes of me. And that when you talk about "cost", for them it is marching in the rain and having their hats knocked crooked. For my sort it is risking a beating, to lose our work, our homes... It is so...different. And for what?'

'For justice. The right to decide how you will be governed and by whom.'

'A prison is a prison, miss. No matter who guards the door.'

* * *

Last night, after my fighting lesson, I felt a low achy pain in my belly. I had had it before, on and off for a few days and thought perhaps the dinner fish was bad. This morning when I got up I found that I was bleeding down my legs. I washed as best I could but more kept coming from inside me so I knew I must have harmed myself most dreadfully. I durst not tell Mrs Garrud for she has been so kind to me and would be mortal worried if I said that I had damaged myself in the fighting.

I walked to Lincoln's Inn, all the while fearing lest my innards should fall out on to the pavement, and when I got there was so pale and faint that Miss Kerr sat me straight down and would have called a doctor.

Mrs Pethick Lawrence ordered hot sweet tea to be brought to me and asked what signs I had of illness. I told her and her face hardly moved, but she patted my hand and said I must not worry and she would ask Miss Annie (who is back at last, praise the Lord) to come and talk to me.

Miss Annie took me aside to the store-room and gave word that we should not be disturbed, then she explained that my bleeding was a sign that I was fully grown up. I thought it strange that I should fall apart so soon, for I am not fifteen and healthy up till now. It seems that what I have is not a wound but occurs to all women and goes on forever, every month till they are old. I have seen Ma with blood down her but thought it was from arguing with Pa. Miss Annie said it came from not having a baby. 'But if all women bleed, how can there be any babies?' I asked.

She looked a bit confused. 'When they have babies it stops. It starts again after. Every month. You will get used to it.' I said I did not want to, for surely there must be some cure? She smiled and said, none that she knew of, but it was not such a great thing and would be gone very soon, and fetched me two pieces of shortbread which she said was the best medicine she knew for it. She has given me cotton pads for my bloomers. What a business is growing up.

Word has come of a new order from Mrs Pankhurst and Miss Christabel. We are to have no more to do with the politicians unless they are on our side. Miss Sylvia was deeply upset by this for it seems they include Mr Hardie, since it is he and not his party that supports the Cause. She has resigned her post as Honourable Secretary. Also we are to move into offices downstairs as Mr and Mrs Pethick Lawrence are quite overrun with all the banners and bills and helpers and all.

There are meetings held two or three times a week now. To save money on printing I am sent out with chalk to scratch news of the time and place upon the walls and pavements. I was chosen, Miss Annie says, because I have the fastest legs for running away and can bend over without getting the backache (this, I think, is due to my fighting, for we start each class with stretching and truly I am getting very springy).

I have at last been to hear Miss Christabel and surely she is the bravest speaker in the world. It was a rough windy night and we were outside the fish market at Billingsgate. At first she made to stand on a chair but the men, fresh from work and smelling like manky herrings, brought out a great wooden chest that they said she might have for a platform. She thanked them and climbed up on it. She spoke of justice and fairness and our need to stand together, men and women, to fight for what was right. 'Shoulder to shoulder, like warriors of old, unflinching, unafraid, unstoppable...' Just as she had the whole crowd eating from her hand there was a mighty thump and the lid of the chest started to heave beneath her feet.

Miss Christabel carried on, though I could see she was unsettled. 'Men have kept from us many things. There is one particular thing that they have kept from us, and that has been the joy of battle. They tell us women cannot fight...'

The lid gave a mighty judder so that she must stand, legs spread like a common sailor's, to keep her balance and hold it down. The men could scarce hold their laughter, slapping each other's backs and braying like idiot donkeys. 'See, she can raise the dead with the power of her tongue,' one yelled, which started them all off again. She straightened up then turned to them, cool as a summer's breeze. 'It seems I can also walk on water,' which brought forth such a cheer from the women about that the men looked fair ashamed, for they had stood her on a box of live eels, hoping to see her thrown into the crowd. She smiled and held out her hands to them. 'And they say women cannot fight!'

All summer long we have been out and about. Often I am sent ahead to beg the landlord of a public house to lend us chairs or a table for the speaker to stand on. It is wondrous how a clean blouse and neat black skirt can make a man polite to you. I am always called 'Miss', and never have to carry the chairs myself, though I could, for my arms are stronger than a wrestler's now, I'd venture.

Once, when a drunkard sought to wreck a meeting, I asked

Miss Sylvia if I should throw him to the ground, but she counselled against it in case it did not work. Probably she was right for I have only practised with a bolster up till now.

Not a day goes by without a fresh pile of letters asking to join. A man was hired to paint WSPU above the window of our office. I asked what it might mean, thinking perhaps it was typewriting. Miss Kerr said, no, it stood for the Women's Social and Political Union. I said I thought we did not like politicians. She explained we did not, but politics and politicians were not the same thing. I did not understand at all, but Miss Kerr can be very dull sometimes when she gets to explaining things so I nodded and said, 'Quite so,' which Mr Pethick Lawrence often does when he is pressed for time.

The Parliament will open again on October 23$^{rd}$ and we shall march.

Is it always to be so? We gather, full of hope, determination... We march. We wait. At length comes some stiff lackey to ask our business (stiff stupid lackey, if he cannot read a banner). Away he goes. Back he comes. 'The Prime Minister regrets...' Well, today he had cause to regret.

Once again it was decreed that only twenty should be admitted. The officials chose them – those with gloves and hat feathers, furs round their shoulders. In they go. Out they come. There is to be no law to give the vote to women.

What would they have us do? Creep quietly away? One lady immediately jumped up on a seat in the lobby and started to complain. Comes an inspector, very smartly, and though we tried to shield her, whips her away to be arrested. No sooner is she gone than Mrs Despard, no less, steps daintily up and carries on. She, too, is taken off, and up pops another. Truly it was like a party game till the inspector (very red behind the ears and sweating like a nag) orders in a whole bundle of bobbies to clear us all outside.

There Miss Annie, seeing Mrs Pethick Lawrence being fairly minced by one of the constables, ran to her aid and was on the spot arrested. Mrs Pethick Lawrence shouted they should let her go, and was herself taken in hand. I could not see them treated so, for they and Miss Sylvia have been my kindest friends.

We had but lately learnt a move with Mrs Garrud and it seemed now would be an excellent time to test it. As the bobby turned away I hooked my foot around his ankle and pushed him hard in the back. This should have made him fall roughly to the ground but instead he turned round, very peevish, and said, 'Don't do that, miss, if you please.' I knew not what to do next, so said as loud as I dared, 'I will if I like,' whereat he arrested me.

After it was done I was very frightened, for all save Miss Annie were ladies through and through, and it was a shock to sit with them at the police station, all in cold stone cells together.

Our names were taken and it was said we must go before the judge the following day. I swear I did not sleep that night for fear of what would happen, but though I was scared to my very toes and beyond, I also thought that I had not disgraced myself entirely.

As I could not sleep I got out of my bed and practised my move some more with the pillow, that next time I may get it right.

The court was very terrible.

We stood, squashed together in a tall wooden dock, no wider than a coffin and not one half so cosy. The judge was horrible – a face like a bad potato with grizzled ringlets down his back and eyes all popping like a Jack-in-the-box whenever one of the ladies tried to speak out for herself.

I think we were not there above ten minutes. A bobby said that we had caused disorder and then the judge chewed his mouth around as though he had bitten a lemon and said a whole lot of things which I did not understand, ending up with 'Two months. Second division.'

Several ladies gasped and Miss Annie reached across and squeezed my arm very hard. I stayed as close to her as I could. She was very kind to me and tried to make light of our situation. She, having been in prison before, told me it was not so very bad, though the food was not of her choosing and it was a terrible waste of time to be locked up when we could be out spreading the word. Miss Billington said that our very imprisoning would do more for the Cause than a dozen rallies. I hoped she was right.

We were taken below stairs and there divided between the cells. Just as we were about to leave there was a commotion on the stairs and a voice called out, 'Here's another to join you, ladies,' and down came Miss Sylvia, looking mighty pleased and angry at the same time. It seems she had protested not being allowed to attend our trial and, for her pains, had been placed before the same foul judge and sent to join us!

What a gathering we were. I wondered who was left to mind the office with so many of us bound for prison.

Mrs Pethick Lawrence looked exceeding ill, and when the

great black van came thundering into the yard, I thought she would faint away with horror. All the way there I could hear her murmuring to herself and weeping, for she hates to be indoors without a window open and indeed we were pressed as tight as letters in a pillar box, with just a tiny slit up high to let in light and air.

Holloway is a vile place. The women who guard us are big and bristly – more like bulldogs than women, with foul rude voices and a joy in bringing misery.

It is very hard for some of the ladies. They feel the want of a fire and hot water greatly. Worse for me, I think, is the lack of air. Although the cells are cold, they are full of dust, so that our noses are clogged with muck and we snuffle and sneeze like hogs at a trough. We cannot see the sky and no streak of daylight enters. Just dirty yellow gloom like a fog. This is probably for the good, for the clothes we wear are too ugly to be borne if we could see them, I'm sure, and scratchier than a flea comb.

Our beds are stuck to the wall and at night we fold them down. Before I came to Park Walk I would have thought them fine and warm, but now I find I cannot rest with sheets like sand and shavings and blankets thinner than a leaf of cabbage.

We spend the day at prayer! And knitting socks. I do not know which vexes me more. I think the chapel, although there we see each other at least, and may smile and nod. Talk is quite forbidden.

The food is all brown bread and beans and soup. In the morning the soup is called 'tea' and in the evening 'cocoa'. At lunch it is called 'soup'. I wonder what Cook would make of such a recipe! I wonder how she is; if she ever thinks of me. She would be truly angry to see what I have come to, I know, but perhaps if I could tell her the reason she would understand. She did not think a lot of men and so might fathom I was trying to make things better.

I am down on my knees thanking her for teaching me to knit. So far I have finished three pairs of socks and will be paid a shilling for each. This is fine wages, since I do not pay my lodging, and I shall give it all to Ma when I am out.

I wonder if she knows that I am here. I hope not, truly, for she would be much ashamed. Say I was no child of hers. And I am not. Not hers or anyone's. I am so far from her now. Grown up. If I am here much longer the bleeding will start. Oh, please let me go home soon. I do not care about a vote.

I heard today that Mrs Pethick Lawrence has been freed. She was ill and taken to the hospital almost as soon as we arrived with 'nerves'. Several of the other ladies followed, till but a few of us remained, all from working backgrounds. I suppose I must count it a blessing that poor people do not get 'nerves'. Miss Sylvia has not had it either, although I found her very close one morning when the Butcher, as we call the wardress on our row, had shouted at her for not scrubbing her cell right, and refused to give her breakfast. As she said, she did not want the breakfast, but it hurt her so to be called 'a useless sloven'. I told her how to do it so they would be satisfied. It is all a trick. You clean the middle and the bits under your bed, for that is where they look. They are too stupid to change their ways and, like horses, can only look sideways and down.

I also tried to teach her to knit, for none of the ladies have earned a penny so far. She took to it most skilfully and would have finished a pair of socks at least, but the governor came and said she could go free, so she was forced to give it over. Some poor prisoner must pad around, one foot bare now, I suppose.

It is not such a bad thing to be a prisoner. In fact, it is so good I would do it a hundred times over if it could all end as this has done. The Savoy! I cannot believe it. Me! Oh, what a feast we had. One of the ladies had arranged it for us, but that was just the crowning of the best day of my life, I think, so far.

We left Holloway at seven in the morning. Even at that hour there was a crowd to meet us, cheering and clapping as we came through the great oak door to freedom. There were cabs to take us home and Mrs Garrud had heated water and Mr Garrud dragged out the tin bath into the kitchen and then was sent away, that I might soak myself in private, with a great chunk of olive soap. I never had such a bath in all my life. I washed my hair till the water turned black for there was nothing but cold in Holloway and it no good for getting out the muck.

When I was done I put on my own dear precious clothes, then, clean and fresh as a princess, rushed off to the office to present myself.

As I walked up the steps I could see that the curtains were drawn which was strange for it was still early in the day. I rang the bell and Miss Lake came to let me in. She gave me the biggest smile I ever saw, which is not like her at all. 'Come in, Maggie. We have been waiting for you.'

I wondered if I should have come sooner, for truly I had lain in my bath till I was crinkled like a prune, but when she opened the door to the office I could see that no work was being done. The lights were on and everywhere was hung with banners saying, *Welcome Home, Heroines* and on the table there was a great cake, with *Freedom and Victory* piped on it in purple icing, and lemonade, and cards from the women's groups all over England, saying, 'Welcome', and 'Well done', and so many brave things that I thought I should weep for not having suffered worse than I did, when poor Mrs Pethick Lawrence had been brought down with nerves and so many others, also.

Miss Annie and Miss Billington (wrapped in her banner, wouldn't you know!) were already there and they hugged me and said I was a noble sister to the Cause, and everybody clapped, and we sang, 'Rise up, women. For the fight is hard and long', which is my favourite, for the tune is 'John Brown's Body' and quite the best in the world.

Many of the ladies quizzed me about Holloway. They said they had to ask for it was likely they, too, would suffer the same fate before long, and it was as well to be prepared. I said it was not too bad, but boring and the food was very vile. I thought to myself that my best help to them would be to start a knitting class, but durst not say it for fear they might be miffed.

I had thought we would go home at half past five, which is the usual time, but six o'clock struck and still we sat and talked. To tell true, I was tired and would have liked nothing so well as to go to my warm soft bed, but just when I was scraping up the courage to ask if I might leave, the doorbell clanged.

'There!' cried Miss Lake, and was once more off at the gallop. She returned with a young woman who came bouncing in. 'Are you ready? Mother is waiting for us there.'

If she had spoken Scottish I could not have been more confused.

Miss Annie told me to put on my coat and we all trooped downstairs and out into the street where four cabs waited, in a line. We piled into them and before I knew it, we were off down the Aldwych and on till we came to rest outside the greatest hotel you ever saw.

'Well,' said the bouncy girl who sat opposite me and was not much older, 'here we are.'

'Where?' I asked.

'The Savoy. We are to have dinner here. Mama has arranged it all.'

We had soup (not like the prison's), quails' eggs, then quails, then fish, a pheasant and a game terrine, followed by lamb and potatoes. Next a sorbet, a dish of thick chewy grass, some veal pie and, best of all, a 'trifle', which was not a trifle at all but custard and cake soaked in sweet wine and red jammy fruit and almonds all in a bowl, and quite beyond compare.

Some of the ladies could not eat it all, but I ate every course and though I thought I would burst at the end of it, I still managed a little plate of fancies that the waiter (looking like a penguin) brought to us as we waited for the cabs to be called.

Miss Sylvia rode with me to Argyle Place. 'Well, Maggie,

did you enjoy that?' she asked as I was climbing down.

'I cannot think of words to describe it, miss.'

She smiled. 'Nor I. How about "wondrous as the feet of Sheba"?' I said I thought that might serve.

I have been home at last. Ma looks better than last time, though she still cannot feed the baby. My new sister is a sturdy thing, quite chubby and a tooth on the way. She seems cheerful but does not really heed when you play with her. Rather she gazes around and then sucks her fingers as she would chew them off.

Alfie is grown taller still. He likes his work and has a new waistcoat which Mrs Grant sewed for him in return for him carrying her coal home every week. It must be hard to live so high up and have no man about.

Pa seemed pleased to see me, though he is never slow to ask how much I have brought and was off down the alehouse before I had shed my coat, even. He is not a bad man, as Ma would say, but nor, to my mind, is he a very good one. He works hard, keeps his hearth, does not beat Ma as much as some men in our street do their wives. Certainly he is not as foul as the politicians, who are not like real men at all, but more the statues that they live amongst – cold, stony, dead of feeling. I wonder how it is that such men came to govern us when I have read there have been women rulers in the past, that should have sent them all away and filled their courts with such as Mrs Pankhurst and Miss Christabel, who are wise and brave and full of laughter. *Then* what a world we should live in.

Evelyn has had the scarlatina but is well again. Will cries as much as ever and still for nothing, as far as I can tell. Lucy was not there. I did not ask after her, though I know I should have. About four o'clock she came in, just as we were setting out the dinner. I had brought a piece of pork and some dried beans and made a stew of it with carrots and an onion. Pa said it smelt like manna from heaven when he got back. I did not think it likely he would know, never having been in a wilderness, and not often in a church, but it was said with such good feeling we all agreed.

Lucy, too, is grown tall, but very thin. Her hair is like string and she has dark rings under her eyes so that she looks quite old and witchy. I remembered how she had teased me with my spots, but I am grown up now and do not feel the urge to twit her. Truth was, I felt quite sorry for her, at least I did until she spoke!

First, she did not like the stew, saying it tasted of nothing but salt, which was not true. I thought she was lucky to be eating such good food, and all paid for by me, and would have told her about the stuff in Holloway, but that I did not want Ma and Pa to know where I had been.

Next she moaned that she had no warm coat to wear. I could see where this was going. She had seen mine hanging in the hall. It was not new, having been given to me by one of the ladies, but it is wool throughout and truly I have need of it when we go on night meetings, and I must stand outside for hours on end in any weather.

I had brought a treacle tart for our pudding. She liked that but complained when Ma gave the last spare slice to Pa. I was surprised he did not belt her, but he merely shrugged and shovelled it down, faster than a steam train.

After dinner she went out again, not stopping to help clear or to wash Will down or anything. Ma was busy with the baby's milk so I had it all to do myself, although Evelyn, who is a sweet thing, came and stood by me and recited the twenty-ninth psalm to me which Mrs Beckett had given her to learn. She had it all by heart and I gave her a kiss and told her I was proud of her, though listening to her, it struck me what strange things there be in the Bible, and how she would be better to learn how to write to the Parliament and to knit than to skip like a young unicorn.

When little Ann was settled Ma came down and said she would make a cup of tea before I went for it was a long walk home, and bitter cold outside. I said I had come on the omnibus and would return so. She raised her eyebrows.

'Well, still, you would like the tea?'

'Yes, if that is all right?' She brought me a cup and one for herself although I saw it had only water. We sat in silence for a while. Alfie was off out playing in the street. Evelyn was showing Will her picture book which I had bought her for her birthday. I thought she was brave to let him near it, for he is the stickiest boy I ever knew, but she is a kind little soul and does not seem to care much for herself.

I asked Ma if she was recovered now from the baby. She said her strength was much improved. There was still a problem with the milk, but Ann was so hardy she thought she could move her on to potato soon and some bread dipped in water.

'Lucy is much grown.'

Ma looked away. 'Yes.'

'Is she a trouble to you, Ma? I saw she does not help you in the house. Do you want me to speak to her? I can, you know. She will listen to me.'

'She will not listen to anyone, save your brother Frank.'

I heard my voice begin to shake. 'Well then, why cannot he speak to her? Tell her she must help you?'

Ma clasped her knees and rocked a little back and forth as though a pain ran through her. 'Because he cares only for his own pleasure and leads others to do the same. You know that well enough.'

I remembered how ill I had behaved towards her when I was Lucy's age – so long ago, as now it seemed, and how Frank had laughed. I was ashamed that I had caused her so much grief.

'I will speak to her. I will tell her that if she does not mend her ways there will be no more presents. She will not like that.'

Ma raised her head and looked me full in the eyes. 'Frank brings her presents,' she said.

My heart sank like lead. 'Why? He never did when I was home.'

Ma plucked a loose thread from her sleeve. 'Frank does nothing for nothing,' was all she said.

There was a great crash as someone slammed the kitchen door. It was Lucy, red and sullen. She stamped right past us, through the parlour and up the stairs.

I called to her, 'Do you not fear to wake the baby, Lucy?' For answer came another slam. She has my nan's room now, and a great mess she makes of it. I ran up the stairs after her. She was lying on the bed, muddy shoes on the blanket, and not for the first time, either, by the looks.

'This is my room,' she said as I closed the door behind me.

'And a fine sight it is.'

She said nothing but stared at me so coldly I could not think that we were flesh and blood. 'Why do you not help Ma with the house?'

'Why should I?'

'It is your house, too. It's where you live. Ma cannot do everything. She has the little ones to care for.'

'Yes and she does not care for me.'

'It's different. You are older. You can care for yourself.'

'How come she cares for Alfie? He is older than I am.'

'You know that Alfie has problems. He does what he can.'

'"Alfie has problems". You never thought that when you spent long hours trying to teach him to read and to do his numbers, which he still cannot fathom.'

'I was wrong. I did not know that then.'

'Did Frank have problems? When you took him away and went to the concert and the halls and off anywhere so that I could not be with you?'

'That's different. You were too young.'

'And you were his "best girl". Do you think I have forgotten?'

I shook my head. 'Lucy... What...? Lucy, I have not been a very good sister to you, I know. But it is different now. I have my own life. You are the oldest now and you must take my place here.'

'And if I will not?'

'You must.'

'Or what?'

'I don't know. I cannot be here always.'

Lucy gave a laugh, but it was hollow and uncouth. 'No, for you may be in prison, like before.'

I felt as though my blood had drained out through the floor. 'Who told you that?'

'Everyone knows. They call you a heroine in the street.'

'Does Pa know?'

'Him, I don't know. Ma does, and Mrs Grant.'

'But she said nothing.'

'Ma nevers says anything. Don't you know that yet? Anything.' With that, she rolled on her front and would not look at me.

I leant against the door. 'Lucy, please listen to me. Let me explain.'

'Explain what? That you have a fine life and fine clothes and come round here telling me to stay and be a slave here? While you can be a heroine and have your picture in the paper.'

'What paper?'

'Oh, did you not know? Ask Ma. She has it hid in a drawer lest Pa sees it. "Suffra…suffra…something, Released from Holloway." And there you are, smiling and waving and driving off in a cab like a princess and the like. Frank bought it for us. He thought it a great jest so, of course, I had to pretend I thought so too or he would have pulled my hair wicked.'

'Frank is not like that.' For all I understood her envy, I could not hear her speak of him so meanly.

She turned on her side and looked up at me with her pale little caterpillar eyes. 'You don't know Frank. Not the way I do.'

I felt a sick cold stone in my belly.

I said nothing to Ma of what had passed between Lucy and me. What good would it do? Lucy is a liar and always has been. I have been beaten often enough for tales she has spun to Pa to ever trust a word she says, so why should I believe her now? Believe what? For she said nothing – only looked. And yet I know. Know in my heart that she *has* taken my place, and for her there will be no escape. So I carry this with me like a great boulder on my back. This knowledge that I cannot share and I go back to my new, my other life, and there I learn to fight injustice towards people I do not know while my own sister sinks into a pit that I have dug.

And the ladies praise me and call me valiant. Some do, anyway. Others, I know, think it wrong for a slum girl to be put in charge of money (I am given ten shillings each week to pay for stamps). I heard Miss Haythorne murmuring what a risk Mrs Pethick Lawrence took in entrusting so much to the likes of me. 'I hope she counts the change, for that young Maggie has a new ribbon in her hair at every meeting.'

'Why don't you bring it up at the next one?' asked her companion.

'What? I can hardly raise a point of order about Maggie Robins' fripperies.'

'No, but you could pretend to admire them and ask her how much they cost.'

'I suppose so.'

I wrote down a list of every ribbon I had bought since I started at Clement's Inn. Beside it I wrote what they had cost and underneath, what I was paid. I stuck it in an envelope, printed the lady's name in my best writing and handed it to her as she passed by my desk.

'What's this, Maggie?'

'An account, miss.'

'Oh?'

'And if it's not too much trouble, miss, please could you tell me how much those black rubber pellets cost that you brought for our lunch the other day?'

Miss Kerr said that Miss Christabel wanted to see me upstairs. I counted the stairs as I went up, sure it was the last time I would ever climb them. She and Miss Annie were standing by the fireplace when I entered, looking very serious.

'Ah, Maggie,' said Miss Christabel, 'I'll come straight to the point. We've had a complaint.'

I said nothing.

'From Miss Haythorne. She says you insulted her... Did you?'

'I don't think so, miss.'

'Oh, come on, Maggie. Either you did or you didn't. Which is it to be?'

'I did, miss.'

'You *did*?'

'How, Maggie?' Miss Annie broke in. 'What on earth did you say?'

'I asked her how much she paid for the rubber pellets she fed us.'

There was a silence. Miss Christabel's face looked as though it was halfway to cracking in two. 'Well, that's certainly a little uncharitable. Why, Maggie? The ladies do their very best to make a nice lunch for us.'

'She was saying I had too many new ribbons.'

'To you?'

'No, not to me. A yard away from where I sat. That I was pinching from the stamp money to pay for them.'

Miss Christabel looked very stern. 'Is this true?'

'I don't steal, miss.'

She snapped her fingers angrily. 'I know that, Maggie. Is it true, that is what she suggested?'

'To her friend. Not to me.'

'What did you do then?'

'I wrote out what I was paid and how much I spent on ribbons and gave it to her. And then I asked her about the rubber things.'

'Thank you, Maggie. You had better get back to your desk. I know how busy you are.'

Halfway down the stairs I was leapt on by a bear. In fact it was Miss Annie. 'Maggie, you are wonderful,' was all she said before she went hopping ahead of me down to the office.

We never saw Miss Haythorne again.

Miss Annie and Miss Christabel are gone up north to a by-election and word comes back that they are cheered to the roof wherever they go. Miss Sylvia has taken charge of the meetings. At first they were quite jolly and more about what songs to sing and who should carry the banners, but of late there has been a degree of arguing. A lot of ladies (mainly older) do not agree with parades and shouting and the like. They believe we must work by sending letters and waiting till someone feels like answering them. Mrs Despard spoke most forcibly on the subject.

'The human race evolves to meet the challenges of its time,

but this is not a process to be hastened. It must distil into the portals of our intellect. Only then can we hope to attain parity.'

Miss Sylvia asked if anyone would like to respond. I was glad to see no one looked any wiser than I.

Often things are said I do not agree with yet I can never find the courage to speak out. One day a lady suggested we should do a lot better if only pretty women were allowed to represent us in public. There was a lot of 'mmming' and nodding about that. Another lady said all the speakers were pretty anyway, so where was the problem? Everyone laughed.

After Miss Sylvia asked, 'What did you think of that suggestion, Maggie?'

'Which, miss?'

'About pretty speakers?'

'I don't know, miss.'

'Which means you do not agree.'

'It's just...' Silence. I feel her eyes upon me. '...if you only have pretty ladies to speak, people will not believe that they are suffering. How can someone in a silk dress with jewels and a fur cape convince a single soul her life is hard? Why do you not get women who mine the coal or tan the leather to speak for you? Women like those in your pictures?'

Miss Sylvia was silent, then she sighed. 'Maggie, why do you not say these things at the meetings for all to hear?'

I said nothing.

'Tell me.'

'Because I...because I do not talk like the ladies.'

The next day Miss Annie came to find me. 'Tomorrow we go to Huddersfield.'

'Huddersfield? Where is that?'

'Far away in the north. We shall go by train. Will you like that?'

'I don't know, miss. I hope so.'

'You'll love it.'

And I did. Hour after hour just watching the whole country roll out before me. Fields thick with grass, covered in real sheep and cows; church steeples poking out of the smoke above towns no bigger than Parliament Square; rivers, soft and ripply, with painted barges chugging slower than the ducks.

To see the places I have only read about rise up, swell into towns, then fade away to tiny dots as we rushed past in our great rumbling locomotive. Miss Kerr had given me a *Votes For Women* flag so whenever we stopped I waved it at everyone on the platform and got some cheery smiles back, as well as some very cool glances, so there are grey people everywhere, it seems.

'But not enough to stay the march of progress.' (Miss Annie's words, not mine).

If I had not seen it myself I would not have believed it possible that so many, men as well as women, could crowd into a hall, and how their rumpus that would have deafened a whole army should melt away so you could hear a pin dropping as she spoke to them.

'Men, women of Huddersfield, I thank you for turning out on so foul a night. And that, after a hard day's labouring to keep food in your littl'uns' bellies and a lump of coal on your fires. Happen that lump was one you hacked out yourself that didn't quite make it to your Member of Parliament's fireplace.' There was a great burst of laughter.

'Well, you have come, and I honour you for it. Your time shall not be wasted, that I promise. I speak first to the women here. You tell me you long for justice, equality, the right to a fair wage for your labour. I hear you, loud and clear, but does that man who each year takes his seat in the great palace of Westminster on your behalf? Your "Government representative"? Does he hear you? *No.* Why not? Because you do not have a vote. And without a vote you cannot influence one hair on the head of this man who gains so handsome a living from strutting around the Parliament buildings like Cock o' the Roost, with a few hundred other peacocks to share his good fortune with. You cannot put him in there. You cannot kick him out. You are but a woman. Therefore I tell you again, y*ou do not count.* Yet where is the man that can sew on a button or bake a pie or sit all night with an ailing child then rise at dawn to make his snap and when he comes home of a night, wash the soot off his back and the muck off his clothes and feed himself and stretch his wages round the rent, the food, the family? If he's here, will he please stand up that we may look upon so wonderful a creature.'

There was much laughter and jibing at this but the men took it in good part, as indeed they had cause to, for Miss Annie went on to say how, without their support it would take ten times as long to bring the politicians round.

'If you men will join with us and raise your voices as one with ours, how then can they pretend this is some idle petty fancy, peculiar to a few flighty women whose tiny brains cannot address themselves to matters of great state? Let them see that you, the true backbone of this mighty country, know how to value and respect the creatures that gave you life and nurtured you. Your own mothers, the mothers of your children, your sisters, your daughters – let this government see that you are not ashamed to call us women your equals. Not ashamed and not afraid. Perhaps then they will learn to manage their own fear. For make no mistake, it is fear that drives them to deny us. Fear that the world will change and there will be no place for them within it. And they are right. For where is the place for ignorance, conceit and prejudice in a just world? The fight may be long and the battle weary but trust me, my dear friends, with your help, your support, your loyalty and above all, your courage we *shall* win through and then we shall look back on this time and say to our children and our children's children, "I made a difference".'

I have heard her speak and I have heard her cheered to the sky itself. As we journeyed back to London Miss Annie slapped her arms down on the table in front of me. 'So what was that about talking like a lady?' she asked.

More and more women are flocking to our support. Some of the letters that come in are so learned I have to take them to Miss Kerr to find out their meaning! How wonderful to know such words and be able to use them. And this year we are to have our own Parliament! I wonder no one has thought of it before. On the day after the Government open theirs, we are to meet at Caxton Hall and open ours. I suppose it will mean more marching. Why do they always open the Parliament in the winter, I wonder, unless it be to discourage the likes of us? Well, they will have to think of better than that to put us off.

\* \* \*

You would think they had been listening to my very thoughts! If cold and sleet and hail were not enough to fright a band of women, then let them be trampled under foot by horses.

Miss Christabel brought the news. 'It seems the Government persists in its refusal. We have been patient. We have been very patient. Perhaps now we should tell ourselves that we have been patient long enough. The time has come for action. *Deeds Not Words* shall be our motto from now on. Let us take our argument to the very portals of government and beyond, into the very heart of democracy. Rise up, women, with courage in your hearts, for Truth will ever triumph when Justice hides its face. Rise up!'

And like a thunderous wave breaking, we all shouted, 'Now!' then, each clasping a copy of our resolution, we were formed into troops like an army and set off for the Parliament, an escort of police on either side. As we marched the whole sky echoed with our singing. 'Rise up, women! For the fight is hard and long,' and even the bobbies hummed along, some of them.

Just when I was thinking how nice some bobbies are, we turned the corner into Parliament Square and there was a bunch of the surliest ones you ever saw. On a shout they came pounding towards us, hoping to split us up, but we gripped hold of each other with all our might so not an elbow could pass between us. At this they became angry and tried to force a way, but as fast as we were parted we joined ranks again so that it was they who were split, and very silly they looked, too.

At last their sergeant blew his whistle. We laughed and told him he could not carry a tune and to show him, sang out with all our hearts, 'Rise up, women!' As we got to the chorus there came a rumbling like thunder. A dark, angry noise. Not like before. The singing stopped.

Round the corner rode policemen on horses – not trotting as of normal, but charging towards us like cavalry. My heart leapt as it would leave my chest for terror.

We fled up on the pavements. They followed. Back into the road and they came after us. I was sick with fear. I do not care for horses when they are still, but to hear them snorting and whinnying, their eyes all rolling back into their heads, their stinking breath on your neck – I thought I should be trampled where I stood.

The walking policemen now began to shove us this way and that, any way but to the Parliament buildings. We scurried hither and thither, clinging to each other like drowning sailors, yet still, little by little, edging nearer, for we were so many that the police, for all their cruelty, could not contain us.

Far away in the distance I could hear Mrs Drummond. 'Push. Push for freedom and a better life.' So I pushed and shoved and wriggled and slithered until at last, breathless, battered, aching, there I was. At the foot of a great flight of steps and, at the top, the mighty Parliament doors.

I fixed my mind on dinner at the Savoy, and galloped like a mad thing all the way up. There a whiskery man in a very odd coat stepped forward to bar my way.

'Who goes there?' he asked. I said I went there, to which he replied, 'In the name of the King, who goes there?' I was not at all sure what to say to this but had no chance to anyway, for at that moment a big strong hand took hold of my shoulder and a voice said, 'Now, miss. Better not go any further. You might get lost.'

My bobby. Not mine, but I had come to think of him like that. Well, not that I had thought of him at all, of course. He stood there, so tall and sunny with his crinkly smile that it was like a beam of sunlight going straight through me.

'I have brought a resolution,' I told him.

He lifted one eyebrow. 'Have you?'

'Yes,' I said. 'And I must deliver it.'

'Who to?'

This I had not considered.

'I must tell you that I am ordered to prevent such a thing,' he said most helpfully. 'And I must request you to descend these steps immediately.'

'If I will not?'

'I shall have to take you in hand.'

'Does that mean arrest me?' I asked, thinking how cold a cell would be just now.

'Those are my orders.'

Down below in the square I saw women being herded and thrashed like cattle, squealing and sobbing beneath the bobbies' truncheons. Still fighting to reach the steps.

'I have to deliver my resolution.'

My bobby sighed. 'Then I must do my duty.' With that, he took me firmly by the arm and led me down the steps. At the bottom he let me go.

'Am I arrested?'

'Not yet.'

I stared at him. 'So I can try again?'

'If that is your determination.'

Back I went, him following. At the top he took my arm and led me down.

When we had done this six times over and I was about to set off once more, he caught hold of my wrist. 'Do you remember when I left you at your office, what I said?'

I thought, or pretended to think. 'That your name is Fred Thorpe?'

He laughed. 'You remembered. But I also said that if I had cause to escort you back there again I should have to note down your name, miss.'

'If I am arrested, you will know my name.'

'Is that what you want?'

'If I cannot have the vote.'

He looked unsettled. 'Prison is no place for such as you, miss.'

'There is no place for such as me if I am not allowed to choose who shall rule over me.' (This is how Miss Christabel would often end her speech and it always got a cheer, but I felt somewhat guilty, for my bobby plainly thought it came straight out of my head.)

'Well, miss, I cannot argue against such principles. You will be in good company, I'm sure, for half the ladies of Knightsbridge will be in court tomorrow.'

As if to prove his word, a cry went up that Mrs Despard was taken and, sure enough, she sailed by us, stately as on her way to launch a battleship, trailed by two shrivelled little policemen who looked as they should be laying a red carpet out for her, not setting her before a judge. I have never seen her look so cheery.

In her wake came a throng of women, singing and waving their resolution papers, and alongside hopped a bunch of bobbies, all sweaty from their efforts and grinning like lunatics. It was hard to guess who had charge of who.

My bobby gave a kind of sigh and let go of my arm. 'Well, if you will be charged, it shall not be by me.' And he was gone. I confess I felt a little put out for I had slightly hoped he might walk with me to the police station. I did not have long to wait, however, for it seemed anyone downwind of the Parliament and wearing a skirt was arrested that day.

The next morning we appeared before another judge (quite as puffy as the first). As there were so many, we were sent before him in batches, twelve at a time. It was gone three o'clock when my lot were called and we had had no dinner. Not so the judge, I think, for his fatty face had gone from white to red. Also his words were fuzzy.

We were sent off to some prison fifty miles from London because there was no more room in Holloway. I was not sorry, for surely there is no place more vile than Holloway?

Well, yes there is. There is Aylesbury, where we were crammed together like sheep in a pen and not near so cosy, by my guess. The food was worse, the warders more foul, and there was no knitting. Only potatoes to be picked off a piece of scrubland called The Garden till our backs would hardly straighten. Chapel, morning, noon and night. If I had known there was so much of damnation in the Bible I would never have bothered with trying to be good. Never a word of forgiveness, only 'Repent. Repent. Repent.'

I have listened to some of the women on my floor. I do not think they are *bad*, like the chaplain would have us believe. Is it *bad* to be so poor you cannot pay a fine for failing on your rent? If you cannot pay your rent, how can you pay a fine that is twice what you owe already? And is it *bad* to lay with a man for a shilling so you can buy food for your children? And if it is, why is the man not *bad* also? The more I learn, the more I think men do not like women. They like horses better, and dogs, for they do not answer back or ask for justice, no matter how hard or how often they are beaten or kicked.

Is that how we should be? To take what we are given and be glad of it, however little or however ill? And if so, why have women been given great strong brains like Mrs Pankhurst and Miss Sylvia and Miss Christabel, who has taken exams to be a lawyer and come top in them, above all the puffy men, and yet must stand before one and be silenced when she questions his law-making?

And if that is right, and 'the proper order of things', as that poxy-faced chaplain keeps telling us, why do we feel it so hard? Surely if we are but creatures to be trained and commanded, we should not mind it, but strive to please our masters? Not rail against our fate and seek for betterment? Why, if we are not to use them, have we been given minds at all? What use are they?

I put this to one of the lifetime women when we were picking the other day. She came as close to laughing as I have ever seen her. 'Ask the chaplain, why don't you?'

So I did. He makes a daily visit in case you had forgotten between lunch and dinner just how wicked you are and deserving of the hell fires for all eternity.

'If it please, Reverend, may I ask a question?'

He looked most surprised, as though such a thing had never been done before. 'Ahem, ahem, ahem. I think I may allow it. Does it concern the morning text?'

I tried to remember what it had been for I spend most of his sermons thinking about what I would like to eat when I get out.

'If it please, sir, yes.'

'Proceed.'

'Please, sir, if women are not supposed to think and determine for themselves, why has the mighty Lord God given us brains?'

Well, you would think he had been struck by one of his own thunderbolts. Pink, pinker, purple went his face so all his scars turned scaly. His mouth hung open like a pocket. Finally some breath comes back into his lungs. 'Foul, sinful child.' He turns to the warder woman. 'See she has nothing but water till she has cleansed herself of this blasphemy.' And off he puffs, so I never did get my answer. I wasn't sure how long it would take to cleanse me, but next morning the lifetime woman slipped me a piece of bread for she had heard him bellowing and was sorry for telling me to ask. I said it was no matter for I had wanted to know the answer.

'And do you?'

'No.'

She shook her head. 'Don't look for answers in this life.'

But I will. And maybe, one day, the fog will start to clear.

While we have been locked up great things have happened. It seems that all the arrests that night stirred the public to action at last, and many have complained at our treatment to the newspapers, so now a Member of Parliament is to put forward a private bill on our behalf! It is not Mr Hardie, either, but another man called Mr Dickinson, so that's two good men in the world – well, three, for I think my bobby has all the makings of a thoroughly good man, and he is handsome, which the other two are not.

Poor Mrs Pankhurst has lost her job. The authorities in her home town said she must choose – either to return and fulfil her duties or resign from her post as registrar. Though she smiles and says it is no matter and the Cause is all, I know she feels it strongly, for she is not a wealthy woman, as some would think.

Mr Dickinson's bill has been thrown out. We held another 'Parliament' to protest. Miss Christabel urged us all to march and keep on marching till we got inside the Parliament.

'Seize the mace and you will be the Cromwells of the twentieth century!'

I did not know who either were, but everybody cheered and off we charged. I think I only escaped arrest for not knowing where to start looking. Since I was getting nowhere I thought I should go back to the office where at least I could type a few letters or stick some stamps on.

It was on my way there that I met Fred Thorpe. He was walking towards me and when he saw me his face broke out in a great golden smile. 'Good day to you, miss. I had feared you might be on your way to court again.'

'I should have been if…'

'If what?'

'If I had not been distracted from my task.'

'How so?'

'I was to seize the mace,' I told him. 'But he was not in his usual place.' (This was only a small lie, for he might very well not have been.)

My bobby looked for a moment as though he would laugh

out loud, but he straightened up and said in a most serious voice. 'Was he not? Well, that is most unfortunate. For you, if not for him.'

I said, 'It is no wonder the bill cannot get passed if men like the mace are absent from their duties.'

He nodded gravely. 'It must certainly hold things back. And where are you off to now?'

'To my office. There is much to do.'

'Will you let me walk with you?'

'Are you not needed to arrest defenceless women?' (I do not know how I got so bold, but Miss Christabel says that is what we are.)

Fred Thorpe shrugged his shoulders. 'I think they can manage without me for today. Truth is, I am not very good at it, as you yourself are witness.'

'Well, at least you are good at finding streets for people,' I said, for I did not want him to think me quite unfeeling.

He smiled. 'And I'm also good at finding out people's names, Miss Maggie Robins.'

I stopped dead. 'How do you know that?'

'Oh, it's easy enough. I saw it in the police station when you went to court.'

'There were fifty or more of us that day.'

'Yes, but only one from Argyle Place.'

'You must be very good at catching villains,' I said, 'if you remember things like that.'

'It's my job. Anyway, I enjoy it.'

'Remembering things, or catching villains?'

'Both. But most of all I enjoy listening to music in the park on a sunny Sunday afternoon.'

'Oh yes. That's grand. I went with my brother once. All the bandsmen had uniforms. They looked like soldiers. And afterwards we had ices at a tearoom and sat outside and watched the swans.'

'Would you like to do that again?'

'Oh yes. But Frank's away at sea. And anyway...'

'With me, I mean.'

I stared at him.

'We could go this Sunday if it's fine. Or are you off getting arrested somewhere?'

'Not on a Sunday. The Parliament men don't work at weekends.'

'Well then?'

I felt all pink. 'I don't know. I've never...'

'Been out with a bobby before?'

I could have said 'with a man', but instead I just nodded like a great ninny.

'You'll come to no harm, Maggie. I promise you. And I'll see you safe home after, so you don't get lost.'

I laughed and he smiled, too. 'I'll call for you at three o'clock.'

My heart started pounding in panic. 'What if it rains?'

'We'll go to a gallery. Did your brother ever take you to one of those?'

'I don't think so. Do they have ices?'

He smiled. 'I'll make sure of it.'

He left me outside the office. I hoped no one was watching for I really did not think I could take more twitting just right then.

When I got in Miss Kerr and Miss Lake wanted to know

what had happened at the rally, who had been taken, if any were injured? I was ashamed that my head was so full of Fred Thorpe and Sunday that I could hardly turn my thoughts to answering them.

It is as well I am so busy for else I should go mad with trying to decide which blouse to wear and whether to have my hair up in a roll, or brushed straight down with a ribbon at the back to keep it neat. Straight is easier, but a roll makes me look much older – at least sixteen, Mrs Garrud said, when I tried it out on her. I wonder how old Fred Thorpe is. At least twenty, I would say. He must be to be so fine and confident, and to know so many streets and to go to galleries. He will very quickly tire of me. I asked Miss Sylvia if she had any books on music I could borrow and she brought me a whole pile, but they are full of black squiggles with only a little bit of writing so it is more a mystery than ever to me. Perhaps I should pray for rain, but then my hair will get wet and go all straggled like string.

I am the happiest person who ever lived. Today at three o'clock exactly came a knock on the door. Mrs Garrud was on her way to open it but I jumped right past her down four stairs together and begged her not to trouble herself.

There stood Fred. For a moment I could not think why he looked different, but then I realised he had real clothes on, not a uniform. He looked twice as handsome. I had on my best blouse that has tiny flowers across the bodice and round the cuffs and a new blue skirt and jacket that I went out and bought yesterday for thirteen shillings and fourpence in Oxford Street. More than a week's wages! I should not have done it but I will have no chocolate for a month and that will make up the money. I wore my hair down with a blue velvet ribbon although you could not see it under my hat.

Fred smiled when he saw me and offered me his arm. I was all right about that for I have held Frank's arm sometimes and also Pa's when he is acting the clown. We walked down to the corner of Argyle Place and Fred said, 'What do you think? Too cold for the park?'

In fact, it was rather cold and my new jacket not as warm as I would have liked. I said, whatever he thought best. 'Well then, I think we should aim for a gallery. Portraits or landscapes?' I said, whichever he thought best, at which point Fred stopped walking, turned me round to face him and said, 'I'd like best for you to stop trying to please me and say what you think, Maggie.'

'But I was never in a gallery. How can I know what I would like?'

'True. Well, let it be portraits then, for they take less time to look at.'

This seemed sensible to me. I told him how Miss Sylvia had painted my portrait.

'May I see it?'

'I haven't got it. She has it in her studio.'

'Is she a good painter?'

'Wonderful. She made me look...well, like me, I suppose.'

'Then I should certainly like to see it. I shall buy it from her and put it in a locket round my neck. Why are you laughing?'

'Because it is the size of a paving slab.'

Next thing he is dragging along the street like a hunchback, pretending he has a paving stone round his neck. People turned to stare and nudged each other but he did not care at all. I said, 'You will be in rare trouble if your sergeant sees you now. He will not want a madman in his force.'

Fred stood upright again. 'He has a tribe of them already. One more won't make a difference.'

'One person *can* make a difference,' I said, without thinking, for it is a slogan on the bottom of our pamphlets.

Fred looked all serious. 'I suppose you must believe that or you couldn't do what you do,' he said.

The gallery was not a bit as I had expected, not that I had known what to expect. I had thought, I suppose, that it would resemble Miss Sylvia's studio – all mess and paintbrushes and oils with their lids left off. Instead it was high and light with huge wide walls painted white, and along them picture after picture, all of people and sometimes with some bug-eyed little dog sitting, smug as a chaplain, on its mistress's lap.

Some I liked greatly. One of an old man with a skinny child by him. He reminded me a sliver of my grandad, for he had kind crinkly eyes and wispy hair and brown spots under it like the map of the Holy Land that Mrs Beckett had up on the wall of the Sunday School. There were a mass of gentry and dotted round them, their whey-faced children. Pale waxy copies, eyes dull inside their pointy heads, all ruffs and jewels and velvet. Like flowers that never saw the sun.

Fred asked me what I thought.

'It is all very clever.'

'You don't like them?'

'They are not...like Miss Sylvia's.'

'But they are here, and hers are not. So maybe it is she who should change her style?'

I could not let that by. 'These are here because a man has painted them. There can be no other reason.'

Fred looked quite taken aback. 'I had not thought you would be so against our sex.'

I shook my head. 'I'm not. Truly. I have three brothers of my own. How could I be against them?'

'But that is your family. Do you really think all other men are hopeless?'

'No… No I do not. You mistake me. I am just angry that one man can paint the same face six times over and be here, with great white walls, and fame and everything, and someone like Miss Sylvia who can paint you so you would think it was a mirror, is forced to work long hours in a tiny room with no proper light and sleep in that same room, and *still* cannot get her paintings in a gallery.'

Fred was quiet for a long deep moment. 'Would you like to have an ice, now?' he asked.

'If that is all right with you,' I replied.

He took me to a splendid tearoom in Regent's Park from where we could see the zoo animals and the people strolling along, laughing and chatting together and poking sticks through the bars to tease the poor creatures. The monkeys jabbered and grabbed at them and if they succeeded, snapped them in half and chewed at them. Other animals ran away. Only the elephant took no notice.

The waitress brought us the menu which was a foot long at least and covered in wavy writing saying what the different cakes were, and more ices than I had thought were in the world. We had chocolate sponge and then strawberry ice to follow. Fred asked what I would like to drink. There were sodas, and ginger ale and all sorts but I said, 'Tea, please,' because, after all, it was a tearoom and I thought it might be rude not to drink some.

He told me about his sister, Clara. How she has a beautiful singing voice but may not use it for her father says music is a vanity.

'Surely not church music?'

'Yes, anything. Plain, everything must be plain and simple. That way sin cannot get a foothold, he says. Why are you smiling?'

'I was just thinking he should meet the chaplain at Aylesbury who found sin in every breath we took and every blade of grass we trod upon, and there's not much plainer than a prison.'

'Well, that's the sort of righteousness that drove the Quakers away in the first place. They grew tired of being preached at by hypocrites who only got their office by preferment and cared about as much for Christ's teachings as the people who killed him.' He looked quite agitated. 'Would you like another ice?'

I blushed for I had eaten mine very fast. 'No, thank you. It was so lovely I was afraid that it would melt.'

Fred smiled. 'That's no reason not to have another.'

This time we had vanilla. I was so stuffed I could hardly stand when it was time to go.

'Would you like to walk a little?' he asked. Though it was cool, the breeze had died, so I said, yes, I thought I should. He gave me his arm again and I thought how someone looking from the tearoom might think that we were sweethearts. This made me feel most funny.

We strolled across the grass. There was the great grey elephant standing stock-still in its cage, its mighty ears spread open like sails to catch the wind. It had not moved.

I said, 'It's as though it's listening.'

'And watching.'

'Yes. Waiting for something.'

'Like a bun coming over the bars?'

I laughed. 'Maybe. Or something a bit more exciting.'

'Two buns. It'll have a long wait.'

'Elephants don't mind waiting. They live so long it doesn't matter.'

'Lucky old them,' said Fred. 'I hate waiting. I like things to happen when I want them to.'

'So do I. I do hope we get the vote soon. There are so many laws I should like passed.'

'What laws?'

'Oh, hundreds. Free hospitals, free schools, free buns for elephants…'

'How about votes for elephants?'

I laughed. 'Why not? They've got bigger brains than men have.'

'Yes, and they'd be a lot harder to arrest.'

He asked me what it had been like in prison. I told him how frightened I had been at first but that after a while it just got boring.

'I read that some of the women were made very ill by it.'

'Yes, but they were ladies, you see. Not used to such conditions. For me it was not much worse than home except the warders, who are harder than bailiffs, some of them.'

'Still, I do not like to think of you in a cell, Maggie.'

'No more do I, but if it is for the Cause, I have no choice.'

'You do have a choice,' he said most firmly. 'You can choose not to be involved in what can only bring you to trouble.'

'"Stay home and mind my hearth", you mean?' (This is what Miss Sylvia says to stir the women to action).

'Is that so wrong?'

'It is if you haven't got one, like half the women of England.'

'I see you have been well schooled by your employers.'

This riled me. 'My employers are also my friends. They are not all rich fine ladies, you know. Mrs Drummond has a whole family to look after, and Miss Annie was a mill girl herself. They are fighting for justice, that is all. For people like me and your sister.'

Fred lowered his eyes. 'I'm sorry. I was wrong to speak as I did. Of course you must fight for what you believe in. It's just – it just seems to me that you have taken on too much. The Government will not give in and a few hundred women marching will not change a single thing.'

'If a single person can make a difference, how much more can a few hundreds?'

He frowned. 'Is that what Miss Sylvia says as well? Or is it Miss Christabel, or Mrs Pankhurst?'

'No,' I said. 'It's what I say.'

We walked a while in silence and I wondered if I should leave go his arm now we had quarrelled so badly, but when I went to wriggle my hand away he took hold of it with his and looked straight down into my eyes. 'Am I to be forgiven?'

I said I thought it was I who was in disgrace.

'Why? For standing up for your beliefs? That is what I admire about you most.'

I felt quite tingly. 'Yes, but you do not agree with them.'

'Not all of them, but that doesn't make me right and you wrong.'

I looked up at him amazed. For a man who had bought me two ices *and* a cake, to let himself be so countered! 'Perhaps we are both right?'

Fred laughed. 'Perhaps. Or both wrong. Either way I must take you home or it will be midnight and the ladies will come looking for you and beat me with their umbrellas.'

'They will have no need of that for I am trained in self-defence.'

'Really?' He looked mightily surprised.

'Mrs Garrud, where I lodge, teaches it. It is from Japan where everyone is yellow,' I explained.

He stopped dead and, seizing both my hands, asked most earnestly, 'And will all this fighting turn you yellow, too, Maggie?'

For a moment I thought he was serious, then I saw that his beautiful green-brown eyes were dancing.

'Strawberry ices can prevent it, I have heard,' I told him.

Fred gave my hands a real strong squeeze. 'Then it shall be my duty to supply them. Shall you last till next Sunday, do you think?'

I am the happiest person alive.


There has been violence in the north. One of our speakers was knocked unconscious by a marble thrown by a lout (paid for by the Liberals, Miss Annie said). She is all right now, but every day there are mobs of stupid useless youths hurling rotten eggs and fruit at our women. The police do nothing to prevent it. Miss Christabel said it was all to the good for the local people think such behaviour wicked, and have turned out all the more to give support. I can understand her reasoning, but I still should not like to be knocked senseless by a marble, or a rotten egg, for that matter.

Mrs Pethick Lawrence has worked miracles in the office. We now have a separate department, The Women's Press, for selling pamphlets, badges, postcards and photographs of the leaders, as well as books explaining the Cause. Miss Knight has come to take charge of it and on Thursdays I am her assistant. If we are not busy she talks to me about government things, and lets me read the books so that I really begin to understand how much we are seeking to achieve. The more I learn the more I wonder if it can ever be done, for there are women who have been campaigning for nigh on *fifty* years and still see so little progress. Is this to be my whole life's work?

Just when I was feeling truly crushed by it all, into the office burst Miss Christabel, sparkling as a shooting star. 'Look at this! Look at this! Look at this!' Great big photograph of Miss Annie being carried shoulder high through a crowd of cheering miners. *SUFFRAGETTES SWEEP ALL BEFORE THEM* ran the headline. 'What do you think of that, Maggie? Where shall we display it, do you think? On the wall? On the window? How about Big Ben?'

In five minutes I was back up again. I said so to Miss Sylvia. She nodded. 'My sister is a very remarkable creature. My mother, too.' Probably I was wrong but I fancied she looked a bit sad as she spoke. She has had to leave her painting course. The Cause takes too much of her time and she told me if she could not attend to it properly, she would as soon not do it at all.

Though she works all day and into the night, I think she misses it greatly, for I remember how with a brush in her hand, she looked as if she was in another world, full of calm and peace. And there is certainly none of that in Clement's Inn!

She asked if I was glad to have left being in service. I said, yes, mightily, though I still miss Cook and Mr and Mrs Roe, for they are the finest people in the world. She agreed. 'But nothing is wasted, Maggie, for if you were to marry...' here I was attacked of a coughing fit, '...there is no harm in being able to cook.'

I said my ma was a very good cook and could make a feast of a pig's cheek and a potato. This is not entirely true, for she tends to forget about it once it is stewing and often the dinner boils over. Miss Sylvia asked if I had been home lately. I said, no, I had been much occupied with sending out the circulars. She looked quite anxious.

'Maggie, you must not give over your free days to your work. I will speak to Mrs PL. You shall go home next Sunday, for sure.' I felt quite sick.

'If it please, miss, I should like not to go home next Sunday, if it can be arranged.'

Miss Sylvia looked a lot surprised. 'Why not, Maggie?'

'Because... I think I may be unwell, and little Ann being so tiny...'

'Ah. Well, perhaps the one after. I'm sure your handsome bobby will understand.'

I went redder than ox blood. How is it people always know about your business when you particularly do not wish them to?

'I didn't mean to interfere,' she went on, noting my discomfort. 'I just think it's important to stay in touch with your family.'

'It is. I do…want to. I will go soon, I promise. It is just I had sort of made an arrangement… I do not like to let people down.'

'No, of course not. You are right. Families must not always be put before friends, much as they would like it.'

I thought this a strange thing to say, for I have always been told otherwise. 'But would you not put your mother and sister above all others?' I asked.

Miss Sylvia glanced at me, half ashamed. 'If they needed me, of course I should, but sometimes they expect me to fall in with their plans, no matter the inconvenience. And that, I think, is…unnecessary. Besides I have another sister and a brother. Are they not equal claimants to my time?'

'It is hard when you have a big family,' I agreed.

'Has your young man got brothers and sisters?'

I told her about Fred's sister who may not sing. She said she thought that sad, but that Quakers were generally very good people. She asked me how Fred could be a policeman *and* a Quaker, so I told her he had left it.

'What does his father say to that?'

'I think he is unhappy, but Fred likes music and painting and all things that are forbidden by the Quakers. He especially likes painting,' I added. 'He took me to a gallery.'

'Did you enjoy it?'

'Yes, of course, but I told him they were nowhere as good as your paintings.'

Miss Sylvia laughed. 'I'm sure they were.'

'No,' I said. 'They were not. And Fred and I had a right falling out over it.'

'Goodness. I hope I was not the cause of a quarrel between you.'

'No, no. It was all right. He said he liked me to state my own feelings and stand by them. It was what he liked best about me.'

Miss Sylvia smiled. 'He sounds a very astute young man.'

I had no idea what that meant, but was certain it was good. I should so like her to meet him. I am sure they would be friends.

This Sunday it was fine and sunny. We went to Hyde Park and strolled for miles and miles round it. It must be bigger than some counties, for you can walk for a whole hour and not see the same tree twice.

We talked and talked. It was as though we had known each other forever. Fred is nineteen. I am amazed. I had thought him at least twenty. He lives in rooms with a Mrs Blackett, north of Marylebone. She is a widow and a dreadful cook, he says. He thinks she may have poisoned her husband, not on purpose, with her suet pudding. I was pleased to tell him I could cook most things, including biscuits.

'Perhaps you will cook me a meal one day?' he asked rather wistfully.

'Yes, if Mrs Garrud allows it. I should have to ask.'

'Yes, of course.'

He told me Mrs Blackett has a daughter of thirty-seven who works in one of the great shops in Oxford Street. 'She says she is a buyer, but somehow I don't believe it.'

I said I thought it was strange to buy things from your own shop.

Fred laughed. 'Buyers buy things for customers to buy. How else do you think they stock the shelves?'

I had not thought of that.

He says Mrs Blackett wants him to marry her daughter. This unsettled me. 'And are you going to?'

He burst out laughing. 'Not unless she knocks me out and dopes me. Besides Miss Blackett has been looking for a husband for the past twenty years, I would guess, but never found anyone quite to her taste.'

'She must be very particular,' I said, meaning 'fit for Bedlam'.

'Well, there you are. A humble policeman is not much of a catch, is he?'

I said I did not know and, fortunately, tripped over a sticking up root so did not have to continue. Fred caught my arm.

Our conversation turned to Mrs Garrud's fighting classes, for she teaches us how to fall down and not be hurt by it. Fred was most interested. In the police they learn self-defence, he says, but it is mostly hitting people with a truncheon and blowing a whistle to summon assistance, so he does not think it can be half so useful as what I do.

'What made you want to be a policeman?' I asked.

He thought for a bit. 'I liked the uniform.'

'Surely that was not all?' Though thinking how much I love

my office clothes I could hardly blame him.

He smiled. 'No. Lots of reasons. I had an idea I wanted to serve my country.'

'Why did you not join the army?'

He shrugged. 'There are other ways of serving your country than charging around killing people.'

'Why else? You said there were lots of reasons?'

'To get away from home, mainly, I suppose. I was suffocating. The village is so small and everyone there knew my father. I felt as though I was being judged all the time, compared with him and his achievements. And of course, I could never measure up.'

'I'm sure that's not true,' I said with perhaps more feeling than I should have done.

He glanced at me and smiled. 'Also I heard rumours a beautiful young suffragette was in danger of getting lost in Downing Street and might need rescuing.'

I blushed very red but could not help myself. 'If you had not come along then I don't know what would have happened to me.'

'Oh I expect some other lucky man would have come to your rescue.'

I shook my head. 'I doubt it. That tobacconist was all for pushing me under a cab. It was the road sweeper saved me.'

Fred looked quite angry. 'Why did you not tell me? I would have clapped him in irons.'

'The road sweeper?'

'No. The shopkeeper, of course. No, better – I'd have had him lashed to the back of the cab and dragged down Pall Mall and back three times.'

I said, 'I can see the army would be no place for someone as gentle as you.'

We sat by the river. Some men were diving into the water. They came out mighty quick with their teeth all chattering so it seemed a pretty silly thing to do with Easter not yet on us. A group of young ladies were watching them and clapped like mad, so I suppose that was what drove them in the first place. I was just wondering to myself if I would dive into icy water to catch a man's eye when Fred asked, 'Would you like a man the better if he jumped in an icy river for you, Maggie?'

'Only if I was drowning.'

We laughed ourselves stupid. The bathers gave us a very funny look.

Ma is not well. At first I thought maybe she was starting a new baby, for she looked as sick and yellowy as ever, but when I asked if there was another coming she shook her head. 'Nor will be, Maggie.' I was glad for, God knows, she has enough to deal with Alfie and Evelyn and Will and little Ann, and Lucy who is worse than any of them.

I had made up my mind that I would try to talk some sense into my sister before I left. I had brought her a book. It was called *Enquire Within* and stuffed full of ideas, like how to feed a family for sixpence, what to put on a burn, the best cure for flea bites – everything you could need to know, and more besides. I greatly hoped it would have a bit about the bleeding for Lucy is gone thirteen and sure to start it soon, but I could find nothing. I knew I should have to speak to her straight out for I should not like her to find it out as I did – for all the ladies were kind and gave me shortbread. Ma will say nothing, I am sure. I sometimes wonder if she understands herself, or why would she keep having children, which must hurt a good deal more than the bleeding? And if Lucy's should start when Frank is home… I think he lied about putting a baby in me. I think you have to start the bleeding first. But he knows how to do it. I know he does. And if the fancy takes him…

I wonder if Fred knows how to make a baby. I hope not, for he is the finest man I ever met and I would so love to marry him and be with him forever. But not to have that…to have to…for all Frank says it is a sign of his affection and if I truly love him I will not refuse. I do love him. I am so proud to have a brother that is tall and fine and handsome, when half the men are cripples in my street. To see the girls nudge each other and gaze at me so enviously when we are out. But you cannot live forever at the playhouse, or wandering round the fair in your best clothes. Some time you must go home.

When I was little I believed everything he told me – that I was a fairy he had found in a ditch and brought home to Ma to be her daughter; that he was truly a prince and I was a princess and that one day we would go back to our palace and never be hungry again but I must not tell a living soul. It was our secret. He used to steal potatoes from the market and we would share them when the others were asleep. And when we had eaten the potatoes he would give me a kiss and we would tuck our arms round each other to be warm and pretend we were a king and queen and anything we wanted we could have. It was our secret. And then there was another and another. So many secrets. Only now I hate them.

I do not know if it is because I live in such fine conditions now, but the house seemed to me dirtier and smellier than I had ever remembered it. There were the baby's soiled rags just dumped on the kitchen floor with flies buzzing round them. The pans were stacked up dirty in the sink, and a sack of rotting carrots in the corner which, I swear, were there the last time I was home.

Ma was in the front with Ann asleep in her arms. The back door, having broken its hinge, slammed shut behind me and I was fearful it would wake the baby, but she hardly stirred.

Ma looked up and smiled when she saw me. 'Maggie.'

'Yes. Ma, I'm sorry I've not been home before, but we have been rushed off our feet, truly. Mrs Pethick Lawrence has a grand scheme to raise twenty thousand pounds, can you believe? So we must write to everyone who ever breathed.'

Ma nodded. 'Twenty thousand pounds is a lot of money.'

'More than there is in the world, I shouldn't wonder. I wish I had it.'

'It would be a fine thing.' She shifted the baby and I saw that she had a great mucky bruise on her arm.

'How did you come by that, Ma?'

'What? Oh, this. It's nothing.'

'Did Pa do it?'

'No. No. I don't know what it is – I seem to bruise so easy these days. Mrs Grant says I lack iron in my blood. But what's to do about that, except keep munching lumps of coal? And they're more use on a fire than in my belly.'

I sat down. 'I'll ask Miss Annie. She'll know what will mend you. I've a mutton pie and turnips for our dinner, and a baked custard for after. And here.' I gave her three pounds that I had saved.

'Oh, Maggie, you mustn't give me all your money. You'll have nothing to live on.'

'I will. Mrs Garrud feeds me like she's fattening me for Christmas, and my lunch is never above a sixpence. That's with a jam tart.'

'You're a good girl, Maggie. I'm glad it's turning out well for you.'

I felt a great slap of guilt to be so fortunate, and my own mother sitting in this tip. 'I'll get the dinner on. What time will Pa be in?'

'Four o'clock, he said. Alfie's with him.'

'Where're Evelyn and Will?'

'Lucy took them to the park.'

I was relieved to hear that. 'Is she being better now, Ma?'

Ma was quiet for a moment. 'It's not easy for her, living here.'

'It's not easy for anyone. That doesn't mean she needn't help, and go round acting like it's everyone else's fault. If she minds so much she should come to the meetings and learn how to do something about it.'

Ma shook her head. 'She's a child, Maggie. You can't ask her to see things as you do.'

'I was a child when you sent me to Park Walk.'

'I meant it for the best, Maggie. Surely you know that now?'

'Yes, I do now, but that's because I'm grown up.' Ma smiled and looked down at the baby who was stirring. 'And,' I went on, 'Lucy could have had my post at the Roes but that she was too lazy and stupid to take it.'

Ma sighed. 'She's not like you, Maggie. You're the clever

one. None of the others could have done what you have, with help or without. Even Frank...'

'Yes, and that's another thing. I cannot bear how she talks of Frank as though...as though...' I stopped for Ma was staring at me, almost like she was afraid. I took a breath. 'It is so long since I have seen him, Ma.'

She looked away. 'It's better that way.'

My heart was thumping. 'Why do you say that?'

Ma wiped her hand across her forehead. 'Maggie, I am not well. Please believe me, it is for your own good. I want you to have a chance in life. Away from all this. Away from...what it brings with it. Frank is part of that. He is my son and I love him more than my life, but I know him. I know what he is like. He must be best. If he sees how you are bettering yourself, learning so many things, earning a good wage, mixing with important people, he will dislike it. He will try to drag you back.'

Her words cut through me. I had always thought she loved him best.

'How can you say that? How can you speak so ill of your own son?'

'Because he *is* my son. And because he is like his father.' She slumped back in her chair as though a ton weight was lying on her. 'He is so very like his father.'

I do not think that Ma and I had ever had so long a conversation in our lives.

I watched her drag her feet across the room to fetch the baby's milk. From behind she could have been my gran. Why are you so old? I wanted to cry out. Why can't you be like Mrs Pankhurst? So elegant and beautiful. She has grown up children, too. How can I be proud of you when you are so...worn out by life?

I managed to clean up a bit before dinner. I washed the pans and put the baby's clothes to boil, then swept the floor and flung the carrots out into the yard for dogs or rats to get them. Ma sat on with the baby, one asleep, the other dozing. How they managed it with all the clattering and clanging, I could not fathom.

Pa and Alfie were quite merry when they came in and the two of them fell to chuckling about nothing at all, as far as I could tell, like a pair of buffoons.

The dinner was almost ready when Lucy appeared. She looked flushed and more so when she saw me. At first I thought she had left the little ones to find their own way, but they came in just after, very quiet and Evelyn's face muddy with tears. She ran to me and I swept her up in a great big hug, whereupon Will let out a great big howl, which was only to be expected.

I said, 'How are you, Lucy?' for I thought I should try to mend the fences between us from last time.

'I'm very well.'

Pa asked what I had been up to, to stay away so long.

'Maggie has a lot of work. She cannot come and go as it pleases her,' Ma said quickly.

'Why should it please her to come here at all?' Lucy retorted. 'She doesn't come because she's ashamed of us. Not because she is working.'

There was a silence. Alfie began to giggle. Pa's face had gone very red. I thought he would belt her and serve her right. The two of them sat there staring at each other, Lucy bold as a parrot, giving him glare for glare. Ma glanced across at me. She looked as though she would sink into the ground if she could.

'I'm sorry if that's what you think, Lucy,' I said. 'If it was true I wouldn't be here now.'

Pa looked somewhat calmer. He took a great swig of beer. 'You mind your manners to your sister, Lucy,' he said. 'Or she won't bring you no more presents.'

'I've got you a book,' I told her.

'I don't need presents from you. I can get presents any time.'

Good, I thought, for that's the last you'll get, you little cat. 'That's nice.'

Fortunately the baby started crying and Ma got up to her. I brought in the custard tart but somehow it didn't taste so fine to me as usual. I suppose when you are not starving you notice more the manner of your mealtimes – how people eat, their conversation, the way they are to each other. I could not but think how I would sooner share a plate of grass with Fred than a Savoy dinner with my own family.

Alfie helped me clear up. I would rather he had not for he kept dropping things and giggling like an idiot, but it was good of him to offer so the two of us (two and a half, for little Evelyn was hanging round my heels like she was stuck to them) battered against each other till all the dishes were clean or broken.

Afterwards Alfie showed me a wooden box he had made to keep his money in. 'No one can have it,' he told me. 'All mine, I did it.' I said it was very fine and I wished I had one like it. This pleased him mightily. 'I can make you one.'

'Thank you, Alfie. I would really like that.' I had not meant him to start that moment, but off he went to look for his hammer and soon there was banging and sawing and crashing fit to wake the dead.

Evelyn showed me a picture she had coloured at Sunday School. It was of an angel floating over a lake with a great loaf of bread under its arm. 'It's a manna from heaven,' she whispered. 'It's for you.'

Will gave me a tooth that had been knocked out when he fell over the curb stone. I was sorry he had lost it so soon, especially as it looked to be the only good one in his mouth, but I gave him a piece of barley sugar I had been saving till goodbye time and he seemed to think it fair exchange. I only hope he won't go knocking out the rest to get more sweetmeats.

I asked Ma if I could wash the baby for her. Although Ann is my sister, I seem to have had so little to do with her, and yet she should be all the more precious to me for she is named after someone I truly admire.

Evelyn wanted to help and kept trying to wash the baby's hair (she cannot get enough of hair-washing since Miss Annie's visit). Ann did not like this much and mewed like a drowning kitten but apart from that seemed content enough. She is thriving on the cow's milk which is just as well because I doubt Ma has the strength to suckle her as things are.

It grew time for me to leave and I knew I could not delay speaking to Lucy any longer. I asked Ma where she was. She jerked her head towards the ceiling. 'Maggie, please be…don't… I can manage. Truly. Mrs Grant comes round…'

'I have to speak Lucy, Ma. Not just about the house. About…other things."

Ma sank back like someone who knows she cannot win.

Lucy was sitting by the window threading beads on to a string. She looked up as I came in and then continued with her task.

'Lucy, I have to talk to you about something. Now you are thirteen you are on the way to being grown up.' I thought this might please her, but she merely carried on threading. 'I have to tell you about babies,' I burst out, thinking the sooner it was done the sooner I could go and catch my bus.

She did look up now, frowning. 'Babies?'

'Yes. When you don't have them. It happens when you are grown up, like me. You get a bleeding – between your legs. It hurts a bit, and you get a sore belly, but then it goes again. Till the next month. It happens every month.'

Lucy was staring at me as though I was completely mad. 'Why?'

I had no idea why. 'I don't know. If you like I will ask at the office, and then next time I come I can tell you.'

'Does Ma get it?'

'Yes. No. I don't know. She keeps having babies, so maybe she doesn't. I don't know.'

Lucy was staring out of the window. 'It won't happen to me.'

'It will. It happens to all women unless they are having babies. It stops for that.'

Lucy turned to me. 'I don't believe you. What do you know about anything? You don't even know about babies, where they come from.'

I could feel myself burning up. 'I do so. I know exactly where they come from.'

'Oh, yes. "Ezekiel begat Simeon, begat Daniel, begat Josiah…" Every Sunday. Mrs Beckett telling us how we must study our Bibles and try to be like Maggie Robins who is going up in the world. Up, up, *up*. Not like her stupid sister, Lucy, who cannot be fussed to learn a load of psalms and prayers and so has to stay living in a street full of rats and fleas with one brother daft and another…'

'Another what? What are you talking about? And don't call Alfie daft. Just because he has trouble with some things. He's made a fine box for his money, and he's making me one at this minute.' Lucy gave a snort. I could dearly have clouted her. 'Answer me. Another…what? Will's a whiner. We all know that.'

She frowned as though she had never heard the name before. 'Will? I didn't mean Will. It's Frank I was talking about.'

I ripped the beads out of her hand and threw them all over the floor.

When I went downstairs Alfie had finished my box. It was just like his. Without a lid.

I thought all the way back on the omnibus about what Lucy had said. It is true I do not understand how babies get there. I only know how they don't. And that is the bleeding. I know you cannot have one without a man and that the man must put it inside you, but where does he get it from? And how can it breathe? Perhaps it does not need to breathe in your belly, though when Will was born he wailed as if he'd been holding his breath from the second he got in there. He's hardly stopped since.

I will ask Miss Sylvia if I can borrow her animal books again for I remember they had a picture of a lion with her cubs, so maybe it will tell me how she got them.

My head is so packed with questions, sometimes I think they will burst right out of me and smother me. I am so ignorant. I had thought books would teach me everything, but all they teach me is how little I know, and how much everyone else does. It is like swimming in mud and I cannot even swim.

Still, I have my work. When my mind gets too stuffed with worrying I bury myself in that, for I know now what I am doing and really I begin to think even Miss Lake finds me useful, although she would rather die than say so. And we are so busy.

Miss Christabel says we must all offer suggestions for how to advance the Cause, to which end she insists we read a newspaper every day, and two on Saturday. This was a struggle for me at first, not because of the words, but because of the way they are put together, which often seemed to me a great mishmash with nothing determined and a lot of ink wasted. Also, if you read one paper it will tell you we have the finest politicians on earth and in another it will say we should get rid of each and every one of them. How can you know what to believe?

I asked Miss Lake but she just shrugged and said, 'Think, Maggie. Use your brain. That's what it's for.' My poor brain will be worn out in a sixmonth at this rate. Besides, when I see what thinking does for some of the ladies I wonder if it is such a good idea after all, for there has been a mighty quarrel among the leaders. A mighty, mighty quarrel.

Truly sometimes it seems the greater our success, the greater the discontent it carries with it. I cannot understand it. Money is rolling in. Membership grows and grows. You would think everyone would be happy. Are they? Not at all.

It began slowly. A meeting which started orderly as a church service would end in raised voices (very raised!). I think perhaps some had got so used to bellowing on the streets that it came as natural to carry on indoors if they thought their opinions were not being attended to.

At first the quarrels were about little things – who should be in charge of the pamphlets or who order the programmes, but after a while I noticed the ladies did not smile so much and started to gather in twos and threes to murmur with each other when the meeting closed. Miss Sylvia saw it too, and tried with all her might to persuade them to speak out, to no avail. It took Miss Christabel to bring matters into the open and though she won the day, I think there were many wished it had never come to such a pass, including her own sister.

A special meeting was called. Miss Kerr and I were to take notes. It was a Friday evening. Sweltering. All week long the sun had blazed down without a pause, boiling, endless. Our heads ached, our clothes stuck to us like wet rags. The sky was the colour of brass. Like a furnace. Everything, everyone seemed drained. Even the air smelt like ten people had breathed it first – heat, perspiration, Parma violets – but when we opened the windows the stink from the river poured in like gas so we must slam them shut again.

As the ladies arrived we handed each a sheet of paper:

AGENDA

1)    Miss Christabel Pankhurst to open meeting.
2)    Mrs Pankhurst to address assembly.
3)    Resolution.

They sat in rows, all gloved and hatted like they were attending a funeral – which, I suppose, in a way they were. Nobody spoke, but even in that silence you could feel this great dark swirl of anger. Truly, I feared that night for Miss Christabel and her mother. How little I knew!

At a quarter past seven Miss Christabel appeared, fresh as a daisy in a pale green dress with white embroidered trim. 'Good evening, ladies. I hope I have not kept you waiting?'

Since they had been there a good half hour, half of them wearing velvet, there was a bit of a rumbling.

Miss Christabel passed quickly on. 'Let us get to the point. It is my understanding that certain of you have been unhappy with decisions made by myself and my mother on your behalf. May I remind you that the purpose of the WSPU is to promote and advance the cause of women's franchise by whatever means we deem necessary? Are you saying we have not done this? That we have in some way failed in our duty to the Cause? If this is so, please do make our failings known to us that we may strive to remedy them with the utmost speed and diligence. It is, after all, difficult sometimes to orchestrate matters as one might wish from behind prison bars.'

She paused, smiling so patiently at those damp pink faces. No one spoke. 'Am I to take it that you are satisfied, then, with our conduct as your leaders? In which case I suggest you ratify the resolution to be put before you, confirming your acceptance of our continuing authority, and then I shall be more than happy to close the meeting and let us all escape this appalling heat which I can see is causing a degree of distress to so many of you.'

I had thought that would be the end of it and was starting to put my notes away when Mrs Despard stood up, calm, cool as a statue in her black lace robes. 'If I may address the meeting...?'

Miss Christabel smiled. 'Of course, Mrs Despard. That is what meetings are for.' I wondered about that, for I have heard her silence others for asking just such permission.

Mrs Despard turned to face the meeting. 'First, may I say that there can be no doubt in my mind nor, I am sure, in any other member's, that the contribution of both Miss Pankhurst and her mother to the cause of women's suffrage and our fight for equality cannot be overestimated.'

Several ladies murmured, 'Hear, hear.'

'It is not to deny them their right to decision-making that we have asked for this meeting to be held. It is to verify the status of those other organisers who, at times, have felt that the interests of their own branches have been denigrated in the rush to create and initiate policy.' I could see even Miss Kerr was beginning to struggle with all those long words. 'Our concerns arise from a sense of exclusion, where integration should be paramount. We therefore wish to ascertain and ratify the status of all our members with regard to future events and activities. It is as simple as that.' She sat down.

It is as well Miss Christabel is a lawyer or I cannot think how she would have known how to answer.

She rose, cool and unflustered as ever. 'I have listened to

Mrs Despard's eloquent submission and may I say that I understand only too well the sentiments that have given rise to it. It is a wish on the part of all organisers, no matter how small their membership nor how fragmentary their endeavours, to have an equal say in the running of this giant and ever expanding movement. To stay the enactment of spontaneous protest; to squander opportunity; to ponder and procrastinate while circumstances cry out for action. Immediate action.'

'But surely,' a large plump lady in purple struggled up, 'these actions, Miss Pankhurst, require organisation, planning? What can be wrong with consulting the opinions of the other branches before going ahead? Surely success is more likely to flow from consensus than from ignoring the wishes of the majority?'

'I do not ignore them, Mrs Gallagher. I welcome them. But I cannot wait for them forever. What use is it to my mother and me if we hear of a politician who will speak in Battersea at eight o'clock on Tuesday, if we must write to every branch in the kingdom for permission to protest the meeting? It would take weeks – months, the rate some of our organisers deal with their correspondence.'

There was a distinct rumble at this.

'We do not have the privilege of three posts a day in the provinces, Miss Pankhurst,' a thin lady in crimson called out.

'Much they would avail you, Miss Cateman, for you have yet to respond to one article I have sent you.'

The thin lady turned close to the colour of her suit. 'I have other things to deal with. London chit-chat does not book a hall or paint a poster.'

Miss Christabel's smile faded and for a moment the whole

room held its breath, but she merely folded her hands and gave a little shrug. 'Precisely. Thank you, Miss Cateman for making my point so eloquently for me. As you are occupied with local matters so, too, are we here in London. That is as it should be. You attend to your concerns and leave us to deal with ours, albeit yours may lie with the parish committee and ours with His Majesty's Government.'

Such a clucking and squawking broke out. 'We have a right to be heard.'

'We pay our dues.'

'Are we not all equal?'

'We demand that our representatives be allowed to speak at Conference.'

'Because we do not agree, we have been silenced.'

'We will be heard.'

'We desire equality with women as well as men.'

I could not but think they had a point, for although I am sure Miss Christabel and Mrs Pankhurst know far more than the rest of the ladies put together, it is a little strange that we are fighting for justice and equality, but cannot manage it inside our own movement.

Miss Lake signalled me to open the windows and sure enough, as soon as they smelt the rotting fish, the protesters seemed to calm down a little and begged that I should shut them all again.

Down they flopped. Hot, unhappy, feeling themselves beaten as no army of bobbies could beat them. Beaten by one of their own.

It was then that Mrs Pankhurst rose to her feet, calm and serene as always.

'I have listened to the arguments presented here this evening and it is clear to me that there is only one way out of this impasse.' She reached into her bag and, pulling out a copy of our constitution, tore it into pieces, scattering them like so much birdseed on the floor in front of her.

There was a dreadful silence.

She looked around the room. 'I give my thanks to all of you who have come here tonight. Your past help is valued and if you wish to remain as members of the WSPU, so will your future efforts be, but this you must understand: we are not playing a game. We are not a school for teaching women how to use the vote. We are a militant movement and we have to get the vote next session. The leaders of this movement are practical politicians; they have set out to do an almost impossible task. They are fighting the strongest Government of modern times and the strongest prejudice in human nature. They cannot afford to dally with the issue. Those who cannot follow the general must drop out of the ranks.'

She sat down and for the first time in a week the room felt suddenly cold.

And many did drop out. Mrs Pankhurst decreed all subscriptions must be returned and there should be none from now on. Members had simply to sign a pledge saying no politician could be supported till we had been granted the right to vote.

Miss Sylvia was deeply upset by this for Mr Hardie had done so much to help us. She and Miss Christabel had a mighty row about it one evening just as we were closing up the office. They were out in the hall so Miss Kerr and I, who were the only ones left, did not like to walk past them. Instead

we were forced to linger by the door, pretending to be very
interested in buttoning our coats and making sure the
umbrella stand was straight, and all the time this furiousness
going on outside.

'How can you even think of throwing him over after all he
has achieved on our behalf?'

'My dear sister, we are not "throwing him over", as you so
emotively put it. This is a purely practical and necessary move
on our part. Surely you appreciate that we cannot be seen to
be supporting one party over another unless that party
specifically undertakes to promote the Cause?'

'I appreciate that Mr Keir Hardie has put his career and his
reputation on the line to assist the movement and that this is
pretty poor thanks if henceforth we are to shun him.'

'We are not planning to "shun him". Stop being so
melodramatic. It is merely we can have no more dealings with
the Independent Labour Party until it makes women's votes an
issue. Keir Hardie agrees with me himself that it is the only
sensible strategy to pursue.'

'And what of all the hundreds of women who have
subscribed to the WSPU? Are they to be thrown out, too,
because they have canvassed for Members of Parliament in the
past?'

'No, of course not. Provided they agree to forego all such
activity from now on.'

'And if they do not?'

'Then they must leave.'

'That is ridiculous, Christabel. You are saying, are you, that
women like Mrs Despard and Teresa Billington, who have
devoted themselves selflessly and at great personal cost to

fighting for women's rights, should be made to leave the movement?'

'No one's making anyone leave. They just have to decide whose side they're on, that's all.'

'Yours or women's, you mean?'

There was a silence that could have cracked a mirror, then Miss Christabel spoke.

'I won't continue this discussion. You're obviously overwrought, Sylvia. Perhaps you should try to concentrate on your poster designs and leave the policy-making to Mother and me. I, after all, am a trained lawyer and possibly a little more *au fait* with the real world than an artist like yourself.'

'I know which I'd rather be.'

'Good, because there was never really much choice for you, was there?'

There followed the sound of footsteps and the front door opening and closing. Miss Kerr and I glanced at each other then crept out, guilty as two pickpockets to have eavesdropped on such a falling out.

Orders went out that we must return all subscription payments. This was worse than a nightmare for we had spent so long getting them in in the first place. I was up and down to the post office five or six times a day till the man behind the counter asked if I wouldn't like a job there, since I spent so much time in the place. I was beginning to think I might, for the feeling in the office was very bitter at that time, with ladies coming in to complain about their treatment, and Miss Sylvia looking sadder and more wretched every day.

Miss Annie soldiered on for she was mostly concerned with the working women and so had not much to do with all the quarrelling and agitating of the society folk. She asked me one day how I was weathering it. I said I feared that if things were not resolved soon the whole movement would fall apart. She put her arm round my shoulders.

'Don't you believe it, Maggie. It's like a dog with fleas. It'll bear it so long then, all of a sudden, it has to be rid of them, come what may. So it shakes and scratches itself till they all fall off, and if that don't work, it jumps in the pond and drowns them all.'

I could not but smile to think how Mrs Despard would feel to hear herself likened to a flea. In the end she was not, for she, Miss Billington and several of the other ladies who had been with the movement since the Wednesday meetings, withdrew of their own accord.

I was sad to see them go for all they sometimes frightened me with their cleverness. They set up another movement called the Women's Freedom League which I liked much better for a name than WSPU, but a name is only a name, and there is not cleverness enough in the world to make me desert Miss Christabel.

For all the difficulty and worry of this time there was never a morning I woke without a great burst of happiness. Because I knew that today, tomorrow, Sunday – whenever he was free, I would see Fred. And we would walk and talk, and he would hold my hand or put his arm around my waist, and sometimes, when we stood by the river, or under a tree, or really anywhere that there were no galloping horses, he would kiss me. First on the cheek and then on the brow, but after ever so little time, on my mouth, which is really very nice once you get used to it – like a sort of glorious shivery pain that you don't want to stop. A soft, warm pain melting your insides till you are squishy as a jelly. I have never felt like that before. Maybe it is because I am grown up now. Maybe when the bleeding starts it washes out everything that was there before. Maybe I am a new person. Like a butterfly unfolding, ready to fly away to the sun, leaving its dirty old caterpillar body behind forever. I hope so. I hope so so much. I want to be new and clean and to deserve someone wonderful like Fred, then I would never be afraid of anything again. Or any man.

He is the only man who has ever touched me gently. I did not think that was possible. Even Pa, when he hugs me, manages to bang my elbow or stand on my foot or something. It is as though men are made only to be rough and clumsy, but Fred is not like that. His hands are warm and quite soft and when he squeezes my fingers it is like a secret message, telling me I am safe, he is protecting me. From what? From everything, I suppose, except myself.

I love him, like it is quite impossible to love anyone. My bones ache with thinking about him and when I see him I feel like I could float and never have to touch the ground again. He gets more handsome every day, not that he wasn't the handsomest man who ever lived before I met him, but his hair gets goldener and his eyes greenier-brownier and his smile snowier and altogether he is quite perfect. And he is the cleverest man I ever spoke with – more than Mr Pethick Lawrence or Mr Keir Hardie or anyone, because he is so much younger than they are and I feel sure they would not have known half what he does when they were nineteen.

We go to galleries and concerts and sometimes to a play and

once, an opera! His sergeant at work had given him the tickets, not wanting to go himself, so I wore my blue shawl that Cook had knitted me and off we went like proper toffs.

It was a very sad story about a young seamstress who falls in love with a poet but goes off with a nasty rich old man and dies of consumption. She sang a lot when she was dying which surprised me because Mrs Carter could hardly even speak towards the end, and I could not help thinking if the seamstress had had the vote things might have turned out better, but it is so wonderful to be just anywhere with Fred. I can talk to him like I've never talked to anyone before, even Miss Sylvia or Miss Annie, for though they are my best friends, they are not part of me the way Fred is. When I am with him I feel I can do anything, be anything. Nothing is too great or too difficult for me, and that is because he believes it, too, I am sure. We are like two sides of a coin. Different but equal. That is how all men and women should be.

I wish we were married then we could be together forever. I would do anything for him. Even have babies if I had to. We would have two or three nice children that didn't get ill and a cottage in the countryside (for he took me out to Wood Green one day and it is the prettiest place on earth, with flowers and trees growing wild along the roadside).

I wish I could meet his family for he has told me so much about them and although his father is so strict he sounds a very fine and gentle sort of person, and his sister, too. Well, they must be to have a son and brother like Fred.

But then, if I were to meet his family, surely he would want to meet mine? It is shameful of me, I know, but that is the one thing that clouds my happiness for I know how it would be. Ma would be quiet and seem so shabby to him, Pa would drink too much, Alfie...well, I don't know how he would be. Will would howl, and Evelyn would probably try to give him a bath. Then on top of that – Lucy. Oh, I shall not think about it any more. If it happens, so be it, but not yet. Please, Lord, not yet.

Miss Lake remarked the other day that it was a strange thing for a suffragette to be walking out with a policeman. I asked her, 'How, strange?' She said because they were against us. I said Fred was not and told her how he had refused to arrest me.

'But someone else did?'

'Yes, but that was not his fault.'

'Of course not, but he cannot always look away. What will happen when he does take someone in charge?'

'They will go before the court, I suppose.'

'You suppose! Maggie, do you not see that it is bound to be, the way our campaign is organised?'

I felt quite hot. 'Well, so be it. I thought it was the purpose of the Cause to get ourselves arrested, in which case we should be grateful to the police for their help in the matter.'

Miss Kerr was sorting through a pile of postcards. She said nothing but I could see her smile.

It would have stayed there, I think, but that Miss Christabel happened to be next door. Quick as lightning her head pops round the door. 'What's this? Maggie walking out with a bobby? I didn't know that.'

Miss Lake gave a picky little smile. 'And sees nothing wrong in it, neither.'

I waited, expecting to be torn off a strip but knowing whatever was said, I must stand by my true feelings.

Miss Christabel, however, positively beamed. 'How very sensible of you, Maggie. That's exactly what we need. A foot in both camps. Does this young man talk to you about his duties?'

'Er...sometimes he does, miss,' I stammered. 'Not always. It depends.'

'Of course it does. You wouldn't want him to think you were spying on him.'

I blushed crimson. 'I shouldn't want to think it myself, miss.'

Miss Christabel became serious. 'No, indeed. It was just a joke. Still it would be useful to know a little of the police plans in advance of our marches, don't you agree? It might save people getting hurt. I'm sure your young man would prefer that, wouldn't he, to all this fighting in the streets? After all, he wouldn't want you to get hurt. See what you can find out.'

I went home with a very heavy heart. I can see what Miss Christabel means and I am sure she is right. Fred would do anything to stop the arrests and violence, but to ask me to quiz him and then relay it all back to the office... It fills me with a feeling of...dirtiness, I suppose. And I am trying so hard to get clean again. I will not think about it any more. My eyes are closed.

We have started our own newspaper. It is called *Votes For Women* and costs threepence. It comes out once a month, but we have a smaller one each week that costs only a halfpenny and sells like hot chestnuts.

Mr Pethick Lawrence is in charge and he and Mrs Pethick Lawrence write brilliant articles about the Cause. Miss Christabel tells all about how things are going and what we are to do next, and Miss Sylvia writes about the history of the movement which I find most interesting of all. I read one day how a lady was sent to the lunatic asylum by her own father, rather than let her marry a common labourer she had met while doing charity work. A doctor came to her house on the eve of the wedding and asked her if she would leave off the engagement. When she refused he pronounced her mad and had her carted off in a strait-jacket.

I suppose that's one good thing about being common to start with, no one's too low for me.

One issue had a whole section given over to asking the branch leaders what had first brought them to join our movement. One spoke of seeing children with their toes frozen off for want of shoes; one, of a woman turned on to the street by her husband so he could set up his trollop in her place; another of a mother whose baby was taken from her when she ran away from a man that had burnt her with her own iron for making a scorch on his shirt. Miss Christabel asked me what I made of it. 'That women are no better than slaves to be treated so, miss.'

'Slaves. Exactly. So we must form a slave army and drive our oppressors back to the shores of the Adriatic.'

'Will they not get drowned on the way, miss?'

'I'm speaking metaphorically, Maggie. Downing Street will do for now. Have you heard of Spartacus?'

I said I had not.

'Ah, well you must read all about him. He was the leader of

a slave rebellion in Ancient Rome. He achieved great things.'

'Did he get the slaves set free, miss?'

Miss Christabel frowned. 'Not exactly. He was crucified along with most of his followers, but that's not the point. He was a fine and noble leader. Ask my sister to rake you out a book about him. His strategy was much admired, even by his enemies.'

I thought, admiration is all very well.

'Have you found out anything for us from that young bobby of yours yet, Maggie?'

'No, miss... I... He...'

'Well, don't leave it too long. These young men can be very fickle. You don't want to miss your chance. Next time I see you I shall expect something tangible.'

'Yes, miss.'

Another week goes by and I still have not asked Fred about his work. I know Miss Christabel is right for I can see how it would be truly helpful if we did know more of the police's plans, but I cannot, *cannot* deceive him.

Last night he asked me why I seemed so low. I was so close to telling him, but then I thought, supposing he wants no more to do with me if he thinks I would act against him, so I said, nothing, only that I was not having a baby again and it always made me spiky.

He looked at me so strangely. 'Would you like a baby, Maggie?'

'No, not for the world. How could I do my work? And none of my clothes would fit.'

'But one day?'

'Yes, one day, maybe. If I'm married and have a house of my own with a garden and flowers.'

He laughed. 'You don't ask much. What about a husband? Won't you need one of those?'

I went all pink. 'Yes, but I may not be able to get one.'

'Why not?'

'Because...no one might want to marry me.'

He was quiet for a moment then took my hand and squeezed it. 'Come on. I've found a new gallery. All the sculptures are made of wire. I want to know what you think of them.'

So we go on.

On Thursdays it is my turn to sell the paper. There are a group of us, but the others are volunteers so I am in charge. They are nice people – mostly educated. At first I felt shy of telling them what to do, but they seemed to accept it, so now I am quite unruffled. A few nob ladies complained once about being ordered about by one so young but Miss Christabel snapped right down on them, saying I had earned my position on merit and it was a pity there were not more like me, so that put a stop to that.

On the whole it is fun, for people will often stop and chat to us and wish us well. It is not all good, though, for many a time we have been spat at or called slatterns or worse, and 'whipping's too good for us'. When that happens we look across to each other and wave or smile so that we feel more cheerful again and can carry on. Companionship is such a fine strong thing. I had not realised for though I'm from a big family, it never felt like we were together in our hearts, bound together as we are now.

The suffragettes are my true family. My sisters. And I am

theirs. At least I think I am. Just sometimes it seems to me that however hard I try I will always be a little on the outside. Like a clever pet – praised, admired for what I am. What I am, being less than everyone else. Yet why? For we have so many different sorts – nurses, teachers, social workers, seamstresses, washerwomen...all drawn together for one great purpose and I am part of it. Surely that should be enough for anyone?

To begin with many are terrified of having to stand on a corner and shout like a newsboy, but I always stay with them the first time and by the end of an hour they are bellowing like fishwives. 'Votes For Women'. 'The Truth For A Penny'. 'Deeds Not Words'. Those who are good are recruited to our list of speakers. I wish I had the skill but I would just shake and mumble like an idiot, I'm sure, if I ever had to do it.

What everyone agrees on is that of all the speakers in the world, Miss Christabel and Mrs Pankhurst are the finest. The first so glorious – like a fizzing firework, full of passion, wit, brilliance. 'These "Honourable Gentlemen" may try sham pledges, but they will not get the better of us, because they are fighting with crooked weapons and we are fighting with straight ones; we are fighting in a just cause and they are fighting in an unjust cause; we have courage and they have none.'

The second so gentle and calm, yet like a willow that may bend and sway but will not, cannot be broken. 'I say to you women: put aside all fear, fight with the courage that you have had through generations of suffering, and believe me that while you and I may die in the struggle, victory is assured, and out of our struggle, even by the laying down of our lives, will come a time so wonderful for humanity that we can only dimly see that beautiful future.'

Laying down of our lives.

1907 is nearly over. Surely, soon they must give in?

I have never liked Christmas before. Indeed there was no Christmas at our house, except Pa would go to the alehouse and not come back till he was too drunk to see a hole in a ladder. I know Jesus was born then and I truly suppose he had not much better a time of it than we did, what with cows and oxen sniffing round him. On top of that, lambs, and then real kings that must have put the Blessed Virgin in a dither. Ma is bad enough when the parson comes round to bless each baby, so what it must have been like to have kings hanging over you…!

This Christmas was entirely perfect. Fred bought me two presents. One, a fine leather purse, softer than silk and of the most beautiful brown colour you ever saw. I like brown now. But not for a dress.

The other was a book of poems. Fred loves poetry – all kinds, funny, sad, romantic, and often asks me why I do not care for it. I say I do. Some of our women send verses in to be printed in *Votes For Women* and I have always thought them very clever.

'But is that all the poetry you have come across?'

'Yes, I suppose it is.'

'Ah.'

Now I see what he means. It is like someone drawing back a curtain and a whole magic world just waiting for you on the other side of it. From now on I shall read nothing but poetry,

apart from my newspapers, and history books and animal...
No, I shall just have to learn to read quicker.

I bought him a knife. He had never said he wanted one, but
I had no idea what to buy him and had wandered the whole
length of Oxford Street looking for something he might fancy
and there it was, in a window display, shining up at me,
glinting in the sun. It was fifteen shillings. I have never spent
so much on a present for anyone before. After the man had
wrapped it up for me, calling me 'Madam', which was worth
at least a florin, I felt guilty, for it was more than I had spent
on my whole family together. But then I considered that they
would have nothing at all for me and it would discomfort
them if I should make a show of giving them expensive gifts
when they could not return them. Besides, I was taking home
a ham and a whole bag of candied fruits so it will not be such
a poor time for them at all.

Fred was to go to his father's house on Christmas Day. He
said they did not mark it with any celebration, but his cousins
would call in and he should like to see them again.

Some of our helpers who had nowhere to go were asked to
The Mascot which is the name of the Pethick Lawrences'
house in the country. Oh, how I should have loved to be one
of them for I have heard it is very fine and there is a great
garden with a swing. I have seen those at fairs in Battersea
Park. They are the most wonderful objects. When Fred and I
are married and living in Wood Green we shall have a swing.

He was pleased with his knife. At least I think he was. He
looked most surprised when he opened it, and just sat there
gazing at it.

'Do you like it?'

He nodded. 'It's beautiful. What made you buy me a knife, Maggie? Is my hair too long?'

I said, just for a joke, 'No, but your trousers are,' and made to slash at them. Fred caught me by both my wrists and pulled me right up close to him so I could feel his breath, hot against my face. 'I'll take them off if they bother you.' We stared at each other and my heart was like a galloping whirlpool for I knew what he wanted… His eyes were bright and strange like a tiger waiting to pounce. I could see myself in them, a piece of flesh to be torn apart and devoured. And the worst of it was, I wanted it to happen. I wanted to be his. Only his. But then he would know. I know he would know. And he would hate me. He would leave me. And I could not bear it.

I dragged myself away. 'No. It was a joke.'

Fred dropped his head into his hands then sort of sighed. 'I was joking too, Maggie.' He kissed my forehead gently. 'I shall use it to cut my meat at Mrs Blackett's. It must be nearly strong enough to saw through logs and that is what is needed.'

We walked into Trafalgar Square, him holding my hand. I wished I could really understand what his fingers were saying. And more than that, I wished mine could speak back. 'Forgive me. I never meant to. He was bigger than me. Stronger. I don't know how to mend it.'

People were singing carols and collecting for the poor. He gave them a shilling. It was a small shiny man with the tin. He looked at me as he expected me to give some money too. It rankled me somehow so I asked, 'Do you believe in votes for women?'

His face went all puffy. 'We are collecting for widows and orphans.'

'There might not be so many if they had the vote.'

Puffy turned to plum. 'God has ordained that men should command and women obey.'

'God created all mankind equal.'

'Exactly – mankind.'

'Does that not include women?'

Much rattling in his throat. 'There is a divine order to things. In that order men have been placed above women. Just as women are above animals and animals above fish. That is how it is and how it should be.'

'Why?'

'Because...because that is how it is. Men are superior in every respect to women. Their beings, their intellect...'

'But it is they who make widows and orphans through their fighting.'

'Through their labour. War may be a part of that.'

'Do you think men have bigger brains than women?'

He sighed crossly. 'It is a known fact.'

'Just as elephants have bigger brains than men?'

He snorted and turned away. Fred was grinning all over his face. 'Tell you what, Maggie. When you lot do get the vote I'll lay ten to one you end up Prime Minister.'

I laughed. 'Can't you just see it? "All be uprising for the Prime Minister, Miss Maggie Robins".'

'You might not be a "Miss" by then.'

'No, but I shall still be a Maggie. Is that a name for a Prime Minister?'

Fred shrugged. 'It would serve as well as any other, I should say.'

We bought some roasted chestnuts and sat on a wall outside

one of the galleries to eat them, then it was time for Fred to catch his train. I went with him to the station. What a messy rowdy place, full of people shouting and blowing whistles and great belches of steam spouting up like an angry whale.

I waved as it set off and Fred hung out of the window waving back and blowing me kisses and I saw how other women were looking at him and thinking how handsome he was. I felt so proud and happy that if someone had asked me just at that moment, I would have said, 'Yes, I will be Prime Minister one day.'

The next day I went home. I had bought a rag doll for Evelyn with wool plaits so what was the first thing she did? The wool went all straggly and we had a fine time trying to braid it up again.

For Will I had some wooden bricks which he first chewed and then threw at everyone, much to Pa's annoyance who threatened to chuck them in the fire.

I had a pipe for him and a shawl each for Ma and Lucy, though Ma's was softer by far. She straightway wrapped it round the baby which vexed me considerably but I said nothing. She still looks pinched and skinny but at least there are no more babies in sight.

I gave Alfie a spotted necktie which made him look quite the dandy, we all agreed; at least it did when we had showed him how to knot it, and not in a bow like his laces.

When she saw how big the ham was Ma asked if she might invite Mrs Grant to eat with us. I said I would run round to her house and fetch her. At first Mrs Grant said no, fearing she would be depriving others, but I told her if she did not come we would be throwing the leavings in the street for it would not keep (not true, but it worked).

On the way back I thanked her for all she had been doing to help Ma out. 'It's a lot for her to manage till her health is mended. And I fear Lucy does but little.'

She glanced at me. 'Has your Ma spoken to you about Lucy, Maggie?'

'Not really. I wanted to thrash it out with her but Ma almost begged me not to. She is too soft on her by half, I think.'

Mrs Grant sighed. 'Lucy has taken up with some bad company. She is a good girl at heart, but somewhat weak in her judgement, I would say.'

I remembered what she had said of not needing presents. If she had taken to thieving I think Ma would die of shame. 'What sort of bad company?'

'Well, I cannot be sure. But I have seen her more than once with friends of your Frank's. Fellow seamen.'

'Oh well,' said I, much relieved, for Mrs Grant is something of a prude, 'if they are Frank's friends he will make sure they bring her no harm.'

Mrs Grant said nothing, but her expression was far from happy. She asked me how I thought my ma was looking.

'Not well. Too thin. And last time I was home her arm was wicked bruised.'

'She has something wrong in her blood. I'm sure good nursing would cure it, but where's that to be got without money?'

'I would pay for it,' I declared, fearing she thought me unwilling. 'I have told her so.'

Mrs Grant nodded. 'I know. You are a good generous

daughter, but all you provide her goes on the family or the rent or such. She will not use it to buy medicine for herself. I have told her it is foolish for if anything should happen to her...'

I stopped her. 'Nothing will happen to Ma. I will make sure of it. I will find a cure for her. She will be well again. I have made up my mind.'

Mrs Grant smiled. 'I see you are a true suffragette.'

So, a new year. 1908. And it has not started well. Mrs Pankhurst has been attacked! By a mob of drunkards down in Devon, wherever that is. Miss Sylvia says it is because she persuaded so many to vote against the Liberal man, he lost his seat. Lost his brain, more like. For what sort of man would set a bunch of hooligans to beat a lady? And one so gentle and dignified? I wish I had been there. I would have thrown them in the air like pigeon droppings and trampled them in the mud when they came down.

Every day we hear of some meeting or other where these Liberals have refused our women entry. I wondered just what they did stand for, apart from denying women their rights, so I looked it up in Miss Lake's great leather dictionary. *'Liberal: (Polit.) Favourable to democratic reform and individual liberty; progressive.'* When I had looked up all of that I showed it to Miss Sylvia. 'Perhaps we should send a copy to the Parliament. To remind them what they believe in,' I suggested.

Miss Sylvia laughed. 'I tell you what, it would make a very good slogan.'

The next time I saw her she had made a whole poster from it, of a fat man with his foot on a woman's neck. Round his hat was written 'Liberal'. All along her back was written 'Liberty'.

Today Miss Sylvia brought her brother, Harry, to the office. He is a lovely jolly boy, full of pranks. He told me how one night he had charged all round Manchester scrawling *VOTES FOR WOMEN* over the Liberal man Churchill's posters and then gone to one of his meetings just to see his face. 'Like a great bulldog. All crumpled and surly. Arrogant, too, for he fancies himself an orator and will not give way for anyone.'

I let him have a go on the typewriter which annoyed Miss Lake for he managed to twist the ribbon and all her letters came out splodged. I said it was me so Harry went haring off and came back with a great iced bun by way of thanks. He is the perfect mix of Miss Christabel and Miss Sylvia – energy, wits and warmth.

Miss Sylvia popped her head round the door and asked if he was driving me mad. I said, yes, completely, for he had got sugar all over the typewriter. He laughed so hard. 'Well, I shall go off and find someone else to annoy. Who should it be?'

I said, 'Try the Prime Minister.'

'I'll do my best,' and away he went, taking half the furniture with him.

Miss Sylvia helped me set it right again. 'Harry will never make a ballerina, that's for sure.' I said I did not think Frank or Alfie would either, but Will might for he is so altogether droopy.

The two of us have often talked about our brothers together. How they tease and torment us but still we love them. Miss Sylvia told me once how when Harry was very small she showed him a drawing she had made of him and that in his excitement he had torn it. 'I shook him, Maggie.

Shook him till he howled. After I was so ashamed I cried myself to sleep. Swore I'd never say another unkind word to him or anyone. Would be good and kind forevermore. But if you ask him now if he remembers it, he will tell you, "No".'

So I told her about me throwing Alfie's apple in the fire and how, but for Pa, he would have gone after it.

'We are a fine pair of sisters and no mistake,' she said. 'To think our colleagues call us "Sister" and are proud of it.' We laughed so hard Miss Lake put on her 'Some of us are trying to work' face, but that just made us worse.

Harry has thought of the most magnificent plan. We are to do a Trojan horse. I did not know this story but it seems thousands of years ago some Greeks were fighting each other over a beautiful woman who had been stolen from her husband, and they got bored of the war and pretended to go home, leaving a great wooden horse outside the walls of the city they had been attacking. The enemy, thinking it was a gift, dragged the horse inside and in the middle of the night all the Greeks, who had not really gone away but were hiding in its belly, got out and captured the city.

We are to do the same. Well, almost. We shall not actually capture the Parliament, which is a great pity, in my opinion, and we are going inside two furniture vans, not a horse, but for the rest...

Crammed up against each other, clutching our petitions, scarcely daring to breathe, jittery as trapped sparrows.

Horses clattering, hooves like muffled gunshot on the cobbles. On we rumbled, for eternity.

And then eternity was over.

The jolt of reins, stamp of hooves. Silence. No breath. No movement.

The doors flew open. There before us, the Parliament building.

And between us and it, a forest of bobbies, dark, not moving, waiting to swallow us up.

As the members arrived they parted for them. We followed. Then they swooped, grabbing necks, arms, hair; swinging us round like kittens to be drowned, hurling us at the ground. The sound of splitting bones. The hiss of pain. The Black Maria.

I fled down a side street. Ran all the way to Caxton Hall. Miss Annie was just about to address the meeting. I rushed up to her.

'It's all gone wrong, Miss Annie. Everyone's arrested. And horrible beatings.'

'Sit down, Maggie. Catch your breath.'

She strides on to the stage. A storm of applause. She holds up her hands. 'Ladies, fellow suffragettes, please listen to what I have to say. Today I have a special request to put to you. As we feared, many of our number have been arrested at The House this morning and may well be on their way to prison as I speak. They are brave true warriors of the Cause. Some will have endured prison sentences before. For others it will be a new and dreadful experience.

'One thing you may be sure of, they will not be from wealthy families. We all have seen how the bobbies back away from a lady in furs. Well, let us show them now that ours is a movement for *all* the women of Britain, high and low. Let the world see that we stand together, shoulder to shoulder, and when it does, those who oppose us shall have just cause to be afraid.'

Up they all rose.

The papers next day looked like they had attended a fashion parade. Hats, furs, velvet cloaks, fans even. A smarter set of people could not have been found at the opera. More arrests and the judge has threatened a new law, or rather a very ancient one – the Tumultuous Petitions Act, (was there ever a sillier name?) saying that thirteen shall be the most people allowed near the House of Commons in a procession. Or else three months in prison.

On hearing of this Mrs Pankhurst straightway called for twelve volunteers and off they went, cheered to the rafters by the rest of us.

So much for a bold departure. Not an hour later word came back that Mrs Pankhurst herself had been arrested. This sent a true shock through us all, for we had never thought the police would lay a hand on her.

Six weeks in Holloway, even Mrs Pankhurst. And in the second division, which is for common criminals. There is no justice in this world. Or perhaps a little, for now the papers are finally coming to our aid. They say such treatment is wrong. Suffragettes are not thieves, but political prisoners and so should be placed in the first division, (which is much better for you may read and talk and wear your own clothes).

There was a poem published in the *Daily Mail*, very funny like a nursery rhyme and praising Miss Christabel's brilliance to come up with the Trojan Horse. When I showed it to her she smiled deeply. I was surprised she did not remember it was her brother who had thought of it.

Mrs Pethick Lawrence organised a week of fund-raising. So many schemes! Some ladies gave tea parties and charged a sixpence to all who came. Others sold embroidery or paintings they had done. Those too poor for such things merely gave up their favourite food for a week and paid the cost of it to the Cause.

Mrs Garrud decided we should give a display of fighting and charge a shilling to let people watch. Fred was by when she suggested it and was very taken with the idea. He even threatened to bring his friends from the constabulary, but I think he was teasing for they would hardly like to contribute towards paying our fines.

He said at any rate *he* would come, and would buy two seats so that he could stretch his legs out. I was not very happy about this because my coat is shorter than anyone else's and the thought of Fred sitting there watching me trying to break a pillow in half was not my idea of fund-raising. I even offered to give up chocolate instead, but it seemed Mrs Garrud had her heart quite set on it, so on the Friday evening I and the rest of my class – two ladies from the Poor School, some nurses from the asylum and a very fat lady who plays the cello at people's funerals – all lined up.

Fred had brought someone with him. A kind-looking man, somewhat older, with a ginger moustache.

We started by showing some exercises – bending and twisting and the like, and then we did some slow movements to show how we would break people's necks if they annoyed us in any way, and then we each killed a pillow with great deep thrusts and slashes and cries of 'Aaagh! Thwaagh! Thwackkkk!' which Mrs Garrud insists we make as she says it frightens an attacker more than being kicked.

I durst not look at Fred but when I did (we had our hands over our eyes, showing how to gouge them out) he was sitting with his chin in his hand, looking as studious as he was attending a lecture, and likewise his companion.

When it was done everybody clapped and Mr Garrud made a speech to say that all the proceeds from the evening were to go towards the Cause. He then passed round a hat. Fred and his friend put in a whole handful of coins between them and seemed to think it money well spent, for they were smiling like a couple of loons, as Mrs Drummond would say.

Then Fred held out his hand to me. 'Maggie, I would like to introduce my friend, Mr Edwin Neal, to you. He has been most impressed by the performance.'

'I have indeed,' said Mr Neal. 'And I'm mindful to send some of my men to train with Mrs Garrud.'

'Why, sir? Do you meet with a lot of violence in your profession?'

'I never used to, but of late it has grown quite out of order.'

'Are you a soldier, Mr Neal?'

At this they both broke out laughing.

'No, Miss Robins. I am a police sergeant.'

Afterwards Fred and I went for a soda at the corner house. I asked why he had brought Mr Neal with him.

'He gave me the tickets for the opera and besides, he is a friend.'

'Yes, and a policeman.'

'I am a policeman.'

This flummoxed me somewhat. 'But before that you are Fred, are you not?'

'Are the two so very different?'

I had no answer. 'What did you think of the display?'

'Amazing.'

'By that you mean "stupid", I suppose?'

'I do not. I mean I had not thought you capable of it.'

'Of bursting a pillow?'

'No. I was well sure you could do that. Of...'

'Of what, then?'

He looked at me and though I know he was jesting, he said, 'Of wanting to hurt someone so much.'

Wonderful news! A Liberal!! Member of the House, a Mr Stanger of Kensington, who must be exceeding courageous to go against his own government, has put forward a private bill to give us the vote. 'The Women's Enfranchisement Bill'. Not only that, but it has gained one hundred and seventy-nine votes and will go forward for further discussion. If it passes that, it will be made law, Miss Lake says.

We held a great meeting at the Albert Hall and all the more stirring for, centre stage, an empty chair was placed, and on it a placard, *Mrs Pankhurst's Chair*, lest any should forget she was that very moment imprisoned for her bravery. Or so we had believed.

Suddenly the great wooden doors at the rear burst open and there she stood.

'Women, as you see, I am back!'

A great cheer went up. Everyone rose to their feet, handkerchieves waving till the hall looked like a field of flowers, every colour under the sun. Mrs Pankhurst smiled and waved too, then turning to her chair, removed the placard and laid it on the table in front of her. 'I'm sorry I'm late,' she said, and sat down as though she had just got off an omnibus, not been released from that terrible place.

There was more money collected that afternoon than in all our week of fund-raising.

Mrs Pankhurst and Miss Christabel are gone north again. There is a man they particularly dislike (the same Churchill, whose posters Harry writ all over) and he supports a bill to stop the barmaids working. Why? Why must he take work from those who need it? Does he think they labour so of their own free choosing? Does he believe they would not rather ride around in carriages and dine with the nobs as the ladies of his acquaintance do, than pour beer down the necks of rough rowdy menfolk? It is said seven thousand of them will lose their jobs if he succeeds. Does he say what they will do then? How they will live? How can he be so blind? I hope he is beat and beat rotten.

And so he has been, but what of that, for he offs up out of it to another town and two months later is back in the House.

One of Mrs Despard's ladies got it into her head to follow him from meeting to meeting ringing a great brass muffin bell every time he opened his mouth to address the crowd. At first this was thought great good fun and the papers showed many a picture of her, but in the end the people got sick of it and so they voted him in for not having heard a word he said.

Worse than that, though – poor grey old Sir Henry Campbell-Bannerman is dead and replaced by that monster and our greatest enemy, Asquith. What is his first act? To kill stone dead The Women's Enfranchisement Bill.

Mr Pethick Lawrence brought us the news. Miss Christabel turned quite white with fury when she heard it.

'How can he? How can he do this when one hundred and seventy-nine members have given it a second reading? One hundred and seventy-nine. What possible excuse has he come up with this time? A sign from heaven? A ram caught in a burning bush, bleating "No votes for women?" An eleventh commandment: "Thou shalt not have justice"?'

Mr Pethick Lawrence laughed; no one else dared to. 'Well, you are not far wrong, Christabel, as I understand it. His reasoning is he cannot be sure it is the wish of the whole country's women to gain the vote.'

'What! Processions, meetings, petitions, the press – what will it take to unstop his ears?'

'As you said, a sign from heaven, I should think.'

Miss Christabel fair snorted with contempt. 'Well, let it be a thunderbolt. The man's a charlatan, a cad, a reprobate. What does he take us for? Idiots?'

She stormed out, slamming the door so hard all Miss Kerr's letters for filing went flying.

Mr Pethick Lawrence shook his head. 'Poor Christabel. It is a wicked blow, to be sure, but our task now is to think of ways to counter it.'

I asked, 'How can he know women do not wish it, sir, for he has never asked?'

'No, indeed, Maggie. Nor will he, if he can help it. He thinks to avoid it by concentrating on granting the vote to more men.'

'Well, how does he know they want it, for he's never asked them either?'

Mr Pethick Lawrence nodded thoughtfully. 'You're right, Maggie. He's never asked. Perhaps it's time that we did.'

Mr Pethick Lawrence has come up with quite the most brilliant idea. 'Women's Sunday'. We are to take over Hyde Park for a whole afternoon and show the people and the Government just what we are fighting for.

Dozens of new people have been brought in to help with the arrangements. We have had to take two more rooms at Lincoln's Inn just to squeeze them all in.

There are to be seven processions, each coming from a different part of London and all meeting together in the park at an appointed hour. Billboards the height of houses with giant Miss Christabels and Miss Annies beaming down from them. We are sent out to factories, hospitals, restaurants, schools, shops – anywhere with working women, to spread the word.

We have our own special colours now: purple, white and green. Mrs Pethick Lawrence explained they stand for Justice, Purity and Hope. I wonder what Mrs Beckett would make of that. She said nothing pretty could ever be good as well.

The shops have gone quite mad for us and are packed full of ribbons, scarves, bonnets, all in our colours. Newspapers are crammed with articles and advertisements for the great day. Fred gave me a doll he bought off a vendor in the street. It is rubber and dressed just like a tiny suffragette. I asked if I might give it to Evelyn and he said, of course, 'But this *you* must wear', and gave me a little package all wrapped up in tissue paper. It was the most glorious silk scarf, purple, green and white stripes, softer than a baby's skin. Well, I can hardly bear to save it till the day, but I must be strong.

A company has sent Mrs Drummond a whole uniform with a sash lettered, 'GENERAL' across it and a peaked cap and everything. She says it is just what she needs for she is in charge of the processions and no one will dare gainsay her when they see her all dressed up. Miss Kerr and I agreed that it would be a brave man who tried to, anyway, but she looks mightily fine in it, and a man from the *Daily Mail* came specially to take her photograph.

Extra buses and trains are ordered, for thousands are expected. Stewards have been chosen to sort them into line as they alight, and Miss Sylvia asked if I would be willing to assist her. She has charge of St Pancras which is where Fred caught his train at Christmas. She says I shall have an official sash. I asked if I might still wear my scarf and she said, certainly. I showed it to her and she agreed it was quite the finest she had seen. She suggested it would look well around my hat (I have a new straw summer one). I tried it and it is just perfect. Oh, please don't let it rain on the day.

Fred took me to the variety theatre last evening. Can you believe it, halfway through a curtain was dropped and on it were pictures of Miss Christabel and Mrs Pankhurst and a great big notice telling about The Day. I cheered and cheered, so much so that when the comic came on after, he looked straight down at me and said, 'I hope you're going to cheer like that for me, pretty miss', and everyone laughed and cheered some more. I went redder than a radish but something mad happened in my head and I answered right back to him, 'I will if you come to Hyde Park on June 21ˢᵗ and bring your family with you.'

He looked quite stunned for a moment, but then he laughed and said, 'I reckon I shall have to now. Don't let them suffragettes beat me up, though, will you?' which made everyone laugh all the more.

I replied, 'Well, we won't throw any eggs at you, that's for sure,' and there was a great burst of laughing and cheering and I felt quite as though I had made a speech at the Albert Hall, I was so up in the air.

Afterwards as we were walking home Fred asked, 'Would you have liked to be an actress, Maggie?' I said I had never thought about it for, in truth, I had not. What would a girl from my street be doing dancing and singing for her supper?

'Why do you ask?'

'Because I think you would do very well at it. You answered that man back as though you had been working the halls all your life.'

This worried me, for actresses are not considered respectable in the main. 'I do not think the life would suit me.'

Fred smiled. 'Maybe not. And yet I cannot make you out. Sometimes you are so quiet and timid I think a leaf would frighten you, and then other times you are...like tonight.'

I knew when he called me timid what he was thinking of – that I will not let him touch me where he wants to. I cannot. Not yet. But when? When?

I said, 'Was I wrong to answer him back? It was only for the Cause. I would not have spoken otherwise.'

Fred nodded. 'The 'Cause' is very dear to your heart, isn't it?'

'Yes.'

'Dearer than anything else?'

'I do not know. Why do you ask?'

'Because one day you may have to choose, that's all.' Seeing my anxiety he drew me right up close to him and kissed me all slow and beautifully. 'But not tonight,' he whispered. 'You do not have to choose tonight.'

I shall never forget that day. June 21st 1908. It is carved on my memory forever. There will never be another day like it.

The sun shone, no cloud in the sky, the birds sang in their trees and I swear it was 'Fight on, Women' they were chirping as we passed below in our great ranks, as wide as the road and a mile long, at least. Thousands and thousands of women, all dressed in white with purple and green sashes and ribbons, and flowers in their hats. A great field of violets and gardenias waving gently through the streets.

A million bobbies (thereabouts) lined the way, but they, too, were happy, smiling, joking with us as we passed. I wondered how it could be that men who had ridden at us with chargers could now be marking our route so peaceably. Maybe they were not the same ones, but in my heart I think it must be as Fred said: you can be two people at once. Perhaps we are all like that. He thinks *I* am, I know. Maybe he is right. Maybe I am a thousand people. Perhaps I should have been an actress, after all.

Twenty huge wagons snowy with white rosettes served as platforms for the speakers. In the middle of the park a great pantechnicon towering over everything; Mr Pethick Lawrence stood on top to order the proceedings. Around him a mob of pressmen and a bunch of nobs desperate to see (and be seen, I should not wonder).

As two o'clock drew near crowds began to swarm towards the platforms, and nowhere greater than at Number Eight, for this was where Miss Christabel was to speak. No sooner had she stepped up than a gang of loud-mouthed idiots came shoving through to the front and started to yell and holler so that her voice was all but drowned. Still she continued, and as word got out that it was the famous Miss Christabel Pankhurst speaking, hundreds more came thronging round the wagon, their cheers noisier than the idiots' ranting. And how she stirred them up!

'By our actions we have exposed this government not only to the contempt of our own people but to the contempt of the whole civilised world. We suffragettes pity, indeed almost despise the women who can stand aside, who take no part in the battle. It is we militants whom men respect. If you cannot be recognised as a citizen, it is best to be in the front, fighting for a citizen's rights.'

Over the whole park people were clustered, listening, cheering, picnicking. Full of sunshine and goodwill and hope. Policemen sat with suffragettes, nobs with shop assistants, coalmen with *cooks*.

I saw her first. Sitting with a cloth spread out on the grass, all by herself and tucking into a veritable feast of cold meats, brawn and pastries. I flew across the grass.

'Cook...'

She looked up and for a full half-minute seemed not to recognise me, then her hand went to her mouth. 'Maggie? Maggie Robins?'

'Yes, of course. Who did you think it was?'

Cook stared at me. 'A lady.'

I did not know whether to be glad or not. 'I am surely not so much changed?'

'You are indeed, young Maggie. I should not have known you, had you not spoke.'

I felt I could hardly say the same to her as she had not changed one bit, unless to be even stouter.

'Are Mr and Mrs Roe here, too?' I asked.

'They are. Somewhere. Off listening to that pushy girl with all the curls, I think.'

I had not heard Miss Christabel described thus before.

I sat down on the grass. 'It is so good to see you. I had not expected you would like this sort of thing.'

Cook handed me a pork pie. 'I'm not sure I do, but the Master and Mistress were set on it, and that Miss Sylvia kept on at me, and in the end I thought it simpler to come than not to. And it's a fine warm day for a picnic. You look half starved. Have some of this brawn. I made it fresh yesterday.'

We talked of the old times. Cook said Jane, who had taken my place, was as dim as a dormouse and much given to the sulks, which made me think Lucy would not have done so ill there, after all.

She said Mr Roe had had an attack of the gout but I was not to mention it for he disliked to be reminded. Mrs Roe she hardly ever saw, always out gadding (for this, I took her to mean, promoting the Cause). She asked how I was getting on in an office and I told her about learning to type. This amused her greatly. Lord knows why.

'That is a very fine hat you're wearing, Maggie. And if I'm

not mistaken that scarf around it is silk.'

'It is, Fred...a friend gave it to me.'

'A friend, eh? And what does this friend do by manner of employment?'

'He's a policeman.'

Cook looked truly stupefied. 'How did you meet him? Stealing the Crown Jewels?'

I did not think it wise to go into detail. 'Not exactly. I was lost. He showed me the way home.'

'A policeman's respectable enough,' Cook declared. 'You could do worse than that. Does he want to marry you?'

I felt quite shocked. 'We have never spoken of it. I have not known him very long. He is a friend, that's all.'

Cook made her mealy face. 'A friend with more money than sense if he's buying you silk scarves and means nothing by it.'

Mercifully I was saved further questioning by a loud cry which was Mr Roe spotting me. He came hobbling through the crowd with Mrs Roe all but skipping to keep up with him. 'If it ain't Miss Fish Polisher herself. How are you, my dear?' He grasped hold of my hands and practically wrung the blood out of them. 'Quite the young lady now. And what's this?' He tugged at my Steward's Sash. 'Are we to hear a speech from you, too? That Christabel Pankhurst can surely draw a crowd, can she not? Voice like velvet, mind like a razor. And our Sylvia's no slouch, is she? Stirs the people's hearts – half the women were crying. Well, well, well. What a day. And here's our Maggie, looking fit to lead the lot of them. Eh, my dear?'

Mrs Roe gave me the kindest smile. 'Indeed she does, and from what Sylvia tells me, it won't be long before she is doing just that.' She patted my arm. 'Oh yes, Maggie, Miss Sylvia keeps us in touch with everything, and she is particularly warm in her praise for you. I think she feels you are her star pupil.'

There was a snorting sound from Cook, signalling the start of her black look. 'I was Cook's pupil first,' I gabbled. 'Without her guidance I would be as dumb as when I first came to your house.' The look softened a little. 'And my ma still speaks with longing of her currant bread.'

'In that case,' said Cook firmly, 'she shall have this one.' And she wrapped a whole loaf in a piece of muslin and thrust it at me. Poor Mr Roe looked quite crestfallen for it has always been a favourite with him, too.

Somewhere a clock struck. Mr Roe examined his pocket watch. 'Not long now. I hope you're in good voice, Maggie. We are depending on you to show everyone how to shout.'

'I think, sir, you would be better at it than I.' This sent Mrs Roe into fits of laughter for it is well-known that Mr Roe bellows mightily when he is annoyed.

It had been decreed that at five o'clock exactly there would be a Great Shout. It was to be so loud that even if the Asquith man was in Africa, he would surely know whether or not the women of Britain wanted the vote.

I had been instructed to make my way to Miss Annie's platform, to help lead the cry. The nearer I got, the more I quaked for I had no good idea of how I should persuade people to join in if they were not so minded.

I need not have worried! If ever folk were of a mind to holler their heads off, they were that afternoon. Pressed around the platform like they were watching a boxing match, hundreds of them, cheering, stamping their feet, throwing their hats and their children, some of them, high in the air.

Miss Annie spotted me. 'Quick, Maggie. Get up here with me,' she called and hauled me up on to the platform beside her. 'What about this, Maggie? What do you reckon old Asquith will make of this?'

'If it was me I'd leave the country and never come back, or else give in tomorrow.'

'Tomorrow may be a bit soon for him, but he surely cannot hold out much longer.'

Just then, from what sounded like the gates of heaven itself, a mighty trumpeting of bugles burst into the air. This is how it will be on Judgement Day, I thought. Miss Annie seized my arm, her excitement shooting through me like a million red-hot needles. 'Ready?'

'Ready.' I had never felt less ready in my life.

'You take that side, I'll take this.'

'What shall I do? What shall I do?'

'Just lift your arms up high over your head and yell, "On a count of three. One. Two. Three".' I must have looked as sick as I felt. She squeezed my shoulder hard as she could. 'Pretend you're Miss Christabel.'

The bugles fell silent. There was a moment when it seemed to me that all the world had stopped and nobody moved or breathed. I looked out across this ocean of upturned faces and there, not ten rows away from me, stood Ma. Staring up at me like I was some kind of holy vision. So proud. So full of wonder.

I lifted my arms, slowly, like a great bird preparing to fly. 'On a count of three,' I hollered. 'One. Two. Three.' And all through the park the sound rang out, echoing round and round like the cry of a million Israelites entering the Promised Land. *'VOTES FOR WOMEN. VOTES FOR WOMEN. VOTES FOR WOMEN'* caught on the summer breeze for ever and ever.

And I thought, look, God. See what we can do.

Then everyone cheered and clapped each other on the back and started to gather up their things and make for home. And I got down.

Ma was sitting on the grass with the baby, Will piling daisies on to her feet. Alfie was giving Evelyn a piggyback round and round a tree. Pa gave me a funny look, but I could tell he'd been at the beer.

'Hullo, Ma.'

'Maggie.'

'You came then?'

'Yes. We're all here.'

'Even Lucy?'

'Oh yes, Lucy couldn't wait. They should be back in a minute. They went to look at the banners.'

'They?'

'Yes. Oh, here they are now.'

I looked. Lucy was strolling across the grass, her arm linked to a tall young man's in seaman's dress. She was gazing up at him like there was no one else in the world.

It was only when they got nearer that I saw who it was.

When Frank caught sight of me he let go of Lucy's arm and started to run towards me. He swept me up in his arms and twirled me round and round till I had to beg him to stop for fear I would be sick.

He told me he had seen me leading the crowd and nearly

burst for pride of being my brother. 'Wasn't that so, Lucy?'
But her face had gone back to mouldy and her lip stuck out
like a ledge. Frank laughed. 'Lucy, what's that for? You know
I've not seen Maggie for nigh on three years.'

She softened a bit and said she did not care at all but that
her head ached and wasn't it time to go home?

'What? When we've only just met up. You go home if you
want to. Maggie and I are going on a bend.'

My heart jerked. 'No. I cannot. I'm sorry. Truly. It is
impossible. I... I must help clear up. There is a deal to do.'

Frank smiled. 'That's all right. I'll help you. Then we can go
to the fair and I shall buy you... What shall I buy you? What
shall I buy my darling Maggie, Lucy?'

Lucy scowled like she'd lost a diamond down a drain. 'Why
must you buy her anything? She has money of her own, and
to spare.'

'Ah. Jealous. Naughty little cat.' He pinched her cheek. I
heard her gasp. Frank gazed at her, all innocent. 'Did that
hurt? Shall I kiss it better?' Velvet lips across the bright red
blotch. 'Now run along home. Ma needs you to help with the
tiddlers.'

'I want to go to the fair.'

'You have a headache.'

'Not any more.' Her face puckered up like a squeezed
lemon. 'Please let me go with you. Please, Frank. I never go to
fairs. Maggie goes all the time.'

I knew I must prevent it. 'Lucy, Frank is right. Go home
with Ma. I cannot go to the fair either so you've no cause to
fret. Frank can go on his own and buy you all a present.'

He turned to me and I could feel his eyes melting me down

like candle wax. 'But I need you to help me choose, Maggie. I cannot choose on my own.'

'I...' My voice, weak as a sparrow's. 'You always did before, Frank.'

His eyes burnt deeper into me. 'Even so. I need you to help me, Maggie. Or are you too good for me now, with all your fine friends and fine clothes and all?' He reached out to touch my scarf. My precious scarf. I pulled away.

'Frank, I can't. I have arranged something else. If I had known you would be here...'

'I didn't know myself. Well, never mind. I'm sure whatever it is can wait. After all, I am your long lost brother. Don't I come first?'

I looked at him, so handsome with his dark, dark eyes and gleaming teeth, laughing, teasing, expecting – always expecting. I thought, is that the right of handsome people? To always have their way?

But Fred is handsome, yet he expects nothing. Perhaps he is not handsome. Perhaps he is beautiful. That poem he read me. 'Beauty is truth, truth, beauty. That is all we know on earth and all we need to know.' Do handsome people like poetry? Or does it ask too many questions?

I shook my head. 'I made a promise.'

Eyes like a wounded deer. 'Well then, so be it. I must not stand in your way, Maggie. I am sorry you have no time for me now.'

Guilt. More guilt. Never ending. 'That is not true, Frank. If you had sent me word...'

'What is so vital it will not wait?'

'I am meeting...a friend.'

'Well, good. Let her come too. We shall make a merry party, the three of us.'

'It's not…'

Silence. I could feel his eyes on me, as I had so many times before. Pleading, persuading, promising. "Just this once." "Just this once, Maggie." "The last time. Just this once."

'I'm sorry.'

He gave a little shrug. 'As you wish, dear Maggie. I shall just have to make do with poor little Lucy, shan't I, my sweet?' His finger coiled around a strand of her hair. I saw her wince as he caught a tangle.

'Lucy must go home with Ma. She can go with you another day perhaps?'

'There are no other days. We sail tomorrow on the evening tide. Gibraltar, then there's talk of the West Indies. After that, who knows? America, maybe. I shall not be back this year.'

'Why is that bobby staring at us like that?' It was Lucy spoke. She pointed across the park to the bandstand. 'Now he's coming over.' Everybody turned.

I felt the blood draining out of me. Lucy smiled like she had won a hundred pounds. 'Perhaps he's going to lock our Maggie up again.' Fortunately Pa was too drunk to take her meaning, but Frank took a step back suddenly, like someone had struck him in the face.

'Fred,' I said, and I could hear my voice shaking, 'I'd like you to meet my family.'

Fred held out his hand, smiling. Pa shook it without the faintest idea why he was doing so. 'I'm very pleased to meet you, sir. Maggie has often spoken of you and Mrs Robins to me.' Ma made a sort of hiccupping noise and glanced at me in horror. I shook my head so she knew it was just manners made him say so. He would have shaken her hand, but the baby got in the way, so he shook Will's instead, then Alfie's and Evelyn's who did him a beautiful curtsey and said, 'Maggie's going to be King when she grows up. And I'm going to be Queen.'

'In that case…' Fred took off his hat and bowed right down to the ground. 'Your Majesty.'

'Only if she learns her letters,' I said, which set her off reciting them like a little parrot.

Lucy practically jumped on him. 'And I'm Maggie's sister,' as though it was the most important thing in the world.

Fred smiled. 'And your name is Lucy. Am I right?'

'Yes,' said Lucy, real surprised. 'How do you know?'

'Maggie's told me about you.'

'What? What did she say?'

'Oh, that you are thirteen and good at singing, like your ma.'

Lucy went all pink. So did I, for I never said such a thing, only that her voice was better than mine which is not saying much.

Lastly he turned to Frank. Frank stared at him long and hard, hands stuffed in his pockets. Pa thumped him on the shoulder. 'Take the gentleman's hand, Frank, when he offers it to you.'

Slowly he obeyed. 'So you are a friend of Maggie's?'

'Yes, that's right.'

'How long have you known her?'

'Two years about. Is that right, Maggie?'

'Oh, about that,' I said, although I could have told him to the hour when we first met.

Frank smiled all warm and friendly. 'Well, I'm pleased to meet you, Constable. It's good to know my sister is in safe hands while I'm away. I'd never forgive myself if anything happened to her. We're very close, the two of us. I expect she told you?'

'I know she is very fond of all her family.'

'Yes she is. Very fond. And very close. Specially to me.' He clicked his fingers at Lucy. Next they are off across the park without a backward glance. I felt sick.

Pa gave a mighty belch. 'Time we was gone. I've ate nothing but pickled onions and a lump of cheese since dinner time and it's a mighty long walk back to Stepney.' This was enough to set Will howling. I gave Ma a florin and told her to be sure they took the bus, but quick as ninepence Pa had hold of it and was off to buy himself a tub of winkles. Fred was all for giving her another but Ma would have none of it so they all set off, trudging across the grass, Will wailing, Evelyn skipping and Alfie kicking everything in sight. I knew I should run after Ma with another florin, but I had set my heart on buying a new book of poems I had heard of, and I thought, they are used to walking, it is nothing new, and maybe Pa will give them some of his winkles. Then I thought, what will Fred think of me if I let them go, so I did run after them and Ma looked so relieved I swore to myself I would never be so mean-spirited again.

After they had gone, we walked back across the park and along under the trees. The ground was covered with tattered paper and shreds of torn ribbon, burst balloons, muddy from trampling. Neither of us spoke.

By the Round Pond we sat down. Fred took my hand and

held it between his. 'Thank you,' he said, so quietly.

'For what?'

'For letting me meet your family.'

I nearly choked. 'Did you *want* to meet them?'

He laughed. 'Of course I did. I was afraid you were ashamed of me, the way you never let me go home with you.'

'Ashamed of *you*...!' I stopped, for it was plain what I was thinking. Fred put his arm round me. 'I always wanted a big family. Brothers, sisters, aunts, cousins...people to care about. And to care about me.'

'You have your sister. You care about her, surely?'

'Yes, I do, very much. But there's only one of her. You've got so much choice.'

I laughed. 'It's just as well, for I get very tired of some of them.'

'Well, they certainly adore you, Maggie. Little Evelyn wants you to be King.'

'Only so she can be Queen.'

'You'd make a fine ruler.'

'Why would I?'

He sighed. 'Oh, because you are strong, and fair, and good, and generous, and people love you.'

Sometimes you say things that you never thought you would. 'Who loves me?'

Fred smiled. His eyes were so golden green I could have melted into them and drowned quite happily. 'Your ma and pa, and Alfie and Evelyn and Waily Will' (You would think Will would hold off just for an hour!) 'Lucy, I am not sure.'

'Oh, Lucy! She is just a mean little cat. She always has been. But did you like my family, Fred, apart from Lucy, I mean?'

'Lucy is a fine girl – will be.'

'Maybe. A hundred years from now. But what did you think of...?' My courage failed.

'Frank?'

'Is he not handsome?'

'Very.'

'He is kind, too, and generous. Everything you could hope for in a brother. Everything and more...' I heard the lies come tumbling out. If I could make Fred believe them perhaps that would make them true. Madness on madness. But I loved Frank. I loved him. Nearly as much as I loved Fred. You cannot stop loving someone because you love someone else more. You have to grow your love. And I wanted Fred to love him, too. Because if Fred loved him, that meant I could too. 'Would you not like him for a brother?'

He was silent.

'Don't even answer for there is no need.'

I looked up at him and for a moment his eyes seemed darker than before and, indeed, he did not answer, though he took my hand and held it very tight.

You think sometimes that your life is so perfect that it cannot get any better, and that day in June, I thought that. I knew that Fred loved me, though he had not said it. I could sense it in every hair on my head, bone in my body. He did not need to tell me and, indeed, it would have lessened it if he had, for we understood each other so completely that we were like one person. He was me and I was him. And at last I was free of Frank.

That summer was a busy time for us, but a jolly one.

Victory was in the air. The public was on our side and the Asquith man was becoming more and more a figure of fun.

Mrs Pankhurst and Miss Christabel had sensed that what the people liked was a show and they made sure we always gave them one. So it was, when two ladies who had broken the Prime Minister's windows were freed from Holloway, it was decided that women, rather than horses, should draw their carriage through the streets. This was a big mistake and very silly, in my opinion, for whoever thought six women could replace six horses? Still we learnt a lesson from it. The next time there were fifty women and it was great fun for we all took a turn.

One of the papers asked how many men it would take to achieve the same and offered a ten shillings prize for whoever came up with the answer. A writer called George Bernard Shaw hazarded that it would take five hundred, because men would have to talk about it to all their friends and then go to the horse sales to study the form, and so forth and altogether, by the time they had hired a man to train them for the task and hired someone else to look after their business while they were away pulling the carriage... He is quite a funny man and writes plays, Miss Kerr told me. If he is lucky enough to get one performed I shall certainly go and see it.

Miss Annie has been put in charge of the West Country. I miss her so much, although she sends regular news with often a note for me, for I think she thinks of me a little as a sister. We are all sisters, of course, but some more than others.

Still the Asquith ignores us. Another great rally. A thousand handbills: *HELP THE SUFFRAGETTES TO RUSH THE HOUSE OF COMMONS.*

It seems the word 'rush' was worse than treason and immediately officers came to arrest Mrs Pankhurst, Miss Christabel and poor Mrs Drummond, who is with child and can hardly give over being sick long enough to do treason on anyone. All day long bobbies, reporters, visitors tramped all over Lincoln's Inn, getting in each other's way and under each other's feet, but Mrs Pethick Lawrence had hidden them on the roof where no one thought to look and at least Mrs Drummond could be sick in peace for a few hours.

At six o'clock they appeared like magic and when they had had their photographs taken (poor Mrs Drummond looking quite green) they were marched off to Bow Street by Inspector Jarvis who is sweet on Mrs Drummond, although he may not be now she is such a funny colour.

That same afternoon a lady came to the office, offering to help. She said she would not demonstrate, but would be happy to speak to Mr Gladstone on behalf of the prisoners. Miss Lake muttered to Miss Kerr that she thought it a great cheek for the lady to suppose that she could achieve what Mrs Pankhurst could not, but Miss Kerr hushed her down and said the lady was a real Lady and had a brother who was a Lord.

The Lady smiled at me on her way out and I thought she had a very gentle pretty face although her ears stuck out more than I should wish. She did not look at all like the Ladies in the gallery pictures, so I think Miss Kerr must be mistaken. Also, I cannot truly believe a real Lady would care about others who were only women.

News arrived that Mrs Pankhurst and the others must spend the night in the cells because no judge could be found to let them out. This was a wicked thing, for they had no blankets or food or warm clothes with them and there are no beds in the cells, only hard wooden benches.

Mrs Pethick Lawrence said it must not be, and she rushed upstairs and collected a whole pile of bedding so that at least they need not die of cold. She asked if I would go with her to Bow Street for she does not like to be there alone since being put in the Black Maria van. We were just about to leave when a cab drew up and out stepped the Lady, looking mighty low for it seemed no one had listened to her.

Hearing we were on our way to the police station, she asked if she might accompany us. On the way she told Mrs Pethick Lawrence that till that day she had been merely interested in the Cause. 'But what I have witnessed today convinces me that I must do more than stand and watch. Real injustices are being done to women, and if I have any influence, any power, any compassion for my fellow human beings, I must put my shoulder to the wheel and cease to be a spectator to the suffering of others.'

I thought that very beautiful. If I ever am called on to make a speech that is what I shall say.

What a lark! When we got to Bow Street, what do we find? Mrs Pankhurst, Miss Christabel, Miss Sylvia and Mrs Drummond (looking much cheerier) sat round a great long table, white linen cloth, candles in silver holders, the sparkliest glasses you ever set eyes on, dining off partridges and oysters and a whole fruited jelly!

They had sent telegrams to such politicians as had befriended them before, and one had arranged with The Savoy to send over a dinner. Not only a dinner, but three starchy waiters to serve it! The poor young bobby left on watch did not know whether to salute them or arrest them.

The benches in the cells were draped in the finest silk sheets and coverlets so that, if it had not been for the bars on the window, they might have been staying in a palace. The Lady looked so confused as we entered with our great pile of blankets and bread and cheese that I think she was wondering if she was back home again.

They were charged with 'circulating a handbill likely to cause a breach of the peace'.

Miss Christabel called upon Mr Gladstone and Mr Lloyd George to be witnesses. They were very stuffy and dull and seemed not to understand a word that was said to them, which was hardly surprising for the judge spent the whole time interrupting and telling them they need not answer the question. Since, being Parliament men, they must have spent a lifetime not answering the questions that were put to them, they seemed quite content to obey him.

When it was her turn Mrs Pankhurst spoke most movingly of her work with the poor and homeless and told of all she had seen of their suffering. I was stood near the back by the door and I swear the sergeant guarding it had tears in his eyes. Not the judge, of course, who sentenced them to three months in the second division. I hope there is a heaven and hell and I am stood behind the judges when we all line up at The Reckoning.

While Mrs Pankhurst and Miss Christabel were in prison the Pethick Lawrences and Miss Sylvia took charge of the office. I must say that it was somewhat better organised than when Miss Christabel is there! I suppose it is because she is too clever and her head too full of wonderful speeches to be altogether bothered about paying bills and ordering stationery and the like.

The Lady has called in on several occasions. She is called Lady Constance Lytton and truly does have a brother called Lord Lytton. Imagine! A real Lord. I wonder what he looks like for I still think Lady Constance looks just like a normal person.

It seems she is working hard to bring her nob friends round. I can see it is a very good thing to have someone so highly placed on our side and, indeed, she is so genteel and gracious in her manner that it would be a very silly nob ignored her, but then most of them are, it seems to me.

She attends the weekly meetings and though she rarely speaks, what she says makes more sense than a whole half hour of some of them, ranting on about what colour pocket to keep their stones in and whether an umbrella is 'an instrument of violence'!

She never offers herself for the protests, I have noticed. Miss Kerr said it was because it would bring disgrace on her family if she were charged, but I have seen how her face pales when others talk of prison life and I think she fears it dreadfully. I warm to her so much for this, for it means I am not the only coward in the WSPU.

Mrs Drummond was released early, for her expecting was making her very ill. She said Mrs Pankhurst, too, had been moved to the prison hospital and she feared very much for her spirits in that dreadful place. She decided that the best tonic would be a demonstration.

One of the helpers made us prison dresses – green serge

with thick black arrows up them. Truth is, I hated mine. It scratched and tickled like fury, but the reporters were out with their cameras so I tried to look like I felt like the Queen of Sheba.

Mrs Drummond led the way, riding with Miss Sylvia, and we followed on, handing out leaflets and singing our hearts out with a brass band to keep us in tune (mainly). Hundreds of bystanders tagged along. Round and round the prison walls we tramped, singing and shouting encouragement to those within.

When at last we came to the hospital Mrs Drummond signalled everyone to stop. 'Three cheers for Mrs Emmeline Pankhurst, the noblest, bravest soul in all this land.'

What a cry went up! The people of London like to shout, for sure.

No one could be certain, but we thought we saw her shadow at a window. I pray it was her, and she slept the better for it. It is a terrible thing to be so alone and feel yourself forgotten.

At the beginning of December a strange thing happened. The Lloyd George man said he would address some Liberal ladies concerning women's votes. We do not get on very well with these ladies for they are against demonstrations and would rather just write letters and sit round tables talking, but it was decided that some of us should certainly attend to see what, if anything, he had to say.

We sat at the front in our prison dresses and made no sound, merely staring at him till he turned all sweaty and started dragging at his collar like it was stitched to his neck.

He had not got two minutes into his speech when one of our number sprang up with a speech of her own. The stewards tried to get at her but she had hold of a horse whip and kept flipping them away like they were so many bluebottles. After that every time the Lloyd George started, someone else interrupted, till the whole gathering seemed more like a music hall than a political meeting.

But there is a smell to a music hall. It is of warmth and beer and tobacco and spiced apples. There were no spiced apples that night, only sick, cold hatred between men and the women who might have been their wives if they only listened to them for half a moment. And from a music hall it grew very soon to a battleground, with the monstrous scurvy stewards hauling those women out by their hair, striking them about the head, ripping their clothes... And all for asking for justice. *How, how, HOW* have these animals got control of us? They are fit for nothing but to be thrown in the Thames and let them sink to the bottom and drown.

What is happening to me, that I wish death on people I have never known? Reverend Beckett would be proud of me. 'Their sins shall be visited upon them, even unto the third and fourth generation.' Do Reverends have sins? Or do they lay them off on those who are bound for hell anyway?

The press has not been kind to us of late. Seemingly the reporters think it our fault that men are driven to violence when we only ask for what should be ours of right. A number of women have formed themselves into a group to oppose the Cause. Naturally, they, none of them, have to earn a living or keep a family in boots and victuals, so I suppose they have no need to think of those that do. How Christian! But they have taken on a very powerful army and will learn to be sorry for their actions.

I fear sometimes I am not very Christian either.

Mrs Pethick Lawrence came rushing into the office two days before Miss Christabel was due to be released from Holloway. 'The most dreadful thing! Oh, ladies, I really don't know what to do about this one.' We gathered round.

A great procession had been organised to greet Miss Christabel and my first thought was that she was not to be set free after all.

'They are out.' Mrs Pethick Lawrence flapped her arms. 'They are out. Released early. I don't know what to do. Mrs Pankhurst as well. Both of them. Out. And no procession to greet them. Oh, what a mess.'

Mrs Drummond burst out laughing. 'But this is marvellous. Wonderful news. Better out without a greeting, than in and waiting for one, would you not say, dear lady?'

Mrs Pethick Lawrence immediately calmed down. 'Yes, of course. What am I at? Of course. Thank goodness for someone with a bit of sense, Flora. Sometimes I swear I am losing my mind entirely. I shall just have to cancel the procession. Are we too late to get word out, do you think, or shall I have to send them home as they arrive?'

'No need to send them home at all,' declared Mrs Drummond. 'Why don't we move the whole shebang to a hotel and instead of a march, have a meal? I'm sure I know which I'd prefer.'

Mrs Pethick Lawrence positively glowed with relief. 'That's

a brilliant suggestion, Flora. I shall set about it at once.'

I could have kissed Mrs Drummond, although I greatly wished Mrs Pethick Lawrence had not left her in charge of the menu for, her being expecting, there were a deal of pickled walnuts and curried mutton faggots to be got through before the pudding, and that, semolina with dried figs, which is not a favourite of mine.

When we had done eating, Mrs Pethick Lawrence rose to say how happy we were to have our leaders back amongst us and how deeply we had missed them during their absence.

Mrs Pankhurst stood up to reply and we all cheered, expecting her to urge us on to greater acts of defiance, whatever the ordeals awaiting us. Instead, she said nothing of the fight ahead but, speaking in a low still voice, recounted how, once you had been in prison it was like being two people. One for outside, who was brave and fiery and made bold speeches at great gatherings, and another for inside – alone, silent, deserted.

Everyone clapped when she had finished, but I could see, looking along the tables, that only those who had been through it had any idea of what she really meant. Just for one tiny second I felt that I was her true comrade at last and not just an ignorant working girl from Stepney.

Scarce a day goes by now without some article or report about the movement in the papers, even the ones the nobs read. Several groups of professional people have formed their own branches. There is The Artists' League with many of Miss Sylvia's friends in, The Women Writers' League, and my favourite, for they are so funny and pretty and generous beyond all reason, The Actresses' Franchise League. They have actors in it, too, and sometimes the men make speeches which are quite wonderful to hear because they boom and fling their arms about and really it is just like watching a proper play – better, sometimes. Everything they do is so full of colour and noise and excitement and they do not stand on ceremony, but talk to us office girls quite as if they had known us all their lives.

I should so like to have been an actress. Fred says I am one, for he never knows which me I will be when he next sees me. I love him so much it hurts. Yet still I cannot let him... He is so kind and patient, says we have all the time in the world and he can wait, but I can see that he is made unhappy by it. We have been walking out for over a year now. In my street there would be at least one baby on the way by then, married or not.

One night when I was sitting on his knee in Mrs Garrud's parlour he reached around and tried to undo the buttons on my blouse. I was off his knee faster than a lightning bolt. He just sat there staring at me, a look of such confusion in his eyes.

'Why do you do this, Maggie?'

'What?'

'You know what. Why will you not let me love you as I long to? What is it that you fear so? Do you think I would hurt you? How could you believe such a thing?'

'I... I do not know. I know you would not mean to hurt me but...'

He held out his hand. 'Come back, Maggie. Sit on my knee. I swear I will not touch you if you do not want it. See.' He spread his arms wide. 'I shall not move.' I crept back and he was true to his word, sitting with his arms stuck out like a scarecrow's. Just then Mrs Garrud's girl came in to put some more coals on the fire. She stared at us like we were fresh from Bedlam. When she had gone we fell into fits of laughter. I flung my arms round his neck and buried my face against his shoulder. 'Can I put my arms down now?' he begged.

'I think so.'

He folded them round me and just cradled me like I was a little hurt child. 'Oh, Maggie.'

'I'm sorry.'

'And now you're crying. I've made you cry with all my clumsiness.'

I wiped my eyes. 'You're not clumsy. You're…not… You're…not like other men. That's all.'

Fred gave a sort of sigh. 'No wonder you're crying then. But I fear you're wrong on that count. I'm just like other men.'

'Then it is me that's different.'

He kissed my ear. 'Yes, you are different. Different from every woman who ever lived. That is why I love you. Everything about you. Every part of you. Every hair on your head. And if I have to, I will wait forever till you love me the same way.'

I cried some more.

When he had gone home to his cold narrow room (he says he thinks it was once the meat pantry) I went upstairs to my warm soft bed. I took my clothes off and hung them on their hangers. Then I went to the mirror. I am not at all beautiful without my clothes. Indeed, if there is nothing blue or green near to my eyes I look like a boiled crab, so pink is my face. But the rest of me is not pink. It is pale – like cream – and soft and round. I have seen pictures of ladies in the galleries, some without their clothes on. I swear Fred takes me there on purpose. I hate it, for they never have hair where I have got it. I do not know if it is a disease that I have hair in all the wrong places and so much of it. I would ask Miss Annie but then she would know I have been looking at rude pictures and would never speak to me again. How could I let Fred see me, even if I wanted it, for he would think me an ape or very close?

I hate my body. I hate it. Every part of it. It is cursed. I will not think about it any more. My eyes are closed.

So on with my work.

Mrs Pethick Lawrence became nervous that there were so many new branches of the Women's Freedom League starting up, the WSPU would lose members to them. She put out a call in *Votes For Women* for new leaders to come forward and be trained because, as she said, there were so many young women in England who had more time on their hands than they knew what to do with. She gave me a copy and asked me to read it first and tell her how it struck me. I said it was very fine and would surely inspire all manner of ladies to apply.

'But... Maggie?'

'Excuse me, ma'am?'

'There is a huge "But" in your reply. Tell me where it leads.'

I have worked at Lincoln's Inn for nigh on two years now and I know who to trust and who not. Mrs Pethick Lawrence, I trust.

'You are right, ma'am, to say that there are ladies without occupation who would willingly step forward to become leaders...'

'But…'

'But you will find no one from the working classes because they cannot afford to leave their jobs.'

Mrs Pethick Lawrence became very thoughtful. 'Give me that back, Maggie.'

Half an hour later she handed me the new script. It was the same as before but added at the bottom: 'It may be some girl will read this and say: "Oh, I wish I were fortunate enough to be in an independent position – but I must work for my living."'

'Well, if you feel like that, write, or better still, come and see me or some other member of the committee. Every would-be organiser has to undergo a training and testing of three months and during that time a sum to cover board and lodging expenses is paid to her.'

She smiled at me. 'Will that do, do you think?' I felt truly startled to be asked and then listened to in this way.

'I'm sure it will, ma'am. I hope you did not mind me saying?'

Mrs Pethick Lawrence shook her head like a wet dog. 'I certainly do not, Maggie. I am most grateful. Just one more thing I would ask of you.'

'Anything, ma'am,' I said, relieved to be let off so lightly.

'You do promise me that you will apply, don't you?'

Ma could hardly believe it when I told her I am to train to be a leader. She kept starting to speak then stopping again till in the end I said, 'Ma, are you pleased or displeased? Just nod your head or shake it for I see you will never form a sentence again in your lifetime at this rate.'

She smiled and then suddenly she broke out laughing. I can't remember when I last saw her do that. Not since I was very little. Before Samuel... She laughed and laughed, and poor Will who was in the middle of trying to pull her hair out just sat there and stared as though he'd been struck by lightning. At last she stopped.

'Oh, Maggie. It's more than I ever dreamt. I am so proud of you,' and she sort of flapped her hands around as though she did not know what to do with them.

'And I am to keep my wages while I train so you need not fear for that.'

'It would not matter,' but I could tell she was relieved.

It was a Thursday when I called and the house empty but for the little ones. Even Evelyn was off at the Poor School. Ma says she is doing really well and has twice gone out the front to say a psalm. I said if she carried on that way I should soon be enrolling her as a speaker.

I heated us a pie for dinner. Little Ann has two teeth and though they looked sore to me, she makes no fuss. I fed her so Ma could eat in peace, if you don't count Will snivelling for he had burnt his mouth on a potato. When we had done I brewed some tea and we sat by the hearth talking. I asked about Alfie. Ma says he is still at his job and is sweet on a girl in the bakery. He goes in every day to buy a bun and she gives him the one with most sugar on it. She says it is a good thing he has such a hard job or he would be fatter than a Christmas hog by now.

Lucy has started work cleaning at the alehouse. I said I hoped she kept it cleaner than she does her own room or she would be out of the job pretty fast.

Ma sighed. 'She likes it there. I wish she could find something else, for to tell the truth, there are some rough types drink there.' I wondered if she meant Pa! Though he is a lot softer than some of the men in this street.

When it was time to go Ma came to the door with me. She had that look of wanting to say something but not being able to. Usually I would have gone not knowing, but since we had been so warm together that day I said, 'What is it, Ma?'

She fumbled with her shawl. 'Nothing. Only I just wanted to... Frank did not mean to be cold to you that day in the park, you know. He was very sorry for it after.'

'It was nothing, Ma. He was disappointed I could not go out with him, that's all.'

'Yes, of course. That's all it was.' Suddenly she threw her arms round me and hugged me to her. 'Thank you, Maggie.' I could think of no reply since I did not know for what I was being thanked.

'Bye, Ma. I will come again soon.'

She smiled and turned to go back in. On the back of her neck, just below her ear I saw a shiny white lump.

Part of my duties in my training is to organise 'knocking at the door'. This means sending people to call on the politicians at home. Mrs Pankhurst's sister, Mrs Clarke, went to the Prime Minister's house itself. She was arrested for her pains. It seems strange to me that a person can be charged for knocking at a door. Soon they will be arresting the delivery men, I daresay, and then the postman. I said as much to Mrs Pethick Lawrence and next I know she has got her faraway look. 'I think you have given me an idea, Maggie. Yes, a very good idea.'

Me and my ideas! I am only to be delivered to the Asquith man as a human letter! Fortunately I am to have a companion for I really think I should die of fright on my own.

Miss Annie's sister, Jessie, was put in charge of us. At ten o'clock the three of us went down to the post office and Miss Jessie marched straight up to the counter, bold as brass. 'I want to send a human letter.' The poor man behind the counter looked mighty confused. He went away to ask his superior and we could hear a load of laughing from the back room. When he came back he brought a form which Miss Jessie had to fill in and then, after she had paid the threepence, we set off with a telegraph boy – a jolly lad who said it was the best job he'd been given since he started.

We must have made a peculiar sight, him in the middle, one side my helper holding the address, and me on the other with a giant placard: *VOTES FOR WOMEN – DEPUTATION – HOUSE OF COMMONS – WEDNESDAY.*

We were stopped at Downing Street by three policemen but when the lad showed his papers they let him through. No sooner is he in Number Ten than he is out again, followed by a frost-faced butler. 'You must be returned.'

'But we have been paid for.' He would have none of it. We told him it was the law he should accept us, but still he shook his head. In the end we gave up, but not before the reporters had clicked and flashed away with their cameras and sure enough, we were on the front of every paper next morning.

Fred came charging round to Mrs Garrud's with his copy. He said every man at his station had bought a paper that day and that he had been much ribbed for walking out with a piece of female mail. (I can see that would be funny the first time.)

'But they all agreed you were the prettiest letter they'd seen in a long time.'

'I don't suppose that will stop them blacking both my eyes if they get the chance, will it?'

'Maggie, we're not like that at Marylebone. You know we're not. Besides—'

'Besides what?'

'I told them you'd been stamped enough already so I'd deal with anyone who tried to do it again.'

Mrs Pethick Lawrence is to lead the deputation on Wednesday. We are to book no engagements for her after that date as it is reckoned she will surely be arrested. I think I must try for it, too, as I cannot bear to think of her in the van without anyone she knows nearby.

Wonders, indeed! Lady Constance is coming, too. She came into the office the other afternoon and asked to see Mrs Pethick Lawrence. Miss Sylvia took her upstairs and when the three of them came down they were all smiling, though Lady Constance looked a little nervous, it must be said. 'Lady Constance has decided to join us on the 24th,' said Mrs Pethick Lawrence. 'We must make sure we take good care of her. Maggie, I shall ask you to stay by her on the night.'

I was so taken aback that I leapt out of my seat and did not know whether I should curtsey or what. Before I could decide Lady Constance stepped forward. 'I shall try not to let you down, Maggie', she said most gravely and held out her hand to me, just as if I was her equal. I saw that she expected me to shake it. This I did, but in a very wavery silly way, murmuring about 'me letting her down, more like and it being a very great honour', as if being beaten with a truncheon was the finest thing that could happen to you. She must have thought me an enormous fool.

Not just a fool, but a failure, for surely I failed Lady Constance that night. 'Stay by her'? 'Take good care of her'? What could I do? Hold back the sea? Beat a path through the middle of a hundred butchering bobbies? Force them back with a single glare? Maybe Miss Christabel could do it. Or Mrs Pankhurst. But not me. Not Maggie Robins. There are no miracles in me.

Such a rough, cruel night. The weather was foul and foggy and we had scarce left the assembly hall before the police began to jostle us, crushing us together so that there was hardly room to move. I stuck close to Lady Constance and tried to pretend all was well and this was normal practice.

She said nothing but just pressed silently on, head down, as though she were struggling through a tunnel. I caught sight of her face beneath her hat. She looked very frightened. I urged her to move faster for if we could clear the main crowd she would be able to rest and recover herself a little, but even as I spoke a great thug of a policeman flung himself between us, thrusting us apart. I heard her cry out. When I looked round she was holding her head and staggering. She seemed close to fainting. I fought to get back to her but the crowd kept surging forward, dragging me away. I durst not shout her name for fear the bobbies would hear and seize her. Further and further she was sucked into the swirl, hands clutching the air like a drowning sailor. Then she was gone. The last I saw was her black hat bobbing like a piece of driftwood, this way and that until it, too, disappeared.

Sick to my very soul, I struggled on as best I could, but it was a wild ugly business. The police acted worse than Liberal louts, picking us up and flinging us like rags back into the crowd. Some women fell directly in the road, others had their heads cracked against the walls. The people, horrified, helped us up and formed a shield around us, begging us to give in. On we went. On and on. And all the time me wondering what had happened to the Lady and cursing myself for not being able to save her.

I was never so glad to be arrested. I had begun to fear it would not happen and I must keep pressing forward till every bone in my body was shattered. I never thought to be glad to see a prison cell, but that night I was. And the gladder by a million miles, for when I got to the police station there was Lady Constance, slumped on a bench between Mrs Pethick Lawrence and Mrs Despard. I thought they would chide me for taking such poor care of her, for she looked truly wiped out – worse even than they did, but they nodded in a weary sort of way and whispered something to Lady Constance. Slowly she opened her eyes and, seeing me, smiled so kindly and tried to raise her hand in greeting before I was taken through to where they put the poor women.

So now I am back in Holloway. I should be used to it. More socks, more soup, more praying. Lady Constance and Mrs Despard are in the hospital wing. They have shorter sentences. I know it is the way of things and I should be glad, for poor Lady Constance suffered grievously that night, but it is hard not to wonder why ten women may be charged with the same offence and the rich and famous go home after a few days, while poor, sorry creatures such as myself must grind away our time a full two months. I wonder, when Miss Christabel's new world is on us, whether it will be any different.

I am always low in prison. I pass the hours dreaming about freedom – my cottage in Wood Green, with a swing and flowers, and Fred coming home of an evening, and us sitting together and being safe and happy. But then the shadows come and I think, how can I go on like this? How can I spend half my life in prison and the other half with the man who puts me there? I know it is not Fred, and he would never, ever do that, but how long can he keep himself free of it? It is his duty, just as this is mine.

Does he even think of me when I am away? Would it not be better for us to part, for I am sure if things continue thus, I shall be forced to betray either him or the Cause. And, God help me, I do not know which it will be.

Free at last! I am like a mole coming out of its tunnel, blinking in the sunlight, sniffing the clean air after long weeks in the damp stinking earth. And what things have taken place in our absence! The movement is a great snowball rolling downhill, gathering more and more snow as it travels till it is so huge and powerful that castles would fall before it. I did not think of that. I read it in a pamphlet.

Suffragettes have chained themselves to the grille in the Ladies' Gallery in Parliament, so now it has had to be closed, then to statues in the House of Commons, and to railings. Miss Kerr said the Asquith man is hated everywhere for there has been a demonstration by men without work as well as all of ours. I could not help thinking if they all took to being ironsmiths they should have occupation enough to keep them going a lifetime.

Some women from Lancashire came down for a deputation and this, too, ended in violence. One of those who took part was in the office on my first day back. Her name is Miss Davison. She is monstrous clever and knows it. She has a degree from Oxford and never tires of telling us or rather, showing us, for all her talk is full of Greek and Latin. We know this because she translates it for us after. I had it on my tongue to ask why she did not just give us the English and be done with it since she plainly thought us all fools.

She is full of ideas on how things should be done, and done better. One of the ways, it seems, is for each last one of us to go to prison and when there, make as much fuss and trouble as we can so that the King himself will be forced to take notice.

I asked her which prisons she had been in herself. She said, 'None, at present, but *nihil ad rem*, what of that? I shall be there shortly and then I shall light a fire under them.'

I thought, yes, well, wait till you've spent a week on slops and stale water and see how many fires you light then.

Fred came to call for me on my first night home. He looked tired and anxious and though he took my hand and squeezed it very tight, I could tell there was something bad coming. He took me to a corner house and bought me a great big slab of chocolate cake as he always does when I have been in prison.

'Maggie, I must talk to you.'

I could hardly bear to look at him for I knew what was coming. 'Maggie, while you were away I did something you may not like.' Then I did look at him for I thought he was going to tell me he had found another sweetheart, and who could blame him? What use to a policeman is a girl who spends half her life urging people to break the law and the other half imprisoned for her troubles?

'I went to see your ma and pa.'

The chocolate turned to vinegar. 'What?'

'I went to see them. When I knew you were gone for two whole months – I was afraid they would worry if you did not visit…'

'They are used to it. And now you have told them the reason. Pa will never let me through the door again.'

'I did not tell them where you were. I just said you were away. Now you are in training they did not think it odd, although I do believe your ma knows as much of your activities as I do.'

I was silent for a moment. 'Yes, she will know from Miss Annie or Miss Sylvia, but Pa knows nothing. He would go wild if he did.'

Fred took my hand. 'I promise you he learnt nothing from me.'

'Were they not surprised to see you?'

'Yes, a little. They made me most welcome. Evelyn offered to wash my hair and Alfie showed me a box he was carving.'

'That house will look like a funeral parlour if he makes many more.'

Fred laughed. 'There were rather a lot, but the baby sleeps in one and Will has another for a boat, and your pa keeps his boots in another.'

'Was Ma well?'

'She seemed a little tired. Her neck aches, she said.'

'How was Lucy? Was she there?'

Fred hesitated. 'She was there.'

'As sullen as usual, I suppose?'

'No, not sullen. Not at all.' He looked away and I could see that he was flushed.

My heart turned over. 'Oh, why did you have to go? Why could you not have let matters be?'

Fred sat staring at his hands like they were someone else's. 'I went because I care about you. That is all.'

'And now you see how my family lives, you no longer care?' A distant voice coming out of my head, not mine at all.

'No. No. How can you say that? Lucy is Lucy. She is not you. They are none of them you, but they are a part of you, and if I cannot be with you, see you, they are all I have. Can you not understand? You, you have this Cause of yours, and all your comrades and fellow suffragettes, but when you are gone and locked away, I have nothing but my fears, my dreadful apprehensions. That is why I went.'

For the first time in my life I understood that love could hurt as well as heal. He looked so lonely, hunched up over his fists and I thought, yes, I have taken everything from you and given so little in return. I touched his hand. 'Thank you.'

'For what? All I have achieved is making you angry.'

'Not angry. Anxious, I suppose, but not now. Now I see the reason. You are the best man who ever lived, Fred. Whatever happens, that is what I believe. Now and forever.'

We walked home neither of us speaking, each a million miles away in our own thoughts. When we came to my door he turned to go. I caught hold of his arm. 'Will you not come in?'

'Maggie, it's very late. Mrs Garrud will not welcome a visitor at this time of night.'

'Mrs Garrud is not in.' It came out so fast. Like a bullet. And sure, Fred looked at me like I had fired one. 'She's away visiting her sister. Mr Garrud is home but he will be in bed at this hour.'

Fred cleared his throat. 'Maggie, I don't know.'

'Why not?' I could feel the courage dripping out of me.

'Well, because it's not entirely proper for…for… Maggie, I don't know I can trust myself, that's all. I really don't, and that's the truth.'

My head was swimming, half panic, half this great quivering urge to be truly his. To belong to him. To show him how much I loved him. To give him something back.

'Please – just for a little while.'

He looked at me for a full minute, I swear, then oh, so slowly, he nodded his head. 'I should like that, Maggie. Very much.'

We went into the parlour. I lit the lamps and poked around at the fire that was all but out. 'Shall I make some tea? Would you like a cup of tea?'

Fred sat down on the settee, like he was waiting to be interviewed for Chief Constable. 'That would be very nice.'

I scurried off and made some. As I came into the hall I bumped smack into Mr Garrud. 'Oh, it's you, Maggie. I heard voices. Thought we might be being burgled.' He chuckled for we all know no one would dare to burgle the Garruds' house unless they wanted to end up as mincemeat. I stood there with my tray with two cups and a plate of cinnamon biscuits on it, going redder by the second.

'I'm just…I…some tea…biscuits…'

Mr Garrud nodded. 'Yes, by all means. He works hard, your young man. And that landlady of his is no cook, from what I hear. Well, good night, Maggie, my dear, and don't get cold, the pair of you, for that fire's nearly out in the parlour.' And off he went, up the stairs without a second glance. The whole world was pushing me in one direction. Did I want to go? I don't know.

Fred had quit the settee and was standing by the window, peering out through a crack in the curtains. He turned as I came in and seemed terribly pleased to see the biscuits.

'Mrs Garrud will not mind us having them, for I gave her the recipe from Cook and can easy make some more,' I wittered.

'Oh, good. They look…very good.'

'They're cinnamon.'

'Oh. Good.'

I set down the tray. Fred did not move.

'I have made some tea.'

'Oh. Good.' He glanced once more out of the window. Again he cleared his throat. 'I think there will be a frost tonight.'

'Yes, it was very cold out. So will this tea be, if you don't drink it soon.'

He came away from the window and stood by the tray, staring down at it so hard that I thought he had forgotten I was in the room. Indeed, I began to wish I was not.

'Would you like some sugar?'

'Yes. Yes, please. Just one spoonful.'

How I wished I could do with so little, for then I would surely not get spots.

In goes the sugar. We both stir our tea.

'Will you have a biscuit, Fred?'

'Yes. Thank you.'

I picked up the plate. I know not what happened, for I am strong as an oxen, but I dropped it. All over the rug. Biscuits everywhere.

'Oh.'

Down we go on our knees. Suddenly we are face to face.

'Maggie...'

'I love you, Fred.'

'I love you.'

And then we were kissing like we were the last two people on earth, clinging so nothing could come between us, his fingers fumbling with a thousand buttons. I went to help him but he shook his head. 'Lie back. Lie still.'

I lay back on the rug, eyes half closed, my heart beating fit to burst. A shiver of cool air. Me. My flesh. Air. I heard him catch his breath. I felt his fingers touch my skin and though he did not hurt me, it was as though lightning had run right through me. I gasped. He looked at me then, very gently, he bent down and began to kiss my belly. I could feel his lips, his tongue, lower and lower. It was like drowning in honey. I wanted it to last forever.

He kissed every part of me. I don't even know if it was kissing. More like melting my soul. My whole inside was shivering and burning at the same time. Somewhere a clock struck. The fire was long dead in the grate. We lay together as though we were one being.

I asked, 'Am I a woman now?'

'You were always a woman.'

'Like Ma, I mean. A proper woman.'

He smiled and kissed my nose. 'Nearly.'

'Will I have a baby?'

'No.'

'Are you sure?'

He leant up on his elbow and kissed my fingers one by one. 'Yes. Maggie, you will never have a baby from me till we are married. That I promise you.' My heart leapt higher than the sky.

He tucked my shawl around my shoulders. 'You must get to bed. And I must go home. Or Mrs Blackett will be after me with a frying pan for waking her up.'

'Yes. Must you? Go? I'm not tired. Not even a bit.'

He laughed. 'Neither am I, but I will be tomorrow when I have to be on duty at half past seven.'

I went with him to the door, him carrying his shoes for fear of waking Mr Garrud. As he turned to go I caught hold of his hand, his beautiful warm, strong hand. 'Fred... I... Thank you.' He smiled.

Next morning I went back to the office, and though nothing had been moved or changed while I was in prison, the curtains seemed suddenly brighter and the chairs more comfortable and everything – even the dusty old reeds in a pot by the door – looked fresh and welcoming and new. Or perhaps it was me. I listened to all that had been going on – how Miss Davison had been chased by a great big dog when she went to nail up a poster, and how a group of mill girls had got all the way into the Parliament lobby, pretending to be tourists, and all sorts of wonderful things, but all the while my heart was singing, 'He loves me. He loves me. Love is so wonderful. I am nearly

a woman. When we are married I will be a real one. It cannot
be better than nearly being one, surely? Supposing it is? I shall
die of happiness on my wedding night.' Miss Lake asked me
what I was beaming about. I said, 'Oh, just to be free again,
Miss Lake.'

She humphed and said that was all very well but there was
a deal of work that had piled up in my absence and perhaps I
would like to make a start on the backlog. I wonder if Miss
Lake has ever been nearly a woman. I wonder if any of them
have. I cannot think so or they would not be so cross about
men all the time.

Miss Sylvia came rushing into the office today, quite pink with
excitement. She is usually in a rush but hardly ever happy
about it. 'Oh, Maggie, goodness knows how I am to do it. It
is so huge and really there is next to no time. Still, it is such a
challenge I would never forgive myself if I turned it down.
What I need now is...' and she was off, burrowing through
the cupboards like a bloodhound on the trail of a cutthroat.

I was desperate to know what was going on so after the
third crash and a rather loud *ouch!* from the storeroom I
asked Miss Kerr if I should check if Miss Sylvia needed any
help.

'Oh, yes, do. And try not to let her destroy the entire
place, will you, Maggie? Those files took me months to sort
out.'

Miss Sylvia was slumped against a cabinet, thumbing
through a pile of postcards. All around lay posters, banners,
photographs, newspapers. Had I not known her better I
would have said the place had been hit by an earthquake.

She looked up as I entered. 'What I'm thinking of is a mural along the main wall made up of panels, you see. What do you think of this?' waving a picture of an angel with a bugle at me. I said I liked it very much.

'But for the mural? For the main motif?' Head in her hands. 'Oh, I knew I should never have said yes. I haven't an idea in the world. Blank. Completely blank.'

I said nothing, feeling just as blank myself. At length she raised her eyes again and gave a great helpless shrug. 'Maggie, you must think me mad.'

'Not mad exactly...'

She laughed. 'But near enough to make no difference, I know. No, it shall be done. I can do it. With help I can do it. I just have to think it through logically.'

'I would very much like to help, miss, if you would like me to, only...'

'Oh, I should. Only what?'

'Only I don't know what you're talking about.'

Miss Lake came in to see what we were laughing about. She went out again very quickly when she saw the state of the room but not before her face had quite iced over.

There is to be a great exhibition. The Prince's Skating Rink has been taken for three whole weeks and Miss Sylvia has been put entirely in charge of the decorations.

She has rented a studio in Fulham just for that. 'You are most welcome to call any time you like,' she told me. 'Why don't you bring your young man?' (knowing he likes paintings).

Fred was most keen when I told him. 'We can go tomorrow after I finish at the station. Why are you smiling?'

'I was just thinking of what your fellow officers would say if they knew where you were going.'

'Oh, well, I could always say I was doing it to spy on you.'

I tried to laugh.

When we arrived we could hardly believe our eyes. Great canvases, twenty feet high or more, were stretched along the walls, and working at them like Hebrew slaves, a team of students from Miss Sylvia's old art college, some tottering on rickety old chairs, others balanced on planks between two stepladders to reach the top. She said they had all been at it day and night and still could not be certain to be finished.

Fred was truly enthralled. He even offered to lend a hand, for some of the helpers looked extremely tired. Next thing, we are both of us wrapped up like fishermen in great oilskin smocks and splashing away at a great high bunch of angels till our arms felt fit to fall off.

Miss Sylvia was really pleased with our efforts. She said she was sorry she had no cake to offer us but if we would like to come again on Saturday, she would make sure she had some in. Fred said he would come anyway. I think he fancies himself as a painter, although to speak true, his hair was yellower than his angel's when he had done. Why do angels always have fair hair? Fred has, and he is an angel. Mine is dark.

I have been charged with arranging the programmes. I had not believed so much could go on in one hall. There will be bands, dancing, fortune-tellers, displays, stalls... A rich American has promised us an ice cream soda fountain. I am not sure what this is, but Miss Davison said it was like nectar from the gods which, I daresay, she has drunk on many an occasion.

Mrs Garrud is to mount a display of jiu-jitsu. She has asked me to be in it and though I have tried to think of every excuse, she has been so good to me I dare not disappoint her. She has promised to find me a longer coat.

It has been a triumph! *Triumphus spectaculosus!* Guess who came up with that! So many visitors, and such joy and cheerfulness all around. There was a whole stall full of different sorts of jam. I bought three pots – raspberry, bramble and a yellow one called 'lemon curd' for Cook. Miss Sylvia promised to deliver them to her for me and the next day came back with a sheet of Mrs Roe's writing paper. It said: 'DEaR MaGGE, ThaNC yo FoR Mi JaM. CooK.' Well, I thought, I would never have made a schoolteacher.

One table was entirely covered with the most beautiful hats in the world, with a great long mirror for ladies to admire themselves in. Whenever things went quiet I and two or three other helpers would rush off over to it and try as many on as we could before the real customers appeared. Mr Pethick Lawrence spotted me one day when I was swishing around in a great feathery straw.

'Do you like that one, Maggie?'

'I do, sir, but I think maybe I would need a big car and servants to go with it.'

He laughed. 'Maybe you're right. More for a Prime Minister's wife, perhaps?'

I took it off right fast.

At the end, when the clearing up was done and the money counted, Mr and Mrs Pethick Lawrence took all the office staff out to supper. After the ices they both made a short speech to say how grateful they were and how proud of us all. They gave special thanks to Miss Sylvia who went red as strawberries and said she could not have done one thing without her helpers. I felt like standing up and saying, 'That's not true, for I know Miss Sylvia and she would have painted the whole hall single-handed if she'd had to,' only I lacked the courage.

Mr Pethick Lawrence then made a great show of getting ready to go home when his wife caught him by the arm and said, 'My dear, haven't you forgotten something?' And he looked all surprised and confused, but not very convincingly – more like a man in a comedy.

'Ah, yes, my dear. Now what can it be?' And down he goes under the table and pulls out the biggest cardboard box you ever saw. He opens it up and inside, can you believe, he has bought each and every one of us a hat from the hat table. And they are all different and all quite, quite beautiful. Miss Christabel's was purest white with a mass of violet feathers, Miss Sylvia's the softest green, oh, all so beautiful. I was half fearful when it came to my turn that I should have the straw with all the feathers, but instead I had a lovely blue felt with a dark blue ribbon and the tiniest pale blue veil. I could have cried with happiness. Mr Pethick Lawrence whispered to me as he gave it to me, 'I hope you are not disappointed, Maggie. I just didn't think you'd like to marry Mr Asquith.'

'I should rather be dead, sir.'

He smiled. 'No need for that, I hope.'

I told Fred when I showed it to him. He looked at me hard, as though he was trying to make up his mind about something.

'Blue is much better,' he said at last. 'And very suitable.'

'Suitable for what?'

'For a policeman's wife, of course.'

A policeman's wife. And a suffragette?

Last night I lay and looked at my blue hat. I have hung it on a hook right opposite my bed so I can gaze and gaze at it till I fall asleep. It is so fine. So soft. So beautiful. Fit for a real lady. But I am not a real lady, nor ever will be. My best hope is for Fred to make me a real woman. There is no shame in that. The shame is in being wed to one of the Asquith's policemen. What am I to do? I *cannot* give him up. I cannot.

I will not think about it any more. My eyes are closed.

I suppose, because everyone had worked so hard and put so much into the exhibition, we all felt a little flat and dull afterwards. It was difficult to start back over, knowing as we did that we were not much nearer our goal than we had been a year ago or even two.

Mrs Pankhurst noticed this and was not pleased! Orders went out that we were to attend every by-election, every political gathering where a Cabinet Minister was present. Up and down the country we were to be ahead of them, drumming up support before they had even stepped off the train or out of their smart black cars.

The Liberals had got so afraid of us that we were banned from their meetings altogether and had to think of clever ways to get inside the halls. The actresses were brilliant at this.

I wrote to see if they could give us advice on how to disguise ourselves as men and they decided they would do better than that, and organised classes for us where we learnt to walk like men, talk like men (well, lads), and, all in all, behave like men. Miss Davison suggested we put a bucket in the middle of the room and all practise spitting, but it was generally felt that even the commonest men would not dare spit with a Cabinet Minister on the stage. She was a bit miffed at this and went off to practise on her own.

The politicians are as frightened as mice and go everywhere with an army of bobbies to protect them. In Sheffield the Asquith had to be sneaked out through a back door like a stolen sack of potatoes. The papers had fine fun with that, some suggesting he might be booked to appear in the pantomime for he was so good at magically vanishing himself.

June 29<sup>th</sup> is to be our biggest demonstration yet. We are to petition the King. I cannot believe the Parliament will allow us through though, for every time we try a new way they find a law to use against us and those they cannot find, they invent, it seems to me.

Miss Wallace Dunlop, an artist friend of Miss Sylvia's, has made a great rubber stamp with the words of the bill on it and stamped them on the wall outside the House of Commons. The first time it smudged so she was let go, but she went right back with a second one and there it is: *IT IS THE RIGHT OF THE SUBJECT TO PETITION THE KING* in purple letters all along the wall of St Stephen's Hall.

This is my first real night as an organiser. Yes, I have been trained and put in charge of printing and lists and arranging stalls and even paying some bills, but tonight I have my own team – eight women, two of them nobs, and all instructed to

follow my bidding. I feel sicker than when Fred first came to
see me fighting.

We are to break the windows of the Foreign Office and,
because it is feared we will meet with rough treatment, we
are all parcelled up like china vases. Padded vests and
woollens, and inside our skirts in a hidden pocket, a bag of
stones. I am twice the size I was this morning. If Fred should
see me now I think he would never buy me another piece of
chocolate.

He is on duty tonight, I know, and dreading it. I wonder
sometimes how he can do his job. He says there are other
ways to stop a crime than hurting someone, but it is a message
he has yet to sell to his fellows. Not all of them. Many of the
bobbies are family men and truly hate to see the women flung
about and beaten. The trouble is they are the ones who hang
back, while it is the wild young bloods that lay about us with
their belts and truncheons.

What can it be in a man that he must loose his anger on the
weak? Do they fear us so much? I hope so, for that would help
me to bear it.

I am no leader. I am worse than useless. At the very moment
when we should hurl our stones I find three of my ladies are
shaking like leaves and cannot find their pockets. I say,
'Sisters,' (we must always address each other as such, though
it is very hard when you know half of them are wearing silk
camisoles) 'make ready.' Comes this whinnying sound like a
half-dead horse, and one of them has a pot of smelling salts
up her nose, with the others hanging on her heels to be next.

The Foreign Office, to be sure, is a mighty fine building and

I can understand that it is a shame to ruin its beauty, but it is *only* a building.

I said, 'What is it you fear? To be arrested or to throw a stone at a window?'

Much shivering.

I thought, well, if they will not do it, then I must, or the whole team will be disgraced. I pulled a stone out and without another word, flung it as hard as I could.

Can you believe that in a building that is more window than wall, I managed to miss? My stone bounced off the bricks and clattered away into the basement. Within nobody stirred. Nobody even turned from their chattering. Nobody noticed.

Suddenly, like a bullet, something flashes by my head and next we know, there is an enormous explosion, or so it sounded, for it was the shattering of a huge, tall window, ceiling to floor. I turned and there, looking as though she had just been crowned queen of the whole world, is my timidest lady, still shivering, but now with excitement and delight.

The others, seeing what smelling salts could bring about, were after her, raining down stones on that building till there was not a pane of glass at ground level.

I grasped another pebble and flung it like I was sending it to the end of the world. We threw and we threw till our arms were fit to fall off and then we were marched away singing to the police station. And all the while the reporters popped their cameras and the crowd cheered and cheered and, I know not why, I thought of Jesus riding into Jerusalem on Palm Sunday, and I wondered if they would still be cheering one week on.

*    *    *

Good old Holloway! I am in the same cell as the first time I was brought here. How strange to think how many have lain on this splintery plank since then or sat on this rickety chair. On the underside is carved *Fight On and God Will Give The Victory* all rough and crooked, and today I was given a spoon with *Christabel Forever* scratched on the handle. I thought perhaps if I got a fresh one I might write *Maggie Forever* but no one would fathom that so I shall put *Sylvia* instead. I bet, if she is brought here, there will be a whole canteen with *Emily Forever* from Miss Davison.

Word has gone out that Miss Dunlop has been released. She refused all food and took only water for four whole days in protest at our treatment. By the end she became so weak and feeble that they would not even care for her in the hospital and sent her home.

In chapel this morning a note dropped on my prayer book. *Hunger strike commences tomorrow morning, 8 o'clock. Pass it on.* So we are all to do it. Oh Lord, give me strength, for all that keeps me going in here is the thought of my next meal.

Today was truly dreadful. Breakfast time passed well enough, for the bread is so foul that it takes little resolve to refuse it, but by dinner I was starving. So much so that when the wardress brought in the soup it smelt as good to me as Cook's. I drank a lot of water and turned my head to the window so that I need not see it. After an hour she took it away, thank God, for although it was chilled and floating in fat I think I would have had to eat some, had it remained much longer.

Usually I look forward to Exercise but today I felt tired and cold and had to drag my feet round the yard. All of us looked pinched and weary but when we saw each other we all smiled and raised our hands in salute and after that I felt a good deal stronger. I thought, these are ladies; they have education and money and fine houses. Why should they care about me with my nine stupid psalms and my knitting and cooking? And I knew in another world, the world outside the prison walls, they would not see me, would not know I was born. But here, in this great burial ground of freedom I was what they were – a tiny breath of air. Escaping.

By supper I was past caring, my stomach cramped in knots as though someone had kicked me. I drank more water and finally fell asleep but my dreams were all of pork and chocolate cake and warm sweet milk. I woke a dozen times, aching with hunger, and it seemed to me that in the morning I should have to give in, no matter what.

As it happened I had no choice for I was so stupid with fatigue that I had not finished scrubbing my cell when breakfast came round and so the wardress passed straight by without a word.

I am ashamed to say I cried and cried till the chaplain came by and told me God was punishing me for my wicked ways, which so vexed me that I asked him why God should punish me for following our Lord's example. He went very purply red and roared, what did I think I was talking of, taking the Lord's name in vain? I said I was not, only our Lord had gone without His food for forty days and nights in the wilderness, and it was generally agreed to have been a fine thing He had done at the end of it.

The chaplain went stamping off. I think if he could he would have had me whipped, not for taking the Lord's name in vain, but for knowing my scriptures better than he did.

The time passes so slowly. I cannot knit, my hands are trembling like an old woman's and my fingers ache and clack when I try to bend them. My head is thumping. I am so cold. I have nearly finished my water. My belly feels puffed out yet there can be nothing in it. I managed to pull my belt in a whole hole! That cheered me up for, though Fred says I am quite perfect as I am, I would like to trim my waist another inch.

I must have slept. There has been no sign of dinner and yet the guards are calling us down for Exercise. We all look bruised with weariness, great dark circles round our eyes, hair stiff and dirty for we drink our washing water to keep from fainting. A dozen of us, dragging ourselves round the yard. I saw some of the other prisoners staring at us. I had always thought them poor wretched creatures but today they looked a sight better served than we did.

Miss Garnett, who is a good brave soul, winked at me and whispered, 'Courage. The battle will soon be won.'

I felt like answering, 'And if it is not?' but doubt is a worse sin than murder in our movement so I nodded and tried to smile.

Later, when we were back in our cells I heard a tapping on the wall. I tapped back.

'Can you hear me?' came a faint voice.

'Yes.'

'This evening, when they have taken away the supper we are to break our windows. Miss Christabel has organised photographers. When the clock strikes eight. That is the signal.'

'How?' was all I could think of.

'With your shoe. With anything. Can you do it?'

'I do not know. I am very tired. My arms hurt so much.'

There was a silence. 'Well, it is up to you. I was told you were one of our leaders.'

I waited until the brute had closed the door. They have given us fish for supper, hoping, I suppose, that the smell would make it harder to resist, but tonight I scarce noticed it. I took my knife (bent piece of tin, more like) and hacked and sawed at my wobbly chair till I could turn one leg in my hand. I wriggled it and wrenched it and finally it broke away clean with a snapping sound that could be heard in the Governor's office, I would not wonder. I held my breath, fearful that the brute would come barging back in, but it is a long floor and she was away down the other end.

I tucked the leg back in place but it looked so crooked I felt sure it would be seen, so when the wardress came for my tray I sat full square on the middle of it with my legs spread out like a fishwife. She glared at me and I was terrified she would make me stand up as we are supposed to when they enter, but I think she was near as tired as I was for she said nothing but just slammed out of the cell, rattling her keys.

I waited a few minutes and when it seemed that all was quiet for the night I got off the chair and pulled the leg off again. It made a sturdy weapon.

There was another tapping on my wall. 'Are you ready?'

'Yes.'

'Five minutes.'

How she knew, I cannot tell but I thought I should get myself in position for it would be a sorry thing after all my pains if I should miss the signal.

It was then I understood why I will never be a leader. The window is high up in the wall. To break it I would have to be on a level and the only way I could achieve such a thing would be – to stand on my chair.

I could have wept. Indeed, I was closer than I care to say, but then my neighbour tapped again.

'Two minutes. Stand by.'

I thought, she thinks I am a leader. How can I fail her, and all the women who put their trust in us?

I pulled down my bed, set the chair on top of it, slanting it against the wall like a ladder, and clambered up till my nose was rubbing against the bars, clasping my chair leg like a truncheon. My head was spinning and little black dots came darting at me like angry flies. I could feel the strength soaking out of me. It was then I heard the prison clock. A great clanging chime, iron cold. One, two, three… At the last beat there was a pause like the world holding its breath then, from far away I heard a voice. Thin, tinny, a Punch and Judy puppet. 'Votes for women', and all through the block came this wailing, wandering cry, 'Votes for women'. But there was nothing weak about the sound that followed. Glass, glass, glass, shattering, crashing into the hard stone yard below. I hoisted my chair leg and struck as hard as I could. The panes held firm and I feared I was too weak to break them. The chair swayed beneath me. I grasped the bars and clung with all my might to keep my balance, then raised the wooden leg and smashed it down on to the window. Smashed it and smashed it, again and again.

I broke seven panes. That is the most of anyone. I am to be taken before a magistrate in the Governor's office.

What a horrible watery man was the magistrate. Eyes paler than his pus-coloured skin. 'Close confinement. Seven days.'

This is a terrible place. No light, only a murky glow from the passage. Double iron doors – as if I had the strength to break out of a paper bag, let alone a prison cell! God help me, how can I live in this dungeon for seven days? And if I die who will ever know it or mourn for me?

Now I am drenched with crying. Fred, I love you so much. I am sorry I am grown so ugly and dirty and cannot keep even my own spittle down. I am disgusting. My skin is like wafers and my bones are poking through my clothes. My hair is falling out in handfuls. My beautiful brown hair that you loved so much is lying on my pillow and my shiny white teeth are yellow with slime. I hope I do die. I would rather be dead than Fred see me like this. Or Ma.

Today the doctor came. He said I must stop my fast and take some nourishment or he would not answer for my fate. I could not speak for dryness but made a sign that I would like some water. He raised his hand and one of the brutes came over to him. He whispered something to her. She nodded and went away, then came back with a covered cup with a spout like Nan used to have. She hauled me up and put it to my lips.

I have been moved to the hospital. I have broken my fast. There was milk in the cup.

*  *  *

Mrs Pethick Lawrence had organised a great reception for us on our release, with a band and reporters and masses of people cheering. Out we all came and they clapped and sang and waved their banners, though I think they were a little shocked by how we all looked.

Miss Sylvia tore right up to me. 'Maggie, we are so proud of you. It has been all over the papers how you chopped up your chair and smashed your windows. Fred has been round at the office every day to hear how you are.'

I positively shook. 'He is not here?'

She took my hand. 'I thought you would like to rest a little first?'

Miss Christabel had also come to meet us for it seems we 'Hunger Strikers' are quite famous. She looked so beautiful in her lilac gown with the purple feathers round her snow-white straw. I thought perhaps she would like to ask me how it had been in 'close confinement', for she must surely stand in danger of it herself, and I was right for she made her way towards me after a while.

'Maggie, how are you? A bad time, as I understand?'

'Not the best, Miss Christabel, for sure.'

She smiled. It was like a beam of the purest sunshine. 'And I hear you broke seven panes? That is truly impressive.'

I felt a great warm glow flushing through me.

'But you broke your strike? Why was that?'

'I was... I did not know... I thought it was water.'

'Of course. That is what I had supposed. You must be more wary in the future. The authorities will always seek out the weakest link in a chain. Well done.' And she was gone.

* * *

Mrs Garrud prepared me a bath and put me to bed with a hot stone wrapped in flannel to warm my feet. I cannot get warm. She says it is because I have not eaten for so long, but I am not hungry any more. She brought me some warm milk with honey in it which I sipped as best I could, but my stomach churned and churned and I thought I should be sick. She told me to rest and she would fetch the doctor to me but I begged her not to, for I never want to see another as long as I live. They are foul, deceitful creatures with smooth tongues and wicked ways.

One day on and I am feeling so much better. Today I had a coddled egg and then later some bread mashed in milk. Mrs Garrud helped me wash my hair again for yesterday I could do no more than sluice it.

Miss Sylvia called round with the papers. 'I thought you would like to see how things are turning our way at last.'

It was true. Though some still insisted we were nothing but criminals and should be treated as such, many were coming to the view that our cause was a just one and in any case that it was cruel and barbarous of the Government to punish us with prison. There were lots of articles about the window-smashing. '*We understand that one of the female vandals broke seven panes, no less. Put her in the stocks, we say, till she has learnt her manners.*' I felt like writing back and saying, 'Is it manners to shut someone in a black hole for seven days?' but then I found another that said I was a '*latterday Joan of Arc*'. Joan of Arc is a great favourite with Mrs Pankhurst and Miss Christabel so I asked if I might cut it out to keep.

'Of course. Keep them all if you like.'

'No. Just that one, please,' for I did not want to remember my week in hell.

I asked when I was expected back in the office. Miss Sylvia made a face. 'Not until you are strong and well again.'

'I am. Much stronger than yesterday and tomorrow I am sure I shall be fine.'

'Well, fine or not, you are to go to Mr and Mrs Pethick Lawrence's country house to convalesce. One of our women will drive you down. It's all arranged.'

I was quite dazed. I know that some of the ladies have been taken there after prison, but *me*! My heart started jumping. 'I cannot go, Miss Sylvia. Really, I cannot.'

'Why ever not, Maggie?'

'Because…because I must go home to Ma. I have not seen her for so long.'

'She knows all about it. She thinks it a wonderful idea.'

'But… I do not know what to do in the country. I shall not know how to behave. And I have no clothes for country living.'

'Maggie, calm down. It's not a shooting party. It's to give you time to get your strength back, that's all. Nothing will be required of you. You may read and walk in the gardens – anything you like.'

'But I am fine, truly I am.'

Miss Sylvia became serious. 'Maggie, you are not. You could hardly walk when we brought you back yesterday. Mrs Garrud was in tears after she put you to bed. Now is that what you want? Do you want your ma, who has made so many sacrifices for you, to see you like this?'

'Like what?'

'Like this.' She went over to the table and picked up a hand mirror. She held it in front of me.

I should not have known myself. My eyes looked twice as big as normal, staring out at me from hollow treacly circles. My skin was dry and flaking, my hair like wire, splitting and coarse...

Miss Sylvia put her arm round me till I had done crying. 'You will soon be well again. Believe me, Maggie. One week from now and you will be good as new, I promise you.'

I could not think it would be so.

She got up. 'I will leave you to rest now.' At the door she turned. 'Maggie, it is not just for your sake we are sending you to convalesce. The Cause needs you, and needs you to be strong. It is a long hard struggle we have before us still. You do understand what I'm saying, don't you?'

I nodded. When she had gone I cried some more, because I knew she meant we would have to go through it all again.

In the evening Mrs Garrud brought me some broth and when I had drunk it she bathed my face with a cloth and brushed my hair and tied it back with a purple ribbon. 'You have a visitor.'

'Who?'

'Who do you think?'

I shook my head. 'No. I cannot see him. Please... Tell him I am unwell, anything... Please.'

'Maggie, why? He has been beside himself with worry. You must let him speak to you at least.'

'No. No. No. Another time. I am too tired. Oh, please, Mrs Garrud...'

'But why not?'

'I cannot bear for him to see me like this. I cannot bear it.'

Mrs Garrud nodded. 'What if I light some candles and turn down the lamp? He will not stay long. He knows you are very tired. He loves you, Maggie.'

'He will not if he sees me now.'

Mrs Garrud sat down by the bed. 'I have been married to Mr Garrud for twenty-two years. Do you think in all that time he has never seen me sick or ill or worse? Once, when I was starting out my classes I turned wrong and fell and hit my head on the wall. I was senseless for ten days. When I came to he was there, sitting by my bed, his face all stained with tears. He grasped hold of my hand and said, "Edith, I feared I had lost you. I am the happiest man alive." It was a week before I found out I was entirely yellow with the jaundice. I asked him about it after and he said, "Oh, yes, I suppose you were. I never noticed".'

Fred came tiptoeing into the room in his great bobby's boots, for he had come straight from being on duty. Halfway across the room he tripped over the jug that Mrs Garrud had used to wash my hair and it went clanging away like a church bell. This made me laugh.

'I was trying not to wake you. I cannot see a thing in here. Has Mrs Garrud got no oil?'

'I preferred the candles.'

'Oh. Well…' He sat down. I looked at him. He was gazing at me as though he had never seen me before. I thought, so much for candles! Slowly he leant across and, taking my face in his hands, kissed me, oh so gently, on my cheeks and then my forehead. 'Oh, Maggie, I have missed you so much.'

'Yes, I missed you.'

'The ladies told me what was happening. I did not know how to bear it. I almost went to church to say a prayer.'

'Don't talk to me about church. Or chaplains. Not prison ones, anyway.'

'No. They say you are to go to the country for a few days. Till you are recovered.'

'Yes. I have got a bit thin.'

'I've brought you some cake, and chocolate, and flowers. Mrs Garrud said I should leave them downstairs for now in case you were...Oh, God, Maggie, you look so...'

I felt my hopes go crashing down like the prison windows. 'So...?' All those words – 'ill, old, vile, ugly', the lot.

He reached across for my ice-cold hand and pressed it to his lips. 'Beautiful. So beautiful. I am the luckiest man on earth.'

The country is all I could have dreamt and more. I was driven down here by a very funny lady, Miss Holmes, who kept quipping all the way. She told me she had nearly landed Mrs Pankhurst in a ditch on her first outing, she was so nervous. 'I'd taken a wrong turning and it was nearly dark and we were running late. Mrs P tapped me on the shoulder and said, "Vera dear, if we are not there in five and half minutes you will have two thousand women to answer to", so I slammed my foot down just as we were going round a corner and skidded and if there had been anything coming the other way, we should both have been in paradise by now. Or whatever the alternative is.'

'Holloway,' I said and we just fell about laughing. I should so like to learn to drive a car.

I cannot begin to describe my treatment here. If Holloway is hell, then The Mascot is paradise.

I was greeted on my arrival by Mrs Cliffe, the housekeeper, Mr and Mrs Pethick Lawrence being still in town. 'Welcome, Miss Robins. We are so looking forward to having you here.'

She led us through to the parlour where we had a cup of tea and then a real maid came and showed us up to our rooms. Mine is decorated with wallpaper, yellow and white stripes. It is like something out of a palace. I have a great china bowl with a jug, patterned in yellow and blue flowers. My sheets are softer than velvet. I have my own dressing-table with a mirror, though this is a fright for I can see how freakish I am become, though my hair is shinier now and not falling out so much, so I have hope that I may yet improve.

For our supper Mrs Cliffe brought us soup, then venison with peas and carrots and then cheese and afterwards, strawberries picked that very day, she said. To drink, we had *wine*. It was dark red like blood and I did not think I liked it much, but after a little while I started to feel properly warm again – the first time for weeks.

I slept that night like I had never slept before. When I woke the sun was pouring through the curtains. For a good minute I could not remember where I was and then there was a knock on the door and the maid brought in a great jug of hot water for me to wash in. She poured it right into the bowl without spilling a drop and I thought, that might have been me if I had stayed with the Roes.

I would have liked to talk to her but she moved so quickly and never once raised her eyes to me. I wondered if it was because she thought I was a nob, but then I caught sight of me in the mirror again and I knew it must be because I looked so awful.

Miss Holmes had to drive back to London after breakfast but first she showed me all around the garden which is huge – nearly as big as a park, I would say, and with pathways overhung with roses, and lawns and trees and a special wooden house called a summer-house with cushions and chairs and bats and balls and skittles and all sorts. And a swing! I wonder if I shall dare to try it.

There is even a sort of cage with a net strung across the middle which Miss Holmes says is for a game called tennis. You have to hit a ball backwards and forwards across the net. She says it is very jolly and if she comes down again before I go she will teach me how to play it.

Inside the house is almost as beautiful as out. There is a great drawing-room with a piano. I tried a few notes when I thought there was no one about. After a while I could do a whole verse of *Fight on, Women, for the fight is hard and long* so I thought it would be a fine idea to sing it, too. I had just got to the third line when, like an echo, I heard another voice joining in. I never had such a fright. I spun round and there, standing in the doorway, was Miss Christabel, no less. I fairly leapt out of my seat.

'Don't stop, Maggie. You're doing a grand job. How are you? You're looking much better. We shall soon have you back on the road, shall we not? I trust you've read your newspapers this morning? Of course you have. I'm only joking. Where's Mrs Cliffe, do you know? I need to bring some women down from Aylesbury. The hunger strikes are working a treat. Questions in the House. Do you know, there was a whole column in *The Times* yesterday? Saying how it can render a woman infertile if carried to excess. That should raise an eyebrow or two, wouldn't you say?' Fortunately I did not have to say, because she was gone.

There is a library here. I have spent the whole afternoon examining the books and it seems to me that there is all the knowledge known to mankind contained among those shelves. I asked if I might borrow one and Mrs Cliffe looked most surprised. 'Of course you may. You are a guest. You may do whatever you like.' Well, I knew that could not be true but I thanked her all the same.

It is very strange being here all by myself. I should be frightened in such a great house but it has such a warm, good feeling to it, as though it wants me to be here.

After my supper Mrs Cliffe brought me some photographs to look at. They were of Mr and Mrs Pethick Lawrence when they were younger, in the garden of the house, surrounded by children – scrappy toothy little mites that might have come from Stepney.

Seeing my surprise, Mrs Cliffe explained that they had first met when working in the East End and that, after their marriage, they would often bring whole charabanc loads of children down so that they could have a real holiday and feel some sunshine on their faces. I understood then why she found nothing odd about me.

Before I went to bed she gave me a tiny thimbleful of a golden brown liquid. 'To help you sleep, dear.' I thought it must be medicine so screwed up my eyes and swallowed it in one. Lord, did it make me cough! When I was right again Mrs Cliffe said, 'It's probably better to sip it next time, Maggie. Besides, the master would be very put out if he saw his best brandy disappearing so fast, I can assure you.'

So now I have had brandy. It is a very good drink and makes you glow like a furnace all through. Perhaps I should ask the prison doctor next time if he will prescribe some for me, just to stop the cold.

Next morning after breakfast (hot rolls, jam, butter, cold ham, a boiled egg) I went back to the library. There were three or four newspapers laid out so I thought I should read at least one or Miss Christabel might not be so generous about it next time. I picked the smallest.

I found a book of poetry by a man called Byron and after dinner (soup, a whole trout, potatoes and a strawberry jelly) took it down to the summer-house. I sat the whole afternoon with my feet on a little stool just reading and reading, with the sun dripping down on me like honey and a cool soft breeze whispering in the trees.

Poetry is surely the finest thing in the world. There was one about a man locked up alone in prison for fourteen years. What could be more awful? And yet, when they finally came to let him out, he did not want it. 'Even I, Regained my freedom with a sigh'. I shall learn it by heart so that next time I am Close Confined I can repeat it to myself and maybe be a bit braver.

At five o'clock the maid brought me out a pot of tea and some cream sponge cake on a tray. She asked if I would like a bath before dinner. I am sure she can be no older than I am but she was so respectful I hardly knew how to reply.

'The Master and Mistress will be down about seven, I am to tell you, miss, and you will all dine together this evening.'

'Oh no...' I said, which was not at all what I intended. 'Then I should like a bath very much, please.'

'I will prepare one for you when you are ready.'

'Oh… Thank you.'

'And shall you like me to help you dress after, miss?'

I do not know what my expression must have been. 'No, thank you. I can do that. I used to be a maid.' She looked up at me so strangely. 'I know what you are thinking,' I blathered. 'You are thinking that cannot be true.'

The girl blushed. 'No, miss, truly. I was just wondering…'

'What?'

'Why anyone who could have been a maid would want to do what you do.'

As I lay in my bath I thought, if only you knew.

The days have flown by. I have put on near all the weight I lost and if I keep this up I shall need a wagon to take me back to London, not a car. I have written to Fred every day. I had hoped to have a reply from him, but I expect he is very busy. I have had two goes on the swing. It is the best feeling in the world to sway backwards and forwards with the sun on your back and a warm soft wind in your face. That must be how angels feel when they are flying.

I have read four books of poems, one about a king called Arthur who lived at a magic time and had a round table where all his noble knights sat, so that no one could be greater than the others. We could do with a round table at some suffragette meetings, I am thinking, for there is a load of arguing goes on about who is in charge of who, although in the end, the knights quarrelled anyway and poor Arthur died and went away in a barge with three wailing queens.

I have committed six poems to heart. I could not learn all

the prison one for it is twelve pages long, but I know a good few verses.

Mr and Mrs Pethick Lawrence stayed the weekend and Miss Sylvia came down on Saturday and we all played tennis. It is a wonderful game although I do not understand the rules one bit. Mr Pethick Lawrence was my partner and Mrs Pethick Lawrence and Miss Sylvia were against us. We won by miles. Miss Sylvia is a bit soppy at running and Mrs Pethick Lawrence could not find her eye-glasses.

Then we had lemonade and sat under the trees to cool down and everyone said how well I looked, and how they were looking forward to having me back in the office. I said I was quite well enough to return but they said, no, a few more days would do me no harm, so here I am, feet up, book on my lap, sun in my hair. Maggie Robins, the Queen of Camelot. Oh, for my knight in shining armour.

And he has come. The maid, whose name is Lucy! came hurrying out to the summer-house at half past ten this morning to say a young man had called and should she send him out or would I like to receive him in the drawing-room? Well, I beat her back for I rushed across that lawn like I was shot from a bow. Through the drawing-room, the library and straight out into the hall. Fred was standing with his back to me, studying a painting, light streaming on to him through the stained-glass window. His hair was full of flames. I just gazed. He turned and his whole face lit up like diamond sparks, mystic, wonderful. He held out his arms. 'Maggie...'

I think the maid was a bit shocked. I cannot help that. Queen Guinevere was just as forward when Sir Lancelot returned from seeking the Holy Grail. I think he was gone a bit longer than two weeks but it seemed like forever to me and anyway she didn't have to watch.

This has been the most perfect day. Mrs Cliffe asked if we would like to eat lunch (dinner) in the dining-room or should she pack us a picnic to take down to the lake?

We sat by the water's edge and Fred took off his shoes and socks and dipped his feet in, so I did, too, and after I had given over screaming for it was so cold, it was quite lovely. Fred tried to catch my foot between his own and we had such a tussle that I nearly fell in and had to smack him (but not hard) and he caught hold of my hand and kissed it, then my arm, then my shoulder, my neck...so now I am nearly a woman again. Oh, he is so lovely.

I told him about King Arthur. He knew of him already and agreed that he was quite the best king who ever reigned in our country. I asked him if he thought women would have had the vote in Arthur's time. He smiled and rolled on his back so that all his muscles sort of rippled like a beautiful wave. 'They wouldn't have needed it, Maggie. The men were theirs to command.'

'Are you mine to command?'

He reached up with his hand and touched the skin of my neck so it tingled like a firework bursting. 'You know I am.'

I lay down beside him. 'Well, that's not fair. We must be equal. That is what I am fighting for.'

He tickled my nose with a piece of grass. '*You* are, Maggie. I would not vouch for your fellows.' I would have questioned him about that but he seemed to think kissing would be better.

After tea he had to catch a train back to London.

He said he had received all my letters and had started to answer each one of them but could not get his thoughts out, so that is why he came to see me. I said I should be home soon for I could not bear to be away from him much longer. He made me promise that I would stay as long as I was ordered. I said, 'Why? Am I still too ugly to come back?'

He shook his head. 'But if I could, I would keep you here forever.' He didn't say why.

Happy. Today I am perfectly happy. I must remember how this feels in case I ever lose it.

# PART THREE

## 1909–1910

All summer long the war has continued, for it is a war now. We can no longer pretend that fine words and promises mean a thing. There will be no vote for us until the Asquith and all his slimy kind have been beaten.

They complain that we challenge them at church, at dinner, when they are on holiday, but if they will not receive us in the proper place, what can we do? They cannot ignore our demands and expect us to respect theirs. Anyway, now they must go around with an army to shield them. Sneaking in and out of their meetings, scurrying away into the night like sewer rats. And so we go on with our protests: window smashing, taunting the politicians, storming Liberal assemblies. Paying the price. And the price is always prison. Prison, then hunger strike. Recovery, protest, prison. On and on.

Some days I think I shall run mad. For where is it getting us, all this endless rebellion? I see women in the street, in the shops, through the windows of their homes, going about their business without a single care or thought for the struggle we are engaged in. Sometimes I want to cry out, 'Look at me. See what they are doing to me. Look at my hair, my skin, my bones sticking through my garments. And it is for *you*. For you and your children. Why can you not stand by us? Why do you turn your backs?' And then I think, they look so calm, so peaceful, so contented. Perhaps they do not need the vote after all. Women have lived for thousands of years without it. Why should they want it now? Besides, people do not welcome change, it seems to me, for I have only to move the chairs around in the office for everyone to start fretting and moaning about how much better it was before.

Before. What is this magical 'before' when everything was fine and no one went hungry or died or got beaten with a truncheon? When did it exist? I think, never, unless in a poem like King Arthur and his knights. But we must not think of 'before'. Only of the future. Tomorrow, when we have won. Tomorrow and tomorrow and tomorrow.

Mrs Pankhurst is forbidden to go on any more deputations till the courts have ruled on what to charge her with. For once they have not found a law yet to counter her.

The Women's Freedom League has taken over the protests. Perhaps it is as well they do it, for so many of us are so wrecked we have no longer the strength for such a thing. Once fine strong women trudge about like crones, dull-eyed, aching, frozen – always frozen. I would rather fall in the Thames in darkest winter than lie on a Holloway plank with no food inside me. It is like a block of freezing iron binding my ribs to my backbone. Sometimes I think my soul will fall out the other side. There is no blood flowing beneath my skin. Everything is frozen.

I have been hungry before. At home there was never enough to fill us all, and Pa and my brothers got first pickings, but even at the worst times it was never like this. This endless starving of ourselves. It is so contrary to everything that life should be. To turn your back on nourishment, on all you need to live and keep on living. To watch your body failing bit by bit. My bleeding has quite stopped now but there is no baby in me, that I know. I told Miss Annie. She said hers had, too. It was a 'side effect'. 'Side effects', it seems, are little fiddling nuisances that can occur as a result of certain actions. 'Like getting your skirt splashed if you stand too near the gutter on a wet day,' she explained. I wondered if losing your hair and your eyelashes and being able to count each rib in your body were side effects, too.

One day as I was sitting in the park waiting for Fred to come off duty, a mother came by with her little girl, about four years old, I would guess. They stopped right near me and brought out a bag of crumbs to feed the ducks. As the child took hold of it, the bag split open and half the bread spilt on the ground so I bent down to help her pick it up, but when I held it out to her, she screamed and ran behind her mother's skirts, and would not come out till I had moved away. I heard the woman soothing her. 'No, no, Emily. She's not a witch. It's just the way she looks.'

I fled home, scurrying along the pavements, eyes down, scarf round my head to hide my horrible face. Still I could see my scraggy fingers gnawing at my coat buttons. Once I glanced in a shop window and there I was, one, two, three of me. Three witches scuttling like rats to find a hole to hide in.

Fred came round to the house that evening. 'I thought we were to meet in the park?'

'Yes... I... I got cold.'

'But it's warmer than it's been all week.'

'Yes. I don't know... I... I'm always cold. You know that.'
I did not mean to sound so pettish.

Fred frowned. 'And you know the reason. You are half starved.'

'Whose fault is that?'

He turned away impatiently. 'Mine, I suppose. Since I must carry all the ills of the world on my shoulders.'

'Who do you blame then, if not this government and its loyal servants, the police?'

'I suppose we cannot find fault in your wonderful leaders, who send you time and again into this torture?'

'They endure it too, you know. You speak as though they did not.'

Fred gripped me by the shoulders. They crackled like old twigs. 'I know they do, Maggie. But it is their choice, do you not see? And it is not yours. That much I am sure of.'

I felt the tears coming, as they do so often now. His arms were round me in a second, sharing his warmth, keeping me safe. He kissed the top of my head. 'I hate to see you like this. You know I do. If I thought it was doing any good...all this window smashing, stone throwing...'

'But it is. It is. Every day we are in the papers. It is the only way... Miss Christabel...'

'It is *not* the only way, Maggie. It is a stupid way. The worst possible way. Yes, you are in the papers, but what do they say? That it is a scandal. Nothing short of vandalism. That the suffragettes are no better than hooligans. How much good do you think that does your cause? I can tell you. None. People who once believed in you are sickened by all this violence. You are playing into the Government's very hands. You are giving them the bullets they need to shoot you down. Does Miss Christabel ever consider that when she is planning her next act of brilliance?'

'But what can I do? What can I do?' I sobbed. 'It is my duty, my work – my way of life.'

'Your first duty is to yourself, Maggie. You will be no good to them dead or infirm. Is that what you want? What Miss Christabel wants? Because that is how it will end if you do not look to your health. I say nothing of our life together, for it seems you care nothing for that these days.' He stopped but I could feel his anger sparking right through into my pitiful bones. I don't think I had ever felt so hopeless.

I answered, 'I do think of it, Fred. It is the only comfort I have in my life, night or day. It is the only thing I feel sure of in this world. And if you take that away, there will be nothing.'

He dropped his hands. 'Oh, Maggie. Why do you do this to me?'

'Do what?'

'Make me feel so guilty.'

I stared at him. 'Why should you feel guilty? It is me that is causing all the trouble.'

He smoothed my bracken hair. 'You are doing what you believe in. That is enough for anyone. But it grieves me so much to see you so skinny.'

'A girl called me a witch today.'

'Who was it? I shall handcuff her to a runaway carthorse.'

I laughed. 'I don't think you should. She was only little.'

'Then I shall handcuff her to your broomstick. Teach her to mind her manners.'

'Do I look like a witch, Fred? Tell me the truth.'

He cupped my face in his hands and kissed my nose. 'I've never met one, but if I ever do, I hope she looks just like you.' I took what comfort I could from that.

At our next meeting I dragged up all my courage and when it came to questions I stood up. After a while Miss Christabel spotted me and signalled that I should speak.

'I would like to ask, on account we are a peaceful movement, is it not against our principles to cause so much damage to other people's property?'

Miss Christabel looked at me in huge surprise. 'Do you have an alternative, Maggie?'

This threw me. 'What would you like us to do instead?' asked Lady Con (as we all call her now).

I knew I must not say I did not know. 'I am only afraid that someone will be hurt one day, and then the public will turn against us.'

Miss Christabel smiled. 'It is a risk, certainly, Maggie. But should that happen, perhaps it will be time to remind the public of our suffering in Holloway and all the other prisons. I do not think that a graze from a tiny stone can quite equate say to the damage done to Lady Con by a week without food.'

Madness is my middle name. 'I do not know that Lady Con feels hunger any worse than the rest of us, miss.'

Miss Christabel looked at me so patiently. 'You are right, Maggie, and clearly *you* feel it more than most, or you would not have broken your fast on the very first occasion.'

I sat back down.

Afterwards Miss Sylvia came over to me. 'How are you,

Maggie? It's so long since I have seen you.'

I said I was fine apart from my hair falling out and my belly swelling like a pumpkin after each trip to prison, and all for throwing a stone into a grating (my aim is not improving).

She nodded wearily. 'I would prefer a more peaceful approach, myself. What does Fred make of it?'

'He hates it. He hates any violence, and this he thinks is so pointless. Worse than that, for he says it turns people against us.'

'Yes, it does. Even our own supporters. I have letters every day from women wishing to resign their membership. They want justice, of course they do, but not if innocent bystanders are harmed as a result.'

'But Miss Christabel *is* right – we do suffer far more than they do.'

'But at least we have the choice.' She shivered suddenly. 'If only everyone could choose what came to them.'

'Is that not what we are fighting for?'

Miss Sylvia smiled her strange sad smile. 'Yes, of course. I was thinking of the things we cannot change, like illness and...well, illness.'

'Are you ill?' I asked, for in truth she looked horribly pale.

'Not me. Harry.'

'Is he not well?' I remembered how full of energy and life he had been that day in the office and with his plans for the Wooden Horse.

Miss Sylvia shook her head. 'He has polio. It is paralysing him, joint by joint. Like some vile snake creeping through his body. Oh, he is in the very best hands and Mother is going on a lecture tour to America to raise funds for his treatment. I'm sure all will be well in the end.' She bit her lip and stared hard at the ceiling, and I knew she did not believe one word of what she said.

'He is young and a fighter. They are the best to conquer illness, are they not?'

She tried to smile. 'Yes, yes, you are right. It's just...very hard to see someone you love suffering so and not be able to do anything. That is the worst. Oh, why him? Why not me? Why couldn't it have been me?'

'You cannot mean that?'

Miss Sylvia looked me straight in the eye. 'Yes,' she said. 'I do.'

I was ashamed, for now I see what loving someone truly means.

Something terrible is to happen.

In Birmingham two of our women climbed on to a factory roof opposite the building where the Asquith was to speak. From there they flung stones and slates on to the roof of the hall, and generally frightened the vile man half to death, it seems. They were only captured after fire hoses were turned on them.

Their sentence was wicked – four months' hard labour. Immediately they began to fast for that is the surest and quickest way out of prison, but they have not been freed and word has come out that they are to be fed by force.

I cannot imagine how awful this must be. How is it done? Miss Kerr said she supposed they would be offered such fine food their wills could not resist it, but Miss Davison said that was nonsense, and she had heard of it being employed in distant times to torture traitors. Though I do not heed one half of what she says, I asked her what she meant.

She said the prisoner was tied to a chair and a piece of iron pipe thrust down his throat and then boiling oil was poured down the pipe into his belly. I know she thinks me a silly ignorant creature, but did she really suppose I would be fooled by that? I asked her if she truly thought that was like to happen to our sisters. She went all huffy and then came back with, 'If it does, so be it. I am ready.'

I said, well, I was certainly not. Justice was one thing and boiling oil was another, which made Miss Kerr giggle so much she got the hiccoughs. Miss Davison flung her a wild look and went stamping off to frighten someone else.

I used to think that there were so many things in life I would love to do. Going on a train was one of them. Being in a newspaper was another. Loving a man who did not beat me, wearing fine clothes, reading books.

All these I have achieved, but there is a price for everything. Tonight I must lay beside them pain, mortification, disgust, filth, shame, and most of all, fear – sick smothering fear that comes over you like a great thick blanket, choking the breath out of you. So much fear that I thought I would die of it. Now I know that there is no mercy in heaven for me.

All my life I have prayed and hoped that someone would look down on me and see that I was trying. And that for that I would be pitied and maybe, at last, forgiven for it all. Now I see this will not happen. Some sins are too bad. Lying with your brother is one of them. Or perhaps it is the baby he put in me then took away. Perhaps that baby is crying out for vengeance, for what became of it? Was it a boy or a girl? Where do babies go when they are pulled out of you too early?

I was brought here on Friday. We had gone on a train to Birmingham. I had, as usual, thrown my stones and missed everything in sight. I had, as usual, been arrested. I had, as usual, been taken to court and then sent on to prison.

The following morning came a man in a long coat, accompanied by five or six brutes. It makes me smile to think we called them 'brutes' for denying us food and fresh water. What is there left to call a woman – one of our own sex, who will tie your feet to a chair and your arms to its arms and crush your nose between her fingers so that you cannot breathe and when your mouth bursts open, fill it with swill not fit for pigs and clamp your lips together so that you half choke, half drown; who will listen to you choking and strike you over and over in the back so that the filth roars back up, tearing your throat like a razor, and then down again into your shrunken stomach, which hurls it back till the vomit comes flying from your nostrils in a great porridge of blood and bile and pus all down your sopping stinking clothes, for you cannot save yourself from wetting; who will leave you lying in your own foulness while she moves on to the next cell to start the game again?

A doctor, yes, for they are vile creatures, but a woman? Are these who we are fighting for? Tonight I have no more faith, no beliefs, no hopes. Tomorrow I shall be seventeen. Well, let that be all, I have had enough.

\* \* \*

This morning I was taken to the Governor's office. I feared it was to begin again and I knew I could not stand it. Could not. I stood before him.

'Margaret Robins, you are to be released this afternoon. Return to your cell.'

At a quarter before two I was taken to the prison gates and turned out into the street. In Birmingham. I had no money, no ticket for the train, only my foul filthy clothes that I had splashed with cold water to try and rub the sick away and failed, as I have failed at everything else. No one to meet me. No grand procession with horses and bands and women waving banners. Nothing. I sat down on the curb. A policeman came up to me and asked me my name.

'Maggie Robins.'

'Then I must ask you to come along with me.'

I tried to get up but there was no strength left in me and I sank back. He raised his arm and I knew he was preparing to strike me. I just sat there, too weak to move, too smashed about to care.

Footsteps running. 'Maggie? Oh God, Maggie. What have they done to you?' Fred, crouching beside me. 'Maggie? Do you hear me?' Like he was speaking to a child. 'Maggie, give me your hand. That's right. I've come to take you home.'

I looked at him but he was ten years older than two weeks ago so I knew I must have died. He glanced up at the other man. 'My thanks.'

The bobby was staring at me, frowning. 'It cannot be right,' he said, then shook his head and turned and walked away.

Fred carried me to a waiting cab. Outside the railway

station he bought me a strawberry ice. I threw it in the gutter.

It was dark when the train arrived in London. I know now why I have been freed. It is to say goodbye to Ma.

I sat by her bed. Her neck was swollen and disgusting, like a great onion was bursting through her skin. She could hardly speak. Lucy attended to the young ones and, though she did not say a word to me, I saw that she was trying. My darling Evelyn came running to me as we opened the back door. 'Ma's got a bad neck.'

'I know, sweet.'

'Have you come to make her better?'

Fred swept her up into his arms and set her on his shoulders. She squealed with happiness. 'Let me down, let me down.'

'Only if you count to twenty.'

Off they went into the cold evening air. Inside all was stuffy, rancid, rotting. Pa was clamped in the corner like he had been nailed there.

I climbed the stairs.

Her eyes flickered as I came in. I saw that she did not like my looks. I sat down by the bed. Saw her waxy skin, sweat-drenched hair, eyes dull with pain. I remembered Miss Sylvia's words: 'Why couldn't it have been me?' But I didn't want it to be me. I didn't want it to be anyone. I wanted to save her. Make her well again. I wanted to tell her all the things I never had. How much I loved her. That I was proud to be her daughter. That I never meant to...but the words would not come. They stayed locked inside my head.

'Ma, I am so sorry I have not been home.'

She stirred.

I took a breath. 'Ma, I am giving it up. The Cause. There is no point. I will come home and nurse you back to health, I promise you.'

She turned her face away.

I tried to straighten the sheet. She flinched as it brushed against her skin. 'Ma, Fred has asked me to give it up. I love him. He is a good man. The best that ever lived.'

Still she faced the wall.

I knelt down beside the bed. 'Ma, tell me what you want. I know I have not been a good daughter to you. I have been selfish and vain and just because I brought money home, I thought I was better than you – all of you. But I knew nothing. Tell me what to do, and whatever you say, I will do it.'

Then she did look back, and through her croaky blistered throat she whispered, 'Fight for us, Maggie'.


Mrs Grant helped me lay her out. I wanted to do it alone, but since I had never done it, it made sense to let her show me. She did not interfere, just gave advice.

I washed Ma's body gently with soft soap. She was swollen all over with great bulging lumps. Her breasts were shrivelled like an eagle's claw had raked them. Her skin was greasy yellow.

I thought, how can a person live, even for an hour, with a body that turns against them? Is this how I shall end? And I thought, if she had been rich she could have been cured. The rich do not die covered in bruises and swellings, between rough sheets in dark, stinking rooms with no one by to wipe their sweat away or cool their fever. They do not leave a family without a mother.

All night long I have lain awake. I am needed here. I cannot desert the little ones. Pa will ignore them and Lucy... Who knows? Ma cannot have wanted me to forsake them, even for the Cause. I must stay. I know I must. Yet now, lying here on this flea-bitten mattress with Lucy's feet in my face I cannot help thinking of my beautiful room in Argyle Place. Of all my learning and typewriting and adding up accounts. Is it all to go to waste?

Oh, Ma, forgive me. Tell me what to do. Tell me what to do. Tell me how to cry for I have forgotten.

The parlour was dark, save for a streak of moonlight on the coffin. Such a cold light. The very wood looked lifeless, dry as bone – none of the rich warm swirls of Argyle Place. Only rough raw planks, splintered at the seams, and a coarse linen cloth to shield her from their scraping.

Clouds crept across the moon and blacked her out. Took her away.

I found some matches and a stub of candle. I sat by her till dawn. Waiting for her to answer.

We buried Ma this afternoon. She is near Mrs Grant's daughter on a little hill behind the church. In the morning I took Evelyn and Will to the river-bank and we picked some flowers for them to lay on the grave. They had mostly withered by the time Reverend Beckett had done preachifying, but it was no matter for Fred had bought a whole bunch of white lilies that near covered the coffin, and there was another great pile from Miss Sylvia and Miss Annie. I saw Mrs Beckett eyeing them most greedily so I shall go by the church tomorrow morning and see if she has nabbed them for the altar.

Afterwards we went home and Mrs Grant and I served tea and cold meat with pickles to everyone. Will liked it so much he asked if we could bury someone else tomorrow. I slapped him, so for once in his life he had something real to cry about. Lucy spent the whole afternoon making cow's eyes at Fred, for all the good it did her. Alfie's girl, Edith, is a sweet-natured creature. She had brought a cake from the bakery that she had paid for herself and when the others had gone she stayed and helped me clear up, poor Mrs Grant having fallen to weeping. I gave the poor soul the baby to hold.

I walked with Fred to the bus stop. I know he would have stayed, slept on the floor, if I had asked him. I did not. I watched him mount the stairs. He always likes the open deck. Says you can see forever. He turned to wave to me. My hand waved back. Is this what it is like, being dead? I have remarked every single thing today, and felt nothing.

Pa had been at the ale when I got back. He was slumped by the hearth holding Ma's shawl that I had given her and snivelling. I thought, if he wipes his nose on that I shall spit.

Mrs Grant was somewhat recovered. 'Maggie, your Pa and I have been talking...'

'Oh?'

'It is arranged. I will help with the baby and little Will and Evelyn. Lucy can continue her job and Edith says she will call every evening and put them to bed if I cannot do it.'

I stared at her. 'What are you saying?'

I must have looked mighty wild for she became nervous. 'So that you need not worry. You have enough to deal with...'

I shook my head. 'I must come home. I cannot continue. That is all finished. Over. This is where I belong now.'

Mrs Grant looked agitated. She glanced at Pa.

I have never thought much of my father. I knew he would not care who did what, so long as his food was waiting for him and his shoes cleaned, but he pulled himself out of his chair and came to me. He put his hand on my shoulder. 'No, Maggie. It shall be as Mrs Grant says. It is what your ma wanted.'

I looked at him and it was as if a great iron cage had disappeared from round my heart and I could feel again. I burnt with anger, enough to set his skin on fire with just one breath.

'How do you know what Ma wanted, Pa? When did you ever bother to ask?'

He took a step back. 'Maggie...'

'No don't bother to answer, because I know the answer. *Never.* You... You let her die. She could have got well. She could have got better.'

'Maggie, no...' He fended my words away as though they were blows. 'Tell her, Agnes.'

Mrs Grant put her hand on my arm. 'No one could cure her, Maggie. It wasn't something that could be stopped.'

'I could have stopped it. I could have found someone. Been here... She was young, she didn't have to die. Why did you not send for me? Fetch me home? I could have...'

What could I have?

Pa turned his head to the window, staring out, great shoulders hunched. 'It's as I've said. You're to go back to your work. It's what your ma wanted. This is not your home any more.'

Everyone was very kind in the office. Miss Sylvia said I should take time off if I needed to, but I did not. I wanted to be working. Miss Christabel said that was sensible of me and kept me harder at it than ever. Night and day, fighting, writing, agitating, up and down the country, always on the move. Not thinking.

I sent money now. Did not visit. I wrote to Mrs Grant, always with a little note for Evelyn and she would send me back a picture or a verse she had learnt and ask when I was coming home. At first I dreaded getting them but after a while I got used to it and what had been a cut became a graze.

And we were so busy.

Mr Hardie speaks every day in the House of the torture, asking how in a civilised country such savagery can be allowed. It seems now they are using tubes which they force down the prisoner's nostrils and pump food into her that way. I have met women who have suffered this. Though they smile and try to make light of it, I can see how dreadful is their suffering. Their noses are swollen and so inflamed they can hardly breathe but rather snuffle, and their eyes are shot with blood from retching. They cannot swallow and their hands shake continually. Their voices are tired and crackling. And yet they go on and on.

Mrs Pankhurst looks quite ashen. I think she fears we are

going to lose the battle after all, for how can we fight barbarians? And it is barbarians that rule this country. Always she has told us that human life is sacred. All human life. So, though we are beaten and abused, we may not strike back. 'Our weapons are not those of the gun, the whip, the truncheon. Our only armour is the truth, our shield, the justice of our cause.'

I asked Miss Christabel if we might not even defend ourselves, for I am a fine fighter now and can kick a pillow half across a room. She said, no, for then we should lose the support of the public. I thought, well, much good this support has done us so far. We are no more than a circus show to them. They may shake their heads and cry 'Shame' but which one of them sleeps less sound for knowing a woman is being slammed to the stone floor of a cell and pumped full of slush?

Every day I send out posters showing the awful deed. The papers, too, are full of it. Pictures, plays, protests. And through all this Mr Gladstone stands up and jokes. He says there is no serious harm can come from force-feeding, and besides, the remedy is in our own hands. He cannot understand what all the fuss is about.

I have walked four hours round Lambeth to collect signatures from doctors to say it must be stopped. That it is dangerous to the health, inhuman, cruel. All were from home when I called. It is the same wherever you go. No one will speak the truth – that women are being tortured in the name of the law. I think they are waiting for one of us to die. Well, if it is me, what good will that do, for I am no one? And it will not be me, for I dare not go through it again. I do anything, everything, to keep myself safe from arrest. I will stay at my desk till midnight and be back again by seven. Miss Sylvia says I must not work such hours, but Miss Christabel applauds it.

Last night Fred came round to take me to the playhouse. He had saved up specially for the tickets, as it was a piece by Mr George Bernard Shaw, and he knows how much I admire him. I wore my beautiful blue shawl, but for all its finery I looked like a bag of bones. I fell asleep after ten minutes. Fred took me home at the interval. He said it was no matter, but I could see how much I had pained him. I hate myself for being so useless. I cannot look pretty in my best clothes. I cannot stay awake in a comedy. What is the point of me at all?

Mrs Garrud says I am burning the candle at both ends. Fred says I am wearing myself into the ground, and he is right. They do not know the reason. That I cannot face the agony again. I will do anything to avoid it.

Miss Christabel has called for volunteers to go to Newcastle. The Lloyd George man is to address a Liberal meeting. Needless to say, first off the starter's post was Miss Davison who is turning quite purple with frustration at not being arrested. She told me she practises force-feeding herself every evening before she goes to bed. I suppose this means pushing a strawberry down her throat without biting, for her skin is as clear as ever and her voice as loud.

Lady Con has again offered herself. Truly she is a brave creature for I believe her fear is as terrible as ever, yet she refuses to yield to it. Surely that is greater courage than to rush blindly into battle, caring only for glory and your picture in the paper? Indeed, I think her photograph on the front page would be a worse punishment far than the two or three days she spends in Holloway each time she comes before the court.

Nobs are not like other people. Once when she was in the cells, the matron came and said it was time to get ready for court, but the bobbies would not depart. Miss Sylvia told me Lady Con stripped right down to her waist and washed in front of them. I would rather die. She also told me Lady Con has carved a 'V' on her chest for 'Votes' or maybe 'Victory'. Surely that must have hurt most terribly?

I have never seen a woman's chest except my own, and Ma's when she was feeding and after she died. Mrs Beckett said they were sinful and we should never ever speak about them. Reverend Beckett said they were God's gift and should be valued above all else. He licked mine to show how much God loved me. I know now how much God loves me and it is not worth the licking.

Miss Christabel has asked me to be part of the protest. She came to the office one evening when everyone had gone. I was preparing *Votes For Women* for the printers. She asked me whether I should not like to write an article to appear in it. I said I did not think I could.

'Why not? You are as literate as half the women in the movement now and that without the benefit of proper schooling. It would give great heart to others such as yourself if you could.'

'Well, I will gladly try if you would like me to.'

'Ah, but what shall you write about, do you think?'

I supposed I should try to tell about my work.

'Yes, yes, but office work is office work, although you do it very well. I was thinking of something more…vigorous.'

'Like my fighting lessons, you mean?'

'You could mention that, certainly. It would be no bad thing if more of our women learnt the art. But, as you know, Maggie, the vital issue now is our battle against force-feeding. I would like you to give an account of your own experiences.' I felt cold all over for I have struggled so hard to forget them.

'What do you think about that?'

I knew there was no choice. 'I will try, if that is what you wish, Miss Christabel.'

'Excellent. I am sure you will do it very well, although since it is such a long time since you were last in prison and the methods have been changed, do you not think it would be a good idea if you were to join the others up in Newcastle? That way it will be fresh in your mind.'

My voice went from me. I could not speak. Miss Christabel was smiling, her head tilted in that quizzical way that makes her every request seem reason itself. 'Of course, Maggie, as you know, there is no compulsion on you to offer yourself for imprisonment. Everyone will understand if you do not feel yourself up to the task, and though it is for working women above all we are fighting, it is a fact that few of them show the strength and dedication needed for such sacrifice.' At the door she turned. 'I had always believed you one of those very few.'

I suppose I should be glad. I was stood outside the Palace Theatre in Newcastle waiting for the Lloyd George, four stones in my pocket, each wrapped in a message of defiance. Not five feet from me is Lady Con, Mrs Brailsford, wife of a famous newsman, and next to her Miss Davison, positively hopping with excitement. Suddenly from far away round the other side we hear a cheer. He has only gone round the back to save himself a meeting with us.

I felt quite sick with relief but, of course, there is no relief in this struggle. Up sweeps another fine black motor. I saw Lady Con step out in front of it, shouting at those inside that they should cease to torture innocent women. Next goes her stone, right past the door and never a scratch.

Miss Davison is struggling to find her pebbles but she is so worked up she drops them all over the pavement and goes scrabbling after them round people's ankles.

I thought, I could drop mine likewise and no one will know the better, but then I thought, is this what Miss Christabel means when she says the poor have no stomach for a fight? Am I to be her proof?

I took the biggest flint in my pouch and flung it with all my might. Straight into the little grating on the front. There was a terrible scrunching sound and the car stopped dead. Out got a man with a great twizzly moustache, curled enough to feed him down his own nose, I remember thinking. He looked mighty angry. Anyone would think it was him I had struck, and not a silly hunk of metal.

Off to the cells. It was a filthy place, the worst I have seen, and at midnight came all the drunks from the alehouses and piled in next door to us, singing, shouting – fortunately their accents were so strange we could not fathom what they were saying, though I am sure it was not for the ears of Lady Con.

One month in the third division, which for Lady Con and Mrs Brailsford means three days in the second. For the rest of us! I wonder that I thought the last time bad. I knew nothing, suffered nothing to this torture. And Miss Christabel asks me to write of it.

How? Where are the words?

Handcuffed, my arms behind my back; dragged by my hair along stone passages; flung down steps, knelt on, slapped, head ripped back and clamped between two vicious fists. My mouth torn open with metal pegs, stretched till my lips split like rotten fruit. Wedged apart. And then the tube. A great snaking coil of filthy vomit-stained rubber crawling down my throat, swallowing me up. Fighting for breath, retching, choking. A distant desolate shriek that comes from outside of me but is me, is all that is left of me. The slurp of the curdled slops plopping into the tube. The daggers of light screaming towards me, the iron band tightening round my brain. How do I write about that?

Miss Christabel says never mind. She does not need the article now. Lady Con has written most movingly of her experiences in prison. She will use that instead.

*Another* election. The Commons have quarrelled with the Lords over taxes. I suppose we do not pay enough to keep them in their scarlet robes and carriages and castles? I have been sent up to Manchester to help with the campaigning.

Fred came to see me off at the station, but though he squeezed my hand like he would like to take it home with him, he did not kiss me. His eyes were dark and anxious. I waved and waved as the train drew out, but he did not wave back. Just stood and watched till I was out of sight.

I was to go first to the City Hall to hand out pamphlets but news came as I arrived, the speaker was delayed. The organiser was near frantic. 'Someone must speak. We have three hundred out there. Promised a London speaker. We cannot fail them at this late stage.' All eyes turned to me.

'I cannot do it,' I stammered, quite stiff with terror. 'I have never spoke to more than ten, and that very badly. I would not know where to begin.'

'Why have you come then?' asked one fierce-looking woman with a twitchy eye.

'To help. That's all. To help.'

'Well then, *help*,' she roared and the very platform quaked beneath me. I wonder any politician can deny these northern women!

At half past seven the curtains on the stage were drawn back and there below us was a sea of faces – men, women, nobs (not many) – just faces for as far as you could see.

There were four of us at the table, the organiser, her assistant, the fierce woman and me. One by one they spoke. There was much clapping and stamping for the fierce woman who told how she had tipped a pint of beer over the head of a local councillor when he dared to suggest she was not his equal. Indeed she could have led an unarmed army into battle I believe, for none would have dared refuse her. At last she finished and after more cheering, the hall fell quiet. The organiser rose. 'Tonight we have a speaker all the way from London to bring us news of our esteemed leader, Mrs Pankhurst and her valiant daughters, and to tell us how the campaign is going down there.' Cheers. 'I ask you to welcome Miss Maggie Robins.'

Clapping. I climbed to my feet, legs of jelly, hands shaking, no breath inside me, my mind as blank as it had been wiped with Mrs Beckett's chalk rag.

'Good evening. I have come up from London today.'
Silence.

A lone man's voice. 'Why, chuck?' Great gales of laughter.
When at last it died away, I tried again.

'I have worked in our office at Lincoln's Inn for…a long
time.'

'That's nice.' Off they go again. The organiser is looking
desperate.

'Get on with it,' yells another.

The fierce woman is on her feet. 'It makes you wonder why
they send 'em to us. Done nothing. Knows nothing. Comes
here to tell us what's what.'

Wild cheers and whoops. Slow handclap for me.

I looked out at their grinning faces and back at hers, so
sure, so full of scorn.

'You are right,' I replied. 'I know nothing, I have done
nothing, because I *am* nothing. I am nothing because
whatever I do, whatever I learn, whatever I try to pass on to
others, counts as nothing as long as I have no voice, no choice
in what I become, in how my life is governed, in how my life
is lived. I am nothing. And so are all of you.

'Do you not see what it is like to be faceless, without a
voice, without the right to decide your own destiny? To be
nothing – less than animals, yet expected to work, to pay
taxes, to drag out your miserable lives in the service of the rich
and powerful? What reason have they to change the laws for
our sakes? What good will it do a fat man with money in a
bank to share it with the starving at his doorstep?'

I heard a faint 'Hear, hear,' from near the back.

I went on, 'This lady is right. I am young, I am ignorant. I have no right to be here, but I am. All I can offer you is my beliefs. That women are not animals. Should not be treated as such. Should be free as men to choose who governs them and how. You ask, 'What have I done?' I have failed. Failed, because men – doctors, they call themselves, who are meant to heal the sick not torture them, have thrust rubber piping down my throat and poured stinking rubbish through it into my belly. And I could not stop them.'

Silence.

'I have thrown stones at windows and missed, every single time.'

Laughter.

'I have had Men of God tell me I must burn in hell for wanting justice.'

'God bless you, girl,' came a voice.

Everyone cheered.

'I have lost the person I loved best in all the world to an illness the rich could cure but the poor could not. Because the poor are nothing.'

Fred was waiting for me on the platform. He looked happier than when he had seen me off, but still not the Fred I knew and loved the best. He kissed me on the cheek.

'Well, now you are famous, Maggie.'

'How "famous"? What do you mean?'

He pulled a newspaper from inside his coat. I could scarce believe it. There, on the front page was a photograph of *me*, my fist in the air (I cannot remember raising it). *NO LONGER NOTHING* ran the headline and, beneath the picture, an account of my speech. '*Grown men weeping*', it

said. Well, I thought that a bit foolish for those that did had
been drunk, but all the same I felt a great warm glow flooding
through me.

'I wonder if Miss Christabel has seen it.'

Fred glanced at me, his eyes weary. 'I'm sure she has,' he
said.

'I hope so. I do hope so.'

'Why? So she can send you on even more dangerous
missions? Your imprisonment will be worth much more to her
now people know who you are.'

I felt shocked right through. 'That is a wicked thing to say.'

'Is it? True, though, I'll warrant.'

I did not know what to make of his remarks. I said, 'Are
you angry with me for having my picture taken? I did not
know they were doing it, I can promise you, or I would have
worn my yellow blouse.' We stood there glaring at each other
in the middle of the platform. A porter struggled by with a
trunk on his back.

''Scuse me, Gov, Miss... Do you think you could kill each
other on someone else's platform? Only I've got another four
of these to shift and the train leaves in ten minutes.'

Fred is so hopeless. Whenever he is trying to look all cross
and serious something always makes him laugh. Once he
started I could not hold off long, although I did not like him
talking about Miss Christabel like that. It is almost as though
he was jealous.

We went to our tearoom. Where we had gone that first
Sunday, after the gallery. Fred does not order anything now
without asking me. I said I would like a slice of chocolate
sponge. He had some too.

'I have a piece of news for you, Maggie.' His face told nothing so I knew not, good or bad. 'I have been offered promotion.'

'Promotion to what?'

'Sergeant. I was waiting to hear when you went away.'

'Is that why you were…?'

'I suppose so.'

'Well, that is wonderful.'

'There is money in it. A hundred a year if I stay in London.'

'And if you do not?' I was still hankering for our cottage in Wood Green.

'Seventy-five. But it is enough, is it not?'

'Enough for what?'

He smiled at me and I came over mushier than in the Manchester hall. 'Enough for two to live on?'

I flung my arms round him. 'It will be near twice that, Fred, for I have fifty now, less what I send my Pa.'

He was quiet for a moment then reached for my hands. 'Maggie, if I am a sergeant, you cannot go on as you are.'

I stared at him. 'Why not?'

'Because while I am a constable I can avoid it. If I am made up, I cannot.'

'You mean you would take us in charge?'

'I'd have no choice.'

I love Fred. I love every hair of his head, every breath of his body, but I slapped him. So hard I think he wondered if day was day and night was night.

He rubbed his poor cheek. 'Not sergeant, then?' was all he said.

\* \* \*

I am on the list of speakers! At our monthly meeting several of the committee remarked upon my visit to Manchester. Miss Sylvia said it was a double triumph, for northern women were famously hard to impress. That much I certainly could vouch for.

Miss Christabel, too, was very generous in her praise, and said she had always known I had what it took. Her saying so meant more to me than a whole book of compliments from anyone else.

This past six weeks I have visited fourteen towns! I have spoken to labourers, countrymen, seamstresses, coal miners and, once, a party of Americans who were on a tour and thought they had tickets for the music hall! Well, we gave them a good show and I think they went home happy. Especially when we all sang 'Rise up, women, for the fight is hard and long' to 'John Brown's Body' at the end. They clapped and stamped and put more money in the collecting plates than we had got in the whole of the week before. Miss Davison said it was because they were too dumb to understand our coins, but I think it was because they were good, true people. I heard one say, 'No American would stand to see his womenfolk so treated.' For a new sort of people they are a sight more civilised than the British.

This election will be like no other. Poor Mr Churchill has spent so much on guards to save him from a bag or two of flour that he can scarce afford the cost of holding a meeting, and when he does, ten to one, one of us will get in and ruin it for him. I have heard of late he has taken to raising his hat to our ladies when they meet. The newspapers say he and the Lloyd George are half persuaded to support us, for they see that we shall win in the end and, I suppose, fear to be on the wrong side when victory comes!

Mr Bernard Shaw has written to *The Times* a most brilliant letter. He told how the Gladstone has said our torture is not torture but a perfectly decent way to be fed and that no one suffers from it in the least. He has therefore invited the Gladstone to the most splendid banquet that ever was, only insisting that, with a cinematograph machine hard by to picture it, the cruel beast shall take each morsel through his nostrils.

Fred says a lot of his colleagues will not arrest the women any more for fear they will be force-fed in the prisons. They think it is quite wrong and not in keeping with the law, though they cannot say as much. 'Why can they not say as much? It is surely their duty to uphold the law?' I quizzed him.

'Yes, it is, but it is the judges send the women to prison, not the police. It is not within our power to say what happens inside a jail.'

'So it is enough to turn your backs and pretend it is not happening?'

He stood stock-still in the middle of the pavement and swung me round to face him. 'Maggie, that is not true. You know full well I have never denied how wicked I think this force-feeding. Never once.'

'No, but you do nothing to halt it.'

'What would you have me do? Shoot the Prime Minister? I am a constable. That is all. I cannot say to the judges, "Stop sending these women to prison. I do not think it right".'

'Why not? Other people do.'

'Who?'

'Lots of people. Famous people. Mr Bernard Shaw, Mr Keir Hardie.'

'Yes, and how much difference has it made? If the Government will not listen to them, do you truly think they will pay any heed to Fred Thorpe, Junior Constable, Marylebone High Street?'

I felt something snap that the man I loved, of all people, should be so feeble.

'You'll never know, Fred, for you are afraid to try.' With that I marched off down the street quicker than I ever walked before. He did not follow me.

The next day came a long brown envelope addressed to me at the office. Inside was a cutting from the Letters Page of *The Times*:

*Sir,*

*As a junior ranking constable with the Central London Police, I wish to state my unreserved detestation of the cruel and inhuman practice of force-feeding, presently being visited upon women prisoners for their part in the fight for Women's Enfranchisement. Whatever the rights and wrongs of their cause they should be entitled to fair and Christian treatment at all times even, or perhaps particularly, within the walls of our penal institutions. I speak only for myself in this when I say that when I swore my Oath of Allegiance to the Crown, I little thought I should be upholding the rule of torture.*

*I remain, Sir, your obedient servant,*

*Frederick Thorpe.*

I showed it to Miss Kerr and Miss Lake. They were strong in their praise for Fred's courage. I asked if I might pin it on the notice-board and was just doing so when Miss Christabel swept in. 'What's this, Maggie? Have you been writing to the papers?'

'Not me, miss. My...'

She peered past me. 'Well, that is very good news, Maggie. My congratulations to your young man. He is obviously someone of principle and good sense. What a pity he is not a little higher up the ranks, then think what currency we could make of it. Still it's a very good start. You must be very proud of him.'

'I am, miss,' I said, thinking I would be if I could be sure he would ever speak to me again.

I need not have worried. When I left the office that evening he was waiting for me just as though nothing had happened. I ran to him.

'Fred, you must forgive me. I never meant... I am so proud.'

'What of?'

'Your beautiful letter. It is wonderful. Quite the best ever written.'

'I couldn't be sure of that.'

'Yes it is. I have shown it to Miss Christabel. She thinks so, too, and if she does, it must be so. It is on the board for everyone to see.'

Fred looked a bit rueful. 'It's on the board at the police station, too, but I don't think my colleagues feel quite the same about it. In fact I know they don't.'

'Why not? They should. They are probably just jealous. Wish they had written it themselves.' This made him laugh a good deal, but not in a very cheerful way.

* * *

Miss Davison is happier than the day she was born. She has excelled herself by getting shut in a cell with two beds and shoving them against the door so the brutes could not enter. Well, clearly they do not need to be inside a cell to do their work, for they went out into the prison yard and turned an ice-cold hosepipe on her through the bars till she was all but drowned.

Miss Christabel has taken down Fred's letter and covered the board in clippings about the affair. It made for grand pictures in the papers and Miss Davison, of course, is full of how she will do it again and again if ever she gets the chance. All I hope is Miss Christabel will not decide we are all to copy her, for it seems to me some of these ladies are in a contest for who can harm themselves the most.

Does Miss Christabel read my mind? Organisers' meeting. 'Miss Davison has set an example we should all be proud to follow', looking straight at me, or so it felt. I stared at my hands. 'It does seem to me that we must continually be looking for new ways to attack the Government. The public is fickle, remember, and easily bored. There is no point in our expecting the press to keep publishing the same old stories. Yes, meetings. Yes, processions. Yes, hunger strikes. But we need more. More. More. We need to keep our faces constantly before them, be it through protests, petitions, disruption.' She lowered her voice. 'My dear sisters, I know how some of you have suffered, are suffering for the Cause... My heart goes out to each and every one of you. Believe me, when you weep, I weep. When you cry out in pain, I cry out with you. When you are slapped and beaten, I, too, am bruised. But do not let it be in vain. Do not let it be for nothing.

'Take the example of these courageous souls and make it your own. Miss Davison endured saturation with freezing water. Lady Con has been arrested four times in the past year, yet bravely returns to the fray. Mrs Brailsford has personally put herself at risk of arrest on several occasions, with all its consequences for her husband's position. Do not leave it to those who perhaps have a better claim to privilege than some of you, to show you the true path to nobility.'

We sat there, watched by this woman whose shoelaces we were not fit to tie, each feeling…what? Guilt? Determination? Inspiration? I know what I felt as I forced my arm into the air. Dread.

'Yes, Maggie?'

I stood up. My hands were shaking and my voice as well, but I knew if I did not speak, my thoughts would turn in on me and I should lose my mind.

'I just want to say that I admire very much the ladies you speak of who work so hard for the Cause and put themselves and, I suppose, their reputations at risk in doing so.'

'Indeed they do.'

'I do not run that risk, I know, for my name means nothing to the rich and those who care about these things.'

'You can still do your bit, Maggie. You need not fear on that count.'

'But I do fear, Miss. I fear because, though Lady Con may be arrested and sent to prison a dozen times, a hundred times, she will not go through what I and the likes of me must. You tell us, Miss Christabel, how brave these ladies are and how we should try to copy them in every way. Well, let them copy us, too. Let them be put a month in the third division and be kicked and dragged by their hair and hurled from one side of their cell to the other. Not sit with the matron reading newspapers and discussing what flowers to sow along the hospital borders till they're let out three days later with 'nerves' and 'flutters' and the like.'

There was a silence. Nobody looked at me. Nobody except Miss Christabel who, for the first time ever in my experience, seemed completely lost for words. Not for long. With a little shrug of her shoulders she collected up her papers and tucked them into a folder. 'Does anyone have anything else they want to bring up, because if not, I'd like to close the meeting. I'm due in Rochester at seven this evening and I need to pop into the printers on the way.'

End of meeting.

Everyone scurried off. I was to turn off the lights and lock up so at least I could shut myself away till they had all gone. When I thought it was safe I came out.

'Maggie.'

I fairly leapt. Lady Con was still sitting there. She looked at me with her grave blue eyes and I felt worse than if I had kicked her.

'I'm sorry,' I muttered. 'I should never have...'

'Yes, you should. If we cannot open our hearts to each other, what hope have we got of convincing anyone else?'

'I never meant... It wasn't against you, Lady Con... It's just that sometimes I feel as though everything I do is counted useless. Not good enough. I do try. But Miss Christabel's right. I am not a lady. I have none of the courage and bravery that goes with being one. I am not made like that. The best I can do is try to bear what comes to me. I cannot go seeking for worse. I simply cannot.'

'I understand that, Maggie. I do not know that I could dare do one half of what I do if I truly believed I should be tortured as you have been. I tell myself it is not the case, but in my heart I know that my name protects me, and always will. So don't ever tell yourself that a "Lady" is a finer person than a woman without a title. We have all your weaknesses and fears. More, probably, for we have never been truly tested, nor will be while rank is valued above merit in a human being.'

We went our ways. I thought, if life had turned out differently that lady and I might have been friends, for we understand each other. I have never felt that with any of the others, except Miss Sylvia and Miss Annie. Miss Annie because she is working class, and Miss Sylvia because…I don't know. It is as though in amongst all these fine noble people she feels my loneliness, how outside I am of everything, and sometimes I think she shares that feeling. I can make the right noises and do (occasionally) the right things, but I am like a creature from the circus. They can dress me up and teach me a thousand tricks, still in the end I will be only what they have made of me, nothing more. The real me does not matter to them. Perhaps it is just as well.

Miss Sylvia came to the office this evening. I was alone, marking up the new calendar. I had not seen her for weeks. She looked drawn and wretched, but so do we all with the election coming up and so much to be done.

There was some cake left over from Christmas so I fetched her a piece, saying, 'Well, now it is my turn to feed you up, just as you did me back at Park Walk.' I thought it would make her smile. To my horror, she lowered her head into her hands and started to sob – not really making any noise, just sort of gulps.

I flew to her. 'Miss Sylvia, what is it? What has happened? Is your mother arrested?'

'No,' she was rubbing her eyes with her sleeve like she used to in the studio. 'Harry. My brother, my dearest brother... Oh, Harry...'

'Is he worse? I am sure he will soon be cured. Quite sure of it. Your mother has found him the very best doctors, has she not?'

Miss Sylvia raised her great dark eyes and stared ahead of her. 'Oh yes. The very best. Always the best. Always too late.'

Word came that no one was to speak to the family about their loss. We were to behave as normal in their presence. Indeed they bore their pain so bravely a stranger would not have guessed they were in mourning. Miss Christabel worked as I had done after Ma died. Speaking, writing, organising, tearing up and down the country to rallies. Never quiet, never still.

I noticed that she would not travel by train if she could help it. One day I booked tickets for her all the way to Liverpool and she almost threw them back at me.

'Maggie, how many times must you be told? Vera will drive me. That is all there is to it.'

Miss Kerr came over to me afterwards. 'You must not take it to heart, Maggie. You were not to know.'

'Know what?'

She sighed. 'Miss Christabel was on a train when she learnt

of her father's death. I think, what with Harry...'

'I'm so sorry, Miss Kerr. No one told me.'

'Well, no, why should they have? Yes, it must have been terrible. To see it like that. On the back of a stranger's newspaper. She and her mother were on their way home to him. But they were too late.' I understood then the meaning of Miss Sylvia's words.

I have always been afraid of Mrs Pankhurst. Not because she has ever been anything but kind and generous to me, but simply because she seemed to me to be so far beyond anything I could approach or reach for in this life. She was like a sort of goddess – calm, wise, noble, gracious, elegant beyond my dreams. Not like any other person in this world.

Yesterday I was sent round to a hall with some leaflets that were needed for the meeting. Not finding anyone out the front I made my way to the room behind the stage where speakers wait. At first I thought it empty, but then I saw someone huddled in the corner, arms drooping, head lolling against the wall like a broken marionette. It was Mrs Pankhurst.

She looked up as I entered, then pulled herself to her feet and came slowly over to shake my hand. 'Maggie, good evening. What have you brought? Ah, yes. Thank you. Thank you.' She took the leaflets and stood motionless just holding them. I asked if there was anything she would like me to help with. For a moment she did not seem to hear, then she shook her head. 'No, thank you, Maggie. Everything is arranged. You need not stay.' She tried to smile.

All evening I could not rid myself of that image. Mrs

Pankhurst, the greatest, bravest, most spoken-of woman in all the world, crumpled, hopeless, lost in a dusty room behind a damp dirty stage. Fighting for something she may never see.

Miss Sylvia went away for a while. She had been so close to her brother and it had been she who had nursed him and stayed with him during those last dreadful months.

I thought of how we had so often talked of our brothers together. It was a bond between us, a happiness shared. Now she has none, and I have three. I would swap them all to give Harry back to her, just for a year. Just for a day. To cure her pain. Is that a sin? Very likely. But does not the Bible say, 'A life for a life'? It does not say whose it should be. Surely, though, if we could choose who lived and who died, would that not make us equal to God? Or to the devil?

Perhaps it is as well that we cannot. God knows, I am near enough to the devil already. I need no further shoving.

Sadly the Liberals won the election again, but only just, and it had one good result – they were so frightened by the people turning against them in such numbers that they finally allowed a bill to let *some* women have the vote be put before them. Mr Pethick Lawrence explained it to me. It is called the Conciliation Bill, and will give women the right to vote if they have property and are not married. I could not see how any woman could own property without a husband, but it seems it can be so. Though hardly ever.

There was such jubilation in the office when the news came through. 'Of course, it is only a start,' Miss Christabel insisted. 'We must not raise our hopes too high yet.' We nodded soberly and tried to look as though we would never have dreamt of doing such a thing. Suddenly her face broke out in a great glittering smile. 'But it takes only a chink in a dam for the torrent to break through. And we have made that chink at last. At last victory is in sight. A whole new world will soon be ours for the taking.'

How we cheered and danced and hugged each other. Even Miss Lake who doesn't like people too close to her in the main. She went quite strawberry-coloured when Miss Christabel flung her arm around her shoulders and gave her a squeeze. You would have thought it was a handsome man had done it, the way she blushed. Still, maybe I would have, too, had Miss Christabel put her arm round me.

Fred was nearly as excited as I when I told him. 'But this is wonderful news. The most wonderful news. This requires at least…three ices and two pieces of cake.'

'Two ices and three pieces of cake. I do not want to get fat.'

He laughed till I thought he would fall over.

Afterwards we walked by the river and he held my hand like when it used to be worth holding. As we came to Westminster Bridge he stopped. Across the water we could see the Palace of Westminster, the Houses of Parliament.

'Maggie.'

'Yes?'

'Do you remember that night you took me back to your lodgings?'

I stared at my scrawny knuckles poking out from my scrawny hands at the end of my scrawny arms. It seemed so long ago.

'Yes.'

'Do you remember what I said to you that night?'

'You said so many things.'

'I said I would not give you a baby unless we were married.'

My whole body stiffened like a rod.

'Now that your cause is won...'

I raised my hand to stop him. 'I cannot have a baby any more, Fred.'

'What do you mean?'

'It is a side effect, Miss Annie says.'

'A side effect of what? What are you talking about?'

I looked at him. 'Of the starving. And the torture. I have... I...there is no more bleeding.'

It was like a light going out in his eyes. 'You are barren?'

'Yes.' I could not bear to see him so unhappy. 'So it will do no harm if I lie with you, if that is what you are asking. I will not be disgraced.'

This time he slapped me. 'Don't you ever speak like that again, Maggie Robins. Children or no children, I want you for my wife. And I will not lay one finger on you till that day comes. So let it not be long.'

We both cried. And then we held each other close and pretended we didn't mind about the babies, for though I did not greatly want them, it made me sad to see how much he did.

That night I lay in bed and thought how I should soon be married and all this life would be behind me. No more pug-faced judges, prison cells, starving, torture, suffering. It would fade away into my memory like some cruel nightmare. And with it, too, would go the laughter, the hope, the striving, the comradeship, the longing for a new tomorrow. Now victory was in sight.

*  *  *

But it was not. The chink in the dam was soon sealed up again. Mrs Pankhurst said we should bide our time and see what came of the Conciliation Bill. Demonstrations ceased. We put on weight, regained our health. I started to bleed again. Life seemed so nearly good. For a little while.

Yet what came of it was what always comes of anything we are promised. Nothing.

The Government delayed and delayed, then fell out with the House of Lords until it looked as though Parliament would have to be dissolved and another election called. Fortunately we were saved from this, thanks to the King, who managed to fall ill and die before they got round to it.

Everywhere was gloomy, the shops all draped in black and many of the people, too. I could not see that it was such a sad thing for he was old and caught his fever on a holiday, so at least he had had a nice time first.

Fred and I watched the funeral procession and then had a picnic by the river. Some of the people passing tut-tutted at us and said we should show more respect, but I do not see that dead people can mind what you eat particularly, and besides, if we are to believe the churchmen, the King was probably up with all the angels having heavenly manna by then.

Mrs Grant wrote to say that Pa would like me to visit. At first I thought I would not for we should be bound to quarrel, but in the end I did and was glad of it. They were all so happy to see me and mighty happy to see a mutton pie and strawberries!

Little Evelyn is grown quite tall and very pretty. She reminds me so of Ma with her grey eyes and wavy brown hair. Like Ma once was. Baby Ann is walking though she does not talk yet. Will shouts at her all the time but she does not mind him. Just smiles. Mrs Grant fair dotes on her.

Alfie is to marry Edith just as soon as he has saved enough for a proper bed, he says. I am surprised he does not build one, but he is still not good with numbers and it would be a sorry thing if it turned out the size of the coal box.

Evelyn cried bitterly when it was time for me to go. I promised I would come again soon if Pa agreed it. He came with me to the door.

'Maggie...'

'Yes, Pa?'

'I am glad to have seen you.'

'Yes.'

'I would have...wanted...wished to... I never meant for you to stay away so long. I just wanted...'

'What, Pa?'

'I wanted you to be free. For your ma's sake. For her. Because she never was.' He stared past me like he was looking for the words in the street lamps. 'And she should have been, Maggie. She was clever like you, bright as a star. I felt like I'd seen an angel the first time she walked by me coming out of church. It seemed like a miracle she could feel the same about me, but we married so young, and we had so little, and then you children came and the spirit just drained out of her. I watched it going, drop by drop, and did nothing. I didn't know what to do. I couldn't give her back her life, her freedom. I wanted to. I just couldn't.'

I nodded. 'I know Pa,' though I had not known, for I had not believed him capable of such feeling. Had not known him. Had not loved him enough.

Is that how it would be if Fred and I were wed? Not a house in the country with a swing. Just a stinking hovel in some back street with babies sliding out of me like shelled peas. No, never. I would rather die. But surely Pa never thought that was how it would end for him and Ma? If she had hopes, he must have had them too. If she loved him, he must have been loveable, not the great lumpen drudge he has become. So when did it go wrong? Why? How can I stop it happening to me? *Fight on and God will give the victory.* But will he give it to us?

In June we held a giant procession for we had a new king and queen and with them, new hope. The Conciliation Bill had been read on June 14th and passed without a murmur! No one doubted that by autumn the struggle would be over.

Everyone came from all over the country, and it was so grand and beautiful and peaceful. Like when we first started. Like Women's Sunday.

How good it will be if we can keep on like this. Mrs Pankhurst says she is sure we are almost there. Two more readings and then the bill will go to the Lords who, she promised us, are far too dim and cowardly to gainsay the House of Commons.

The Asquith is doing all in his power to delay it but there are too many against him now, I truly believe. Although the rat, Churchill, and that pasty Lloyd George, with his whiney sing-song voice, have gone to great lengths to destroy the bill by saying it was not fair to all women which, of course, it is not. But, as Miss Christabel says, 'It is better than nothing'. And once *some* women have the vote, it cannot be long before the rest of us do. I am convinced of it.

Fred has written to his father to see if he may take me to meet him. Although he says we will be married no matter what, I know he would cherish his father's blessing, and so should I. I feel for the first time in so many years that things are truly going to work out right. And I can do a double flip. Mrs Garrud says it is amazing after all I have been through. I tell her it is that that has made me strong.

Hope is a strange thing. It lifts you up, high, higher...and then it drops you down. So quickly. But always there is a little drop left. Like a seed, ready to grow again when the time is right.

Fred has had a letter from his father saying he will be glad to meet me. He is so cheerful. We are to go on November 20$^{th}$. It is his sister's fifteenth birthday though, of course, we may not take presents. I asked Fred if I could bake some biscuits and he said it was worth a try! If not we will eat them on the way home.

It was not to be. I was a fool to think otherwise. I remember Reverend Beckett preaching one Easter about the thieves who were crucified beside Our Lord. He said one of them repented but the other could not – scorned Lord Jesus and said if he were truly the Son of God he would save himself *and* them. Reverend Beckett said that man was born of darkness. 'Some people are born of darkness and can never be saved. They are the children of the devil. Fear them, for they will destroy your soul. They are destined for eternal darkness.' I never thought then he was talking about me.

\* \* \*

A Special Meeting. There is talk of a fresh election. If so, the Conciliation Bill will fall. We are to march upon the House. Only those chosen are to go. No one old or ill or still at school. There will be no more talking. We have been denied too long. We have had enough.

Mrs Pankhurst came to speak to us. She walked among us like a ministering angel, joking, encouraging, inspiring. Is this how the disciples felt when Jesus came amongst them? Is it a mortal sin to even wonder? What if Jesus had been a woman? How would the world be then?

She said we must keep on, no matter what. 'In quietness and assurance shall be your strength. All your other kind of efforts have failed, you will now press forward in quietness and peaceableness, offending none and blaming none, ready to sacrifice yourselves even unto death if need be, in the cause of freedom.'

'Even unto death'. I thought, what good will freedom do me if I am dead?

November 18<sup>th</sup> 1910. Black Friday, they are calling it. Why? Why do they do this to us?

Escorted by bobbies all the way to Parliament Square, suddenly they are nowhere. And who takes their place? Savages. Great brutish louts who seize us by the hair, the neck, the arms, flinging us at walls, pavements, cobble-stones; slapping, kicking and, if it is to be believed, dragging some of our women into alley-ways and forcing themselves upon them. And these were policemen. These are the men who serve beside the man I love. And he is one of them. Ordered by Mr Churchill to turn us back. This creature, this politician who has smiled and nodded and pretended to be our friend. I do not understand why Jesus would choose to come on earth as a man for they are less than cockroaches.

All of them.


This morning I went to Marylebone. To the police station. I asked to speak to Fred. His friend, Sergeant Neal, came out of his office and asked could he help me? I said, no, my business was personal. He sent someone to fetch him. Fred came down. His face was pinched with fatigue. 'Is it about last night?'

'It is.'

'Maggie, we did not know. No one from here was involved. Not one of us. You must believe that.'

I said, 'Yes, I do. But you are all policemen and so were they.'

'We condemn it. Condemn it with all our hearts. It should never have happened. Been allowed. Those men are a disgrace to their calling.'

Something inside me burst. 'You condemn it so much that you close your eyes and hide yourselves away, Fred. Is that "protecting the people from villains?" I would call it "protecting villains from the people". How long can you go on like that? A dog cannot serve two masters. You ask me to give over the Cause. When have I ever asked you to give over being in the police?'

'Never.'

'No, and I never will, because if you cannot see how wrong it is, I am not the one to show you.' I turned and came away. So now my choice is made.

# PART FOUR

## 1910–1913

I am working harder than ever. It is the only way. Every time I hear a man's foot on the stair I pray it will be Fred, come to take me back, to forgive me for treating him so wickedly, to tell me he understands what makes me say the things I say, act as I do. And he does. He is the only person on this earth who has stood by me always. When I was beaten, starved, tortured, hideous, he picked me up and loved me anyway. He showed me what life could be like. How there could be music and painting and poetry and laughter in amidst all this cruelty and poison. And I have thrown it all away.

Perhaps if I went to him, explained... What? That I made *him* choose because I had not the strength to do it myself? And he had.

Miss Christabel has just returned an article I passed for the printers.

'Really, Maggie, are you sleeping on the job? Where are the quotation marks, the commas? You've even let "Asquith" by with a small "a". Whatever we think of the man, we must at least spell his name right.'

'I'm sorry, Miss Christabel.'

'Yes, well, I can see you're tired. What about if I ask Mrs PL if you can pop down to The Mascot for a day or two? Put some colour back in your cheeks.'

I said I would rather not just at present.

'Fair enough, but we must have more attention to the job. This election may be the turning point. Even the men are starting to rally round us now. Poor Alfred Hawkins had his leg broken being chucked out of one of Churchill's rallies. Still, do them no harm to find out what it feels like for a change. I'll leave this with you, shall I?

'Oh, by the way, are you still seeing that bobby friend of yours? Because if so, perhaps you can wheedle the names of some of his thuggee colleagues out of him. Lord Lytton plans to raise last Friday's abomination in the House. Not that he got anywhere after the Jane Warton business.'

'Which business was that, miss?' I asked, to change the subject.

Miss Christabel flapped her hand in front of my eyes. 'Wake up, Maggie. Surely you heard? Oh, no. I think you were in prison. Lady Con got it into her head that she was receiving special treatment on account of her social position, so she cut off all her hair, dressed herself in rags and got herself arrested as a seamstress called Jane Warton.'

'What happened?' I asked, feeling quite sick.

'Oh, dreadful. They fed her without any medical checks. Same as the rest of us. What they didn't realise is she has a chronic heart condition. She'll never recover. Our first real martyr, you might say. We're all so proud of her. Anyway, back to what I was saying. See what you can glean. There has to be some use in consorting with the enemy.'

The words burst out of me. 'He's not the enemy. He's the truest friend I ever had.' But she was gone. And I thought, what need of an enemy, with me to fight for you?

Tonight I went back to Marylebone police station. It has been a fortnight and I cannot think, cannot eat, cannot sleep. I cannot live this way. I asked if I might speak to Constable Thorpe. I did not know what I would say. Sergeant Neal came out of his office.

'I'm sorry to disturb you yet again, Sergeant Neal.'

'It's not a problem. What can I do for you, Miss Robins?'

'I wanted... Is it possible?...I know I shouldn't... Can I just please speak to Fred, just for one moment? I promise I won't be long.'

He was looking at me in a funny way – surprised – shocked, even. Embarrassed. 'Did you not know?'

'Know what?'

'I felt sure he would have... He isn't here, Maggie.'

'Oh, I'm sorry. I thought he was on duty Wednesday evenings.'

'He is... He was.'

I stared at him.

'He's gone, Maggie. Left. Resigned from the force.'

'But where... Where has he gone? What did he say? Surely...'

Sergeant Neal shook his head regretfully. 'He didn't say anything. Only he had had enough. It wasn't for him. He was tired of being a policeman.'

I went round to his lodgings. He had left the week before. The landlady's daughter, Miss Blackett, answered the door. I could see what Fred meant. She scowled at me when I asked if she knew where he had gone. 'He didn't say. I expect he'll be writing to me with his address as soon as he's sorted, though. Not that I shall be able to pass it on.'

'No, of course not. But perhaps if you could just...'

I saw her looking at me, looking the way the wardresses do before they come marching in with their straps and manacles and funnels scaly with rotting mucus. Triumphant. The Chosen Ones. Come to visit judgement on the sinners.

Inside and out, these Chosen Ones are everywhere, it seems to me. And what sort of a God is it that chooses them? Am I not a thousand times better to be one of the Rejected when my fellows are Miss Christabel and Miss Annie and Miss Sylvia? Better to be next to them in hell than with Miss Blackett and the brutes in heaven.

I turned and walked away.

So this shall be my life now. The Cause. It is so much easier, better, to be dedicated to one thing and one thing only. Before I was always torn between my love for Fred and my duty to my work. As Miss Christabel said, 'A dog cannot serve two masters.' Well, I am no better than a dog but I shall serve this cause harder than anyone ever did. I will make Miss Christabel proud of me, and Mrs Pankhurst, too. I will make up for all my weakness and cowardly behaviour in the past. Nothing shall ever frighten me again, for to be frightened you have to be afraid of losing something and I have nothing left to lose.

Things are going well again. Men as well as women are flocking to the Cause. There are plays about suffragettes, songs, poems and every day the papers are full of it. Mrs Pankhurst's great friend, Dr Ethel Smyth, has written a piece of music specially. It is called 'March of the Women' and when we first heard it a lot of us thought we would rather hear cats fighting on a tin roof, but we are all to learn it in time for our next demonstration, before the coronation. If we sound as bad as the choir that sang it to us I should think the Parliament will give us the vote just to go away.

The Government has some plan to count everyone. I cannot think why. What difference does it make how many people there are unless you intend to feed them or educate them or cure them when they are ill, and for sure this government will not do that.

We are to avoid it (you can only be counted in your own home, it seems. A bit like poor Mary having to go all the way to Bethlehem, I suppose, and we all know what trouble that started).

Great events are being arranged to occupy us on the day. There are to be concerts and parties and dancing – anything to keep us out till past counting time. Miss Sylvia and I are going to go roller-skating. You have wheels tied to your feet and then you skid round and round forever. At least I shall, for no one has told me how to stop. Miss Sylvia says if we get tired she knows at least three parties we can go to. One with a fortune-teller. I am so looking forward to it. Perhaps the Government can be persuaded to count the people every month. It is just the sort of thing they like to spend their time on in order to avoid the proper business of the day. Wait till we get the vote. Then they will have to work for their money. No wonder they fight it so hard.

This Prime Minister, Asquith, is surely closer to the serpent than any man born. With all the country on our side, and half the world, to judge from the letters pouring in, he ups and changes the bill that was to give us our rights at last. In its place, the Manhood Suffrage Bill. Votes for all. Oh yes. All men!

Mrs Pethick Lawrence was close to tears. 'After all this time. All our efforts. The suffering. The imprisonment. The… All for nothing. Nothing. Worse than nothing.'

'But if this bill is passed, will that not pave the way for our own?' Miss Kerr sort of whispered.

Mrs Pethick Lawrence threw up her arms in despair. 'No. A thousand times, no. Do you not see, if all those men who are without a vote are granted one, do you truly believe they will continue to side with us? To fight on our behalf? Once they have achieved their goal?'

Miss Kerr looked very chastened. 'They might.'

Mrs Pethick Lawrence gave a mournful sigh. 'If only I had your faith, Miss Kerr. However, experience has taught me that altruism is a preserve of the Chosen Few.'

I looked up 'altruism'. *Unselfishness.* I can only think her Chosen Few are not the same as mine. And if they are not, then maybe neither is anything else. Maybe none of them think the same as me. Want the same things. Would that be so surprising? I am from a different world. I could live a hundred years amongst these people and not be one of them. I read somewhere that there was a queen who, when she died, they cut her open and found the word 'England' carved right across her heart. Well if the same thing happens to me, they will find 'Stepney' writ on mine. And how they will laugh.

Oh, I am so tired. So tired of it all. Fred, I miss you so much. I am so alone.

\* \* \*

Today I thought I should go mad. I had thought and thought so hard, lain awake half the night trying to persuade myself out of it. In the end I decided if the sun was shining in the morning I would do it, but if it rained or was even a tiny bit cloudy, I would not. I was woken by the sun on my face.

It was a beautiful card. A giant green tree all covered in silver tassels with presents laid at the foot of it and a family – boy, girl, mother and father all gazing at each other and smiling. Inside it said, 'May the blessings of the season be with you.' I had wanted to write something extra but, though I spent half the morning scribbling little messages, none of them seemed right, so in the end I put, 'with love from Maggie'. On the envelope I wrote: Constable Fred Thorpe, Hadlow Village, Buckinghamshire. At lunchtime I ran all the way to the post office before I had time to change my mind and posted it in the great box outside.

At half past two Miss Lake came bursting into the office. 'You'll never guess what. Miss Davison is arrested.'

This was nothing new.

'Why?' I asked.

'Oh, a very audacious thing. She put a lighted taper into the pillar-box outside the main post office.'

I felt my throat tightening. 'What happened?'

'Well, two bobbies rushed forward and dragged her off to the police station.'

'To the things in the box?'

'Goodness, I don't know. Burnt to a cinder, I expect. What a whiz idea, though.'

\* \* \*

I went home for Christmas. Mrs Grant was there and wearing one of Ma's old aprons. I know it was wrong of me but I spoke sharply to her. Not about that – something stupid like the way she sliced the mutton. She looked so wretched that I could have bitten my tongue off. Lucy thought it a great joke.

Later I said I was sorry. Mrs Grant looked so relieved. 'Maggie, I understand. It was foolish of me. I did not think. I had left my apron at home and did not want to spoil my best skirt, that is all.'

We both knew this was not true, but Ma is gone now, and Mrs Grant has had more than her share of grief. Why should she not scoop a ha'p'orth of happiness out of what comes her way? Pa seems a sight better tempered, and the children are clean and fed and Mrs Grant is past the age for birthing, so where's the harm? It's a hard life for a woman without a man.

Thankfully no one asked about Fred. Too busy eating. I dreaded that Lucy would say something but she held her peace till the evening when I was getting ready to leave. Then she showed me a pretty blue bangle. 'Guess who gave me this?'

I shrugged. 'Pa?'

She snorted with scorn. 'When did our Pa ever give anyone a present?'

I took a breath, 'Frank, then?'

I swear if the Asquith needed a female serpent for company my sister Lucy would serve. Her slitty pale eyes fair gleamed. 'Fred.'

'You are a liar.'

'Am I? Am I? Well, why don't you ask him yourself? If you can find him.'

I could not help myself. I took hold of her hair and shook her till she screamed like a boiled cat. Pa came running and pulled me away, but not before I had a fistful of her scraggy locks.

'What's this? Maggie, let go. What are you thinking of? Leave go your sister *now*.' So I did because if I had not, I would have killed her.

Lucy hauled herself into a corner, whimpering like some half-eaten rat.

Pa shook his head in despair. 'What is it between you two that there is never a moment's peace when you are together?'

'Ask her,' I spat.

'I'm asking you.'

'Nothing. There is nothing between us. Nothing.'

Bull's-eye! I broke the whole of the front window, all full of dummies daubed in jewels and silk and top hats. There they stood, sprinkled with glass like diamond dust, their proud bony noses poked up at the sky as though nothing had happened, and I swear they looked more real than the nobs they copy.

Mrs Pankhurst had fooled the Government into thinking we would gather on March 4th. While they were stretching their brains round how to crush us, we flocked into the West End on the 1st and broke every shop window between Marble Arch and Tottenham Court Road.

Better still, my stone went into Marshall and Snelgrove where that pickle-faced crow, Miss Blackett, works. Buyer or not, she will have her work cut out to clear that lot up.

The police, expecting nothing, were slow to come after us

although when they did arrive they looked in no mood for jokes. I had told my team to run straight for Mrs Garrud's. As fast as we got there she had us out of our clothes and into fighting garb, our weapons hid beneath loose floorboards in the studio. Seconds later came the screech of whistles and furious thumping on the door.

'Quick, girls. Bicycles.' And down we went on our mats, peddling the air for all we were worth. Mr Garrud let them in. Six great bobbies came thundering up the stairs and there they stopped, great whiskery chops hanging open.

Mrs Garrud, cool as a cucumber, turns to them. 'May I ask the reason for this interruption? Girls, you may lower your legs now. Just lie on your fronts and practise your breathing.'

One crimson-faced sergeant steps forward. 'I beg your pardon, ma'am, but we had information that some suffragettes were seen entering this house. They have caused a pile of damage to the Oxford Street shops just now and it is our duty to try to apprehend them.'

Here my breathing turned into snorts for I was trying so not to laugh. Mrs Garrud sent me for a glass of water. On the way out one of the bobbies peered at me real hard. I did a cartwheel right under his nose so he would have something worth gawping at.

When they had gone we fell about laughing.

If the Government thought because of the 1st they could forget about the 4th…! Knightsbridge took such a knocking! Glass, glass, glass. So many arrests. I know not how I escaped it. Perhaps it is because now I know so many back streets and side-alleys. So different from when I first came to London. I almost never get lost now.

What I would not give to be back to those days. I must not think like that. 'Times change. Life moves on,' as Miss Christabel would say.

Times certainly changed this morning. I had hardly drawn the blinds when there was a clanging on the doorbell and in came four detectives to charge Miss Christabel and the Pethick Lawrences with 'Incitement', and now Miss Christabel is fled to France. I can hardly believe it. That she would leave us.

We are like a rudderless ship, tossed this way and that in a stormy sea with no lighthouse to guide us to calmer waters.

I did not think of that, I am happy to say. Miss Davison came up with it and insists it goes in the next edition of *Votes For Women*. If there is one, for with Mr and Mrs Pethick Lawrence arrested, I do not know how we shall sort it. I begin to wonder if Miss Davison uses so much Greek and Latin because her English is so soppy.

One wonderful thing has come out of all this. Miss Annie is back to run the office. Each weekend she travels to France and returns on the night train with Miss Christabel's articles and new instructions for us.

Stone throwing is the order of the day. The prisons are full to bursting. It is a strange time. Half of the public support us and half are against so much violence, for though Miss Christabel insists that we respect all human life, she urges us constantly towards greater and greater destruction of property. She says it is the only way, and if the Government pays no heed when its offices are attacked, then we must go further and destroy their very homes.

I do not like the thought of this. Desks and typewriters are one thing. Where a man lives with his family is another altogether.

And yet today I would gladly destroy the home of Judge Lord Coleridge and everything about him from his flee-ridden wig to his fat flat feet. Nine months! Mrs Pankhurst, Mr and Mrs Pethick Lawrence. 'Conspiracy and Incitement'.

'But what is that?' I begged Miss Sylvia. 'They have never thrown a stone between them. Nor harmed anyone. Except with their truth and courage.'

'I know, I know, Maggie. It is a dreadful sentence. Quite awful.' She looked so pale and exhausted, but I had to know.

'Please tell me what it means. I need to understand.'

She sank down in a chair. 'It means... I suppose it means trying to force other people to do your bidding, whether they want to or not.'

'Like the politicians, you mean?'

She nearly smiled. 'I'm afraid so.'

The feeding has begun again. Terrible tales come out of women bleeding from their ears, unable to swallow, their vision wrecked, limbs cracking over pumped up bellies. I daily give thanks that I am needed here and cannot leave the office. Every day comes news of some fresh torture. A 'doctor' has writ that women are mad by nature and nothing can alter it! I wonder if he thought them mad when they answered his every bidding, or if he has come but lately to such lofty thinking.

Miss Davison, who managed to get herself arrested merely for going into the post office (a thing I do every day without a second glance from anyone) has thrown herself down the stairs at Holloway and is in the prison hospital, mightily wounded.

Miss Kerr telephoned the news to France. Back comes the order, 'Tell Maggie she's to write a whole column in Miss Davison's honour. Make sure it gets the front page.'

I said I would not (only to Miss Kerr).

She looked terribly worried. 'Oh, please, Maggie. I'd do it myself but I haven't a minute free at the moment.'

'Why can't she do it herself? She does everything so much better than anyone else.'

'Oh, Maggie, that's not very generous. Miss Davison is such a very brave soul. Surely you should feel proud to be asked to write her praises?'

'I've no doubt I should, Miss Kerr. But I don't.'

She said no more but when Miss Annie got back the two of them were talking together for ages and then Miss Annie came looking for me. 'Maggie, what's this, you don't want to write our front page for us?'

I was ready for her. 'It's not that I don't want to, miss. I just don't think I'm up to it.'

'Of course you are. We wouldn't have suggested it else. Miss Christabel was most particular. She says you have a fine way with words.'

'Not Latin and Greek ones, miss. And I'm sure Miss Davison would expect a deal of those.'

'Miss Davison is in no condition to choose at the moment, Maggie, and I'm sure if she were, she would like nothing better than for you to chronicle her deeds in your own distinctive way.'

I thought, that she would not, for it would make for pretty spiky reading.

'And besides,' she went on, 'Miss Christabel desires it specially. Don't worry about the filing. I'll get someone else to finish it for you.'

By three o'clock I had got no further than: *Miss Emily Davison has been taken to the prison hospital again. Sadly. She threw herself down the stairs and is much hurt by it. Sadly. She has done things like this before.*

Miss Sylvia called in with some press cuttings and she and Miss Annie came to see how I was getting on. Poor Miss Annie looked quite desperate when she saw. 'It's fine, Maggie, so far. But couldn't you try and go a little bit faster? We need it at the printer's first thing tomorrow.'

'I'm sorry, miss. It just doesn't seem to be coming quite as it should.'

'No, well, do your best. If you can't finish it in time I'll just have to stay late and see what I can come up with.'

'Yes, miss.'

When she had gone Miss Sylvia popped back to me. 'Maggie, I have a suggestion. Tell me if I'm being stupid, but why don't you pretend you're writing about Mama? I know how much you admire her, and it would be such a shame if the front page was...well, a bit...dull, if you see what I mean.'

I was off like a rocket and finished by ten past four, although Miss Sharp who has taken over the paper for now, did ask I remove the line about 'withered old bones' and 'a lady of advancing years'. I have still not forgiven Miss Davison for burning my Christmas card to Fred.

Perhaps it was meant to be. Perhaps I should be grateful to her. I only know I am not.

Oh, Fred. Where are you? Why did you go? I miss you so much. I have got back my body nearly. I am healthy again. My arms are strong and firm like before, my hands are soft. I'm no longer a witch. And every part of me is aching for you. For all the things you were going to help me be. A wife, a mother, a woman. Now I shall never know any of them.

But I have my work.

Mrs Pankhurst and Mr and Mrs Pethick Lawrence have been released at last. They are gone abroad to recover. Today a Labour Member of Parliament challenged the Prime Minister, calling him a torturer and a murderer. His name is Mr Lansbury and he was thrown out for his pains.

The Government has done a wicked thing. The wickedest of all. It has sent the bailiffs to The Mascot to take away the furniture and sell it to pay for the court cases. My heart is sick when I think of that most beautiful of homes being torn apart by villains and thieves, for that is all bailiffs are, and the worse for they carry the law with them in their thievery. I did not think such a thing could happen to a gentleman and lady, like Mr and Mrs Pethick Lawrence.

And now the shopkeepers are at it, too. Saying they must be paid for their windows and it is for Mr and Mrs Pethick Lawrence to bear the cost of it. They are like dogs picking at the flesh of a great fallen lion. Well, a lion may fall but he may rise again and then beware, those dogs.

I showed that to Miss Sharp and she gave me that funny fierce look of hers and said, 'Not bad, Maggie. I think we might find a space for that.'

\* \* \*

Miss Sylvia came to the office tonight. I was about to lock up. We had had a busy day for tomorrow there is to be a great meeting at the Albert Hall to welcome home Mr and Mrs Pethick Lawrence. God knows, they have been greatly missed.

I could see she was troubled.

'I have bad news, Maggie. Dreadful. I wanted you to know before it becomes public for it affects you – all of us, very deeply.'

My heart started pumping. I did not dare to think what was coming.

'My mother and Christabel have had a secret meeting with Mr and Mrs Pethick Lawrence in France. They discussed the bailiffs' writ and all that that means. It seems that if the Government insists on applying it, it will be entitled to charge every penny of damage our movement causes to the Pethick Lawrences personally.'

'But why them? Why not all of us?'

'Because they have been found guilty of Conspiracy, so every deed may now be laid at their door. Besides, they alone have sufficient means to be worth hounding through the courts.'

'What will happen?

Miss Sylvia sighed deeply. 'It already has. Mother and Christabel are bent on pursuing a violent course, no matter what. There have long been disagreements on that subject. It has reached the point where the Pethick Lawrences are no longer prepared to lend their name to such activities. Mrs Pethick Lawrence is a Quaker, after all.'

'A Quaker?' I squawked.

'Yes, and a pacifist. They both are. And so, in my heart, am I.' She stood up. 'But I am also a Pankhurst.' And though she did not say it, I knew she wished she were not.

So the Union was split. We moved to premises in Kingsway and because we no longer had Mrs Pethick Lawrence to hold us in check, the office became noisier, and madder and more disorganised, and so did our supporters. Mrs Pankhurst counselled no caution, except in the matter of human life, and that not our own. It is odd that for one who cares so deeply about the safety of others, she seems so reckless with ours. And Miss Christabel even more so. Perhaps a broken head looks less painful from across the water in France.

I did not mean that. Sure, without her the whole movement would crumble into dust. I remember Miss Sylvia saying once how the militants had 'injected the thrill of life' back into the fight, when it had all but sunk into a 'coma of hopelessness'. And that is thanks to Miss Christabel more than anyone. She is the inspiration and force behind our every move. I am ashamed of myself for even thinking as I did.

Gone, too, our magazine. Mr and Mrs Pethick Lawrence continue to publish *Votes For Women* and have found great favour with those who prefer a more peaceable approach. That will not do for the militants, naturally, so a new one has been started, *The Suffragette*, full of fire and brilliance, but without their calming influence it often reads more like a hellfire preacher's ranting than a plea for fairness and justice.

The Labour politician, Mr Lansbury, who called the Asquith a torturer, has shown himself a true hero, resigning his seat and seeking re-election as an Independent, hoping to further our cause. Miss Sylvia admires him mightily and has made him one of her speakers. He is to stand at the by-election in Bow.

I went down to help. The people loved him, and but for his old party making trouble against him, he would have won, I am sure. Now the Tory has got in. In Bow! His name is Blair and he has to be told what to say all the time.

Miss Sylvia is quite down about Mr Lansbury losing. She says the people of the East End deserve someone like him to stand up for them. She has had an idea. To gather a deputation made up only of working women from all over the country and take them to speak before the Lloyd George and Sir Edward Grey, who is now quite white, but has grown a little softer with the years. Mrs Drummond is to take charge so whatever happens it will be exciting! Miss Annie is going too. There is to be a tailoress and a laundress and a pit-brow woman. A fisherwoman is coming all the way from Scotland. Good thing Mrs Drummond is going, so at least one person will understand what she is talking about.

Miss Sylvia asked if I would be of the number. I thought it a strange request. 'What can I say? I work in an office and am paid good money.'

She said, 'Tell them where you came from.'

When the women had spoken, of how they worked ten hours a stretch for half of what the men earned, of how they swung hot irons from dawn till dusk because men could not stand to do it, of how they dressed the dead from the mines and cared for the children left behind, nursed the sick, stitched till their fingers bled, sweated over boiling tallow vats, choked on cotton dust till their lungs filled like pillows, it was my turn.

I could see they were surprised to see me rise. Indeed I was quaking so heartily I feared I should fall down dead in a faint, for my feet and hands were tingling as when the prison butchers tied me to the torture chair.

Then I thought, these men are not my torturers. How can I fear them when I have endured so much worse? So I gripped my snivelling drops of courage and began. 'Excuse me, sirs, I know I am young and have little knowledge of the world or how it should be.'

'I would imagine that to be true,' muttered one of them.

'But still I know that it is wrong for a woman to watch her children die, as my mother did, for want of medicine and victuals, and coal to light a fire. To have to choose between her ma and her pa, who shall stay and who go to the workhouse. To have a baby made on her year in year out, and when she is too ill for any more to...' I stopped. 'To have no power over her life and let it slip away as though she had never been, because she counted for nothing to those who could have made things better. There must be good men in the world, sir. And I know there are. Who would rule justly and seek to change such misery. They are the men we would vote for. How can that be wrong?'

They listened. And heard nothing.

There is to be no bill at all. The Parliament has ruled that to include women in the Manhood Suffrage Bill would so alter it that they must throw it out and start again. Well, if they do not do so soon they will have to start the whole country again,

I think, for there is so much damage done, it cannot last much longer. Messages carved in golf courses, telegraph wires cut, windows smashed, the Crown Jewels attacked!

Miss Sylvia is gone into the East End and will hardly come near us, so dismayed she is by all this destruction. Still the orders come. More breaking, more smashing, more slashing – pictures, posters daubed with slogans, houses fired, railway stations bombed, a cannon shot off at Dudley Castle!...

They have burnt down our tearoom in Regent's Park. I walked up there last evening when I heard. A little crowd had gathered, the people gazing and shaking their heads. 'Next they'll be burning us in our beds,' one man said.

'Stick 'em in a barn and set light to that. See how they like it,' said another.

'There'll be lives lost.'

'So long as it's theirs. Mad, they are. Worse than mad. Wicked.'

I thought, are you the ones that picked us out of the gutter and sent us on our way with all your cheering? Have you changed so much? Or have we?

When they had gone I went and stood in the ruins, by the window where Fred and I had sat and looked out at the great elephant, and it was still there, waiting.

A new law has come in. It has a long name, but Mr Pethick Lawrence calls it 'The Cat and Mouse Act' when he writes of it, and that will do for me.

A prisoner who starves herself will no longer be fed, but released until such time as she is recovered, and then taken back to prison to complete her term, and so on forever, or at least till her sentence is served.

There is a great outcry against such cruelty. I know I should condemn it, and indeed I do in public, but my heart sings with gratitude inside me for I would rather endure ten years in prison than to hear the key in the lock and smell that festering rubber snake, clotted with sick and the dried-out blood of my sisters, and know what is to come.

Poor Mrs Pankhurst is made very ill by so much starving and is gone into the country to recover. There are some who say she never will. This I do not believe for if pure force could destroy her she would have been laid low long ago. Her spirit drives her on and it will not yield till the battle is won. I shall ask Miss Sharp if that can go in next month's *Suffragette*.

I saw a man today on the street. From behind. He was walking along the Aldwych, swinging his arms the way Fred used to do when he was acting the fool. He had fair hair and a strong straight back. I started to run. I ran and ran till I came level with him. He turned and looked at me. He was older than my pa. I went into a shop.

I do not know whether to be pleased or alarmed. Miss Sharp had given me a whole quarter page to fill and what happens? We are raided – all the copy seized and taken away as 'evidence'. Of what, no one seemed very sure. That we can spell? Surely soon it will come to that, for every day the arrests become more whimsical. The printer – for printing! Miss Kerr – for opening the door. It must be that, for she has done nothing else all day. I wonder what the police did before our movement was formed, for they have time for nothing else, it seems, but to harass and torment us.

What a happy time this must be for house-robbers and pickpockets since there can be not one bobby free to apprehend them.

Miss Roe, who is in charge while Miss Annie awaits trial for telling the truth, says she has found a printer and we are to cobble together as much as we can.

Why is it, some people cannot leave you alone? Just when I have the hardest task of my life – to write two whole columns, and that with only a day to do it, into the office comes Miss Davison, all full of brilliant ideas for the summer fête which is weeks away. As usual, most of her plans involve a lot of work for others and a lot of praise for her. I thought I should scream if she asked me once more about where to order flags from, and when *The Suffragette* was published I saw that I had put three 'm's in Emmeline and could truly have kicked myself for mortification. I only hope Mrs Pankhurst is too ill to read it. I did not mean that. I just do not want her to think me a stupid ignorant girl, even if I am.

A man called Bodkin is trying to stop us publishing altogether. He says it is 'inflammatory'. I asked Miss Kerr what that meant and she said 'setting fire to things'. I thought, well, perhaps he is right for half of England has been burnt down lately, but the public is furious and there was a great rally in Trafalgar Square to defend the freedom of the Press. Thousands came and afterwards we went on to Hyde Park and had a great laugh, making speeches (which we are forbidden to do just now) and as soon as the police arrived the crowd would hold them back till we had run to another part of the park and started again. I declare I could hardly speak for panting by the end of it, but it was such a lark – like at the beginning, except there was no Fred striding through the people to take my hand and walk with me beside the great Round Pond. I have almost forgotten him. It is only sometimes it comes on me.

Last night I lay in my bed and thought what a mad wild world I have entered. I closed my eyes and tried to remember how life had been before I met the Pankhursts, but try as I might, I could not bring it to mind. It seems they were always there, even before I knew them or knew one thing about what they were fighting for. Why else did I struggle to learn my letters, to be best at the psalms, to be fastest with my numbers? Why was I strong when others were ill? Why did I thrive while others failed? What was it for?

We have been much involved in arranging the summer fête. It is to be a fine affair, with cakes and jam and lace and handkerchiefs and all manner of delicacies for sale. Strawberries and cream and gentle music playing in the background. A children's dancing display, bell-ringers, painted eggs and a (very spiteful) pig to bowl for. And everywhere great bursts of flowers so that you would think you were in Paradise or very close (apart from the pig).

And all the while we are preparing for this comes news of another church burnt, a train destroyed, a garden hacked to bits with scythes. And Mrs Pankhurst, in, out of prison, every time weaker, more frail, more racked with pain. Her voice, that filled the Albert Hall, leaking from her like a punctured balloon. Only her smile, that bright brave smile pouring courage into all who see it, remains unbroken still.

I have been put in charge of the pig. I begged Miss Roe to find someone else but she said there was no one free and, besides, I was the strongest. I wished then I had been bolder to offer myself for hunger-striking.

We have spent a wretched day, the pair of us. The pig is in a pen with straw which it continually fouls so that I have to keep climbing the rail with a shovel to clear up after it. This the children find more exciting than anything else in the pavilion and they hurtle around me, positively screeching with laughter as I ferry to and fro with my steaming stinking buckets.

All day I have prayed that someone would win it, but it seems we have to wait till the show is over unless someone beats all others by a clear ten points.

At the end of the day as I was nailing back a banner which had dropped into my pen for the third time, I heard a voice behind me. 'Maggie, I need two flags. Where can I get two flags? It is most urgent.'

Since it was Miss Davison, of course it was most urgent, because everything always is.

I said, 'I believe there are some in the office, but it will be locked now.'

'I must have them. How can I get them?'

I was tempted to say, 'Why do you not walk up the wall and break in through the roof, Miss Davison?' for I was sure she would think nothing of it.

'I do not know. Do you need them tonight?'

'No, not till tomorrow, but early.'

'I must go by the office first thing to collect some more leaflets. Will eight o'clock suit you?'

'Yes, oh yes, that's brilliant, Maggie. Thank you so much.

Eight o'clock. I'll be there. Good night. And well done with the pig.'

'Well done with the pig'! I am surprised she does not translate it into Latin.

She is there already, waiting for me. Big bright eyes, almost mad, you would say, but so hopeful. Always so hopeful. Is that what madness is? Hoping? For things that will never come?

I unlock the door. She bounds past me up the stairs. We find the flags.

'Two?'

'Two, yes please.'

'What are you going to do with them?'

She smiles. 'You'll know soon enough.'

'Are you going to the show today, Miss Davison?'

For a tiny moment her face seems troubled but then back comes the mad hopeful smile. 'Not today, Maggie, I'm off to the Derby, but every day after. I've still to bowl for that pig of yours.'

I say, 'Well, you could not do me a greater favour than to win it.'

She laughs. 'They say one good turn deserves another. Here.' She reaches into her pocket and gives me a florin. 'How many goes will that buy me?'

'Ten.'

'Oh, I should be exhausted by so many. How about if you have five turns on my behalf? Then tomorrow I can take the rest?'

'If that is what you would like, I should be happy to.'

Already a thought comes to me that I am strong enough to win the prize and who better to pass it on to?

'Yes, I should.'

I collect my leaflets. Miss Davison looks round the office as though trying to place it in her mind. As we go down the stairs she says, 'Maggie...'

'Miss Davison?'

For a moment she says nothing, then, 'I do envy you, you know.'

I stare at her. 'But why?'

She shakes her head. 'I don't know. I suppose because people need you. I always wanted to be necessary. Never quite managed it.' She laughs. At the door we part.

'See you tomorrow. I'm counting on you to win that pig for me.'

I smile. 'I shall do my very best, miss.' I watch her trotting off towards the station, flags bundled up under her coat.

We were packing up for the night. I was bouncing with joy for I had won the pig on my third 'Miss Davison' throw. If that was not enough I had spent the day feeding it treacle toffee so that she would find out just how exciting it is to clean up after a pig more stinky than a newborn babe. 'Well done with the pig, Miss Davison!'

Miss Kerr brought the news. She is a quiet soul and does not like to put herself forward so when I saw her – standing so awkward in the middle of the hall, her face screwed up, hunched over like she had been punched, just sobbing – I knew something awful had happened.

We gathered round.

'There has been a terrible accident. Miss Davison – Emily Davison – she... I do not know the details but it seems...'

Miss Sylvia led her to a seat. 'Take your time, Harriet. Compose yourself. Tell us what has happened.'

I remember thinking, if she has got herself arrested and left me with this pig to look after...

Such a sad day. Emily Davison, she that I had watched so cheerfully setting off just a few hours before, flags flapping like petticoats from under her coat, mad hopeful gleam in her eyes, was now lying unconscious in a hospital bed, broken to pieces by the King's own horse.

The news had come through in a telegram. Miss Kerr had been alone in the office when it arrived. She had telephoned the hospital but they could give her scant information, except that a lady called Miss Emily Wilding Davison had been admitted suffering from 'multiple fractures and contusions'. Miss Kerr had asked the cause of them but was told they did not know. It was on her way to the Empress Rooms to find Miss Sylvia that she had seen the headlines: *Suffragette Brings Down The King's Horse.*

There were various opinions of what had happened. Some declared she had thrown herself directly in the path of the oncoming mount, others that she had merely tried to grasp its reins and become entangled in them. One bystander swore she had already tried to halt two horses before the King's, another that she had cried out 'God has sent me', before flinging herself on to the track.

I think the truth was that no one knew what happened. The pictures showed a horse down, a woman twisting away from it, her hat spinning in the air like a child's quoit. A horse, a woman, a lilac hat. And a thousand people looking the other way.

She died on June 8th, four days later. 'Misadventure', the inquest said though I have heard people call it suicide. I do not believe them. Miss Davison wanted to live. She wanted to live forever. That was her misfortune.

No one could be found to bury her. All those clergymen – so bold with their words till someone asks them to hold to them. 'Self-murder is a crime against God.' So, presumably, is torturing his creation to the point where such crimes happen.

Only one, a good kind man. Mrs Pankhurst dragging herself from her sick-bed and, for her pains, ripped away to Holloway before the funeral. Her carriage driving empty behind the coffin. Lilies, the scent of lilies, white against white. Blood red peonies, purple and black sashes. Marching, the soft shuffle of feet, no words. And over it all the banner flies: *Fight on and God will give the Victory*.

I asked Miss Sylvia if she still believed that. She gave a shuddering sigh. 'I have to. Yes, I do, truly I do, but sometimes… Such…waste. A life – wasted. Why did she have to do it? There are so many other, better ways. What is gained by this, but a family bereft of a daughter, and friends bereft of a colleague? It was all so…unnecessary.'

I sold the pig to a butcher. He gave me three pounds and a haunch for roasting. I took it home to Pa. He was mightily pleased and said I should stay to eat with them, but I did not want to.

They all looked well. Alfie is halfway through building his

bed. Unfortunately he is doing it in the front room which leaves little space for anything else and there is more dust from the shavings than in a desert, but Mrs Grant just smiled and put her finger to her lips when I asked how she could bear it. 'He's a good lad. The kindest born if you don't cross him.' I knew what she meant, for he is a good head taller than Pa now, and broad, too, so it is good sense to leave him be.

Will has a broken head from falling from a railing he was swinging over. Evelyn said he was dead for 'near five minutes and then he opened his eyes and started bellowing.' Being Will, he's scarce stopped since, but it is a mighty bruise so perhaps for once he is not to blame.

Mrs Grant thinks baby Ann cannot hear. That is why she does not heed the endless racket in the house. I asked her how she could tell and she said Mrs Benson down the road has two deaf, and recognised the signs. No wonder Ann has no words, poor soul, yet she looks as bonny as a princess. I asked about a cure. Mrs Grant said she did not know. It would take a doctor to say. I said, 'She is better off deaf than let a doctor near her', but then I thought, what will her life be if she cannot speak? A life without music and laughter and words? She is my sister and she deserves better than that.

Lucy, on the other hand, deserves a good slapping, though from the look of her, that is what she has been getting. Her eye was quite purple and she had a scratch on her cheek like a tiger had gone for her. I asked her where she had got it but she just turned her head away and rolled her eyes like it was the stupidest question ever.

I found a piece of clean muslin and told her to bathe it lest germs take hold, but she would have none of it and was off out of the house not ten minutes after I arrived.

I asked Mrs Grant about it. She shook her head, not wanting to tell me. 'Lucy has been in a bit of trouble. It's nothing. Over now.'

'What trouble? Fighting?'

She nodded.

'Who?'

'A woman – girl – sloven, if you ask me. Lucy was spending time with the brewer's man and it turns out he's married and got three children at home. His wife, if that is what she is, gets wind of it and comes down the alehouse to put young Lucy straight. Anyway, Lucy being Lucy will have none of it and the two of them fall to it like wildcats, so I heard.'

'And what's the outcome?'

'Oh, he's gone off back to his wife, but Lucy's pretty sore about it. She's not been that well lately, either, but the liquor she pours down her throat at that alehouse it's scarce surprising.'

On the way back I wondered if Lucy had ever been happy.

Tonight, I know not why, I took down the book of poems Fred gave me that glorious Christmas a lifetime ago.

When he first went away I read it over and over, as though somehow I could reach out to him through its pages, cling on to him through another's words. I suppose that is what books are for, to unite people who will never meet – never meet again. But for me the agony grew worse, not better, so I put it by. Shut it away. Closed my eyes.

I was right to, for nothing has changed. The pain came back, ripping through me like an arrow. I heard his voice, his laughter, felt his awful loneliness, as sure as if he had been sitting next to me. *'Remember me when I am gone away'*. How can pain last so long? And be as raw and wicked as the second it began?

I have buried the book at the bottom of my cupboard, wrapped in my suffragette scarf.

How long do memories last? My whole life seems to be floating by me, all my mistakes, wrong deeds, cruel words, and the good things, too. Coming top at Sunday School, Clement's Inn, clothes, money, Fred... There I stop. I am nineteen years old. I cannot live my whole life looking back. I must go forward in hope and sureness of victory at the last. Shoulder to shoulder with my comrades, bravely facing each new ordeal... I even think like a pamphlet now.

What do I think? Maggie Robins, nineteen. Office worker, vandal, convict, suffragette. Old Maid.

Is it not strange to live in a society of women? Of course there are convents, but there the women are given over to religious life and anyway get married to Our Lord, which must be interesting. Some schools, I know, take only girls for pupils and they are taught by only women teachers, but still they go home at the end of the day where they will see their brothers and fathers and other menfolk.

Here it is almost as though men do not exist, except as the enemy. The Grey Men, distant foes, not real as Pa, say, or...other men are real. They do not smell of beer or baccy, they do not fall down drunk on pay-day, they do not lug coal on their backs or take care of you when you are lost or buy you chocolate cake or kiss you...

How can all men be judged against these pitiful shadows? And yet over and over again I hear it from my comrades: 'Men are useless. Men are fools. Men are savages.' How do they know? And why do they go all shaky and fluttery if a gentleman stops by the office to offer his support?

I asked one lady who was particularly loud on the subject if she thought all men vile.

'Not all, Maggie. But most of them, certainly.'

'How many do you know?'

'I don't have to know them to know I despise them,' she snapped. 'I know I don't want to be hanged. I don't have to try it to make sure.'

This brought forth screams of laughter.

'Are we to gather you're fond of the species, Maggie?' twittered her companion.

'Well she was courting that bobby for ages so she must see something in them,' chimes in a third.

'Bobbies are the very worst. I'd rather marry a pig,' comes back the first, looking very pink about the gills.

Still – still I cannot hear him spoken against like that.

'That's good for it's very likely what you'll have to make do with, miss,' I practically roared, which brought Miss Roe charging into the room to see what was happening.

'Ladies, ladies, what's going on?'

We all fell silent, looking sulkier than a row of camels.

'Well it must have been something to have you all shouting at each other. I could hardly hear Christabel down the telephone from France. Is it anything I can help with?'

Then we all felt guilty for Miss Roe works longer hours than anyone and has been very ill as a result of it.

'It was my fault, Miss Roe, ' said the pig wife. 'I was rude to Maggie and upset her.'

Well, I can be noble too. 'No, miss, it was all my fault. I should never have spoke as I did.' So the other two poke their twitchy little noses in and say they were to blame as well and poor Miss Roe looks as though she would happily see us cut each others' throats if we would only give her ten minutes' peace to get on with what she was doing.

So now I am marked for a 'difficult creature'. I suppose I am. If not 'difficult' then 'different'. Nothing can change that, it seems.

But still I wonder, what will these helper ladies do when it is all over? When we have won the vote? Will they consent to marry these men they so despise? Will the men want to marry them? What will they do? What will I do? Where will it end? And when?

Mrs Pankhurst is refusing water as well as food in prison. Some say she has also taken to walking up and down her cell till she drops in sheer exhaustion. Her courage is beyond understanding. Yet how can we ignore what is happening to her?

Once the high point of a meeting would be the cry, 'Mrs Pankhurst is free.' The curtains would sweep open or the doors fly back and in she would stride like the breath of life itself.

The other night we were gathered in a hall near Kensington when word came round that she was on her way. You could have lit the whole building with the excitement in the air. We waited and waited, hardly daring to breathe, aching for that moment when she would step into the spotlight and our lungs would explode with cheering.

The ladies on the stage were whispering amongst

themselves. At length there was a rustling of the great black
drapes at the back and slowly, slowly they began to pull
apart. A great roar rocketed round the auditorium, cheering,
clapping, stamping feet, then just as suddenly it died away.
Died to a sickening, deathly silence for there before us,
slumped in a cold iron wheelchair was a skeleton, scarce
more. A papery old woman, skin stretched over jagged
cheekbones, bulging rocks beneath glassy wandering eyes,
hands clawing at the blanket tucked around her like a
shroud.

A great sort of sigh sounded round the hall. Like something
dying. That something, I thought that night, was hope.

But it was not so, for four days later Mrs Pankhurst was
back on her feet inspiring us, urging us on as though the police
were not at the door waiting to drag her back to torture. 'The
only recklessness that suffragettes have ever shown has been
about their own lives. It has never been, and it never will be,
the policy of the Women's Social and Political Union
recklessly to endanger human life. We leave that to the enemy.
Be militant each in your own way. And my last word is to the
Government: I incite this meeting to rebellion.'

How could we let her down?

There is much debate in the press for the voters do not like
to see women racked and broken by the very government they
have put in place. Some think it 'uncivilised', 'barbaric',
'unsporting'! Others say, 'Let them starve. Give them food, if
they will not eat it, so be it.'

The Government takes no notice. Perhaps they are waiting
for us all to die then they need not worry about giving women
the vote at all. But if we do die, where will their next lot of

voters come from, for there will be no children to follow on? These are wild thoughts. For now all that matters is surviving. I know I can, but what of Mrs Pankhurst, so frail and getting weaker every day? If only there was a way to protect her.

I mentioned this to Miss Roe. 'You mean like a bodyguard? To stand between her and the police, Maggie?'

'Well, I suppose so.'

'That is a brilliant idea. But we should need some very strong women and they would need to be properly trained.'

'Perhaps Mrs Garrud could be persuaded...?'

At last! I have a chance to prove myself again. To make my mark. To show them I am truly worthy of the Cause.

There are thirty of us and we train each Tuesday in whatever place is considered safe from spying eyes. We do drill – marching in lines and stamping (this seems silly to me, as if anything will tell the bobbies we are coming it is the sound of thundering feet).

Mrs Garrud has undertaken to instruct everyone in jiu-jitsu and I am her assistant. It makes me smile to see how little I must have known when I first started. Some of the girls scarce know their left hand from their right which, though it makes us laugh when we are practising, will prove a sore problem if we are ever called upon to attack.

Miss Christabel has taken on a new cause – women of the street. She says it is wrong to blame them and not the men who use them. I am surprised she thinks so, for she always told us we should act for ourselves and not be slaves to others, although hunger is the hardest master of all, I suppose.

The clergy are mighty pleased with her and gather in great

black clumps to burble their support. It would be wrong of me to think perhaps this is just great cleverness on Miss Christabel's part and not something she greatly cares about in truth. It is certainly strange to have the churchmen on our side. I suppose they do not count as real men so do not have to be shunned as others are. For me they are as bad as the politicians – worse, for they think themselves so saintly.

Miss Sylvia was waiting for me at my lodgings tonight. She was in the parlour and Mrs Garrud went straightway to bring me a cup of tea, then left us. I knew at once it must be something bad.

'Maggie, I came as fast as I could. Your sister is very ill. She is being cared for now and we all hope so hard for a...happy conclusion.'

I tried to muster my thoughts. 'Mrs Grant told me she thought she could not hear.'

Confusion spread across her face. 'Lucy?'

'Lucy?'

'Lucy is gravely ill. She had an operation. It did not go well. There is a chance... She is in the Bow Infirmary. Miss Annie has sent for the medicines they prescribe.'

'An operation?'

She looked away. 'Yes.'

'What sort of operation?'

Miss Sylvia took my hand and now she did look at me. 'You remember how I once said it would be so good if we could change things? But we cannot always?'

'Yes.'

'Lucy was to have a child, Maggie. The man, it seems, has

disappeared or wanted nothing to do with her. In her fear and distress she went to a...what can I call her?

'The woman tried to pierce the baby with a button hook and pull it out. The hook was not clean. Lucy's blood is poisoned.'

I heard a cup go clattering to the floor.

We went by cab. Fast as it was, it seemed to take forever.

The infirmary, dark and cheerless, blocking out the evening sun's last rays. Along stone passageways, nurses sliding past, eyes downcast. Lamps dim as prison, making everyone look sick. At the end of a long low room, airless and stinking, Lucy crammed on to an iron bed, eyes shut, skin like squashed blackberries, breath like a broken whistle. She did not stir.

Miss Sylvia went to find a doctor. When he came I saw he was young though his eyes were not. 'I am very sorry, Miss Robins. We have done our best. The operation has not gone as we had hoped.'

'Why? What have you done to her? Why is she this...this awful colour?'

He shook his head. 'The womb was terribly infected. We have removed what remained of the foetus, the unborn child, and disinfected the wounds as best we could, but the septicaemia – poisoning is spreading. She has not responded to the medications we have given her.'

'Well, give her some more. Something different. There must be something. You cannot just leave her – leave her to... She's sixteen years old. She is young. She's only young. She is... She's my sister.' My knees gave way beneath me.

How many more? How many more of my family is God going to take? All of them? And why not me? Because I have to stay and bear it. That is the punishment.

Miss Sylvia was talking to the doctor but I heard nothing. She touched my shoulder. 'Maggie. Maggie, listen. There is just a chance...'

The doctor crouched down beside me. 'I cannot promise...it has not been tried before...'

'What? What? What?'

'In our laboratory we are experimenting with a new bacterial mould. It has been proved to halt putrefaction in the body of a rat but no one has yet tested it on a human being. I cannot guarantee...'

I clutched his arm. 'Will it save her?'

'I cannot tell. Nothing else will, unless you believe in miracles.'

I shook my head.

'You understand there is no certainty that this will work?'

'There is no certainty of anything in this life.'

He almost smiled.

I stayed the night at Miss Sylvia's lodgings. I knew I should go to Pa's but I could not face it. A house full of misery. Evelyn begging me to make Lucy well again. How many times must I let her down?

We sat together by the fire and drank beef tea, and toasted bread and talked. She told me how her East End mission is growing faster than she can keep up with, but that she has never in her life been happier. 'I could not ask for more loyal, willing helpers, men *and* women. We are making such strides, Maggie. I have three women running a reading class for the children that cannot afford Poor School, and others offering to take clean linen to the sick, and a soup kitchen – goodness, it's better than The Savoy sometimes. I should sell the recipe to their chef.'

'You'd be better selling it to Holloway, miss. They've more customers.'

She laughed. 'Yes, well, if you think they'd appreciate it...'

I told her about the Bodyguard and how two of the volunteers had black eyes from trying to swing their batons like David at Goliath and forgetting to let go.

Miss Sylvia has her own bodyguard.

'"The People's Army", we call it. They are quite brilliant. Every time I am speaking and word comes of a raid, they line up close by the platform and as the police come storming on to the stage, they cry, "Jump, Sylvia, Jump", and I just launch myself into the air like a trapeze artist and they catch me and rush me out of the building.'

'What happens if they miss?'

Miss Sylvia swallowed. 'Well, I rather fancy I shall be the main ingredient for the next soup run, but so far, touch wood, they never have. Anyway, it's better not to dwell on what may go wrong, I rather think, don't you? There are too many imponderables.'

'What are those?'

'Oh, things that you don't know about until it's too late to do anything. Things you couldn't hope to change.'

'Like what's happened to Lucy?'

She nodded sadly. 'Yes, I suppose so. Dr Rowan is a very fine physician, Maggie. If anyone can save your sister...'

We were quiet for a while, me thinking, if he is so fine what is he doing in a poor people's infirmary? Miss Sylvia, something altogether different, for at last she raised her eyes from the fire and said, 'I want to tell you something, Maggie.'

I waited.

'When Mrs Grant first came to me to tell me what had happened I brought Lucy here to our hostel, hoping perhaps rest and proper nursing would provide a cure. One night before the fever set in, she could not sleep so I took her some broth and sat with her for a while. She told me then that she thought she would die. I said that was nonsense and that she would soon be well again, but she said, "No, I was never meant to live". I asked her what on earth she meant. How had she come by such a dismal notion? And she said, "My brother Frank told me. When I was a baby my brother Samuel caught the measles and so did I. Frank said he heard my mother praying, 'Please God, take the baby. Not Samuel. Please spare me my Samuel. Don't let him die. Take the baby.'"'

I thought, have you worked among these people so long and still you do not know them? So I told her. 'Women round here try never to love a baby before it can walk. They don't even use its name, just "the baby". So many die, you see, in the first few months, it is better not to waste your affections on what you may lose. Keep them for when the child is strong enough to live. But it was wrong of Frank to talk to Lucy so. She must have vexed him mightily.'

Miss Sylvia was staring at me and I knew she was shocked by what I had said. So I did not tell her the rest.

Lucy is mending. It will be long and slow but it seems whatever worked on the rat is working just as well on her. I must not be mean and say it does not surprise me. Since my talk with Miss Sylvia I have begun to understand how wretched she must have been and I am trying my very hardest to be a good sister. She is moved to the hostel now and I visit once a week and bring her flowers or some fruit, and a magazine, as well as the latest copy of *The Suffragette*, which I fancy she uses to wrap her leavings in for she seems no wiser about our work than ever. I tried to explain to her about Frank not meaning what he had said, but she just turned her head away and covered her ears with her hands.

Evelyn visits every day with Mrs Grant, bringing a new painting so that Lucy's wall looks like a gallery although most of the pictures are of cherry cakes which are Evelyn's favourite at the moment – thanks to Alfie's Edith who is fattening the whole family for the slaughter, I fancy, judging by the amount of pastries coming into that house.

Miss Sylvia met me at the door one day as I arrived. She seemed excited. 'Maggie, I have spoken to Dr Rowan about baby Ann. He thinks he may know what is wrong.'

'How can he? He has never examined her.' Though how I could question his judgement when he had performed such a miracle on Lucy, I do not know.

'He says it is common with the infants round here. They catch an infection early on before they are speaking and it makes a congestion in their ears which stops them hearing. He says it is a simple matter to cure. Of course he cannot be sure...'

I left her holding the bag of plums and ran all the way to our house.

During these weeks I have come to see how much good is done by Miss Sylvia's East End Federation. In a practical way. There is nursing, teaching, cleaning, lessons in how to care for babies, help with finding work, a savings plan that lets people put by money for if they are laid off or injured at work, trips to the country for the children – so much going on, and all of it useful. All of it making a difference.

And I think, it is all very well for me to sit in an office passing on instructions to burn this building, bomb that one... Miss Christabel insists, and of course being so clever, she must be right, that in the end ours is the only way. But it is a way strewn with broken bodies, broken minds, broken dreams, and if, in the end, we should all die for the Cause, which we know in our hearts it may come to, what will be left? A few columns in the national newspapers. A few sombre words from the pulpits. A few shakes of the head, a few hopeless tears from those who loved us.

We are commanded to model ourselves on Joan of Arc. 'Think,' writes Miss Christabel from France. 'Only consider how now, four centuries after her ruthless murder by the English rulers of the day, she is remembered, sanctified, honoured. And where are they? Dead, and all but forgotten.'

And I think, yes, but she was nineteen. So am I. What good is it to me to be remembered four hundred years from now? I want to live. Why is my life worth so much less to the Cause than my death? And all those forgotten nobles went home after they had burnt that young French peasant girl, and ate and drank and ruled, just as they had done before.

I have resolved to ask Miss Sylvia if I may work for her. She is gone to Paris to see Miss Christabel but I shall write to her offering my services. There are plenty could take my place in the office – would happily do so. I know it means I must leave Mrs Garrud and that will be a sore wrench for I have never loved anywhere more than my room with the blue curtains (unless it be my yellow one at The Mascot) but I cannot stay my life in someone else's family.

I can lodge at the hostel and although I think the pay will be far less, so will my costs be, for I shall have no need of fine office clothes and money for cabs and the like.

Tomorrow I will write a letter to Miss Christabel.

It is so long since I have cried. Tonight I wept till there were no more tears inside my body.

I have lost a friend. My oldest truest friend. Miss Sylvia is gone. Split from the WSPU. All contact severed. The outcome of her trip to Paris. Miss Christabel demanding that she forsake the men who had served and defended her so bravely, and rely only on women from now on. Miss Lake says there was a disagreement. I can only guess at its fury. So now Miss Sylvia is cast out. For refusing to bow the knee to her sister.

And I have my answer.

From Miss Christabel Pankhurst
Founder Member of the Women's Social and Political Union
Paris

*Dear Maggie,*

*Of course it is up to you. If you prefer to desert us at this crucial time, forgetful of all the heinous suffering that has been endured by our sisters on your behalf, not to mention your own endeavours which have been most creditable in the main then, naturally, you must go.*

*I will not remind you that my own dear mother lies, at this very moment, close to death, a condition brought about entirely by her profound and passionate belief in the right of every woman, from whatever situation in life, to have a say in determining her own future and that of those most precious to her.*

*Your mother, too, as I recall, was a fervent supporter of our cause and it would be a sadness, indeed, if her hopes for your future in a freer, better world should come to naught.*

*Christabel Pankhurst*

From Miss Sylvia:

*Dear Maggie,*
*Do whatever is right for you. I will understand either way. Remember, there is always a place for you here or wherever I am.*
*Affectionately,*
*Sylvia Pankhurst*

I remember Miss Roe once saying she had writ down all the reasons to stay and those to resign before she took over as Chief Organiser. I asked her how many of each.

'Oh, fourteen, I think, to go.'

'How many to stay?'

'One.'

I asked her what it was.

'Loyalty.'

# PART FIVE

## 1913–1914

Tonight I am to burn down a man's house. I have been chosen specially. It is a reward for all my past endeavours. My loyalty. Choosing the Cause above friendship, wishes, instincts. But I will always follow the light, the shining dazzling light of those who have no doubts, no fear of darkness, hoping one day it will rub off on me.

Miss Christabel sent word specially.

*Dear Maggie,*
*You have shown yourself worthy of the highest trust. I know that in this, as in your previous undertakings, you will bring all your courage and energy to the task, knowing as you do, that the success of our entire enterprise hangs upon the valiant actions of such as yourself. And that failure would be unthinkable.*
*Yours in the Cause,*
*Christabel Pankhurst. Founder Member WSPU*

'The highest trust'. At last. At last I am on the inside.

All summer long I have thrown myself back into the battle.

Baton hurling, stone throwing, painting slogans, carving up golf greens. We even attend the churches of those who have preached against us and sing loudly and lustily throughout the prayers. We interrupt plays, operas, sporting tournaments. One headline likened us to jesters, the licensed fools of old – permitted to be mad, but only for so long.

Mrs Garrud taught the Bodyguard a wonderful African dance. Every time the bobbies rushed at Mrs Pankhurst we swung our hips one way and our batons the other so there was no way they could break through, or there would not have been, had the same two ladies who blackened each other's eyes managed to keep the rhythm for more than six beats together.

Galleries and museums are closed for fear of assault. It distresses me greatly when I hear of paintings ripped and torn apart. Museums I do not mind, for they are full of bits of old iron and cracked up bones, but to ruin a picture seems to me a very wretched thing, remembering as I do how much work goes into one. And if it be a good one, not just 'work' but a drop of someone's soul.

It is odd I have been sent to Birmingham, a city I detest, for it was here I first was tortured. Here that that doctor prised my lips apart and forced his filthy poison down my throat. I have never forgotten him. He was not old like the politicians, nor young like Dr Rowan. He was what I would call a bloodless man. There was nothing warm and vital in him.

He did not see us as living creatures, but objects to be stretched and twisted as a tanner works a hide. Bloodless face, bloodless mind. Bloodless heart, with one hand to pinch my nose shut, and the other to sip his glass of brandy.

As I walked from the station to the lodgings where I am to stay, I passed a gallery – open. I cannot tell why, but suddenly I longed to see something good, untarnished, something worth caring about, for I knew tomorrow a man would be looking at his dreams and memories destroyed and that I would have no right to care for anything ever again.

I went in.

They were not remarkable paintings. Neat water colours, a few splashy fruit bowls, some fierce wobbly flowers. I was about to leave when I saw a little side room and there, leaning against the wall, a stack of canvases, a cloth half thrown across them.

Suddenly I was back in Miss Sylvia's studio, high up in the eaves above Park Walk. I knew that if I lifted that cloth the picture beneath it would be me.

It was as I bent to do so I heard a voice. 'Maggie.'

I turned. Standing in the doorway, the sun, as always, flickering through his hair, or perhaps that was just how I remembered it, was Fred.

We stood there, just gazing at each other. He looked thinner, older. I think I must have too.

At last he spoke. 'I had not thought to see you here. How have you been?'

I swallowed. 'Well enough, I suppose. And you?'

'Well enough. I... I... Why did you not answer my letter, Maggie?'

I stared at him. 'What letter?'

'The one I gave to Lucy. Explaining. Telling you where I

was. Begging you to come to me. Did I not deserve even a word? A refusal I could have borne, understood, but silence…'

This afternoon we walked in a park. It was not pretty, for nothing in Birmingham can be, but to me it seemed the finest in the world with its dull dusty trees and scraps of dried-out grass.

Fred told me he often visited that gallery. 'Not that I like it particularly, but so few of them are open these days and besides, I always hoped…'

'Hoped what?'

'I don't know. That perhaps your picture would turn up there one day. I never did get to see it, did I?'

'I doubt there's many gallery owners would hang a picture painted by a suffragette.'

'No. Although they might, in the hope you would not destroy one of your own.'

It was on my tongue to say, they are the only people we would destroy, but I just smiled.

Fred teaches at a boys' academy. He says he must spend each evening swotting the next day's lesson, for they are bright lads, picked from the Poor School to be trained as clerks and office workers, and if he is not careful they catch him out with their questions.

He was bitter angry that Lucy had kept his letter from me, but I told him how she has suffered of late so he gave up his plan to throttle her – for now, at least.

We talked of oh, so many things. How after he had quit the police he had thought to train as a doctor then found he had no stomach for it. 'Besides, what should I have done if they had ordered me to feed the women in prison?'

'Refused, of course.'

'Yes, well, I should have, but that would have meant another career lost. A man cannot be forever changing or he will end up completely useless.'

I hugged his arm. 'In that case you could have become a politician.'

He said his father had suggested teaching and though he was not a particular scholar, he enjoyed it more than he could have imagined. 'The boys are mad keen to learn and so full of ideas and enthusiasm. I swear I gain more from them than they do from me.'

'Well, if it was anyone but you teaching them, I might agree,' I said, and he just smiled, that great golden smile.

I told him how, after my visit to Marylebone police station, I had gone round to his lodgings and what Miss Blackett had said.

'Well, if she was waiting for my address, she is still waiting.'

'Oh, she's had other things to think about,' and I explained about throwing a stone right through her shop's main window. Fred looked at me in utter amazement.

'You mean you actually hit your target? Is there no end to surprises with you, Maggie?'

I laughed. 'I am a lot closer to my target now, so you should be careful what you say to me.'

He tucked my arm right in close to his. I could feel the warmth of him flowing right through me and I thought, this must be how Lazarus felt when Our Lord breathed him back to life. Born again. A new beginning. Another chance.

And so we walked about and sat and talked and then we went to a corner house and this time Fred didn't ask me what I wanted. Just ordered two great slices of chocolate sponge.

'They have burnt down our tearoom in Regent's Park.'

'And the elephant?'

'We do not harm living things.'

Fred looked at me and I could see now that his eyes had grown old like Dr Rowan's. 'You do not *burn* living things, Maggie. Never pretend you do not harm them.'

I said nothing.

He asked what brought me to Birmingham. 'Or need I guess? There must be a meeting somewhere.'

'Not a meeting. I cannot tell you, Fred, and it is better you do not know.'

'Why? Do you think I would arrest you? All that is over.'

I tried to smile. 'Over for you.'

'But not you?'

'It can never be over till the Cause is won.'

He was silent.

'What are you thinking?'

He shook his head. 'It would only vex you.'

'Nothing you can say will ever vex me.'

'I thought you sounded like a machine, Maggie.'

Although I laughed, his words cut deep inside me. Because I knew that they were true. That is what I have become. A machine. How else can I go on? Tonight I must burn down a man's house. There are no second chances for me.

And I thought, this is how it is. Today is a dream. A brief, glorious dream. But soon I will wake. I am set on a course. I am a cog in a wheel that is spinning too fast to be stopped. I cannot escape. I cannot break free. Not now I am on the inside. 'A dog cannot serve two masters.' 'Loyalty.' 'Even unto death.'

There will be no cottage in the country, no children that do not wail, no talking and reading together of an evening. There is only today.

We bought bread and sausages and cheese and strawberries and a bottle of blood red wine and I went home with him to his lodgings, two fine clean rooms and a little balcony on which he is growing a lot of dead plants, by the look of them. His landlord lives in the basement and has no daughter he needs to marry off.

Fred found some candles and we lit them and sat together watching the sun go down, and after we had eaten he reached for my hand across the table and we looked at each other, deep into each other's eyes and right through into our hearts. And I knew he understood.

He took my hand and led me into the other room.

I did not know loving could be like that. Loving between a man and woman. All I knew of it was pain and fear. Frank's fingers, groping, eager, slippery, putting babies in, pulling them out, rooting inside me – rough, unstoppable. And me, my shift all crumpled up round my shoulders, trying not to cry out, trying to turn away, trying to block my mind. Praying never to be loved again.

I knew so little. Less than nothing. I did not know a man could be so gentle and yet so strong, could make my body sing with every touch and beg for more. Make me part of him. Part of his soul. I did not know it could be like that. I did not know what love was.

He asked me if it had hurt.

'A little. Not very much.'

'I tried not to hurt you.'

'I know.'

'Next time it won't.'

I turned away. He kissed the back of my neck. 'What are you thinking?'

'Nothing. Everything. Why did you come to Birmingham?'

'Because I thought you never would.'

'You did not want me to?'

'Oh, yes, but if you were lost to me, I could not face the agony of seeing you. I was trying to be sensible.'

I turned back to him and saw that he was not a great golden god at all. He was young like me, and he feared to be hurt, just as I do. I kissed his nose. 'We are neither of us very good at being sensible, are we?'

He smiled. 'I suppose not. Tomorrow we can start again.'

'Tomorrow?'

'Tomorrow we will find a clergyman.'

'No.'

He grasped my hand. 'Because of The Cause? I would not stand in your way, Maggie. You know that. I believe in truth and justice, too, you know.'

'I know you do. It is not that. Not just that. I cannot...'

'Cannot what?'

Cannot retrace my steps. Cannot undo the past. Cannot undo the future.

I knew I had one hope. To make him hate me, so that when

I left he would no longer care. I closed my eyes. 'There is something much worse.'

'Worse?'

'I had thought never to tell you.'

'Tell me what?'

I told him then how I had killed my brother, Samuel. How, when Samuel was so ill with the measles, I had heard the Reverend Beckett say he would take me in his Bible class for a shilling a week, and my ma had replied, 'I cannot find it, Reverend, for I have medicine to buy for my Samuel.' And yet the very next week I was called up from my seat in the Sunday School and told I was to go home and learn two psalms by heart and the Reverend would test me on them on the Friday. And so I did, and when he came by I said the two he had set me and one more, *As the hart panteth after the water brooks, so panteth my soul after thee, O God.* And he said that was very good, and I was to attend on Sunday after matins. And at five o'clock next morning Samuel died.

Fred gripped my hand and squeezed it very tight. 'Maggie, you are wrong. So wrong. Don't you understand? This Reverend took you in his class because you are clever. Because he knew he could reap the rewards of his charity. Did he not use you to teach the younger children, to impress the Guardians on their rounds, to clean the classrooms after lessons?'

'Yes, but...'

'You did not kill your brother, Maggie. Do you truly believe your ma would, even for one mad second, have chosen a few scripture lessons above her child's life? Is that all you think of her?'

I started to cry. 'But Samuel died. He died the next day. Because he had no medicine, only a poultice to ease the blisters.'

'There is no cure for measles, Maggie. You live or you die. And if you are poor and have no medicine, most likely you will die.'

'How can you be so sure?'

'Because I have seen it, over and over. My father used to take me visiting. I feared it. Hated those stinking hovels full of illness and decay. I caught everything that was going. He said it would save me from it in later life. I used to think, what good is 'later life' if I die before I am twelve? But I did not. And they did. And if you have a life you must live it. If I believe nothing else, I believe that.'

I curled up close to him and he wiped away my tears and kissed me and told me I was safe now. Would always be safe. Then he asked, 'Have you never spoken of this before, Maggie?'

'Never. Only to Frank when it happened.'

'What did he say?'

'He said he felt very sorry for me and he promised to keep my secret.'

Fred was silent for a while and then he spoke. 'Just as you kept his?'

My heart stopped. I looked at him and saw his eyes were full of kindness and love – and forgiveness, I suppose. 'The things he did to you, Maggie, in return for that silence.'

'How did you know?'

'Lucy told me. Not in so many words, but she made it fairly clear she had taken your place. Besides, I think I'd already

guessed. We used to see a lot of it when I was in the police –
young prostitutes, trained up by their brothers or fathers.'

I started to tremble. 'Is that what you thought of me, then?
That I would end up on the streets?'

He stroked my cheek. 'No, Maggie, I did not. And if you
had, it would have made no difference to me. Can you
understand that? No difference, because it's the real you I
love, not the packaging. The real Maggie Robins, who is
unique and wonderful and braver than any woman I ever met.
That is why you are a suffragette, and Lucy...'

Still I tried to fight him. 'You think she will end up that
way? My own sister?'

He shook his head. 'I hope not, Maggie. All I can say is I
think she enjoyed it more than most girls do, because she went
looking for it everywhere.'

I could not help myself. 'Is that why you gave her that
bracelet?'

He stared at me in astonishment. 'What bracelet?'

'The blue one. She showed it to me the Christmas after you
visited.'

For a moment he said nothing. When he spoke it was like I
had stuck a knife in him. 'Is that all you think of me, Maggie?
Is that all you think of my love for you? That I would buy
your own sister with a bangle?'

'No... I...' My head was pounding. Say 'yes' *now* and it
will be over. This is your chance. You are a suffragette.
Loyalty. A dog cannot serve two masters. Even unto death.

I covered my face with my hands. 'I don't know any more.
I don't know what I think. Forgive me...'

Gently he drew my hands from my face. 'The bracelet was

for you. It was all wrapped up with your name on it. For Christmas.'

I could hardly speak. 'I sent you a card.'

'I never got it.'

I almost laughed. 'No. Miss Davison managed to set fire to the pillar-box I had posted it in.'

Fred frowned. 'Is that the Miss Davison who...?'

'Yes.'

'She was a brave woman.'

'Yes. Very.'

'But foolish. To think such an act would change the politicians' minds.'

The wheel began to turn again. 'Sometimes desperate methods are necessary to achieve one's aims.'

Fred sighed. 'You and I both know that is nonsense. All this vandalism just hardens people's hearts.'

'Perhaps if they get much harder they will crack.'

'Perhaps. But they may not. And then where will all your militant sisters be? Violence is never the answer to anything, Maggie. That much I have learnt.'

'What would you say if I turned militant?'

'I should be very sad.'

'But could you forgive me?'

He was silent for a while. 'I would forgive you anything. Everything. I always will. I cannot help myself.'

I snatched my hands from his. 'No. Don't forgive me. Never forgive me. I do not deserve forgiveness. I am too... I am not...this "Maggie Robins" you talk about. It isn't me. I'm not like that.'

'Like what?'

'Brave and wonderful and...'

'You are to me.'

'I'm not, Fred. I'm not. I'm... I'm so sorry.'

'Sorry for what?'

What could I say? 'For not being me. The me I wanted to be. For your sake.'

He reached over and doused the candle, then he drew me to him and kissed me like his life depended on it.

'You are the "me" I wanted, Maggie. From the night I saw you outside the Albert Hall. Running, your hair flying out in all directions, your cheeks flushed, your eyes shining. You were like a flame lighting up the night. Warming everything you touched.'

'That's beautiful. Like a poem.'

He laughed. 'One of my boys wrote it. I gave him four out of ten for being soppy. Now if you want a real poem...' He rolled out of bed and went crashing around till he found the matches, a candle, an old battered book. It was the same as the one he had given to me that first Christmas. He turned to a page near the end. I saw that it was scribbled over – scribbled over with my name. And the writing was all blotched.

> *'If I might see another Spring –*
> *Oh stinging comment on my past*
> *That all my past results in 'if' –*
> *If I might see another Spring*
> *I'd laugh today, today is brief;*
> *I would not wait for anything:*
> *I'd use today that cannot last,*
> *Be glad today and sing.'*

Be glad today and sing. We lay together in the dark, listening to each other's breathing. When I knew he was asleep I crept away. And went to burn down a man's house.

I remember so little of that night, and yet I remember everything. How my life was given to me then taken away.

A great house, iron gates, walls reaching up forever. My frozen skin tearing on rusty wire as I slipped and slid, running, tripping, crawling, my heart hammering, bursting inside me. My hands shaking so I dropped the matches, scattered them like spillikins, could not find them, could not lay my fire. Crouched, scrabbling in the dark with the dank fog curling round me, soaking me, soaking everything. Then a light. Thin, relentless, blinding.

There were two of them, local men, volunteers – I had been recognised at the station by the prison doctor, he who had first tortured me, the man with no blood, travelling on the same train. His duty to report me.

There being no meetings organised, a watch had been put on all public buildings – the gallery owner remembered me and declared my behaviour suspicious. 'Entering a private room and searching, possibly with a view to hiding a bomb.' All local politicians had been notified and guards put on those of their residences found to be unoccupied.

The men had watched me break in, tracked my progress through the grounds, with every bush hiding some savage beast, every cracking twig the lurch of a mantrap to my fevered brain.

They took me by my arms and dragged me down the steps,

laughing all the while. There they spread me on the manky grass and pulled my skirt high over my head. They took turns to ram themselves up into me, then turned me over and did it from behind. Laughing. The stink of their sweat, their rancid breath, slobber dripping from their gobs into my mouth, my nose, my eyes, callused hands scraping, twisting, squeezing. The pain like jagged glass.

The judge sentenced me to six months, third division. 'Intent to Endanger Life.'

The prison doctor was a witness. He said I was a 'known felon' and that he knew me to be capable of violence. I said I knew him to be capable of the same. The judge ordered me to be silent. The men said they had caught me setting light to a pile of sticks by the main entrance to the house. Fortunately they had managed to douse the fire before serious damage could occur. The judge congratulated them on their bravery and public spirit and awarded them five pounds each from the Public Purse.

It was night again when they took me away. I thought of Fred lying by the window, his arm curled round me, protecting me, keeping me safe, and how I had slipped away from him like water through his fingers. And I knew that by now he would have read the evening paper.

I thought, he will not come looking for me again.

The women here are kind to me. They beg me to eat for they cannot bear to hear the screams. I tell them not to worry for there is no more force-feeding. When I am too weak to stand, the prison must release me and I shall go back to London where I am sure a safe house will be found for me, at least until I have regained my strength. They shake their heads. 'It's not like that here, duck. The doctor enjoys himself too much to let folk go.'

He came in the evening. I had not eaten for four days. I looked at his lizard eyes, flicking around the cell then over me as though deciding whether I was worth the trouble of devouring.

He signalled to two of the brutes who brought in a jug of hot milk and some bread spread with honey. 'I must ask you to eat this bread.'

I said nothing. He poured some milk into a cup and held it out to me. 'At least drink this milk.'

I shook my head.

'You refuse. Very well, I must warn you that, in the interests of the preservation of human life, I shall be obliged to feed you, whether you desire it or not.' He nodded to the brutes who went out and came back with four others. They circled me like hungry crows. He opened his fat black bag. Uncoiled the rubber tube.

I must have cried out for I remember them all looking at me in surprise. He signalled to the women to tie my hands and legs to the chair. I kicked out. I was screaming, 'No. No. No. You have to release me. It is the law. You have to release me.'

He cracked me across the face with the back of his hand. 'I am the law in here, you stupid minx. Will you eat or not? No, I thought not.'

And so it began again. I did not think there remained any part of my body that was not split inside and out, but he found more and tore them, too. He cranked my mouth wide with a metal brace, shovelled the poisonous tubing down my throat, and down and down till I thought he would drag my heart and lungs out with it. He flung the bread into the jug of milk, slurped it around then emptied it, all clods and chunks into the funnel. Down it slithered, like a fat white worm. Then I was sick.

I have been sick every day since. They took me to the hospital. The matron was shocked. 'Who has done this? Not the doctor?'

I shook my head, though if I could have seen him blamed I would have. Later she spoke to him, but he said they were surface cuts and needed nutrition to heal them. So it went on. Torture. Sickness. Sleep – blessed sleep. Days. Weeks. I do not know. And then the dreams. Great red eyes streaking towards me like comets. The walls talking and when I looked they were covered in chocolate-coloured diamonds, stretching their sides till they were tall as the room and I could see the metal pegs holding them wide, ready for the tube.

One day I saw a vicar standing near me, hands clasped in front of him like a shield. His nose was wrinkled so I knew I must have sicked up again. A nurse came in and wiped the floor around him. She brought him a chair and he perched on it and turned his face sideways so he wouldn't have to smell the sheets.

He cleared his throat so hard I was afraid he would set the walls talking again, for they are always worse when there is some commotion. I think he spoke to me. He was asking something about my treatment. Was I content with my treatment? I could not remember what 'treatment' meant so I smiled at him and he got up, looking mightily relieved and went away. The nurse came back for the chair but it was talking to me so I shouted she should leave it and the next minute, another nurse came with a spoon and gave me some syrup.

It is dark all the time now. I do not know if it is day or night, winter or summer. They have stopped the torture but I am as sick as ever. And so tired. They have taken away the syrup so now I cannot sleep, but just lie here waiting for my stomach to stop heaving and it never does.

The nurse says I have had a visitor. I ask, 'Was it the vicar?'

She says, 'No, not him. He doesn't count. A young man. Respectable-looking. He said he had to see you. I told him you were sleeping, but he came back next day and the next. He said you couldn't still be asleep and that he would bring the press around if I didn't let him in.'

'What happened?'

She straightens my sheets. 'I told him you refused to see him. We can't have press men wandering round the hospital, now can we? Now you just close your eyes and go to sleep.'

I say, 'Not any more. I shall never sleep again.'

She looks unhappy. 'Sometimes it does that to you,' she says. I don't know what.

Today another doctor came to see me. He examined me most fully and when he had done he sat down by my bed and looked at me hard. 'You are very lucky. A very fortunate young woman indeed.'

I asked him how he came by that opinion.

'You are strong. Ferociously strong. Anyone less robust would certainly have succumbed. It has been decided to release you early in view of your current condition. You would be wise to have a care what you get up to if you do not wish to inflict further damage on your unborn child.'

So now a child is growing in me. Put there by a beast, a savage, a wild animal. Put there and no one to pull it out again. Maybe it is not a child, but some foul piece of vermin, for what else could such as they be father to? They. I do not even know which one. I do not care. It is there, sewn into me, spreading, swelling, sucking the life out of me from inside my own body. Inside. And I am outside. Once more. For no one knows what really happened that night. They do not know because I am too ashamed to speak of it, and so they think it is my own doing. My own unchastity. My pitiful lack of virtue. I have shown myself unworthy of their 'highest trust'. But they are not especially surprised. Given where I came from.

Miss Christabel has sent word that I may not stay in our London office once the baby shows. She thinks it might upset the others.

*After all, Maggie, they are respectable girls and, though no one wishes to condemn your behaviour out of hand, I do feel a responsibility for their moral welfare, which is hard enough anyway from such a distance, and would not be helped by your continuing presence. I have therefore arranged for you to transfer to our Hornchurch branch at the appropriate stage, where you will be properly cared for until such time as it is all over.*

*I have also asked their organiser to look out for a*

*respectable couple who would be prepared to take the child and rear it as their own. I believe this is quite regularly done in those parts, so do not foresee any great problems in that department.*

*In the meantime, I would ask you to refrain from activity likely to result in arrest, as it is vital you retain your good health for your own and your infant's sake. Also bear in mind that it would be a lot harder to find prospective parents for a damaged child.*

*I will close by sending you my very best wishes for a safe delivery and speedy return to Lincoln's Inn where I am sure you will be much missed.*

*Yours in the Cause,*

*Christabel Pankhurst. Founder Member WSPU*

*PS. Who knows? I may be there before you! Matters are finally going our way, and the use of drugs on prisoners has created a veritable storm for poor Mr McKenna.*

Mrs Garrud says my room will be waiting for me. She has given me some breathing exercises which she says will help with the birthing pains. I did not tell her there are no pains left which can hurt me. My body is like a broken shell packed full with other people's foulness.

She had asked that I might be allowed to stay, but it seems there are fears the press might learn of my condition and use it against Miss Christabel. *'Above all, suffragettes must be seen to be morally beyond reproach.' The Suffragette. May 1912.*

So I am to go to a strange place and stay amongst strangers

and if the child lives it will be taken from me and given to other strangers and then, only then, will I be allowed to return. So be it, but I do not think there is one person in this world who is not a stranger to me now, and I to them.

The months have gone. Mr McKenna, the Home Secretary (what kind of a home must he come from?) persists in his vileness, sending dying women back to prison. He heeds no one. Not doctors, clergy, his fellow politicians. Just smirks away at the photographers like a cat that got the cream. He *is* the cat in this Cat and Mouse Act. But mice breed quickly and perhaps he will wake one morning to find we are too many for him and all his fur has been torn away and his claws ripped out and he is nothing but a scrap for dogs to gnaw on. Now I am hungry again. Always hungry.

How did Ma manage for she was always last to the table? Miss Kerr says such appetite is natural for she has a married sister who eats twice what her husband does when she's expecting. And I don't like chocolate any more. Mrs Garrud made me a special chocolate pudding when I was feeling low the other night, but though I ate it as best I could, I lost it down the sink straight after. Nothing is right about me any more. I cry, I ache, I fall asleep in the middle of the day, wake in the middle of the night, and all the time I eat and eat, as though a million hunger strikes must be repaid inside me.

I am swollen once more like a pumpkin, only this pumpkin has a steam train chugging round inside it. It is strange to lie in bed at night and place my hand across my belly and feel tiny limbs bouncing and bashing at me. Like a chick trying to break out of the egg. I say, 'Wait till your time, little one.

There is nothing good awaits you in this world,' but still it kicks.

Today there is to be a great march to Buckingham Palace. To petition the King! What kind of a king sits in his palace and does not know his subjects are being tortured in his name? Does not care, more like. But why should he care? He does not know us. We are as different from him as coal is from diamonds, though we come from the same beginnings. A beginning is nothing without an end.

I am forbidden to go on the march. Instead I am to catch a train into Essex.

*'Better as little fuss as possible,'* writes Miss Christabel. *'The women have enough to worry about.'* So nothing has been said and tomorrow they will find me gone and forget all about me.

Mrs Garrud wept bitterly in parting. 'Oh, Maggie, I wish I could keep you with me. I hate to think of you alone at such a time. Promise you will write, every week till your confinement. Promise.'

'I promise.'

She hugged me. 'And you have your exercises, haven't you? I have seen it make a great difference. Just keep huffing like an elephant.'

I said I was doing that anyway, all I needed was a grey coat and I should be carted off to the zoo.

She smiled. 'And Mr Garrud is going to paint your room while you're away, Maggie, *and* fix that window catch which he should have made a proper job of in the first place.'

As I sat in the cab to the station I thought, that catch has seen me through a lot.

The driver was fussing and grumbling. 'Roads closed. Sorry, ma'am. That suffragette mob are at it again. I shall have to go the long way round.' I said I did not mind.

It was as we came up Piccadilly to Green Park I saw them. A great horde of mounted policemen marshalling behind the Ritz Hotel. It came to me at once our women would know nothing of it for they were approaching from Constitution Hill. My heart turned sick within me.

'Looks like they're in for a right walloping,' the cabman chuckled. I rose in my seat. 'Let me out. I want to get out here.'

'Eh? What? I'm booked for Liverpool Street.'

'I can pay. I'll pay.' I gave him what he asked. He lugged my bag down and dumped it on the pavement by me. People stared for I must have looked a regular sight, round, hot, angry. I did not know what I could do. I just knew I must do something.

It seemed to me that the mounted men were not yet ready to make a charge. The best I could do would be to cut across the grass and hope to warn the women what was planned. Off I chuffed, half carrying, half dragging my bag, hat clamped to my forehead, dizzy with heat and worry. My heart was beating so loud I kept fancying it the thundering of hooves and broke into a sort of run till I tripped and went hurtling headlong on the grass. A man helped me up most kindly, asking if I had hurt myself. I said no. He asked where I was bound.

'The palace', for there was no time to think of a clever answer. He nodded and said if I wished he would follow behind me with my bag as it was such a hot day, and a woman in my state should not be carrying heavy weights. This seemed like the answer to my prayers.

'I shall head straight for the main gates,' I told him. 'I only wish to look at something. It will not take long.' He smiled and tipped his hat. I rushed off, wheezing and puffing like a locomotive.

As I got to the other side I could see our women massing before the gates. Great crowds had gathered. I fought my way through, desperate for a face I knew. At last I spotted Miss Lake. I thrust my way towards her.

'Miss Lake.'

She swung round, startled and seeing me, positively gaped.

'Maggie? You must get away. There is terrible fighting going on. Get away. Hurry. Into the park. Get away from here. They have seized Mrs Pankhurst. Ripped her from the railings and just hurled her into the van. And it is getting worse all the time.'

I shook my head. 'It will get worse than this, Miss Lake. The horse police are assembling in Piccadilly. Dozens of them, and they will have the hill to their advantage. Please, please warn the women. Tell them to flee. It will be murder, else. Oh, please tell them, Miss Lake.'

Her face was like ash. 'I shall try, Maggie. But please save yourself. You can do no more.' I watched her struggling through the crowd. I knew, too, that she was right. I had done what I could. Of course it was not enough.

I watched from inside the park as the police came galloping, batons swinging, eyes burning, slicing and slashing through the soft summer colours. I saw the women crawl away, bleeding, sobbing, terrified. And when I looked for the man with my bag, he was nowhere.

I took a bus to the Euston Road. Already word was spreading of the mounted charge. Newsvendors sang on every corner, 'Bloodshed outside the palace. Many injured. Mrs Pankhurst detained and near to death', flapping their headlines in the faces of passers-by. I found a penny and gave it to a boy. A hand reached out and whipped the paper away. 'Oi, guv, that's the lady's.'

'Ladies don't read newspapers, lad. Return her her penny and take mine instead. I've got a train to catch.' The boy shrugged and did as he was bid. The man bounced away, sure, confident, bloodless. The prison doctor. I bounced after him.

I saw him go down the steps to the lavatories. For all my exertions I felt suddenly calm. I knew that this moment had been given to me and that I must use it, for there would never be another.

Slowly, slowly he mounted the steps. Neat, oiled, consulting his pocket-watch, adjusting his neckerchief. As his head came level I struck him, first with my purse, coins cracking against his bloodless skull and sending his hat flying. Then as he turned, trying to steady himself, I launched myself at him like a cannon ball, kicking, scratching, biting, tearing at his hair. He sunk to his knees, his arms across his face. He was crying out some weird helpless sob like a stuck pig. I kicked him where he crouched. Kicked him and kicked him.

'That is for the women you tortured. That is for Mrs Pankhurst. That is for Lady Constance. That is for all the women in the world. And that is for me. And me. And me.'

Feet came running. Hands dragged me off him. 'Get her. Get her. She's mad, they all are,' he was squawking.

The newsboy stood gawping. 'Blimey, ma'am. I'd've given you a paper if I'd known you were that fussed.'

I was struggling for breath. 'This man calls himself a doctor. Do you know what he does? He pushes rubber piping down helpless women's throats and chokes them half to death. He pours filth into their stomachs and if they're sick he scoops it up and pours that in as well. Sometimes it goes into their lungs and gives them pneumonia. He drinks brandy while he's doing it. And when he has finished he slaps them across the face and goes on to the next cell to start again. And he tells them it does not hurt. Does no harm. Serves them right.'

The men all stared at me. Bloodless was trying to get up. 'Call the police. What's the matter with you? Call the police. The woman's mad. She tried to kill me.'

One of them, a porter, stepped forward. 'Women don't act like that for nothing, guv. Specially not in her condition.' He reached out his hand to him. The doctor grasped at it, calling him every name under the sun as he did so. As he straightened up the man, with hardly a flicker of his eyelid, brought up his knee. The doctor sank like a sack of stones onto the ground, clutching his stomach, his eyes rolling in agony. The man glanced around him. 'Looks like this gentleman's been the victim of a robbery. Happens a lot round here. One of you best call a policeman while I help this young lady to her train.'

I never caught the train. As we walked towards the ticket barrier I heard a great popping like a balloon bursting inside me. When I looked down there was water all over my shoes.

They took me to the workhouse infirmary. No one asked my name or where I had been bound. They just propped me up on an iron bed with a rubber sheet beneath me and brought towels and bandages and bowls of water and told me to breathe as deep as I could and grip the rails when the pain came.

At first it was not too bad and I tried to remember Mrs Garrud's instructions and huffed and snorted so much I gave the nurse the giggles. She asked if it was helping but I did not know because I had never given birth before.

She sat with me awhile and told me it was not so bad and would all be over soon and then my husband could come and collect me. I showed her my hands. She gave a little sigh and crossed herself. 'So it'll be for the orphanage, poor mite?'

I shook my head. 'It is arranged that a couple will care for it. I do not know who.'

She patted my hand. 'It's as well not to know. Otherwise you'd be forever wanting to see how it was going on. You're young. God will forgive you.'

Then the pains started. Like a rolling blade inside me turning and turning till it had scraped the baby down into my belly, then lower and lower till I felt that my legs would split apart. They gave me a sponge soaked in laudanum to suck but nothing could halt the endless rolling, grating, crushing. I begged them to stop it just for a moment so that I could catch my breath, but they said it was impossible and that it would soon be over. I closed my eyes and clutched the iron rails of my bed. I could not cry out even, for I had not the strength. At last when I could bear it no more the nurse took firm hold of my hand and whispered to me, 'When I squeeze your hand you're to push.' She squeezed and I pushed and pushed till I felt as though my body would burst.

'*Push*,' she shouted. '*Push*.' And suddenly I remembered the day I met Fred on the demonstration and how the police had lined up against us and somewhere close by I had heard Mrs Drummond shout, '*Push. Push* for freedom and a new and better life'. So I pushed, and the baby shot out like a fat red sausage, roaring louder than a lion.

I said I would not see it. They understood and took it to another room where the orphanage babies were laid. Then the nurse came and washed me and brought me a drink of warm milk and told me to rest. I asked if I might write a letter. I felt I must send word to Mrs Garrud and ask if she would tell the office. She brought me some paper. I wrote, 'Baby born. I am still in London. Maggie.' It was the best I could manage.

The next day Miss Lake arrived with a lady I did not know. 'How are you, Maggie? You're looking very well.'

I said I was fine.

'We have been in touch with Miss Christabel. She was most surprised that you had got your dates so wrong, but you are not to worry. She has arranged for you to spend a few days at our Hornchurch branch. The country air will revive you. Miss Clements here is to take the baby.'

'Are you to keep it?' I asked the lady. She looked quite horrified.

'Goodness, no. I'm just the delivery boy, as you might say. No, it's a very nice couple. Not too bright, but kindly. They lost a child to diphtheria so yours has come along just at the right time. They really wanted a boy but beggars can't be choosers and she's a healthy enough little thing. I'm sure she'll do just fine. Have you seen her?'

I said no.

'Probably just as well. It can be a bit of a wrench, especially when you're feeling a bit – you know.'

It was arranged that they would come back next day, Miss Lake to drive me to Hornchurch and Miss Clements to take my daughter away forever.

That night my milk came in. The nurse told me not to worry and that it would dry up soon as I wasn't feeding. I asked what the baby would have instead.

'Oh, we have a few wet nurses come in, and if that's not enough we give them cow's milk boiled. It gives them colic, poor mites, but at least they don't starve.'

So I lay on my bed with milk leaking out of me onto the cold dead sheets, and next door my child, my daughter, cried and howled for want of it. I thought, one night won't harm.

She was in a little iron crib under the window. There were four in all, two sleeping, one wailing and mine, lying on her back just gazing up at the light. They each had a card stuck on the wall behind them. Hers said, 'Robins. Girl. For adoption.'

I bent down and lifted her out, just as I had seen Ma do so many times, holding the head so it would not flop. She gave a little sound like a hiccup. I wrapped her inside my shawl and carried her back to my bed. I could feel her warm downy skin against me, her little fingers opening and closing, her scratchy little nails. I put her to my breast and she straightway started to suck. I felt a great cramping in my belly. I thought, is there no end to pain with these babies? But it was funny to look at her, sucking away like a tiny monkey with her pat of velvety hair, black as coal and her eyes tight shut like she was dreaming.

When she had done I sat her up and patted her back as I have seen Ma do. She gave a great burp and sicked up half of what she had taken. I wiped her down and took her back to the orphans' room. As I went to lay her down, she opened her eyes and reached her tiny arms towards me. I covered her up.

Lying on my bed I could hear her crying, very softly, just for a little while. But babies don't cry softly, so I knew it must be me.

I left a note for Miss Lake. I said I was very sorry for the trouble I had caused.

It was dark when I got to Bow. The baby was wet and howling. Twice I had crept into a park and fed her, the griping in my guts as bad as ever. I had no clothes for her so had to keep folding my shawl in search of a dry patch, which seemed to annoy her greatly.

In Fetter Lane there was a trough for watering horses. I could not help myself. I drank from it. I had never been so thirsty, even on the thirst strikes. Each time I fed her it was as if all the moisture in my body was being drained out of me in one great rush. All the strength. I was so tired.

I thought to myself, what have I done? I am not fit for this. What kind of a life can I give her?

I thought of my room at Mrs Garrud's, clean, warm, welcoming. Of my work. How I should be able to return to the office and carry on as before. How pleased Miss Christabel would be with me for wasting so little time. I knew I must decide.

I made my way along the side streets. There it was. That great cheerless building. The infirmary. I climbed the steps.

Inside I took off my jacket and made a nest for her in a dark corner behind the great wooden door. I knew as soon as she hollered a nurse would come, for it is a great echoey place and a child's cries would ring from the rafters. I laid her carefully down, terrified to wake her. She stirred and gave a little grunt.

I whispered, 'Goodbye, little one. Godspeed,' and kissed her head. She opened her eyes and looked up at me, little hands clenching, and I knew I could not do it. She was too little to be left like this. She needed someone to care for her. A mother. She needed me. And I remembered Miss Davison, and how she had longed to be needed. I thought I owe her this at least.

The lights were all out in the hostel, save one at the back. I knocked as hard as I dared. Footsteps came hurrying. I heard the lock being pulled back and there, blinking into the darkness, hair all over the place and blouse covered in paint, stood Miss Sylvia. I said, 'I am sorry to disturb you so late...'

She gave a little gasp. 'Maggie, is it you?'

I nodded.

She drew me inside. 'Maggie, I am so glad to see you. You cannot believe... And this is your beautiful baby. Mrs Garrud wrote to me about...what happened. I had so much hoped...but she said my sister had arranged matters. I thought I had better not interfere.'

'Yes.'

'Oh, Maggie, quick, come and sit down. Let me get you some food. You must be exhausted.'

'Thirsty, mainly, miss.'

'Oh, well of course, if you are feeding. Excuse the mess, I am painting a mural for the playroom. I have no time during the day.'

And so it was. Within minutes, broth, warm milk, clothes for the baby, a bed for me, a crib wheeled in beside it.

Miss Sylvia was gazing at the baby. 'Would you let me hold... Is it a boy or girl, Maggie?'

'A girl, miss.'

'Oh, but she's so beautiful. Just like her mother. She has your eyes. Well, I expect she does, anyway. Oh, you must be so proud, Maggie. So proud of her. You must let me paint the two of you together. Will you let me do that? Not now, I don't mean. When she's a bit bigger.'

'I... I don't know, miss. That it would be such a good idea... She's... I'm not wed, miss.'

Her face grew serious. 'I know that, Maggie. Forgive me, I never meant to embarrass you. I just... I suppose I got carried away. It's so good to see a healthy baby. And to see you again. I have often thought about you, you know. Particularly since...'

'Since you heard.'

She nodded. 'Mrs Garrud said the baby was going for adoption.'

'Yes. I... Miss Christabel said it would be for the best. Then I could go back to the office. Like before. No one would hold it against me.'

'And is that what you want? It's not too late, you know. If that is what you want.'

I closed my eyes. What did I want? To do the right thing. For who? For me? For the baby? For the Cause?

'I want,' I said, 'to belong.'

She smiled.

'And what are you going to call this beautiful daughter of yours?'

I had no answer for, in truth, I had not thought about it till that moment. 'I'll tell you in the morning, miss. I haven't quite decided.'

That night I fell asleep with a hundred names spinning through my head. Sarah, for my mother; May for my nan; Emmeline in honour of Mrs Pankhurst; Christabel, for strength and courage; Sylvia, because she is my friend, Emily for Miss Davison.

'Well,' Miss Sylvia asked next morning when she had helped me bath the squeaky little horror. 'Will you tell me now what you are going to call her?'

I said, 'Does "Piglet" sound about right?'

She laughed. 'Piglet Robins. She may not thank you in years to come. It's a pity children cannot choose their own names, I always think.'

I said, 'But yours is beautiful. How could you wish for better?'

She made a face. 'I'll tell you a secret, Maggie. Sylvia is my second name. My first is Estelle and I hate it. And next to Estelle, I'll tell you what I hate most.'

'What's that, Miss Sylvia?'

She smiled. 'It's being called "Miss" Sylvia. It makes me feel a hundred. So please, from now on, as we are to work together, please will you call me "Sylvia"?'

I said I would try but it would be difficult with two of them about. She opened her eyes very wide. 'So I shall make

"Sylvia" her second name, too, and call her by her first.'

'And what's that to be?'

'Freda.'

Her face lit up. 'Oh, that's a beautiful name, Maggie. And I know what made you choose it.'

I wondered if she did.

'For freedom, am I right?'

I said she was.


Word came that Miss Christabel wished to see me.

It was arranged we should meet in the office. After the others had gone home. Miss Sylvia offered to come with me, but I said, no, it would be better if I went alone.

How did I feel climbing those stairs, knowing and not knowing what lay ahead? I don't know.

She was standing by the desk, busy with some papers. So cool in her pale blue linen. She did not look up.

'Well, Maggie. What is all this?'

'I'm sorry, miss. I never thought... It was just when I saw her... I couldn't... She's so little.'

Then she did look at me. 'Maggie, sit down.'

I was glad to do so, for truly I was still mighty sore in certain places. Miss Christabel came round the desk. 'Maggie, do you have any idea of the trouble you have caused?'

'I'm truly sorry, miss. I know you took great pains to find my Freda a decent family...'

'I certainly did. And what's this, giving her a name? For heaven's sake, Maggie, let the poor parents choose what they are to call her. They've had enough anxiety as it is. Set aside, we none of us knew where you'd gone till Mrs Garrud sent word.'

Fingers crushed in my palms. 'Miss, I don't think you understand.'

'Understand what, Maggie? I confess your behaviour does continue to baffle me, even after all this time.'

My dress was sticking to me. Sweat, milk, dripping, leaking. Soiled. I saw her distaste.

'I'm not giving her up, miss. I'm keeping her. That's what I've decided.'

For only the second time in my life Miss Christabel seemed lost for words. Not for long.

'Maggie, listen to me. I understand you may feel some attachment to the infant. It's very commendable, but think. *Think* what you're saying. Do you seriously intend to jettison all we – you have worked for, not to mention depriving a deserving and respectable couple of their chance to rear a child in a Christian environment, for a...whim?'

'It's not a whim, miss.'

'Well, what else would you call it? There has never been any mention before of your wanting to keep the child. I thought you were happy with the arrangements.'

I lowered my head. 'I thought I was, too, miss.'

'So what has changed your mind? Has the man offered to marry you? Is that it?'

I thought I should be sick. 'No, miss.'

'Then what? Surely you can see that to keep the child would constitute a supremely selfish act on your part? Sometimes sacrifices are necessary. Besides, what sort of life would she have? Born out of wedlock. Do you wish to condemn her to poverty – worse than that, the life of a social pariah?'

'A child needs a mother.'

'It also needs a father. Perhaps you should have thought about that before you allowed yourself to bring such utter disgrace on both yourself *and* the movement.'

'Like when I "allowed" the doctors to torture me, miss?'

'What are you talking about? That's not at all the same thing, as you very well know.'

'Isn't it, miss? Are you saying there's a difference between being held down by prison guards and held down by workmen?'

'What on earth…?'

'The night I was caught. At the Parliament man's house. It wasn't true what they said in court. About the fire. I never lit one.'

'You mean you didn't even…?'

'They found me. Two men found me. I tried. I did try. I just couldn't…'

Miss Christabel was staring at me. Suddenly her hands were in the air. 'I give up. *I give up*. After all your training. After all the endless effort that has been invested in you, not just by me, by all of us…the support, the encouragement, the time… And yet again, you fall at the very first hurdle. What is it about you, Maggie, that you must always take the easy path, while others tread the thorny one?'

It was as though an ice-cold wind had blown over me. I wasn't me any more. I wasn't a dirty, smelly, stupid girl who failed at every turn of the way. I was Ma, and my nan, and that mother burnt with an iron, and all the women for a thousand years who had crept along in the gutter while our 'betters' told us what to do.

'I don't know, miss. It didn't seem so easy to me. Being starved and choked and beaten.'

'Do you think you're the only one, Maggie, to have suffered for the Cause? Because I can tell you, you are not.'

'I don't suppose I am, miss. But maybe I'm the only one who suffered for something else.'

'What do you mean?'

'I mean, miss, I suffered because I wasn't like the rest of you. I wasn't a lady. I wasn't schooled. I wasn't...right. And whatever I did, it was never going to be right for you, was it? Because I'm everything you say you're fighting against. I'm stupid and ignorant and common and, worse than that, I want to live. I don't want to die for this great wonderful Cause. I want to live and see my Freda grow up, and be with her and talk to her and tell her things.'

'Tell her what, Maggie? How her mother forced her into a life of misery; betrayed her friends; cared only for herself...?'

'I'll tell her the truth, miss. She can make of it what she wants. But it's going to be me she hears it from. Because I'll be there when she asks. Not dead in a grave before she knows me.'

'Maggie, you're overwrought. I do understand, you know...'

I stood up. 'No, you don't, miss. You don't understand one thing about me. When I first came here, came to work for the Cause, I'd've done anything for you. Do you know that? Anything. Just for one word of kindness, one word of praise that didn't make me feel like a dog you'd taught to beg. You talk about sacrifices...'

'All suffragettes make sacrifices.'

'Well, I've no more left to make. I'm sorry if I've failed you, Miss Christabel, but you've had everything from me.

Everything I had to give and more. And you're not getting my daughter.'

I don't know if it was right or wrong, what I did. I only know that I stared right into those brilliant, unforgiving eyes for what seemed like half a lifetime, and the deeper I looked, the more I could see the emptiness behind them.

# POSTSCRIPT

## 1918

I have been with Sylvia for over four years now, working in the hostel, teaching, cooking, in charge of the paperwork.

I did not hear from Miss Christabel again, nor anyone in the office, though Mrs Garrud came out to see me as often as she could. She said there had been furious arguments up and down the country, for Miss Christabel had sent out an order that the branches should rid themselves of working-class supporters and deal only with educated women from then on. I could not help but wonder if I was the reason for it. Sylvia said, 'No. My sister sees only her own way of doing things. She cannot cope with anything that challenges her authority. The middle-classes are generally more pliable. And more ignorant.'

I asked how you could be educated and ignorant. She laughed. 'Easier than you think, Maggie. Life is what educates you. Not a dream of life.'

The war came that summer. Freda was cutting her first tooth so between her wailing and the whole country plodding around with long faces, it was not a jolly time.

The strangest thing to me was that, as soon as war was

declared all the suffragette prisoners were set free. Not only that, but Mrs Pankhurst and Miss Christabel turned right round in their shoes and began defending the Government and saying how all young men must join up to the army, and the women must give themselves over to working in factories and digging coal – all the things I thought we had been fighting against.

Sylvia does not believe in war, but that did not stop her working every waking hour to care for those whose sons and husbands were gone to it. It seems so few of them came back and those that did – the same ones we had seen marching away with eyes as bright as diamonds and pride sparking from their very heels – came back broken, crippled, blind – mad, a fair few of them, with eyes that had grown as old as Time.

Frank was lost at a place called Gallipoli. It took so long for the letter to come that he had been dead nigh a year and we all felt wretched for having gone on with our lives without a thought for him lying all that time in a ditch in some distant land. I did not cry for him, but I was sorry. Sorry because, although he had wounded and deceived me, I think he had always loved me in his heart and love is such a scarce thing to come by in this world.

Alfie was sent down the mines on account of his working for a coal merchant and being very strong (and possibly a bit of a danger to his fellows with a rifle!). He is married to Edith and she is expecting her first baby around Whitsuntide.

Lucy married a knife-grinder. I told Mrs Grant I thought it an excellent match for she could be sure of keeping her nails sharp. She laughed. 'You two will be scrapping when you're ninety, I'll wager.' I saw no reason to doubt it. They have two boys who are nice enough little fellows. Well, no they are not. They are scrawny little weasels and seem to get all their delight from pulling Freda's hair. Fortunately she is stronger than them and can easily knock them down and sit on them whenever she chooses. This makes the boys squall, Lucy shout, the knife-grinder sniff and generally, we do not call very often.

Pa, for all his grumbling about children out of wedlock, is Freda's absolute slave. She sits on his knee and tells him all about what she will do when he is dead and the house is hers. For some reason this seems to amuse him. She can do anything she likes with him. Last time we went over he was carving her a wooden elephant from one of Alfie's leftovers. He has already made her a plate with her name carved on it, some bricks and now he is talking about a truck with wheels on! I say, 'Why not just buy her a charabanc, Pa, and be done with it?'

Will still sees life from the gloomy end. Last Christmas I took a box of crackers over and after dinner we all pulled them. He, of course, cried at the bang, but when he found there was a paper hat and a little tin soldier inside he got quite excited, and even more so when he discovered a joke tucked into the wrapping. It was something stupid but to him it seemed the funniest thing in creation. He read it over and over, each time guffawing more wildly. We were all so amazed we could not help joining in till we were all clutching at each other with tears running down our faces. Anyone looking in would think they had come upon Bedlam. I do not think Will is destined for the music halls.

Little Ann truly loved the crackers and chuckled away for hours. It is as though, since Dr Rowan cleared her ears, everything sounds like music to her. She has caught up so fast with her talking. In fact, Mrs Grant says it is impossible to shut her up sometimes, especially if Reverend Beckett goes maundering on in the sermon.

Evelyn is sixteen now. A quiet gentle girl, and so clever. Ma would be so proud of her. She helps us at the hostel when she is not at college. She is learning stenography and typing, and already has been promised a position at a law firm if she passes her exams. I know she will.

It is when I look at her I realise the struggle was not in vain. It would be so easy sometimes to think that all our fighting, all our suffering had been for nothing – when you see children begging in the streets, women still dying in childbirth and their babies with them, half the time, while their men are sent to fight an enemy we none of us know for the sake of some distant prince who knew nothing of us, but it takes just one good thing to revive our spirits and send us onward once again.

Often in the evening Sylvia and I sit together and talk of the old days. We laugh so hard when we recall some of the pranks – roller-skating through the census, dressing up as showgirls to fool the police, emptying flour over the Parliament statues, Miss Billington and her banner... Sunshine, the great rallies, the marches, the colours, the songs, the friendship. So perhaps that was my education, and not the Bible learning and adding up change from the butcher's shop.

We do not talk of the bad times, except to remember those who are gone.

One night, the eve of Freda's first birthday, Sylvia seemed much preoccupied. I asked what was the matter.

'Nothing. I was just wondering... Please do not answer me if it offends you...'

'What? I shall not be offended.'

'I hope not. Truly, I do. I was just wondering if you ever...if...you have thought about trying to find Freda's father? I know how wayward young men can be in these matters, but in my experience it is usually more from thoughtlessness than heartlessness. Many of the girls round here have been safely married once the fathers were made to accept their responsibility for the child. And life is so hard for...'

'Bastards.'

'Oh, don't call her that. It is such a hideous word.'

'Why not? She will hear it often enough, I'll wager. Better that than...'

'Than what? Marriage to a man you do not love? I can see your thinking, of course I can, but sometimes people grow to love one another. With patience and good sense.'

'Freda has no father.'

'Maggie, what are you talking about? She has to have a father. It takes a woman *and* a man to make a baby.'

I flung the sock I was darning across the room. 'Or two? Or ten? Or a hundred? How do I know who her father is? I never saw his face. He could have been anyone. He could have been the King himself and I would not have known.'

Sylvia came and sat by me. She took her shawl and wrapped it round my shoulders for I was shaking so hard I could scarce speak. 'Tell me what happened. Tell me everything.'

So I did.

At the end she sat for a long time staring at her hands, then up she got and went to poke the fire. 'And yet you kept her. After all you had been through. That is a real mother's love, Maggie. Freda will not want for anything while she has that.'

I shook my head. 'You don't understand. It is nothing good in me that made me do it. I could not help myself. I have tried so hard not to love her. I have looked and looked at her and tried to see a stranger, one I should hate for what was done to me that night.'

She waited.

'But all I see is her. Her smile, her gurgles, her crossness when she is wet or tired, her curiosity, her trust. And besides, tomorrow she is one year old and she is starting to walk.'

'What does that signify?'

I was silent for a moment. 'That she has earned the right to my love.'

She asked me if birthing was really as painful as folk said.

'Pretty well, I should say. Though not to a suffragette, of course.'

We laughed. 'Mind,' I said, 'I cannot think how animals bear it. They have six or seven together, some of them.'

'It's a bit different for them, though.'

'Is it?'

'Well, they impregnate each other from behind, don't they? Not like humans.'

After everyone was in bed I crept down to the clinic and found the medical books. There was a great one called, *Embryonic Fertilisation and Development*. It showed how a baby grew inside its mother. I turned back to the beginning.

There were two drawings. One of a man without his clothes, the other of a woman and arrows to show how the baby was made. It was as though a great shaft of light had come out of the sky and entered my brain. How could I not have known? But how could I have, when all my learning came from nature books?

And in the end it made no difference, for there was no way I could ever know which of the three my baby's father was. I only knew who I wanted it to be, and that, no matter what, I would never see any of them again.

Not long after a package came for me. It had been forwarded from Mrs Garrud's. Inside was a letter. It was on plain grey paper, the writing clear and jagged.

*Dear Miss Robins,*

*I hope you will forgive the liberty I take in writing to you. It was the wish of my son, Frederick, that, should anything befall him, I would send you the enclosed items.*

*Though we did not meet, he had spoken much of you to me. Of your courage, your strength, your unfailing determination to bring about justice for yourself and others, no matter how high the cost.*

*I think he believed that I would disapprove of your actions, and, indeed, I do dislike destruction in whatever form it comes, but dislike and condemnation are two different things. We Quakers began our fight in much the same way as the suffragettes. For the sake of our beliefs our forerunners bellowed, argued, battled, were imprisoned and mocked, and it is only now, centuries later, that such as I may worship in quietness and tranquillity because of those brave souls who sacrificed themselves for a future they would not know. So I honour you, Miss Robins, just as I honour my beloved son.*

*As I understand, Frederick was lost in a trench explosion some way from his unit, caused by a shell igniting a stock of ammunition. (He was working as a stretcher-bearer near the town of Arras.) His body was not recovered. His commanding officer wrote most movingly of Frederick's devotion to duty and courage under fire, of his wit, humour and kindness to others,* "And all this, despite his deeply held conviction that war was wrong. It takes courage to fight for a cause one believes in. It takes supreme courage to fight for one that one does not."

*I trust and pray that this may be of some comfort to you in these dark days, and that you will always remember my son with affection and pride, as do I. May God bless and keep you.*

*Edward Thorpe*

Inside the packet were two folded pieces of newspaper and an envelope. I opened one and there was the photo of me that first time I was released from Holloway. The other was of me at the Manchester meeting, my head held high. '*NO LONGER NOTHING*'. They were yellow with age, crumpled, streaked with a fine red mud. I thought, is this the mud Fred died in? Is this his blood mixed in with it? I rubbed it with my finger. The paper tore.

Inside the envelope was a postcard of our elephant, her great body rocklike, unmoveable, her trunk lifted high like a trumpet, looking upwards over the bars, up to where freedom waited. I turned it over. There, in Fred's scribbly writing that he never could keep straight, were some copied lines of poetry. I have learnt them for they are all I have of him and yet what more could he have given me? For in those lines are all the words we never spoke and all the love we might have shared. What more could I have asked?

> When you are old and grey and full of sleep,
> And nodding by the fire, take down this book,
> And slowly read, and dream of the soft look
> Your eyes had once, and of their shadows deep;
>
> How many loved your moments of glad grace,
> And loved your beauty with love false or true,
> But one man loved the pilgrim soul in you,
> And loved the sorrows of your changing face;
>
> And bending down beside the glowing bars,
> Murmur, a little sadly, how Love fled
> And paced upon the mountains overhead
> And hid his face amid a crowd of stars.

I still love books. The more I read, I see how little I knew, but there is great joy in gaining new knowledge, even if some of it shocks and frightens me, and I know I must go on, stretching away into the future, the past, the present to find out why.

'Why what?' Sylvia teases me.

'Just "why?"'

Freda is with me on this. She never ceases with her questions. 'Why? How? Who? What?' Sometimes I am hard put to answer her, then I remember Fred, and how he studied each night to keep ahead of his pupils. And how he thought it was worth it.

I am as happy as I can be. Particularly today for today the church bells are ringing, ringing for life and hope and victory. The war is ended and when the men return they will find a different world from the one they left behind.

Their battle is won and so is ours. Strange that it should take a war in France to end the one at home. But when the men were gone and there was no one left to keep the country going but the women, it finally dawned on those grey felt-filled brains in Parliament that maybe we were not so close to rabbits as the Asquith liked to suppose.

And so, quietly and with hardly a snort or whimper, the vote was granted. To women aged thirty and over. Tucked in amidst a dozen new laws as though it was nothing more than a detail that scarce deserved the mentioning. A detail.

Is that what we were? I was? I am? A detail in history's long march? Maybe. Maybe a thousand years from now it will make no difference, just as what people did a thousand years back is all but lost or forgotten. Or perhaps we shall all be saints like Joan of Arc. What does it matter? Today is what counts. And tomorrow. If you have a life you must live it.

Yes, today I am happy. Freda and I are at The Mascot, invited down while Freda gets over the chicken pox. She has made a great friend of Mrs Cliffe, who quite spoils her. The two of them spent the morning making flour paste animals which Mrs Cliffe then cooked so that the pie was half an hour late going in and Mr Pethick Lawrence pretended to cry for hunger, delighting my hard-hearted daughter!

And here she comes. Little fat legs thudding across the grass to where I sit, wrapped in my coat in the cool autumn sun, looking at the lake, which does not change.

'Ma.'

'Yes, lovey.'

'Come quick. There's a man. He's got a pot.'

'Well, tell Mrs Cliffe. She's in charge of the pots.'

Feet stamping like a little wild bull.

'A pot. A pot like mine.' She waves her arm at me.

'Your spots have gone now, Freda. You're better.'

'This pot. My pot.' The tiny little strawberry under her wrist.

My heart begins a somersault. 'Did he tell you his name, Freda? Did he say what he was called?'

'Limpy.'

'Limpy?'

'He's got a funny leg.'

'Did he have another name?

'Yes, but I have to guess and I can't. He said you would know. Auntie Sylvia sent him. And here.' She hands me a screwed up piece of paper. It says, *'Be glad today and sing.'*

And now I am running.


He is standing in the hallway. No sun, no light behind him. Only the shadows of a winter's afternoon. But the dark has no fears for me now.